WOLFELORD
A Medieval Romance

By Kathryn Le Veque

PART OF THE DE WOLFE PACK
GENERATIONS SERIES

KATHRYN LE VEQUE
NOVELS

ARE YOU SIGNED UP FOR KATHRYN'S BLOG?

You'll get the latest news and information on exclusive giveaways, exclusive excerpts, coming releases, sales, free books, cover reveals and more.

Kathryn's blog followers get it all first. No spam, no junk.

Get the latest info from the reigning Queen of English Medieval Romance!

Sign Up Here

kathrynleveque.com

It's William de Wolfe's (*The Wolfe*) eldest grandchild and namesake, William "Will" de Wolfe in an unconventional romance that is going to break your heart… and then put the pieces back together again.

Welcome to the greatest de Wolfe Pack generation!

William "Will" de Wolfe has the weight of the entire de Wolfe empire weighing on him. Perfection is key. Living up to the grandfather he was named for has been something he's had to deal with his entire life. But Will is strong, noble, true, and powerful… everything a man named William de Wolfe should be.

Except he's living through a personal tragedy no man should have to live through.

Will was very young when he married his wife, Lily de Lohr. As the great-granddaughter of Christopher de Lohr, the marriage forever linked the Houses of de Wolfe and de Lohr. The children born of the marriage are considered to have some of the finest bloodlines in England. But tragedy strikes when pregnant Lily is diagnosed with a terminal illness.

And she wants to pick her husband's next wife.

More than that, she wants him to fall in love with her.

When his dying wife plays matchmaker, how successful can the relationship be between Will and Adria de Geld, the daughter of a de Lohr ally? Lily is determined that Adria should replace her in Will's heart and in his bed, something Adria is reluctant to do but she cannot help but feel the attraction to the handsome, tortured knight. She soon finds out that his torment is not only because of his dying wife, but because of a terrible secret that Lily hides. Will only found out by accident and it is that, more than anything, tearing him to pieces.

A terrible secret that could tear apart two of England's greatest families.

Can Adria and Will's love take flight in spite of the dire circumstances? Or will Will's torment overshadow a truly gifted, intelligent, and beautiful woman who has managed to fall in love with him?

De Wolfe Pack Generations/ Grandsons of de Wolfe series:

WolfeHeart (Markus de Wolfe)

WolfeStrike (Thomas "Tor" de Wolfe)

WolfeSword (Cassius de Wolfe)

WolfeBlade (Andreas de Wolfe)

WolfeLord (William "Will" de Wolfe)

WolfeShield (Ronan de Wolfe) (2022)

De Wolfe Pack Generations

The grandsons of William de Wolfe are referred to as "The de Wolfe Cubs". There are more than forty of them, both biological and adopted, and each young man is sworn to his powerful and rich legacy. When each grandson comes of age and is knighted, he tattoos the de Wolfe standard onto some part of his body. It is a rite of passage and it is that mark that links these young men together more than blood.

More than brotherhood.

It is the de Wolfe birthright.

The de Wolfe Pack standard is meant to be worn with honor, with pride, and with resilience, for there is no more recognizable standard in Medieval England. To shame the Pack is to have the tattoo removed, never to be regained.

This is their world.

Welcome to the Cub Generation.

De Wolfe Motto: *Fortis in arduis*

Strength in times of trouble

Author's Note

Welcome to Will's story!

I thought it would be fun in the beginning to catch a glimpse of Will's mother, Athena de Norville. If you recall, she was Scott de Wolfe's first wife (*ShadowWolfe*). I don't want to give too much away for those of you who haven't read the book yet, but Athena and her sister, Helene, have been key figures (though we never meet them) in several de Wolfe novels. Though we haven't really met Helene in full, you'll get the chance to meet Athena. As my mother would say, she's a pistol…

It was actually quite difficult to write about Athena because she made a magnificent heroine. You'll see what I mean when you read the prologue. Since I wrote *ShadowWolfe* and *DarkWolfe* well before this book, we already know her ending, but to see her alive like this is kind of a punch to the gut. But listen to what she says to her father… and how unique she is… and you'll understand better why things happened the way they did at the end of her life. You'll see why her departure left such grief in its wake and why Paris never stopped talking about her and her sister, up until the end of his life.

Now, on to the story –

This book discusses a serious medical condition for a pregnant woman, something that would have been deadly during this time – placenta abruption. That basically means the placenta pulls away from the uterine wall. Nowadays, it can be diagnosed and the survival rate for mother and child are excellent (which is a good thing because I had it with my second child), but in Medieval times, there was no way to treat such a thing. The signs were there, but nothing could be done, and it was always invariably deadly. A forerunner of a stethoscope is mentioned in this tale, but note that the "official" discovery of that instrument didn't happen until 1816. That's not to say that something similar wasn't used as far back as the Greeks when the practice of medicine began in earnest.

Now, some less heavy notes about this tale. Chris de Lohr appears, the grandson of Christopher de Lohr through his eldest son, Curtis. I need to make some family dynamics clear here – Chris appears in *ShadowWolfe* in 1281 A.D. and then makes another appearance in both *A Wolfe Among Dragons* in 1287 A.D. and *The Red Lion* in 1288 A.D. I was never clear on Chris de Lohr's family – some appear in some books, while still others appear in other books, so to be clear on Chris' family, he has six sons and one daughter.

Chris' wife was born Alys Kaedia de Titouan, a Welshwoman, and goes by Kaedia. She was mentioned in *A Wolfe Among Dragons*. What wasn't mentioned was the family tradition for the women in the family to have English and Welsh names and then go by the Welsh name. Lily breaks the mold a little, not going by her Welsh name, but once Chris de Lohr married into a Welsh family, things became a little complicated. I'm not sure how thrilled Christopher would have been about Chris infiltrating the Welsh bloodlines, but I'd like to think he would have been tolerant. I never really made all of this clear in the books where Chris appears, so now is the time to avoid reader confusion.

But I digress.

Our first mention of Will de Wolfe comes in *Sword and Shields*. That book was written several years ago and, at the time, I had no plans to ever write Will's book, so there are some slight continuity issues between *Swords and Shields* and

WolfeLord. Will also made a brief appearance in *ShadowWolfe*, and that's the book I used for accuracy in this book – mostly how Will married Lily de Lohr very early in life (she was 16 when he married her). He did marry her, but now we find out how that marriage actually went.

Swords and Shields really didn't fit into what I wanted for Will several years down the road – so the years of his marriage to Adria are a little "off". Not terribly, but a little. If I hadn't mentioned it, you probably wouldn't have even noticed. I desperately wanted to fit William de Wolfe, however briefly, into this novel, and he wasn't alive in 1300 when *Swords and Shields* was set. So – don't mind me. With the (literally) thousands of characters and timelines and worlds I have created, I have been known to screw up family ties and timelines on occasion but, in this case, it's deliberate. Let's just call it creative license!

The usual pronunciation guide:
Unusually, I don't think there are any funky names that need clarification except for the heroine – her name is Adria. Basically, pronounced like Adrian without the "n" – so:
Ā-dree-uh (Long "A")

And with that, I think I've covered everything, so I hope you enjoy the rather heavy, beautiful, and emotional tale of *WolfeLord*!

Hugs,

PROLOGUE
MY MOON AND STARS

Castle Questing
1255 A.D.

"**D**OES IT FIT?"
She twirled the ring around her finger, a golden band with an unusual setting. It was set with a moonstone, reputedly from ancient Rome, in a star-shaped mount. Both the moonstone and the star-shaped mount had meaning to them.

"It does. It's so beautiful, but you know I cannot wear it until you speak with my father."

The softly voiced statement came from an elegant woman with hair the color of starlight. At least, that's what her lover had always said – hair that glittered like the brightest star, a brilliant blend of red and gold. That's why he'd given her the moonstone set in the star mount. *You are my moon and stars*, he told her. In fact, that's what he'd had inscribed on the inside of the band – *my moon and stars*.

It was a ring as magnificent as its owner.

That's what Scott de Wolfe thought, anyway.

He'd thought that way since the day he realized Athena de

Norville was something special.

He wasn't exactly sure when that was. A couple of years ago, at least. It was true that he was a few years older than she was, but not too many in the grand scheme of things. They were both adults. They knew their mind and their hearts. But now, they were facing a very real adult problem.

Scott pointed to the great hall, across the bailey from the stables they were sitting in.

"My brother just had to marry your sister for the exact same reason," he hissed. "Your father, my father, Uncle Kieran... they did unspeakable things to him. God only knows what they are going to do to me."

Athena smiled faintly, looking at her big, strong, handsome lover. He was a de Wolfe, from one of the finest families in the north. More than that, he was his father's heir, which meant he'd inherit the great de Wolfe empire. She put a hand on her belly. So would the child she carried.

She was positive it was male.

"I do not know how much longer I can hide my condition," she said, standing up and rubbing her belly. "Helene is smaller than I am, so hers was quickly apparent, but me... I've got the legs of a deer and a long body, so I can hide it better, but not for much longer. Sooner or later, my mother is going to know and when she does, she will tell my father."

Scott grunted, wiping a hand over his face. In the distance, they could hear music and laughter from the wedding feast that was going on this night. A cold, clear night with a million stars in the sky presiding over the very happy union of two great families.

"Come here, Tee," he said softly.

"Tee" was her nickname, spoken softly and gently. Athena moved in his direction, taking his outstretched hand. He pulled her against him, his face level with her belly. She was wearing a garment that was nipped under the breasts so the fabric draped over her torso. Nothing to bind. He put a hand on her belly, feeling the firm roundness beneath. He wrapped his arms around her, planting his face in her stomach and kissing it sweetly.

"I know I should have told your father sooner," he whispered. "I should have told him as soon as you told me, but then I was sent off to London and I spent longer than I had anticipated there. I had hoped to tell him before the babe was still visible, but five months in London prevented that."

Athena ran her hands through his dark blond hair. "Then you must do it now," she said. "I know we have both been waiting for the right time and that time is now, now while he's still drunk with happiness over Helene and Troy's marriage. Mayhap he will not react so poorly. Besides, I want to wear my ring tonight."

Scott sighed heavily. "We shall see," he said. "He showed up this morning and wanted to kill Troy, you know."

"I know."

"He is going to want to kill me, too."

Athena was trying not to grin. "You will not know until you tell him," she said. "Truly, Scott, if you do not, I must. It would be better coming from you."

He knew that. Wearily, he stood up, towering over a woman who was already quite tall. "Shall we do it together?"

Athena nodded. "I think we'd better," she said. "At least I can stop him from trying to kill you. He wouldn't dare do such a thing in my presence."

Scott cocked a dubious eyebrow at her. "You think so, do you?"

She couldn't help but smile now and he broke down, snorting, mostly because it was a ridiculous situation they'd gotten themselves into. While their fathers were focused on the other pair – Scott's twin brother, Troy, and Athena's older sister, Helene, who found themselves in the exact same situation with an unplanned pregnancy, what they didn't realize was that Scott and Athena were in that identical situation themselves, only they'd been better at concealing it.

Still, Scott was nervous. He drew in several long breaths – *in* and *out, in* and *out* – before turning towards the stable entry. Beyond was the yard and beyond that, the bailey and the massive keep of Castle Questing. As he gazed out at the activity, he caught sight of his Aunt Jemma heading in his direction.

The little Scotswoman was his mother's cousin, married to his father's second in command, Kieran Hage. The woman had a heart of gold but the temper of a banshee, as she was affectionately called. Kieran was an enormous man, the strongest man on the border as William de Wolfe called him, and along with that strength came a calm, calculating personality. Matched with Jemma's fire, they were quite literally fire and ice.

Seeing Jemma gave Scott an idea.

"Aunt Jemma!" he called to her, waving her over.

Jemma had a bucket in her hand, eyeing Scott with mild surprise as she headed in his direction. "What are ye doing out here?" she asked. "Yer brother's wedding feast is that way."

She was pointing to the keep. Scott ignored the question, pointing to the bucket. "What are you doing with that?"

Jemma was distracted as she lifted the bucket. "There's no milk," she said. "All of the kitchen servants are busy with the wedding feast, so I've come tae collect some milk for the bairns. They want warm milk with cinnamon before they'll agree tae go tae bed."

Scott fought off a grin. "Since when do you give in to the demands of children?"

Jemma scowled. "Yer own baby brother, Eddie, is leading the charge," she said. "Ye know yer da thinks the sun rises and sets on his sons, so the other children are smart now. They let Eddie make the demands and we must all go along or there'll be hell tae pay with yer da."

Scott chuckled, thinking of his baby brother, Edward, born a scant year before. But he was smart, verbal, and already walking, and their father put a good deal of stock in bright, loud Edward de Wolfe. But thinking about his littlest brother brought about the very reason why he was in the stable, so he took the bucket from his aunt and took her by the hand, leading her into the stable.

"I must speak with you before you fetch your milk," he said. "I need your counsel."

Jemma let the big, blond knight lead her into the confines of the stable. "Me?" she said. "What could I possibly help ye with?"

As they entered the stable, Jemma immediately saw Athena sitting on a stool near a table that held all manner of combs and brushes for the horses.

"I must swear you to secrecy, Aunt Jemma," he said. "You are the only one not affected by the situation, so I must have your oath."

Jemma looked at him curiously. "Ye have it," she said. "But what situation do ye mean?"

Scott came to a pause in front of Athena, turning to look at Jemma. The woman was pregnant with her fifth child and due to give birth in a month, so Scott was hoping she would understand their predicament and advise them. When she wasn't being angry or volatile, Jemma could be wise and patient. But only if the mood struck her.

Scott could only hope this was one of those times.

He took a deep breath.

"You know the situation my brother and Helene are in?" he said.

Jemma lifted her eyebrows. "Their marriage?"

Scott shook his head. "The reason they were prompted into the marriage so… quickly."

Jemma understood immediately. "Ah," she said. "Aye, *that*. And yer brother paid the price for it when he earned himself the Helm of Shame."

And so came forth that terrible, awful name.

Helm of Shame.

It was something greatly feared by all of the sons and soldiers of William de Wolfe, Paris de Norville, and Kieran Hage. They were the greatest knights of their generation, men who had been born and bred for battle, men who had raised their children in the same honorable fashion.

The Helm of Shame was used as punishment for those who behaved ignobly.

It was one of those brilliant, nasty tricks used for punishment on naughty lads or lazy knights. It had all started many years ago at a battle near Whiteadder Water when someone cut the garter off the mail of Kieran's left leg during the heat of battle. The mail slid down and took his breeches with it, and suddenly, Kieran was fighting with his bare arse exposed.

Once the fighting stopped, Kieran was so angry at the rebelling Scots that he refused to pull up his breeches. He left his backside hanging out and made it all the way back to the encampment that way. But it didn't end there. He went to the Scots prisoners and made them all look at his bare buttocks to punish them for their insurrection.

And so, came the Helm of Shame.

As Kieran was walking around, holding up his breeches in the front so his manhood was covered, he came across a knight from Northwood Castle. The young knight was named Corin de Fortlage and he had pulled out of the battle early, pleading exhaustion. Kieran was so angry at Corin that he pushed the man to the ground and sat on his head with his bare buttocks.

He called it the Helm of Shame and told Corin if he ever left the field of battle early again, he would punish him again with the Helm of Shame. It had been particularly ghastly for Corin because of the way he'd fallen on the ground – when Kieran squatted on him, from the angle of his head, the man's testicles were right by Corin's nose.

Corin was always the last man to leave the field of battle after that.

The Helm of Shame was legendary amongst the de Wolfe armies and it was something that Kieran had done more than once. If a young knight displeased him, they were threatened with the Helm of Shame. No one else could do it better than Kieran and the older knights began using it as a threat to the younger knights or misbehaving squires. William, Paris, and Kieran had even used it on their own sons to keep them from being naughty.

Unfortunately, it had been used on Troy when Helene's pregnancy had been discovered and, even now, Troy was in the great hall with his head shaved because part of the Helm of Shame had been to shave his head in an odd manner, leaving just a patch of hair at the top of his skull so he looked like a complete fool. Scott's mother, Jordan, had taken pity on her son and shaved off that weird patch so at least his head was uniform now, even if he was bald.

Scott didn't want that to happen to him.

"There is no delicate way to put this, so I will come out with it," he finally said. "Tee and I are in the same predicament, only our fathers do not know yet. I am not sure how to tell Uncle Paris. I need your counsel, Aunt Jemma. Please."

Jemma didn't react to the shocking news. Scott and Athena kept waiting for her to shriek with surprise, even outrage, but she didn't. She simply looked between the pair of them, digesting what she'd been told. After a moment, she sighed faintly and rubbed her own blossoming belly.

"Well," she said thoughtfully. "If we're being perfectly honest, yer Uncle Kieran and I were in the same situation before we were married and, if I recall, so were yer own mother and father. 'Tis nothing new with the hot-blooded men of de Wolfe and Hage. Even de Norville. That pompous peacock likes tae think he's perfect."

Scott fought off a grin. The animosity between Jemma and Paris was legendary. "You mean Uncle Paris?"

Jemma snorted and turned up her nose, which was usual when discussing Paris. Scott watched her closely, waiting for some measure of wisdom to come forth, but nothing was forthcoming.

"Well?" he said hopefully. "How should I tell Uncle Paris?"

Jemma held up a hand for patience before extending the bucket to him. "Put some milk in it for the bairns," she said. "I'll return."

Leaving Scott holding the bucket, she headed out of the stable. When she was gone, Scott turned to Athena.

"Where did she go?" he wondered, baffled. "Do you think she's gone to tell him herself?"

Athena's eyes were wide. "I do not know," she said. "He'll not take the news well coming from her. Mayhap you should go after her."

Scott wasn't sure about that. Part of him wanted to hide behind his pregnant aunt, but most of him wanted to stop her if, indeed, she had gone in to tell him herself. He wasn't quite sure what to do, so he stood there nervously as Athena took the bucket from him and went to the rear of the stable where the dairy cows where corralled along with several goats and their kids. Scott could hear her milking the cow, the rhythmic sounds of milk streams hitting the side of the bucket. It seemed like an eternity, listening to the sounds of the distant party and the *swish, swish* of the milk, until he could suddenly hear people approaching the stable.

The sound of footsteps did nothing to help his anxiety. He stood his ground as he saw figures coming at him from the darkness.

Jemma was followed by two very large men.

William de Wolfe's features came into view, followed shortly by Kieran Hage. Men he loved and trusted dearly, but men who, only several hours earlier, had done unspeakable things to his brother in punishment for the exact same predicament. He heard Athena gasp as she came back in from the corral, but Scott couldn't take his eyes from his father.

Jemma came to a halt in front of him.

"I told them that ye needed tae tell them something," she said quietly. "If ye want advice, they're the men tae ask, lad. Ye'd better do it."

Scott looked at her, knowing why she'd done it. He'd tried to put the burden of a terrible situation on her shoulders and she'd shirked that duty, quite reasonably so, in favor of the men who could genuinely be of some help.

"What is it?" William asked, half-drunk from hours of drinking to Troy's marriage. "Why are you out here? What is so important?"

Scott sighed sharply. There was no use in delaying the inevitable.

"Because I must ask your advice," he said. "I want to marry Athena, Papa."

A smile spread across William's lips as he looked at Athena, who was handing the half-filled pail of milk over to Jemma.

"I know," he said. "I have known for years. But I am not the one to ask, lad. Paris is in a good mood – go inside the hall and ask him now."

"I want to marry her because she is carrying my child."

William's smile vanished. Years ago, he'd lost his left eye to an archer in battle, but his right eye was still sharp, still keen, now wide in shock.

"She's pregnant?" he gasped.

"Aye."

"But Helene is pregnant!"

"Aye, Papa. Both of them are."

William just stood there, absorbing what he'd been told. But given that he was tipsy, he was in less control of his emotions than he usually was. Scott's muscular body was tense as he prepared for his father's inevitable onslaught. When his father didn't reply right away, Scott hastened to make his case clear.

"Athena is further along than Helene, only she has managed to hide her condition better," he said, looking between his father and Kieran, who didn't seem particularly surprised. "I meant to ask for her hand when we found out, but you sent me to London on business and by the time I returned, several months had passed. I would have been able to lie about it had we married when we first discovered it. But now, I cannot lie about it. She is going to have a child and I must tell Uncle Paris. I want to ask your advice on how to do it."

William's jaw dropped. He looked at his son for a moment before rolling his eye and slouching back against the wall of the stable.

"Oh... God," he muttered. "Another one."

Scott still wasn't sure where this was going so he remained on his guard, prepared to defend himself. "Aye," he said steadily. "Another one. I am sorry for disappointing you, Papa, but I am not sorry for loving Athena. She carries the heir to the House of de Wolfe and I must marry her. I *want* to."

That was true. Scott was a twin, but he was the firstborn twin, the first son of William de Wolfe and his wife, Jordan. That meant the child Athena carried was indeed the heir if it was a male child. William found himself looking at Athena.

Tall and elegant, with golden-red hair, she was a woman of grace and beauty, even at her young age. Scott had been sweet on her for some time, but he'd spent so much time pretending to ignore her, and she him, that he was genuinely surprised that they'd managed to connect. Not only connect, but conceive a child. Both Scott and his brother, Troy, had bedded women and gotten them pregnant. But not just any women – Paris' daughters.

William couldn't help it; he started to laugh. A dry, humorless laugh.

"God's Bones, what animals I have raised," he muttered. "After what happened with your brother today, Paris will be even angrier with you. He's going to be bloody well furious and you know he wanted to fight your brother today. You saw it, Scott. He came armed for battle and Kieran had to talk him out of it."

Scott knew that, for he'd been armed for battle, too, prepared to defend his brother against a very angry father of a pregnant daughter. He looked to Kieran to see the man's reaction. Wise, gentle, and enormously powerful, Kieran was the most levelheaded person that Scott knew. He was hoping the man had something encouraging to say, but Kieran was gazing at him as if completely exasperated by the situation.

"I know," Scott said. "I was hoping Uncle Kieran might have some words of advice. Or… or mayhap help me face him."

Kieran shook his head. "I do not think Paris can take another dose of news such as this, not today," he said. "But there is little choice. Mayhap it is best you do it now, while he is celebrating Helene's marriage and possibly too drunk to do much damage."

Scott nodded, but it was with great reluctance. "Mayhap," he said. "I'm sorry to ask for your assistance, for I know I should face this alone, but the longer we waited, the more difficult it has become."

"Paris is going to want his pound of flesh," William said. "I will not stop him, Scott. You soiled the man's daughter."

"He did not soil me," Athena said, finding her voice. When Scott tried to stop her, she ignored him. "Do you hear me, Uncle William? He did not soil me. If you must know the truth, I seduced him. Does that shock you?"

William looked at Athena. She was a smart lass, deeply compassionate and caring, but she was also bold and arrogant, like her father. She took after him in almost every aspect. She had an unruly tongue when the mood struck her and Paris had difficulty with her at times because of it. She was unafraid to speak her mind, unafraid to do what she wanted to do. But she was also wildly emotional and her mood swings could be tremendous – happy one moment, weeping the next.

That could be a problem.

Paris told William that Athena had threatened to kill herself once when Scott had seemingly rejected her. That was in days long past, of course, but William wondered if Scott even knew that, and if he did, if he was with the woman because of it. No one wanted to test Athena in that regard because being as fearless as she was, she might very well do such a thing simply to prove a point. It was something Paris really didn't speak of, and hadn't except for that one time, but looking at the young woman, William wondered if she'd grown out of those impulses.

He wondered what would happen should Paris become truly irate at Scott.

"You are young and you are in love," William said after a moment. "You and Scott have demonstrated that love. I do not find it shocking, but your father will have something different to say about it. He was irate about Helene and I can only imagine that he will be irate about you. Now... will you go inside with your Aunt Jemma? I wish to speak to Scott alone, please."

Athena geared up for a retort but the expression on Scott's face forced her to rethink it. After a moment, she reluctantly obeyed. It wasn't her instinct to obey, but she forced herself to. She felt Jemma grasp her hand, pulling her from the stable.

With great misgivings, she followed.

The night outside was cold and crisp, a thousand stars overhead. Inside the great hall of Castle Questing, music and light and warmth filtered through the enormous lancet windows, giving off energy into the night. But Athena wasn't thinking about her sister's wedding feast – she was thinking about the man she'd left behind in the stable.

"What do you think Uncle William is saying to him?" she asked Jemma. "Do you think he's truly angry?"

Jemma was focused on the keep. "I think that he is giving Scott advice on how tae inform yer father without causing the man tae blow the top of his head off in rage."

Athena was still uncertain. "I know that I must let Scott speak with him, but what I said in there was true. I *did* seduce him."

Jemma didn't have any discernable reaction to that declaration. "Ye're a bold woman, Tee," she said. "But ye've always known yer own mind. I know Scott isna a whim."

"Never," she insisted. "I love him and he loves me, and our son will be the greatest knight England has yet seen."

They had come close to the keep now, with its music and light and wafts of food on the night air. Jemma didn't comment any further on the situation between Scott and Athena because, frankly, it was none of her business and out of her hands.

"Come inside, lass," she said. "Yer father has spent a good deal of money for this affair, so ye may as well enjoy it."

"My wedding will be bigger."

"Mayhap," Jemma said. "But come inside now and out of the cold night."

Athena followed her inside, but it was only to linger in the shadows, anxious. She knew, at some point, that either Scott was going to come inside or Paris was going to go out to the stable and she wanted to be prepared for what was to come. One thing was for certain – she wasn't going to let her father try to kill Scott as he'd tried to kill Troy, and she wasn't going to let Kieran sit on his head with the ghastly Helm of Shame. Just as Scott would always protect her, she would protect him.

Judgment Day was coming.

She only hoped they would all survive it.

∞

"KIERAN, GO INTO the hall and get Paris."

William gave the fateful command, speaking softly but firmly. Kieran, his gaze lingering on Scott, left the stable without another word. When he was gone, William turned to his son.

"We can only hope the alcohol will numb him enough so that he simply accepts what you tell him," William said to his son. "Let us pray for that because I almost ended my friendship with him today when he tried to kill Troy. I'd hate to have to make that decision twice in one day."

Scott hung his head. Not because he was ashamed of his predicament with Athena because he wasn't. It was because he was deeply remorseful for what his father had to deal with. It wasn't just a situation that involved him and him alone – it was something that involved the whole family.

That was the unfortunate nature of it.

"For your distress, I am sorry," he said after a moment.

"Please believe me, Papa, when I say that I did not intend to disappoint you like this. I fully intend to face whatever punishment Uncle Paris wants to bring down on me, for the situation warrants it. I know it does. But I will not apologize for loving Athena. She is a strong, beautiful woman and she is worthy of being the mother of the heir to the House of de Wolfe."

"She is indeed worthy, but you should have waited until you were married to bed her."

"Did you wait until you were married to Mother to bed her?"

William couldn't lie to his son, but he wasn't going to answer him, either. "We are not speaking of me," he said. "We are speaking of you. When I married your mother, I did not have a father to advise me. My father was long dead, but you have me and I will indeed advise you. You've gotten yourself into a bind, lad. If we all come out of this unscathed, it will be a miracle."

Scott knew that truer words had never been spoken. "I cannot undo what has been done," he said. "There *is* a child on the way. We have already discussed it and we are going to name our son William, after you. It seems appropriate."

That took the raging wind right out of William's sails. A grandson to carry on his name. He was almost swept away with the sweet and happy thoughts of a grandson who looked just like him, but he wondered if Scott had used it as a ploy to soften him. If he had, it was a brilliant move.

In fact, it gave him an idea.

"While I am deeply honored, and you know I am, I would not tell Paris that," he said. "When the man comes in here and you must tell him the truth, tell him that you intend to name the child after *him*."

Scott's brow furrowed. "What?"

"Do it."

"But –!"

"If you want to throw water on a raging fire, tell him. You can always change your mind later."

Scott shut his mouth, eyeing his father but understanding why he said what he did. It was a dirty trick, but it would – or should – calm Paris' anger. At this point, he was willing to do anything to appease the father of the woman he loved.

"Very well," he sighed heavily. "If you believe it is the right thing to do."

William lifted his big shoulders. "I do not know if it is the right thing, but it is the wise thing to do," he said. "Hopefully, Paris will more easily accept the situation. Hopefully, he will be so drunk that none if it will matter but, somehow, I am not holding out the belief that it will. This could go either way for you, Scott – either he will not care because he has already been through this situation once today, or he will explode because it *has* happened twice."

Scott was aware of that. He sat down on a stool that the grooms used, pondering his immediate future. The more he thought about it, the more worried he became. "Do you think he'll do to me what he did to Troy?"

"If he does, you will accept it."

Scott put his hand on his blond head, hating to lose his hair like his brother had. Yet, if that was all he lost, it would be a small price to pay. Hair would grow back. He might even get a slap or two and he would tolerate it. But the thought of Kieran sitting on his head already turned his stomach.

In silence, Scott and William waited, listening to the sounds of the distant party and the occasional cry of the sentries. The horses in the stable stirred now and again, including a charger who had an inordinate amount of flatulence. Scott sat there, listening to that horse fart, torn between disgust with the animal and the apprehension of what was coming. It was the unknown that worried him.

And then, they began to hear footsteps.

They also heard bickering, clearly Paris speaking to Kieran. Taking a deep breath, Scott stood up so he could face Paris on his feet. He didn't want to face him seated on the stool where Paris could easily kick him in the face if he was angry enough. He didn't want to lose teeth. As he watched the stable entry, Kieran appeared practically dragging Paris by his arm.

And Paris did not look pleased.

"Unhand me, you brute," Paris snapped, yanking his arm from Kieran's grip and nearly landing on his arse with the momentum of the pull. But he kept his balance as well as the contents of the tankard he carried, though barely. "What is this all about?"

William cast his son a long look before speaking. "Scott wishes to speak with you in private," he said. "He did not want to compete with all of the guests in the hall, so I asked Kieran to bring you out here."

Paris was weaving around, perturbed and unsteady. A handsome man with graying blond hair, he was the commander of Northwood Castle's army, a great castle in the north and ally to William and Castle Questing. He also happened to be William's oldest and closest friend next to Kieran. The three of them were so close that they even married cousins, officially making them all family. They'd seen life and death and innumerable battles together, but almost nothing as important as the battle that was forming now. Those family ties had already been tested today and they would, once again, be tested this night.

Scott knew it was time to get on with it.

"Uncle Paris," he said. "I'm not sure this is the right time for such a thing, but I find that I must ask. Now with Troy and Helene married, it has occurred to me that I do not want to wait to start my life with Athena. I... I cannot remember when I haven't loved her, or that she hasn't been in my life. I never wish to be without her and I promise that I will make her happy. She will never want for anything and I will be true to her until the day I die. May I have your permission to marry her?"

William and Kieran were watching Paris closely. That's not the tack or the approach they would have chosen to take when there was something far more important to tell Paris. But very quickly, they realized that it was a brilliant tactical move by Scott by gaining the man's permission to marry first.

Then, deliver the questionable news.

Paris looked at Scott, processing what the young knight had said. Beneath that drunken façade, his mind was fairly clear when it came to matters of the family, including Scott and Athena. The pair that had both pined for one another and ignored one another, and this had been going on for years. Scott was a fine lad and Paris loved him like a son. In fact, he had a special attachment to him, as William's first born, and he had been expecting this question for the past two years.

Was it the right time to ask? Probably not, but he had. Attending a wedding had a way of inspiring bravery in those considering it.

But Paris didn't want Scott to think he was too eager to agree.

"I'm not sure," he said. "She is quite young."

"Not too terribly," Scott said. "Women are married at an age younger than she is now."

"But she may not want to marry *you*. Have you asked her?"

Scott blinked in surprise. "Of course I have," he said. "She wants to marry me very much."

Paris shrugged, leaning against one of the supporting posts for the roof of the stable. "I am not certain of this," he said, sounding both casual and inebriated. "Rafe d'Vant has an eye for her, you know. He's an excellent knight from an excellent Cornwall family."

Scott knew enough about his Uncle Paris to know the man was trying to goad him. "Rafe has an eye for someone else," he pointed out. "He has no interest in marrying Athena when he knows she is for me."

He may have had a better answer than Paris was expecting, but that didn't deter him. "There are a half-dozen lords in Northumberland who are better prospects than you are," he said. "Men who have wealth and titles."

"I'll have those someday."

"But you do not have them *now*," Paris said. "De Vesci's heir has looked at my Athena with longing in his eyes. Mayhap I shall ask him if he wishes to pursue her."

Unfortunately, Scott didn't have much patience, especially when it came to Athena and his pride. He knew Paris was just being difficult for there was truly no reason for him to deny him permission to marry her. The families had been expecting it for quite some time, so Paris was just being childish, in Scott's opinion.

That served to fuel his ire.

"Do that and I shall kill him and bring all of Alnwick down around our ears," he said. "Is that what you want? A war?"

Paris took another swig from his cup. "The war will be with your father, not me," he said. "My daughter is quite beautiful."

"I know."

"Many men look at her with longing in their eyes."

"How many men have asked for her hand?"

He had Paris on that point because there hadn't been any. Paris' eyes narrowed. "That is none of your business," he said. "The point is that you may not be her only suitor. She is young and I will not rush into anything."

Scott's face was beginning to turn red and William had

remained silent long enough. He didn't like seeing Paris harass his son in that fashion because it was bordering on mean-spirited.

"Paris," he rumbled. "Either give your permission or deny him. Stop torturing him for your own amusement."

Paris looked at William. "It is not for my own amusement," he said. "Your son wants to marry my daughter. Did he think it was going to be a simple thing? Did he think I would simply shake his hand and thank him for the offer? She has other choices than your arrogant son, you know."

William shook his head at the man, exasperated, as Scott's dander rose. He knew he shouldn't clap back, but with Paris calling him arrogant, he found that he was deeply insulted.

"She does *not* have any other choices," he pointed out hotly. "I am her first and only choice. If you do not want to give me permission, then simply say so, but know that I will not listen to you. I am going to marry her no matter what you say."

Paris drank the last of his cup and tossed it aside. "Is that so?" he said. "You think no other man will want her, then?"

"No other man will want a woman carrying another man's child!"

Both William and Kieran looked at Scott with wide eyes, shocked that he'd just blurted out something that should have been gently delivered. But Paris had provoked him; there was no question in their minds that Paris had unreasonably provoked him.

But now, they waited for the explosion.

It wasn't long in coming.

With a roar, Paris grabbed the nearest weapon, which happened to be a big, iron bar that the smithies used when shoeing the horses. He lifted it like a club and charged after Scott as the man dodged out of his way. Kieran leapt back as Scott raced past him, sticking out a foot and tripping Paris as the man came near. Scott ran through the stable yard as Paris picked himself up, grabbed his iron bar, and took a swing at Kieran. It was a drunken swing, but a swing nonetheless, and Kieran easily ducked it.

"I will kill you!" Paris shouted at Kieran. "I must kill Scott first, but when I do, I'll come back and kill you!"

Kieran was fighting off a bad case of the giggles. "I will be waiting right here."

Paris roared again and stumbled after Scott, who had retrieved an enormous pitchfork that the grooms used to dispense the hay. It was heavy, made from iron and wood, and he held it up to deflect Paris' blow as the man swung at him.

"I'm sorry, Uncle Paris," Scott said, trying to defend himself. "I did not mean to tell you in that manner, but… well, you were being hateful. It just came out."

Paris was on fire. "I'll tell you what else is going to come out," he bellowed. "Your guts when I'm finished with you! I am going to disembowel you right in front of your father! Guts everywhere like a sea of red!"

He was swinging the iron rod recklessly because he was so drunk that his aim was horrible. Scott was trying to stay out of his range, defending himself more than he was actually fighting back.

"If you kill me, Athena really *will* have a bastard," Scott said, dodging a swing that came close to his knees. "Uncle Paris, I love her. I want to marry her. If the child is male, we are going to name him after you. Your grandson will be named Paris. Does that not please you?"

Paris growled. He didn't stop swinging the rod, as Scott had hoped. "You'll not sully my name with the de Wolfe stench," he said. "You cannot name the child Paris de Wolfe. I forbid it!"

Scott was walking in circles around Paris, trying to stay away from the rod. "You are going to have another grandchild with Troy and Helene," he said. "Both of your daughters have chosen de Wolfe husbands. You love my father and he loves you. Stop saying terrible things about the de Wolfe name."

"It stands for animals! Foolish, reckless animals!"

"At least these animals have wealth and property, unlike the de Norvilles."

Paris stopped swinging, his eyes narrowing at Scott. "What did you just say to me, Boy?"

Scott didn't lower the pitchfork and he didn't back down. "I said the House of de Wolfe has property and money," he said. "What do the de Norvilles have except a madman for a father and a life of servitude to Teviot? You're nothing but a servant and that is all you will ever be. You should be fortunate that I am offering for your daughter at all given the state of your family."

"Scott," William hissed, standing several feet away because he'd followed the combatants at a distance. "Apologize immediately."

Scott glanced at his father. "I will not," he said defiantly. "He has spent the past several minutes greatly insulting me and you let him. I love Athena and I am trying to do the honorable thing by marrying her, but all Paris wants to do is insult me and the family name. I won't stand for it any longer."

"He's drunk, lad."

"I don't care!" Scott said, tossing aside the pitchfork and opening himself up to Paris' weapon. In fact, he faced Paris and spread his arms out. "You want to kill me? Go ahead. But it doesn't change facts. Athena is pregnant and I am the father. I am trying to do the right and honorable thing, but you want to kill me for it just like you wanted to kill Troy. You're a fool, Paris de Norville. An old and stupid fool, so if you think you can find a better husband for Athena, go right ahead. I won't stop you. But just know I have lost every bit of love and respect

I ever had for you, so I hope you can live with that."

With that, he stormed off, leaving Paris, William and Kieran standing in the small stable yard. William and Kieran watched him go as Paris stood there, looking at the rod in his hand. When Scott stormed out of sight, William and Kieran looked at each other before returning their focus to Paris.

"He did not mean it," William said. "But you pushed him too far, Paris. You had no reason to behave as you did towards him."

Paris was still looking at the rod in his hand. "No reason?" he repeated. "The man impregnated my daughter. You've had *two* sons impregnate my daughters, William. What does that say about you as a father?"

William's instinct was to hold his tongue because with as brittle as they both were, their lifelong friendship really could end that night. For good. But he didn't like hearing Paris impugning his sons.

It wasn't as if Paris had lived a straight and pious life himself.

"I'm not sure," he said. "I'd be more concerned with the fact that you have two unwed, pregnant daughters. What does that say about *you*, as a father, that you would let your daughters be so unrestrained around men?"

Paris looked at him. "What in the hell is that supposed to mean?"

William shook his head, exasperated, but he was prevented from responding when Kieran put himself between them.

"Enough," he rumbled quietly. "If this conversation goes any further, real damage will be done. Paris, you have left many a deflowered maiden in your wake, so stop pointing fingers. You, of all people, have no right to do so. What Scott did was not ideal, but it's not like you haven't done the same thing and with women you were not in love with, so your outrage is hollow."

Paris' blue eyes glittered. "Are you taking his side, Kieran?"

Kieran cocked an eyebrow. "I'm not taking anyone's side," he said. "But I am pointing out that you are acting despicably. You have every right to become angry and to punish Scott, but you do not have the right to insult him and his father. Stop acting so self-righteous. We have been through this with you once today and, quite honestly, I am weary of your behavior."

"So am I."

It wasn't William or even Paris who spoke. The three of them turned towards the stable yard entry to see Athena standing there with a broadsword in her hand. A big, heavy broadsword that she was handling most ably. The men faced her as she stepped into the small yard, her focus on her father.

"Scott is in the hall, Papa," she said, her jaw ticking faintly. "He will not speak to me or look at me. What did you do?"

Paris didn't like being cornered and he didn't like being questioned, especially by his daughter.

"That is no affair of yours," he said. Eyeing his tall, elegant daughter, the emotion was visible on his face. "Tee... how could you let this happen? Helene, I can understand, because she is weak and pliable. But you... you would make a magnificent battle commander had you been born a man. How could you let this happen?"

Athena could match her father's strength and then some. "It's not his fault, you know," she said, coming closer to him. "I seduced him. You are right when you say that I would have made a magnificent battle commander because I can command men to my will. I commanded Scott to my will and I liked it. Is that clear enough? I carry his child now and I am not sorry. He came to tell you the situation like an honorable man but, clearly, you did not react in kind. What did you do?"

The last four words were spoken deliberately. Paris heard

them, but he was still dealing with the fact that his daughter had admitted to seducing a man. Bold, strong, and willful Athena was behaving like her father had in his prime – seducing women, acting on impulse and passion rather than common sense. She was most definitely her father's daughter.

But his pride wouldn't let him admit it.

"I called him an animal," he said. "Because he is. Both Scott and Troy are animals because of what they've done to you and your sister. Beastly actions from men with no honor."

Athena's eyes narrowed, looking a good deal like her father in that gesture. "Take that back," she said in a hazardous tone. "Take it back and apologize. You will not insult him so."

"After what he has done?" Paris said, incredulous. "After what you let him do? Your mother is a fine, noble woman. I thought you would have learned grace and restraint from her."

Athena cocked an eyebrow. "As you have so often pointed out, I am exactly like you," she said. "I learned to be passionate and selfish, because that is exactly what you are – selfish. You are selfishly thinking about yourself in this situation and not about me. I love Scott, Papa. Does that even matter to you? I *will* marry him."

"It is my decision."

"It is *not*."

Paris waved her off. "I will not have this discussion with you," he said. "You are a lass that knows your own mind and is not afraid to speak it. But in this case, you are wrong. It's my decision whether or not you will marry that rutting bull who has soiled my fragile flower."

It was almost the exact same thing he had said to William about Troy earlier in the day, though Athena couldn't have known that. She did, however, have the same reply that William had.

"No daughter of Caladora de Norville is a fragile flower,"

she said coldly. "And you will not speak that way of Scott."

"I will do as I please."

Athena lifted the broadsword with two hands. "Then you have insulted him for the last time," she said. "I will ask you once more – will you give permission for our marriage?"

Paris happened to look at her, sword raised. He wasn't quite sure what to make of it. "And you will kill me if I do not?"

Athena's response was to wield the sword in a surprisingly skilled move, arcing it over her head and swinging it right at her father. He barely had time to get the iron rod up to deflect her blow.

"Athena!" he said, moving away from her. "What in the hell are you doing? Cease this at once!"

Athena wasn't listening. She leveled off a series of impressive moves, striking the iron rod her father was holding, defending himself from her onslaught.

"Not until you give permission," she said, grunting as she swung the sword at his head. "Give it or face my wrath!"

She went after her father with an astonishing amount of skill and strength for a woman who had not been trained as a warrior. She chopped and thrusted, chasing Paris all over the small yard as he used the iron rod to defend himself, all the while begging her to cease. But she wouldn't. Athena was determined to force her father into giving his consent as William and Kieran watched, open-mouthed.

They'd never seen anything like it.

"What do we do?" Kieran hissed.

William had no idea. He couldn't quite believe what he was seeing. "I am not sure," he said. "She's very good."

Kieran nodded in shock. "*Very* good," he agreed. "If she makes contact, she is going to seriously injure her father, or worse."

William could see that. "Frankly, I am afraid to try to disarm her," he said. "I might come away missing a hand."

They watched as she narrowly missed clipping Paris' forearm. "They can't keep this up much longer before someone is hurt," Kieran muttered. "She said that Scott was in the hall."

They were both thinking the same thing. "Find him, Kieran," William said. "Tell him to come running."

Kieran headed off into the darkness as William monitored the fight, which was becoming more brutal by the moment. Paris, not wanting to fight his own daughter, was simply trying to stay clear of her. He was simply trying to stay in one piece.

But the battle raged on.

At some point, they ended up inside the stable as Paris tried to avoid getting sliced. He stumbled as he tried to flee her slashing, falling to his knees and forced to protect himself by bringing up a stool in order to prevent his daughter from cutting him through the neck. He managed to get to his feet but she continued to chase him, growing progressively weary. She may have been good with a sword, but she didn't have the stamina that a knight had to throw around a heavy broadsword in the heat of battle.

Athena finally backed Paris into a corner and having nowhere to run, Paris simply stood there with the iron rod raised. There was nowhere for him to go and they both knew it. With the advantage, Athena finally lowered the sword, panting heavily.

"Now," she said, exhausted. "Are you going to give us permission to wed?"

All of the drink Paris had been filled with had been mostly burned off during his flight for his life from his very own daughter. He was still tipsy, but not nearly as drunk as he had been.

He lowered the rod.

"Does it mean so much to you?" he asked.

Athena rolled her eyes, exasperated. "Of course it does," she said. "I am willing to cut your head off because you will not give your permission. Why would you ask such a foolish question?"

Paris' gaze moved over her as she leaned against the side of the stall, wiping the sweat from her brow. He could see William standing behind her – the man had moved close to make sure no one really got hurt. He didn't care if Paris' pride took a beating from his aggressive daughter, but he did care if she drew blood.

Slowly, Paris sighed.

"When you were a little girl, you challenged Scott to a fight," he said softly. "Do you remember?"

Athena, still breathing heavily, nodded. "I do," she said. "He and Troy and Hector would travel in a gang and fight other squires and pages and steal their money."

"So you would champion their victims."

"Exactly," she said. "He was a bully."

"So were you."

Athena eyed her father for a moment before looking away, trying not to grin. "I was taller than most of the boys," she said. "I was stronger, too. Someone had to stop them."

"And you decided it would be you."

She nodded, leaning the sword against the stall wall as she faced him. "I did," she said. "Somewhere in the process, I realized that I loved Scott. I have always loved him, Papa, and I would be lost without him. Even if I was not carrying his child, I would still want to marry him very badly."

Paris, by now, was much calmer and more rational. Perhaps just the least bit sorry he'd been such a horse's arse and had driven his daughter to violence. "I know," he said quietly. "I have always known."

"Then why are you resisting?"

Paris took a long, deep breath and slumped against the wall.

"I do not know," he said. "I suppose because you are growing up so fast. Yesterday, you were a young lass who wanted to fight all of the boys and when I woke up this morning, you were a young woman wanting to marry the man you love. You have always wanted to grow up so fast, Tee, and to do everything so quickly. You rush into everything. Mayhap I am simply not ready for you to rush into this."

Athena could hear the sorrow in his tone and it softened her, just a little. "But you let Helene marry."

He lifted his shoulders. "I had little choice," he said. "But neither one of you are of age, Tee. You are young women, that is true, but you've not yet seen eighteen years. And you wonder why I do not want you to marry yet?"

Athena might not have been of age yet, but she was close. Not only that, she was quite mature for her age. She always came across as someone much older because of the way she carried herself, and those who did not know the family thought she was older than her sister when, in fact, she was younger. She had a certain quality about her that made her wise beyond her age, something Scott had seen in her for the past couple of years now, ever since she'd become a woman in every sense of the word. The only person who didn't see her as a grown woman was, in fact, her father.

Sighing faintly, she went to him.

"I know that I rush into everything, Papa," she said softly. "I have since I was a child. I have always felt the urge to do everything I want to do quickly and freely, to live my life to the fullest every single day. It's simply the way I am."

Paris knew why. He'd known why since she had been a young girl. "It's because of those… dreams."

Athena nodded reluctantly. It was well known within the family that Athena had prophetic dreams at times. She was always the one to have gut feelings about a situation or tell her mother an unexpected visitor was arriving and, usually, she was right. She was the lass who saw ghosts in the castles of Northwood and Questing, who would hear things that other did not. She was a woman of many fascinating facets and not simply sword fighting.

She seemed to live her life more hungrily than most because of it.

"Aye, the dreams," she said after a moment. "I've had dreams since I was a girl, vivid dreams of life and death and dying. I've died a hundred different ways in my dreams and the priests have told me that my dreams are omens while others tell me that God is speaking to me. Whatever the case, those dreams have always made me feel as if I must live every single day with vigor and curiosity and passion because one never knows what tomorrow will bring."

"And that is why you wish to marry Scott? To become a married woman so soon?"

"I want to marry him because I love him. I will never love another. Please, Papa."

Paris looked at her. Then, he lifted his hands, cupping her face. "Hector, Apollo, and Helene were born," he said, looking into her eyes. "And then, there was you. There was always something special about you. Mayhap it was because you looked so much like your mother. When I look at you now, I see her so very clearly. Mayhap there is a part of me that always wants to keep you by my side because of it. Is that so wrong?"

Athena smiled at him. "Nay," she said. "It is not wrong. I will never truly leave you, Papa. Don't you know that? I will always be your Tee, in this life or in the next. I will always be your angel."

"Swear it?"

"I do."

He kissed her forehead and dropped his hands. Then, he

stood back, looking at her torso, noticing the flowing dress, concealing her condition. He could hardly bring himself to speak the words, but there was no use avoiding the subject.

"When are we to expect this de Wolfe offspring?" he asked.

Athena instinctively put her hands to her belly and Paris could see, in that gesture, just how much she'd been hiding from the family. He could clearly see her rounded tummy.

"Soon," she said.

"*How* soon?"

"You had better let Scott and I marry in the next few weeks or this child really will be born a bastard."

"Does your mother know?"

Athena shook her head. "I've not told her, but I think she suspects. Mama is not stupid."

Scott chose that moment to make an appearance. Having run all the way from the hall with Kieran on his tail, he was breathing heavily by the time he came to a stop and looked between Paris and Athena in a panic. Kieran had only told him that there was trouble in the stables and when he saw the broadsword leaning against the wall of the stall, his eyes widened.

"What is *that* doing here?" he said. Then he held out a hand to Athena. "Tee, come with me, love. Get behind me. I will protect you."

He collected the sword, convinced that Paris was about to take the weapon to his daughter, but Paris held up a hand to calm him.

"Be at ease," he said. "I was not the one who wielded the weapon."

Scott looked at them both in confusion. "You weren't? Then –?"

"It was your future wife as she demanded I give you my permission to wed," Paris said, eyeing his daughter. "She was going to kill me if I didn't."

Scott stared at him for a moment as his words sank in. "My future wife?" he repeated. "Then I have your permission?"

Paris sighed heavily. "If I do not give it, my daughter is prepared to fight me to the death, so you may have it."

Scott looked at Athena, who smiled brightly at him. Then, she flew at him, throwing herself into his arms as they giggled uncontrollably together. It was the joy of youth and unrestrained love. Paris didn't know if he felt better or worse as he watched.

"You were correct, Scott," he said. "I was a fool. And my daughter is also correct – I am selfish. I suppose... I suppose I simply wasn't prepared to face this moment and it made me angry. I have lost two daughters in one night and that is a great deal for any man to take. Helene and Athena have always been my special little girls and it has always been the two of them, my little blossoms, and now... now, they are becoming wives and mothers and it is difficult for me to swallow. For what I said... mayhap you will forgive me in time. I did not mean it."

Scott had Athena wrapped up in his arms, just where he wanted her, so he could be a little forgiving. "There is nothing to forgive, Uncle Paris," he said. "I was angry. You were angry. I should not have said such things to you and I am sorry, too."

"I should not have called you an animal."

"My father says that it takes one to know one."

Paris' eyebrows flew up in outrage, looking over at William and Kieran, who were grinning broadly. When he saw the grins, he couldn't become too angry, mostly because they were right. That was the trouble with being close to men who had known him in his youth.

They knew everything.

He turned to Scott.

"Then we are a family of animals," he said. "But you are a

fine animal. I knew you when you were born and I have watched you grow up. I am entrusting you with my daughter, mayhap the most important creature in your entire life. May she always be that to you."

Scott's features were full of joy. "For always, I swear it," he said. "Thank you, Uncle Paris. I will not disappoint you."

"I know," he said, watching the pair as they ran off gleefully. He shouted after them. "But do not announce it! I will do that when I return to the hall!"

William watched the pair flee the stable, off into the night. "They will not wait," he said. "They are running to the hall to tell everyone."

Paris grunted. "I know," he said, sighing. He grew serious. "William, I still do not want them naming their son after me, but not because I do not want the de Wolfe name. It is because that privilege is for Hector, my firstborn."

William shrugged. "I would not worry over it," he said. "They only said they were going to name the child after you to gain your favor."

"Is that so?"

"It is. They are, in truth, going to name it after me, as it should be."

Paris rolled his eyes. "God," he muttered. "Another William de Wolfe. Can we stand such a thing?"

William grinned. "He will be the greatest knight England has ever seen," he assured him. "He not only has de Wolfe blood, but de Norville blood. How can he not be the greatest knight?"

Paris hadn't thought of it from that perspective. "You are correct," he said. "I'd not thought of it that way. A knight with those bloodlines will be invincible."

"Indeed," William said, slapping him on the shoulder. "Come on – let us head to the hall so that you may confirm their announcement."

Paris snorted. "Or deny it," he teased. But he quickly sobered. "I am sorry about today, William. I behaved poorly with Troy and I did it again with Scott. How do you tolerate me?"

William glanced at Kieran, who simply shook his head. "I have no choice," he said. "We are family."

"Speaking of family," Kieran said, eyeing Paris. "Apollo has been showing far too much interest in my daughter, Moira. Tell him to stay away from her or he'll not like my reaction."

Paris pointed to Kieran as he spoke to William. "Do you hear this?" he demanded. "This is exactly how I feel with the de Wolfe cubs sniffing around my daughters."

William didn't support him. In fact, he frowned. "And Hector has set his sights on Evelyn," he said, referring to Paris' son and William's daughter, who was barely into womanhood. "If Hector gets too close, I'll cut off something vital. You may want to tell him."

Paris rolled his eyes. "I cannot believe my ears," he said. "Have I not been stressing this very point? Men are animals!"

William grunted. "Hector had better not be an animal if knows what's good for him."

"Nor Apollo," Kieran pointed out. "If he so much as tries to steal a kiss, I'll take it out on his father."

Paris couldn't even rise to the threat. All he could see where a pair of hypocrites. He was about to tell them so, but he just started laughing. They'd accused him of being foolish but, as it turned out, they were just as foolish.

Possibly worse.

The three of them argued and bickered all the way back to the great hall where Paris announced another de Wolfe wedding in the near future. Two months after that glorious and pivotal night, a fat and healthy son was born to Scott and Athena.

Little William de Wolfe had the weight of an entire empire already riding on his tiny shoulders as his grandfathers celebrated the arrival of an heir. Little did they know how close he would come to increasing the de Wolfe empire…

Or breaking it.

Upon Will de Wolfe's shoulders would come the biggest burden of all.

CHAPTER ONE

Carlisle Castle
1293 A.D.

"**K**EEP YOUR SHIELD up, lad. If you lower it, an enemy will take advantage."

A little boy of six years was trying desperately to listen to his father as an older boy, with more skill, cracked a wooden sword over the younger boy's shield. The little boy swung his dull, wooden sword so hard at his opponent that the shield ended up in the dirt. He then launched himself at the older boy, trying to bring him down.

William de Wolfe, known as Will since the day he was born, grinned at his aggressive youngest son.

"Atticus," he said firmly, moving to pull him off of the other lad. "Enough. You cannot attack a man because he makes you angry. You must always keep your wits about you, else your opponent will take advantage of that and kill you."

Atticus de Wolfe was so angry that he was starting to cry, but not wanting his father to see tears, he simply wiped at his face furiously, smearing dirt all over his cheeks.

"He does not play fair," he said, sniffling. "He is taller and he tries to hit me in the head."

Will put his hands on his hips as he faced the boy. "And you do not think you'll face taller men in battle?" he asked. "You must learn patience, lad. You must also learn to fight with your mind more than your muscles. I have told you that before."

Atticus knew that, but he was still eyeing his opponent angrily. His adversary's family was an old friend of the House of de Wolfe, bred from a long line of knights, and he was fostering with Will at the powerful and prestigious compound of Carlisle Castle. When Will wasn't looking, Bradford Payton-Forrester stuck his tongue out at Atticus. The boy lashed out a foot and caught Bradford in the shin, sending him howling.

The lesson was over for the day.

Taking Atticus by the hand, Will pulled him away from his nemesis.

"Truly, Atticus," he scolded softly. "I am ashamed of you. What will Bo and Poppy and Bonny think of your actions?"

He was referring to his own father, Scott de Wolfe, known as Bo, short for *Bodach,* to his grandchildren. It meant *Old Man* in Gaelic, something Scott's Scottish mother had called him upon the birth of his first grandchild, and it had stuck. Will's three children had Bo and Dearest as their grandparents on their father's side, a doting grandfather and grandmother if there ever were such a pair. Bonny, of course, was Will's grandfather on his mother's side, and Poppy and Matha were his grandparents on his father's side. They were all still alive and well, so Will's children – Athena, Andrew, and Atticus – were well-supplied with grandparents and great-grandparents who spoiled them lavishly.

And that was part of the problem.

Atticus, being the youngest of his children, was so incredibly spoiled that the boy had difficulty not having his way in all things.

Like a wooden sword fight.

"Poppy gave me my sword," Atticus said, holding up the weapon. "He has been teaching me to use it. Why can I not go to foster with Andrew, Papa? I will learn much more if I can foster with him."

It was a question Will had heard before but he was distracted by shouting on the walls. At Carlisle Castle, perhaps the largest and most fought-over castle on the English-Scottish border, the soldiers on the walls were always vigilant, all night and all day. There was never one moment when they were not stationed atop the red-stoned walls, watching the magnificent greet landscape for any signs that the Scots were back to try and regain the castle.

It was an extraordinarily active castle, but Will had been the garrison commander long enough to know when his men were worried and when they were not. The castle sat right on the edge of the town of Carlisle and the soldiers had evidently sighted a merchant caravan moving along the main road through town, something that had their interest. The castle itself was a mass of concentric walls, berms, moats, gatehouses, and drawbridges, nearly impossible to penetrate. It had become that way because every time the Scots held it, they fortified it, and when the English took it, they fortified it a little more.

There was probably no safer castle in all of England.

Which was why Will kept his family here – at least, his youngest son and his wife, Lily. So far, they had one daughter and two sons, and Lily was current pregnant with their fourth child. Life was good, Will was content, and the truth was that he didn't want to send Atticus away just yet. Athena and Andrew, his older children, were fostering quite far to the south at Ramsbury Castle, seat of the Duke of Savernake, but he wanted them back in the north where their family was in power, so soon, they would be heading to Bamburgh Castle.

And little Atticus might just go with them.

But not yet.

Will put an enormous hand on Atticus' head.

"You will go to foster soon enough," he said. "Don't you like living here with me and Mama?"

Atticus nodded his little red head. Then, he shook it. "I want to go with Andrew."

Will shrugged, realizing the lure of a brother was greater than the lure of a father. At least, at the moment. He was about to reply, but Atticus caught sight of a knight coming through the inner gatehouse and he took off running.

"Marcellus!" the boy called. "Marcellus, will you fight me?"

Marcellus de Shera grinned at the eager little boy. Tall and handsome, with auburn hair and flashing green eyes, quiet and obedient Marcellus was a favorite of the women in Carlisle.

"Alas, Master Atticus, I cannot," he said regretfully.

"Why not?" the child demanded.

Marcellus pointed to Will. "Because your father has entrusted me with duties that I must fulfill," he said. "Mayhap I will fight you later, before sup."

Atticus wasn't too terribly pleased, but he didn't argue. He saw his nemesis again, walking towards the stable yard because as a page, he also had duties to attend to, and he ran after him.

Will watched him go.

"I am either going to have to send him to foster with his brother so he has someone to play with or I shall have to bring some more children to Carlisle," he said. "He cannot keep commandeering my knights for playmates."

Marcellus smiled. "He's a good lad," he said. "I really don't mind. Except when he insists that he win and I must fall to the ground and die a dramatic death."

Will snorted. "The more dramatic, the better."

"Your son has bloodlust when it comes to a fallen enemy."

Will continued to laugh softly. "He gets it honestly," he said.

"All of the de Wolfes have that particular trait."

"Speaking of de Wolfe," Marcellus said. "When are you planning on departing for Castle Questing and will any of us be going with you for your grandfather's celebration?"

He meant him or the other two knights who served at Carlisle, Sir Hermes de Norville and Sir Ronan de Wolfe. Ronan was Will's younger cousin, a young man with unearthly brilliance as a warrior. At eighteen years of age, he had already been knighted earlier in the year by his grandfather, the Earl of Warenton, because he was just that good. His first assignment had been Carlisle Castle, stationed with his older cousin in command. Somewhat quiet and introspective, but an utterly fearless warrior, Will considered himself fortunate to have young Ronan in his stable of knights.

And then, there was Hermes.

Hermes de Norville was about eight years older than Ronan, so still a young man in the grand scheme of things, but a more aggressive, cunning, wily, and intelligent warrior had never existed. Hermes and his older brother, Atreus, were very close in age and legends within the family for their fight-first-ask-questions-later behavior. The two of them together were like kindling and a spark, so their grandfathers, who were also Will's grandfathers, thought it best to separate the pair when they were knighted lest they kill each other at some point.

Therefore, Will had been saddled with Hermes, whom he was actually quite glad to have even if the man did make him want to tear his hair out at times. But he knew there was no way he was going to keep Ronan or Hermes from the celebratory feast at Castle Questing.

"I assumed that all three of my knights would want to go with me," he said after a moment, a knowing twinkle in his eyes. "Besides – my grandfather is their grandfather, too, and it is William de Wolfe's celebration of the day of his day of birth and nearly every household on the border has been invited, including those with eligible young women."

"Excellent, my lord."

Will cocked an eyebrow. "Are you hearing me, Marcellus? I said eligible women. Something we do not seem to have enough of around here."

Marcellus grinned, holding up a hand. "You know I already have someone who occupies my heart and my mind," he said. "But Ronan and Hermes do not. They need eligible women more than I do."

"Sure they do."

Marcellus started to laugh. "Truly, my lord, I am not looking for a bride," he said. "But Hermes, in particular, says he must marry soon or his father will disown him."

Will's eyes glimmered with mirth. "That is probably true," he said. "Uncle Hector thinks that marriage will settle him down, but the rest of us have our doubts."

"As do I."

Will chuckled. "But let us speak of you," he said. "You speak of this lady who has your heart, but when can we expect you to bring her to Carlisle and marry her? My wife would like another companion."

Marcellus' smile faded a little. "Who can say?" he said evasively. "Now, may I tell your cousins that they are indeed going to Castle Questing?"

He was deliberately changing the subject, as he always did when it came to the enigmatic lady he spoke of on rare occasions. Will was well aware of the woman that Marcellus professed to have a fondness for and he had been for years, only Marcellus had never divulged her name and no one had ever seen her.

It was a big mystery, much as Marcellus himself was.

Marcellus was a de Lohr knight who had come north with

Will when he and Lily had taken possession of Carlisle a few years ago, gifted to Will from Chris de Lohr, the Earl of Hereford and Worcester and Lily's father. Marcellus' grandfather, Leeton, had served the House of de Lohr many years ago, so he was a legacy knight and a very good one. Will considered him a friend, even if the man did keep to himself. He was a private man. Even so, Will had come to the conclusion that the phantom bride was a figment of the Marcellus' imagination.

But he'd never tell him to his face.

"Tell them we leave the day after tomorrow," he said. "We'll travel with a heavily armed escort and leave most of the army here at Carlisle. We'll leave one of the senior sergeants in command – I think Woodrow Decker is a good choice."

"He would be mine, as well."

"Then see to it," Will said. "And you will have the big carriage prepared for my wife and son. Atticus will want to ride with the knights, but he will not, so make sure the carriage is prepared for a six-year-old lad who will be bored to tears for the duration of the journey."

With a smirk, Marcellus headed off.

Will watched him go, looking forward to seeing his father and grandfather in the next few days. It had been a while since he'd seen them both, or the rest of his extended family for that matter, so he was happy to be going. But he knew someone who wouldn't be.

His wife.

Taking a deep breath, he headed towards the keep.

CB

"WHAT DO YOU think of this? Do you think the earl will like it?"

A young woman with gorgeous auburn hair held a piece of blue fabric against her body, showing it off to the woman seated in a cushioned chair.

But the woman in the chair waved her hand.

"It glistens too much," she said. "We must have fabric that is as masculine and strong as Warenton himself."

"But it's quite lovely."

"It's better suited for a lady," the woman in the chair stressed. "In fact, I may have you make a dress for me from it. Where did we get that piece of cloth again?"

The woman with the auburn hair held it up in front of her, looking at it. "Gretna, I think," she said. "Remember? From the man who pays pirates to bring him goods from the sea?"

The woman in the chair snorted. "Aye, I remember him," she said. "The man from Athens? What does he call himself? Kronos or something like it?"

"Karoly, my lady."

Lily de Lohr de Wolfe nodded in remembrance. "The man is a bloody thief," she said. "He has the pirates steal from the other merchant ships. At least, that is what Will tells me. I don't care. I like the fabric, so I bought it."

The woman with the auburn hair grinned as she carefully set the fabric aside, draping it over the back of a chair. She pulled forth another piece of cloth, a woolen fabric that had been greatly softened by using urine. It made the wool quite lovely to the touch, but she hated touching it. It had been dyed to a beautiful shade of green and she held it up for Lily to inspect.

"This one?" she asked.

Lily eyed the wool, leaning forward to finger it but realizing as soon as she touched it that it hadn't been washed yet. She made a face and wiped her fingers off on a kerchief.

"It's lovely, Adie," she said. "Do you think you can sew a tunic in the next two days? I realize that is very short notice, but I could not decide on a gift until now."

Lady Adria de Geld smiled. "I can," she said. "You know there is no one faster than I at sewing a garment."

Lily nodded gratefully. "Even when we were growing up, you were faster than anyone else at Kenilworth," she said. Then she paused, sitting back in the chair and putting her feet on a small stool that had a pillow upon it. Her hands went to her blossoming belly. "Lady Lancaster liked to take credit for your skill, you know."

Adria grinned as she laid out the chosen fabric. "I know."

Lily watched the woman fuss with the fabric as her mind traveled back to the glory days of Kenilworth Castle when she and Adria and many other well-bred young women fostered there amongst royalty. The days before she was summoned back to Lioncross Abbey Castle, her father's seat on the Welsh Marches, and consigned to a much slower life than she would have liked.

Back in the days when she had first met Will.

She didn't consider those particularly joyful days.

"Do you remember the time we went to Coventry and one of the de Nerra sons got into that terrible fight when another knight tried to speak to me?" she asked. "Lady Lancaster used to laugh at the men who would throw themselves at us. Do you recall?"

Adria nodded. "I do, indeed," she said. "Victor de Nerra had a nasty cut on his face as a result. Surely he still bears the scar."

"He was a nice lad."

"He was."

"I wonder what became of him."

Adria shrugged. "He's probably serving the sheriffs of Hampshire," she said. "I think that is the de Nerra lot in life. At least the ones from Selbourne Castle, where he was born."

Lily sighed as she continued to rub her belly. "I think of

those days often," she said. "Days of pageantry and excitement. Do you?"

Adria could hear the longing in her tone. She had known the lovely Lady Lily for many years, ever since she had gone to foster at Kenilworth Castle at around eleven years of age and fourteen-year-old Lily took her under her wing. Lily was sweet and kind, but ambitious. She had spirit and wasn't afraid to speak her mind, but coming from one of the greatest warring dynasties in England, that wasn't surprising. She had the de Lohr boldness, something that people attributed to her great-grandmother, a very lovely but bold woman who had turned the English court on its ear back in the day.

Or, so the stories went.

But Adria knew something a little different when it came to Lily. They were still the best of friends and always would be, but Lily was the kind of woman who should have been entrenched in court life. She should have married a courtier and spent her time in London. Instead, she'd taken a brief fancy to the young and very handsome Will de Wolfe and before she knew it, she was married to the man and pregnant with her first child. And that had ended Lily's quest to be both political and powerful.

Adria was quite certain that Lily had never gotten over it.

"I would not say that I think of them often," she said after a moment. "I do from time to time. I suppose I remember our friends more than I do anyone else, the girls we became close to. But... nothing more."

Lily looked at her, then. "I am sorry," she said softly. "How careless of me. I did not mean to bring back such things as you would probably rather forget."

Adria knew what she meant. She glanced at her, smiling weakly. "There is nothing to forgive and there is nothing to forget," she said. "I do not think of Gerard any longer, at least not in that way."

"Then the pain has gone?"

Adria didn't really want so speak of the knight she'd been so fond of, the young man she had planned to spend her life with. A freak accident had ended her dreams and his life. It had happened in one of the many tournaments that the Earl of Lancaster had hosted. The day itself had been such a normal day and a normal circumstance, and Gerard de Gil had performed well in his very first tournament since being knighted. But shards from a broken lance had pierced his neck brutally, even through the mail he wore, and it had taken him three days to die.

Three long, horrific days.

Adria had spent every moment by his side, tending to the man who had slowly died, his life trickling away like sands through the hourglass. After that, she couldn't bear even thinking of becoming romantic with someone. At twenty years and five, she was something of a spinster.

But it was better than having her heart crushed again.

"The pain is never gone, I suppose," she said upon reflection. "But it has dulled. Sometimes, I cannot even remember his face clearly and that saddens me. Do you remember him?"

Lily shrugged. "I remember that he had curly blond hair and a loud laugh," she said. Then, she smiled. "I remember he liked to tell ridiculous jokes."

That brought a soft giggle from Adria. "They were ridiculous, weren't they?"

Lily laughed softly. "Awful," she agreed. "I do not mean to push you, sweetling, but do you think time enough has passed that you should want to marry now? You know that Hermes has had his eye on you for some time. He comes from a fine family."

Adria cast her a long look. "Hermes de Norville is about as ready for marriage as a wild stallion is ready to be tamed," she said. "Even if he was ready, I would not consider him."

"Why not?"

"Because he is rash and reckless," she said. "I do not think we would make a good match, for we have nothing in common to share. Shall I go on?"

Lily shook her head as she lay her head back against the chair. "Nay," she said. "He is quite rash and reckless. You *could* tame the wild stallion, you know."

"I don't have a big enough whip."

Lily burst out laughing just as there came a knock at the chamber door. She turned to the panel in time to see Will stepping into the chamber. He looked at his wife curiously.

"What are you laughing about?" he asked.

Lily pointed to Adria. "I am trying to convince Adie to marry Hermes," she said. "She says that her whip isn't big enough."

Will grinned, looking at his wife's lady-in-waiting, a woman he'd known almost as long as he'd known Lily. Adria de Geld was a perfect woman if there ever was one, at least in Will's estimation. Petite, with a glorious cascade of auburn hair that tumbled in curls down her back, she had eyes the color of a spring meadow – a brilliant green that always looked tremulous and dewy. She had a pert nose and a mouth shaped like a cupid's bow, a rare beauty indeed. Many a man at Carlisle had commented on the glorious appearance of Lady Adria, and a few had even made advances on her, but she had politely but firmly rejected them.

Hermes de Norville included.

"Hermes is not nearly good enough for her, so stop trying to make a match," he said. "In fact, I came to tell you that I am bringing Hermes and Ronan with us to Castle Questing."

"What of Marcellus?" Lily asked. "Is he remaining here?"

Will shook his head. "All three of them are coming," he

said. "Things are quiet at the moment, so I feel confident enough leaving the majority of the army under the command of the senior sergeants. It will do the knights good to get away and feast with their friends for a few days."

Lily sighed. "I do not suppose I could not go, could I?"

"Nay."

"I did not think so."

Will's gaze lingered on her. "You feel well enough, don't you?"

She nodded. "I do," she said. "Just tired. Quite tired. And I've been having the same odd pains that I had with Atticus."

"What pains?"

She shrugged. "Little stabbing pains that are quickly gone," she said. "Sometimes my back aches. But I had the same thing with Atticus, so I am not concerned."

"What does the midwife say?"

"That it is simply the body adjusting to the child."

Will nodded, though he wasn't terribly comfortable with her aches and pains. Even though this was their fourth child, pregnancy and childbirth still scared him. "I wonder if it has anything to do with the fall you suffered a few weeks ago," he said. "When you slipped in the kitchen yard? You fell right on your backside in the mud."

She was growing irritated with him. "It has nothing to do with that," she said. "I told you – I had the same pains with Atticus. It is perfectly normal."

He wasn't so sure. "Mayhap I should send for the physic," he said. "Just to make sure all is well."

Lily shook her head, exasperated. "If you are speaking of Tarraby, then I doubt he knows more than the midwife does," she said. "The man is a surgeon, Will. He tends the soldiers, removes arrows, sews up wounds. Childbirth is not something he does often and I do not want him poking around."

Will held up a hand to back off before it turned into an argument, which it did fairly easily between them. "He is the most competent physic I've ever seen," he said. "But if you do not wish to see him, that is your decision. It was merely a suggestion. I came to tell you that I'm having Marcellus bring out the heavy carriage and prepare it properly so that you and Atticus will have something comfortable to ride in. I will try to make this journey as easy as possible for you."

Lily wasn't thrilled about the carriage because she didn't want to go, but she didn't fight about it. She simply waved him off.

"I hope Poppy appreciates that I am doing this for him," she said, disgruntled. Then she pointed to the bed where Adria was standing over neat piles of fabric. "Adie is going to make him a tunic as a gift. He will like that, don't you think?"

Will wasn't entirely sure that clothing was appropriate for a man's gift, but he didn't say anything. He just nodded his head.

"That is kind of you, Adria," he said politely. "Thank you."

Adria smiled in return. She genuinely liked Will, a kind and compassionate man. He had always been nice to her.

"I am honored to do it," she said. "I thought I might make a sash for your grandmother out of the leftover fabric. That way, they can match one another."

"Good idea," Lily said, answering for him. "Use Will as a dummy. He is bigger than his grandfather, but you can adjust accordingly."

Adria looked at Will, who rolled his eyes because Lily wasn't looking at him. He hated being pulled into female schemes. She bit off a grin and turned back to the material.

"At your convenience, my lord, but I must get started soon if I am to have it done in time," she said. "Mayhap I can measure you before sup?"

"Of course you can," Lily answered again. "Come back

before we eat, Will."

He sighed faintly, with no way to get out of it. "As you wish."

"Thank you," Lily said. "Now, where's Atticus? Wasn't he with you earlier?"

Will nodded. "He was heading for the kitchen yard last I saw him," he said. "He is playing with Bradford, I assume. Do you want me to fetch him for you?"

"Please."

With his marching orders, Will left without another word and shut the door softly behind him. As they heard his footsteps fade down the steps, Lily looked at Adria.

"We'll be lucky if he returns," she muttered. "He thinks the tunic is a foolish gift for a man of the earl's stature. I can just see it in his face. He hates the idea."

Adria's eyes glimmered. "Shall I run after him and beg him?"

Lily nodded, grinning. "Go," she said. "You know he cannot resist you. When he becomes angry with me, he tells me he is going to sell me to the pirates and marry you instead."

Adria laughed softly. That was an old theme with them and she was used to it. It was purely a jest because everyone knew how dedicated Will was to Lily, although most thought it was simply out of honor. They got along for the most part, but those close to them – like Adria – had seen the love go out of the marriage a long time ago and that was simply the way it was. Two people, married quite young, who had outgrown one another.

It was a little sad, in that sense, but Adria knew beyond the shadow of a doubt that Will really wouldn't sell Lily to the pirates and marry her instead. More than likely, Lily would run off with the pirates and leave Will behind.

But that was only private speculation.

"He has been saying that for years," Adria said after a moment. "I have yet to see him try. Besides – who says I will marry him, anyway?"

"What is wrong with him?"

"Nothing except that he is your husband. I do not want your leavings."

Lily burst out laughing. "He's not so bad as far as husbands go," she said. "Well, sometimes. In any case, you will run after him and make sure he comes to you before sup so you can fit the tunic. If he does not, there will be consequences. Tell him I said so."

Chuckling, Adria did as she was told. Setting aside the fabric, she slipped from the chamber.

They were on the top floor of Carlisle's heavily fortified keep and Adria took the narrow spiral stairs quickly, finally catching up with Will about the time he came off the stairs and into the great hall.

"My lord?" she called after him softly. "My lord, please wait."

Will came to a halt, turning to face her. His hazel eyes settled on her dubiously. "What does my wife want now?"

She cocked a well-shaped eyebrow. "How do you know she wants something?"

He fought off a grin. "Because she always sends you to beg for her," he said. "She still has to come to Castle Questing, so if she's sent you to plead on her behalf, you can go back and tell her I'll not change my mind. My parents and grandparents would be disappointed not to see her."

"It's not that," she said. "She wants to make sure you will come to us before sup so that I may measure you for your grandfather's gift."

"I told you I would."

"I beg your pardon, my lord, but you may forget."

He scowled. "Did she say that?"

Adria shook her head. "Not in so many words, but she sent me to make sure you were going to come. If you do not, there will be consequences. That is a direct quote."

Will made a face. He was a master at making faces to suit his mood or his reaction – long faces, pursed lips, rolling eyes – anything that got his point across. It was really quite comical at times and Adria tried not to smile as the man stuck his jaw out, baring his teeth in a gesture of frustration.

"May I take that as a confirmation you will come?" she asked.

He shook his head, defeated. "Aye, I will come."

"Thank you," she said. But her pleasant expression soon faded. "I also wanted to tell you that I believe it is a good idea for your surgeon to see to her."

Will's expression grew serious. "Why?" he asked. "Is there something the matter that she is not telling me?"

Adria grunted in hesitation. "I do not want to betray a trust, you understand, but her pains are not the only symptom," she said quietly. "You were correct when you said it had something to do with her fall. I believe that is true. I do not wish to be too graphic in my description, but suffice it to say that there has been some blood and there has been since she fell. Not much, but there has been some. The midwife also seems concerned, but Lily is convinced nothing is wrong because she has the same pains with Atticus. This is her fourth child, my lord, and she feels as if she knows her body well enough to know that there is nothing to be concerned with."

Will stared at her for a moment before quickly nodding his head. "You were right to tell me," he said. "I will not betray your confidence, but I will find my surgeon and ask him to examine her. In spite of what Lily says, Tarraby is quite competent. He has studied with the finest physics in London and I am quite fortunate that my grandfather sent him to me when I was injured in the skirmish last year. He has a miraculous touch."

"I agree, my lord," Adria said. "We are fortunate he has remained."

"Indeed," Will said, trying not to feel apprehensive. "I appreciate you telling me about Lady de Wolfe. I will send him to her right away."

"You had better come with him or she may not let him in."

Will sighed heavily. "I will bring him before sup when I come for the fitting," he said. "He can examine her while I am there to make sure she obeys him."

Adria gave him a knowing look before heading back up the stairs and Will stood there for a moment, trying to fight down his concern. Lily had given birth to three children without much trouble, so naturally, she didn't see anything wrong with this pregnancy even though she'd taken a heavy fall last month. She was about two months away from delivering the child, so naturally, he was concerned. Perhaps there wasn't anything wrong, but he wanted a second opinion.

Like it or not, with his surgeon.

Heading out of Carlisle's big keep, he was heading down the stairs leading to the bailey when he heard his sentries taking up the cry. He paused, listening to them shout at one another before a soldier came on the run to deliver a message to him. This time, there was a reason for their chatter.

A visitor had arrived.

CHAPTER TWO

I T HAD BEEN a long time since he'd been to Carlisle Castle.

St. Ansgar de Geld, otherwise known as Gar, rode into the outer bailey of the massive border bastion, reacquainting himself with the sheer size of the place. It had been a very long ride from his home of Alcester Cottage located south and west of Coventry, but he needed to see his only child and he didn't want to send a missive. He hadn't seen Adria in almost a year, but this wasn't a social call.

It was a business one.

He'd come for a reason.

After giving his name to the guards at the gatehouse and stating his business, he was ushered into the outer bailey, which was quite large. There were stables and outbuildings, and structures where the enormous army was housed. He'd been here before but he was always impressed by the enormity of it. The garrison commander, Will de Wolfe, had both royal and de Wolfe troops stationed at the castle, so it was a crowded place.

Gar remembered very well when he'd received a missive from his daughter telling him that she was going north with Lady de Wolfe because the king had appointed her husband garrison commander of Carlisle Castle. The House of de Wolfe controlled nearly the entire stretch of the Scottish border as it was, so placing a de Wolfe son at the helm of one of the largest and most disputed castles on the border was not unexpected.

The de Wolfes were the ones with the money and the power Gar had always hoped for.

The family had dozens of grandsons and cousins floating around and surely there was one his daughter could marry. That was the main reason he'd given his permission, and in light of the fact that she was the heiress to a barony, surely some worthy and rich knight would want her, if for no other reason than she could give him the title of Baron Alcester.

That title was the only thing of value that Gar had.

So, he waited. It was a fine day in early summer and the humidity from the River Eden wasn't too terribly strong this day, not like it would get in the later summer months when the moisture and the bugs would fill the air and make it difficult to breathe. Even this far north, it could get sticky. As he stood there and continued to wait, a stable servant came to collect his horse, so he removed his satchel from the saddle and let the boy take his old rouncey away. The horse was elderly and sometimes unreliable.

Much like him.

"Papa!"

Gar turned to see Adria rushing towards him and he took a moment to drink in the sight of his only child. She was wearing a dark blue dress with embroidery around the rather daring neckline and around the sleeves, which were open and draping. He was rather pleased to see how beautifully she was filling out, as the dress clung to her shapely figure. Surely any man would notice that, which played in his favor.

Perhaps he had more of an asset in her than he'd remembered.

When she came close, he embraced her and kissed her on

the cheek.

"Adie," he said with satisfaction. "Look how beautiful you are. I'd fairly forgotten."

Adria smiled at her father, but it was forced. Their greeting was almost detached, which was normal with them. They'd never been a hugely affectionate pair.

"What a surprise to see you," she said. "Why did you not send word that you were coming?"

Gar shrugged. "I wanted to surprise you," he said. "Besides, it was a long journey and I did not wish to worry you if I did not show my face when you would have expected me to. I move slower these days, I'm sorry to say."

Adria looked at him curiously. "Are you ill?"

He shook his head. "Nay, not ill," he said. "Just... tired. And I've not seen you in quite some time, so there is much to tell you. I do hope my visit is welcome."

"Of course it is," Adria said. "Quite unexpected, but not unwelcome. Please come into the hall. I am sure you wish to sit down on something that isn't moving."

"That would be much appreciated, Daughter."

Adria took him by the arm in a polite gesture and began to lead him towards the second enormous gatehouse that protected the inner bailey and the keep of Carlisle.

"How are things at the Cottage?" she asked. "I've not heard from you in some time, not since the last time I saw you when we traveled to Lioncross Abbey."

Gar was looking up at the walls of the inner bailey, marveling at the sheer size of them. "The house and the lands are the same," he said. "Nothing much has changed."

"And you? How have you been?"

"That is what we shall discuss."

Adria glanced at him, feeling more curiosity at his reply, but she said nothing. She simply continued to lead him towards the keep. Truthfully, his sudden appearance had her on edge because her father could be shifty. That was putting it kindly.

St. Ansgar de Geld wasn't what one would call a noble man. He had some issues.

Purely of his own doing, of course. Gar wasn't a responsible man. He was someone who would rather drink and gamble away money meant for debts or food. His father had been a good man and had tried to set an example for his son, who had been shady at an early age, but whatever lessons the father tried to teach the son had never been learned.

It was something that had driven Adria's mother to an early grave.

Anne de Sauster de Geld had been from a good Cornwall family, marrying Gar de Geld and bringing a fortune with her. She'd tried to be a good wife and mother, but Gar had piddled away her entire dowry and more besides. It was too much for the woman to bear and when she became ill, he couldn't pay for a physic to tend her. She'd died of a cancer, leaving a small daughter and a distraught husband who, in the end, used her death to emotionally blackmail her family for money until they finally cut him off.

Adria knew her father was looking for another pot of gold to tap into.

It was difficult to be truly affectionate with a father who viewed her as a commodity and, quite honestly, that was part of the reason she loved being so far away from him. He was way down towards the south while she was up in the wild north.

And she liked it that way.

They made their way into a big chamber that used to be the great hall, which was located in the keep and had the unique feature of having a massive wall run through the middle of it. Because of the activity on the border when it came to Carlisle Castle and the number of times it had been attacked, the wall in the hall added another layer of security because the opening in the wall could be locked with a big, iron grate, blocking off the stairs leading up to the upper levels. It was low-ceilinged, warm, and smelled heavily of the dogs that roamed the hall in packs, and Adria took her father to one of the well-scrubbed tables, sending a servant running for food.

"There, Papa," she said, indicating the bench. "Sit down and tell me why you've come all the way to Carlisle to see me."

Gar sat heavily, setting his satchel down beside him. "Can a father not visit his daughter simply because he wants to see her?"

"Is that why you came? Just to see me?"

The way Gar looked at her suggested that he was aware that she knew there was some motive behind his appearance other than fatherly love. There wasn't much of that and there never had been.

"You have a suspicious mind," he said quietly.

Adria wasn't going to apologize. "When it comes to you, I do," she said. "I am glad to see you, but I know you did not come simply because you missed me. You may as well tell me now rather than later, so come out with it."

Gar removed his worn leather gloves, setting them on the tabletop. "Can we not just exchange pleasantries first?"

Adria shook her head. "It must be bad, indeed, if you will not tell me right away," she said. "What has happened?"

The servants picked that moment to enter the hall, bearing trays of drink and food. They set them down next to Adria so that she could serve. Their fare included a pitcher with cloudy ale and a platter of raspberries, an early crop of cherries, pickled carrots, cheese, and bread. As the servants departed, Adria poured some of the barley ale into a cup and put it in front of her father.

"Now," she said quietly. "Tell me why you have come. I am

listening."

Gar drank the entire cup of ale in three gulps, setting the cup down and wiping his mouth with the back of his hand. Adria poured him more and he drained half of it before speaking.

"You know why," he said quietly, his gaze averted.

"If I knew, I would not ask."

He paused. "De Brito."

That drew an immediate reaction from Adria. "Not him again," she said in disgust. "What does he want now? Is it about the money?"

Gar looked up from his lap. "Money is not what he wants and you know this," he said. "That was not the deal."

They were only a few minutes into their conversation and, already, Adria had heard enough. "I know what the deal was," she said angrily. "I have already told you that I will not marry him."

Gar sighed sharply. "*I* made the bargain," he said, trying not to raise his voice for all to hear. "You know that Silas de Brito supplied me with enough money so that you could be sent to Kenilworth to foster. One visit to one of Lancaster's lavish tournaments, purposely putting you in Lady Lancaster's sight, and spending four days heaping praise upon Lancaster and his wife before finally broaching the subject of you fostering at Kenilworth."

"I did not ask you to do it!"

"I did it for *you*."

"You did not," Adria fired back. "You did it for yourself. You did it because you were hoping I would make connections at Kenilworth for you and your gambling circle and in return, you promised de Brito that I would marry him when I came of age. Well, I will *not* marry him. I told you I would not when you first told me of your scheme and I will tell you again – I will not marry Silas de Brito. If you came here to ask me again to do it, then you have wasted your time and mine."

Gar watched his daughter from across the table, seeing her angry, red cheeks, the flash in her green eyes. "I am not asking you," he said steadily. "I am telling you. You *will* marry him."

Adria was shaking her head even before he finished speaking. "I will not," she said. "If you try and force me, I will scream the entire time. I will create such a scene that you will be sorry you ever tried. Papa, all de Brito wants is the title I can bring him. That is all. If you pay him back the money he loaned you, then he can find his title elsewhere."

"The Alcester title is an old and prestigious one."

"It is an empty one," she snapped quietly. "It is as empty as your pockets."

Gar didn't like to be reminded of their abject poverty. Adria wasn't subjected to it because she served with the House of de Lohr and they were generous with her, but he didn't have that advantage. He lived in a big house, once rich, now bare and cold and lifeless. He had hoped that his daughter could bring wealth to him through marriage but, so far, she'd been uncooperative and he was starting to lose patience.

"I have come a very long way and you will not disobey me," he said. "You've yet to find a husband at your advanced age, so you must marry de Brito."

Adria shook her head again. "I will not," she said. "I will not be forced into anything."

Gar rolled his eyes, feeling desperate. "Then find a husband," he said. "You are past your prime, Adria. Do you think some man is going to choose you over a young, virginal angel? More than likely not. If you will not marry de Brito, then find a wealthy husband so I can give Silas his money and be done with him. Otherwise, you *must* marry him."

Adria was at her limit of patience with her father. She knew that butting heads with him wouldn't work, so she forced herself to calm. In truth, she was calm by nature, but her father seemed to release an inner demon in her that she didn't like, especially when it came to pulling her into his underhanded dealings.

She was always on the defensive with him.

"Papa, I am sorry that your ill restraint when it comes to gambling has brought you to ruin," she said, trying to be understanding when the truth was that she didn't understand him at all and never had. "I am sorry that you have used your daughter as something to bargain with. Although I am grateful to have fostered at Kenilworth because it has brought me to Carlisle and Lady de Wolfe, understand that I will not let you pull me down into the quagmire that is your life. Baron Alcester used to stand for something fine when Grandfather bore the title and his father before him. It was a title of responsibility and de Geld was a respectable name, but you have destroyed any semblance of what your father and his father built. I will not marry Silas de Brito and I will not marry a wealthy man simply to get money to pay off your debts. I am sorry you came all the way to Carlisle for nothing. Now, if you will excuse me, I have work to do. A servant will show you where you can sleep."

"Stop," he commanded softly when she stood up. "Just like that? You would walk away when I need you the most?"

"You do not need me, only what I can bring you."

Gar looked up at her, pale and distressed. He ran a hand through his thinning hair, trying to think of something to say that would make her stay and talk to him. He finally sighed sharply and looked away.

"You are all that I have," he said. "If you leave me, what will I have? There will be nothing left. I may as well be dead."

Adria knew that her father was very good at emotional blackmail. She'd seen him do it to her mother's family for years so she wasn't going to fall for it.

"If you feel that way, then I am sorry," she said. "You may stay here at Carlisle until you are rested, but then you must go home. I do not want you here making trouble."

He looked at her sharply. "What trouble would I make?"

She lifted an eyebrow. "Knowing you, there would be a game of dice tonight after sup and you would be right in the middle of it, gambling with Lord Irthington's soldiers."

"Irthington? Who is that?"

"De Wolfe," she said. "He was given that title when he was appointed the garrison commander. Henry himself bestowed it upon him. Remember? I told you when it happened."

Gar shook his head slowly. "I do not recall," he said. "So the man has a title, does he?"

"He does."

"And he married a de Lohr," he said, sounding bitter. "That means he is not only the son and heir to a great earldom, but his wife is the daughter of an earl which means he's as rich as Croesus. Some people have all the luck."

Adria didn't want to engage him in that conversation because it wouldn't end well. Her father was the jealous sort.

"He is a good man," she said. "He was born into a good family and he has prospered. You cannot begrudge him that."

Gar eyed her. "He has brothers, doesn't he?" he said. "Cousins? Surely some of them are unmarried."

Adria wasn't going to have that conversation with him, either. She pointed to the food on the table.

"Eat your fill and I will send a servant to show you where you sleep," she said. "There will be a great feast tonight, so do not miss it. But if I find you gambling with the soldiers, I will throw you out of Carlisle myself. Do I make myself clear?"

Gar just turned away from her, pouring himself more ale. Adria's gaze lingered on him a moment before heading from the hall to find Lily and tell her that her father had arrived for a visit. Of course, she would make it sound as if Gar had missed her terribly and had come to see his only child on a social call, but that wasn't the truth. Adria wished it was. She wished she had a father who actually loved her.

As her father had said, some people had all the luck.

But she wasn't one of them.

CHAPTER THREE

"AND HOW IS your father faring, Adie?" Lily asked.
The day was closing in on sunset, the sky streaked with clouds of red and gold. The evening's feast was a couple of hours away yet and Adria had just returned to Lily after seeing to her father's comfort. He tried to speak to her again about de Brito, but she'd simply walked away like she had in the hall. Now, she had the blue woolen fabric for the tunic laid out on the floor in front of the hearth so that she could spot any imperfections and avoid them in the construction of the tunic.

She was also trying to forget her conversation with her father.

"He seems tired, my lady," she said after a moment. "It was a long ride from Coventry."

"Was the weather good?"

Adria looked back to the fabric. "I did not ask him, but I assume so," she said. "This has been a mild month as far as weather goes."

"True," Lily said, popping a raspberry into her mouth. "I was thinking of sending a missive to my family with your father when he returns home. Do you think he will deliver it?"

Adria shrugged. "He should, my lady," she said. "I am sure

he would like to deliver the message and enjoy a day or two of hospitality at Lioncross Abbey Castle."

Lily was sitting in her favorite chair, the heavily cushioned one, with her feet on an equally cushioned stool. That seemed to be her standard position these days. Her hand rubbed her belly gently.

"I wish I could go home," she said wistfully. "I've not been in a couple of years, you know. Not since we came to Carlisle. It seems so far away."

"That is because it is," Adria said flatly, looking at her with a smile on her lips. "It is quite far away, so you'll not be doing any traveling until the babe is born. And what do you think it will be? I've yet to ask you today."

Lily grinned. "I know I change my mind daily," she said. "But, truthfully, I feel like I did when I was pregnant with Atticus, so I think it is a boy. But then I stand up and the babe seems to be lower in my belly than Atticus was. Athena was low."

"So it is a girl?"

Lily shrugged. "It is either Alec or Amalia," she said. "I have decided."

"Have you asked your husband?"

"He will agree with whatever I want."

That was true, mostly. Will was an aggressive knight, a booming commander and a brilliant tactician, but when it came to his wife, he folded like most men did. Before she could answer, however, the chamber door flew open and Atticus appeared.

"Mam!" he shouted, running to her. "Can I bring my dog?"

Lily reached out to stop him from climbing on her. "Bring your dog where?"

"To Poppy's feast," he said. "Can I bring him?"

Lily didn't relish the thought of riding for four days with a squirrely little boy and his energetic dog. She stroked his red head.

"I will think on it," she said. "Where is your father?"

"Here."

Will came in through the open chamber door, looking like a child who was being forced to do something he very much didn't want to do.

He cocked an eyebrow at the pair.

"Well?" he said, spreading his enormous arms. "Do what you must. But know that I am here under protest. And since you are making me do something I do not wish to do, I will make you do something you do not wish to do."

Lily eyed him warily. "What is that?"

Will turned to the doorway, crooking his finger at someone out on the landing. Tarraby de Solis, the army's surgeon, entered the chamber timidly and Lily rolled her eyes.

"God," she hissed. "Must I?"

Will glared at her. "If I must, you must," he said. "Tarraby, tell her where you have learned your craft so that she may be put at ease. She believes you are a simply a barber who cuts into men for pleasure."

Lily was gearing up for a nasty retort, but Tarraby spoke before she could get it out.

"I have attended university in Paris, my lady," he said. "I have also studied in Toledo before I came to Oxford to learn my trade. While many physics and surgeons simply learn the trade from another tradesman as an apprentice, know that I have specifically trained as a physic at university. It is my education that has seen me practice medicine throughout England."

Lily looked at him in disbelief. "You have been educated at university, yet you find yourself practicing your craft on the Scots border?" she said. "Why are you not in London with the king?"

Tarraby, a small man with thin, blond hair and a narrow face shrugged his shoulders. "The king has his own physicians," he said. "They are men of better breeding, finer families, and I have neither. But I served Humphrey de Bohun before I served the Earl of Warenton, and now I serve Warenton's grandson."

It was an impressive resume and Lily grunted. "I see," she said. "Then I am ashamed I never asked before. I thought you were just a soldier who had decided to become a surgeon."

Tarraby shook his head. "Nay, my lady," he said. "I would make a terrible soldier."

"But you are excellent with battle wounds. My husband says so."

Tarraby smiled weakly. "I go where I am needed, my lady."

"And you are needed here," Will said, pointing to his wife. "Lady de Wolfe took a fall last month and she has been having pains ever since. I want you to examine her and tell me if anything is amiss. This is for my own peace of mind because my wife and the midwife seem to think there is no issue."

Tarraby nodded, heading into the chamber with an old, worn satchel filled with his medicaments and instruments.

"My lord, you will leave the chamber," he said, but he looked at Adria, still bent over the fabric. "You will remain and help me, for the lady's comfort."

Adria looked at Will, wide-eyed, but he nodded. She returned her focus to the physic, nodding hesitantly. "As you wish."

Will slipped out, thrilled to have escaped being fitted for his grandfather's tunic – at least for the moment – as Adria shut the door behind him. Tarraby put his satchel on the nearest table.

"Please bring me a bowl, if you have one," he told her.

Adria went into a small alcove in the chamber, one that held a wardrobe for clothing and other dressing essentials including a big earthenware bowl. She emerged with it and brought it over to the surgeon, who poured something on his hands from a phial he carried in his satchel. The liquid dripped into the bowl.

Adria watched him curiously.

"What is that?" she asked.

He didn't dry his hands, but simply shook them out. Whatever liquid he poured on his hands dried quickly.

"It is distilled from grain," he said. "It cleanses the hands."

"For what purpose?"

"To keep poison from transferring from me to anyone I touch," he said. "My teacher in Toledo said that all things must be kept clean if we are to heal properly. I adhere to that rule although I know many do not. You cannot heal a man if you are pushing your own poison into his wounds."

Adria thought that was a rather interesting view. She shrugged and followed him over to the chair where Lily was sitting. He couldn't get a good look at her there so he made her get onto the bed with Adria's help.

When Lily lay back, the examination began.

⚃

HE KNEW THEY were going to find him.

Like a hunter, Will knew that Adria would find him and make him stand still while she measured him for a tunic that he still didn't think was a good idea, but far be it from him to try and change Lily's mind.

She was as stubborn as he was.

As he headed out of the keep, he happened to see Atticus and Bradford playing with their wooden swords again. The small inner ward contained a stone great hall, kitchens, and a chapel built into the wall. The hall in the keep was smaller, low-ceilinged and stuffy, and usually used for smaller meals while the great hall itself could hold five hundred men with ease, double that if they were crammed into the rafters.

Atticus and Bradford were over near the kitchens, where the servants were moving about as they prepared for the evening meal. There was an old, round kitchen servant who tended to Atticus these days because Lily couldn't move around with ease. Will tended his son as much as he could, but he had other pressing duties that required his focus. He could see old Myrtle as she scolded Atticus for skidding around in the mud, the same mud that Lily had slipped in last month. Atticus brushed her off and essentially told her to leave him alone, so she swatted him on the backside and took his sword away. Will grinned as the old woman grabbed him by the wrist and pulled him with her into the kitchen interior.

Poor Atticus was going to have to learn to respect his elders.

Listening to his son howl, his attention turning towards the inner gatehouse, he was thinking on checking the posts before heading to the hall for supper when he caught sight of Adria's father, St. Ansgar de Geld. Will only knew the man slightly, having met him twice before, but what he heard from Lily about the man wasn't good. He was a gambler, one who had managed to blow through the family fortunes, so Will had to wonder what the man was doing here. He hoped he wasn't trying to glean money from his daughter because Will was fairly certain she didn't have any. Lily paid Adria for the dresses she made, but there was little opportunity to make money.

Something about the money-hungry father made Will feel a little protective over Adria.

He knew Lily would have been, too.

"My lord," Gar said pleasantly as he approached. "It is agreeable to see you again."

Will greeted the man who didn't look anything like his beauteous daughter with his stringy hair and red, bulbous nose.

"Alcester," he greeted politely. "You are a long way from home."

Gar smiled, revealing yellowed teeth. "I have not seen my daughter in quite some time and thought to pay her a visit," he said. "I hope it is not inconvenient."

Will shook his head. "You are always welcome at Carlisle," he said. "But we are leaving in a couple of days to travel to Castle Questing. My grandfather is having a celebration of his day of birth and at his age, we are very fortunate to have him for one more year."

"Indeed, you are," Gar said. "The great Wolfe of the Border. My father used to tell stories about him."

"Did he know him?"

Gar shook his head. "Nay," he said. "But he admired him greatly."

"Thank you," Will said. "As do I. Will you go to the hall? Sup shall be commencing shortly and I was just going to check the posts for the night."

"May I accompany you, my lord?"

Will really didn't want him to, but he nodded graciously. "If you wish."

Gar took up pace beside him as they headed out of the inner ward.

"I was hoping to speak with you, my lord, if it would not be too bold," he said. "I have some questions I hope you can answer."

"I will try."

They were passing through the inner gatehouse and Gar looked out over the big moat to the outer ward beyond, packed with soldiers going about their duties as night began to fall.

"I will try to be brief, my lord," he said. "Since you spend so much time around my daughter, I am hoping you can help me. You see, she is quite old for a maiden and part of the reason I have come to visit her is to speak to her of marriage, but she is most resistant. Is there someone special to her that you know of?"

"Why do you ask?"

"Because I was thinking that might be the reason why she is resisting. Mayhap she is waiting for someone that she does not wish to speak of – yet."

Will was uncomfortable with the question because it felt too much like gossip and, truthfully, he didn't pay much attention to Adria other than in a polite manner since she was his wife's lady-in-waiting. It wasn't that he didn't think she was beautiful or accomplished, because she was. It was simply that, as a married man, he didn't look at other women in an appraising manner. Even if he and Lily were more friends than lovers, she was still his wife and he was faithful to those vows.

That meant he didn't pry into the lives of people like Adria de Geld.

"Have you asked your daughter?" he said.

Gar shrugged. "Not directly, but we spoke of marriage and she is unwilling to marry a man of my choosing," he said. "I thought that there may be a man at Carlisle to change her mind. Or… or mayhap you know of a wealthy lord who might like a beautiful wife?"

Will would have thought it was just a normal fatherly question until he mentioned the word wealth. That told him that the man's visit did indeed revolve around something financial.

He wanted his daughter to find someone to feed his gambling habit.

"I do not know of any," he said, trying not to sound disgusted. "Your daughter is a fine woman who will attract a good husband when the time comes. I would not worry over it."

"I am not worried, I assure you," Gar said quickly. "But I will admit that I would like to see her with a home of her own and children at her feet. Every woman wants that, don't they?"

Will nodded in agreement, glancing up at the walls to note that the guards were changing to the night shift. "They do," he said. "Did Adria tell you that Lily is expecting a child at the end of summer?"

Gar shook his head. "She did not," he said. "How many children is this for you?"

"Four."

"Four children with de Wolfe and de Lohr blood. You are building a great empire, my lord."

"I hope so."

"You would not happen to have a brother or cousin looking for a wife?"

Hermes immediately popped to mind, but Will shook his head. "I am sorry, I do not," he said. "If you will excuse me, I must walk the wall. Please go to the hall and enjoy a warm fire and good meal. I will be there shortly."

With that, he pulled himself away from Gar before the man could press him further. He didn't like the feeling he was getting from him, something pushy and greedy.

It was something he couldn't seem to shake.

The more he thought about it, the sorrier he felt for Adria.

∞

"I TOLD YOU that I was fine," Lily said as Tarraby stepped away from the bed. "My husband frets like an old woman."

Tarraby wasn't finished with his examination. He went to his medicament bag and collected what looked like a horn. It was fashioned out of wood and he bent over Lily's belly, putting the wide end of it against her rounded belly.

And he listened.

As Lily and Adria watched curiously, he positioned the odd

horn around her belly, listening for... something. They had no idea what, but he was clearly intent as he did it. Then, he put it away and examined her belly as closely as he could with her dress and underthings covering it. He thumped, poked, and prodded. Then, he tried to feel the position of the child.

"My lady, your husband mentioned a fall," he finally said. "When did you fall?"

Lily lay with a pillow under her head, watching him. "Last month," she said. "A little more than three weeks ago. Why?"

"When you fell, how did you land?"

"On my backside," she said. "Right in the mud."

"And you have been having pains since?"

"Sometimes," she shrugged. "But I had the same thing with Atticus."

"And do you bleed on occasion?"

She sighed faintly. "I have," she said. "But rarely. It is nothing."

"Is it brightly colored or dark?"

"Bright, I suppose," she said. "Why are you asking all of these questions? Is something wrong?"

He didn't say anything. He kept trying to isolate the position of the baby. "Are you having childbirth pains? For example, when the womb tightens as if it is trying to expel the child?"

Lily frowned. "I have had a few of those pains, but I had them with all of my children," she said. "I am not going to answer any more questions unless you tell me why you are asking them."

He glanced up at her. "I am trying to get as much information as I can," he said. "They are all normal questions, I assure you."

Lily was still frowning, but she didn't say anything more. She looked at Adria, who simply shrugged. She didn't know any more than Lily did.

Tarraby finally stopped poking.

"Do you have pain in your back?" he asked.

Lily nodded. "Most pregnant women do," she said. "It is nothing unusual."

"Does your back pain you when you feel the pains in your belly?"

"Sometimes."

"And you feel the child move actively?"

"He is quite active."

Tarraby fell silent as he went over to his table and rinsed his hands again with the distilled grain liquid.

"Were your other children large when they were born?" he asked.

Lily nodded. "Atticus was positively huge," she said. "Why? Is this child large?"

Tarraby nodded. "I think so," he said. "His head is still under your ribs, however. He is not ready to be born yet."

"That is a relief," Lily said. "I still have at least two more months to go."

"I do not think so," he said. "The child feels large enough that he could be born next month."

"That is impossible."

She said it in a clipped manner, as if there was no room for debate. New mothers were often certain in such things, but Tarraby glanced at her as if he wanted to say something but held his tongue. There was something in his expression that was quickly there, quickly gone. He returned his focus to his satchel and packed up his phials and instruments.

"Thank you for tolerating my questions, Lady de Wolfe," he said. "Your child seems well enough."

Lily smiled as Adria helped her sit up. "I told you," she said. "Now you may go tell my husband so he stops worrying."

Tarraby simply nodded, collected his satchel, and left the chamber.

He had a man to see.

In fact, he was rather singularly focused as he headed down to the entry level and out into the night beyond. The sun was down and cooking smells were filling the air as warmth and light radiated from the great hall across the inner ward. He suspected that he could find de Wolfe there so he headed over to the hall, entering to a heat blast as he came through the doors.

Men were eating a hearty stew with beef, cloves, and onions. He could smell the rich scent. Bread and ale were upon the table and the men were laughing and chatting as the evening deepened. A few called out to him, inviting him to join them, but he waved them off, searching for the garrison commander, whom he saw at the end of one of the long feasting tables.

Moving through the smoke and men, Tarraby found Will sitting with Marcellus, Hermes, and Ronan. They hadn't started eating yet, but were simply sitting and talking, passing a pitcher of wine around while everyone else drank ale. When Will noticed Tarraby, he turned his full attention to him.

"Ah," he said. "I see you are finished with Lady de Wolfe."

Tarraby nodded, trying not to seem as if he had come on an urgent matter. But the truth was that he had and he very much needed to speak with de Wolfe. Now was the delicate task of getting the man alone without causing him panic.

"Aye," he said. "If you have a moment, I would like to discuss my findings."

Will nodded, setting his cup down. "Of course," he said. "Did you discover anything out of the ordinary?"

Tarraby looked to the men sitting around and smiled weakly. "I am not sure that Lady de Wolfe would appreciate your men knowing her most intimate details."

Will was on his feet. "How stupid of me," he said. "The truth is that she would murder me in my sleep if she found out. Let us discuss this someplace private."

Tarraby simply nodded, following Will away from the table and out of the hall through a side entrance usually only used by the servants. It dumped out into a small area between the chapel and the hall. There were people around, but no one in earshot, so Will came to a halt and faced the physic.

"I hope Lady de Wolfe was cooperative," he said, a smirk on his face. "She can be difficult if the mood strikes her."

Tarraby shook his head. "She was most cooperative, I assure you," he said. "My lord, I hope that I may be completely honest with you given the subject matter."

"I would hope that you are always honest with me regardless of the subject matter."

Tarraby cleared his throat softly. "That is not exactly what I meant," he said. "Sometimes the truth is difficult to hear and I am not a man accustomed to carefully wording my opinions. I have many years of education and experience behind them and, as you know, I tend to be frank."

The smirk began to fade from Will's face. "I understand that," he said, his gaze on the man for a moment as if sensing what was about to come. The realization made his blood run cold. "Something is wrong. What is it?"

Tarraby didn't take any pleasure in telling Will his thoughts, of course. In fact, this was a difficult case. A new mother, a new child… nay, this wasn't going to be a simple thing at all. He'd been thinking that all the way from Lady de Wolfe's chamber of how he was going to deliver such news to a man she'd been married to for many years. Her husband, father of her children. He was a de Wolfe and she was a de Lohr, two of the greatest families in England.

They were building a dynasty together.

It was best not to beat around the bush.

"When I was apprentice to a fine physic in Toledo, a woman came to him with the same pains as Lady de Wolfe has," he said carefully. "This was a wealthy woman, a contessa in fact. She had her own midwives but about two months before her child was due to arrive, her husband sent her to my master because she had fallen from her horse and was experiencing pains in her belly and back. It was accompanied by tenderness in her belly when pressed and a good deal of blood."

Will was listening intently. "My wife has not fallen from a horse, but she did slip in the mud," he said. "I did not see it happen, but I was told she landed heavily. My God… did she actually harm herself?"

Tarraby kept his manner even. It wouldn't do for panic to set in this early. He had something to tell de Wolfe and he needed the man's attention until the end.

No matter how painful.

"As the weeks went on with the contessa, she continued to bleed and weaken," he said. "The child, who had once been active, gradually lessened in activity until we could no longer feel him moving about. We were faced with a choice – either cut the mother open and take the child or to let God's will be done. Her husband demanded that we take the child by force because he was desperate to have a son, so we cut into the mother to remove the child, but it was too late. Once we opened up her belly, we saw that the sack that provides nourishment to the child had become separated from the womb."

Will was looking at him in horror. "Because she fell from her horse?"

Tarraby nodded. "The blow was too much," he said. "There have been known cases where it has happened before. A woman carrying a child must be very careful because a fall can jolt loose things that are not meant to be jolted."

Will drew in a long, agonizing breath as he realized what Tarraby was driving at. "Like Lady de Wolfe."

Tarraby could see that the man was already figuring this all out. He tried not to appear too sorrowful as he delivered the final blow.

"When the nourishment sack came away from the womb, it slowly killed the child," he said. "It could no longer do what it was supposed to do. Unfortunately, it also meant that the woman was slowly bleeding to death internally. Once the sack comes away from the womb, there is nothing to be done. It cannot be healed. It cannot be repaired. There is nothing to be done."

By this time, the color had drained from Will's face. "Are you telling me that this is what has happened to Lady de Wolfe?"

Tarraby hesitated a moment before nodding. "I believe so," he said quietly. "She is showing all of the symptoms, my lord, the same ones I have seen before. I must, therefore, ask you this – do you wish for me to cut into your wife to remove the child and try to save her life? Or do you wish for God's will to be done?"

It was clear that Will couldn't believe what he was hearing. He stared at Tarraby for several long, painful moments before turning away, trying to come to grips with what he'd been told. Shock didn't quite cover it. Grief and agony did, but he couldn't seem to react with either. He was struggling desperately to control himself. It seemed like a small eternity before he returned his focus to Tarraby.

"Are you certain of this?" he asked hoarsely. "Are you absolutely certain?"

Tarraby shrugged. "I have seen the same symptoms before, my lord," he said. "Can I guarantee this is the issue? I cannot. But I am fairly certain this is the case."

Although Will had expected that answer, to hear the confirmation was still something of a shock. The fact that Tarraby didn't seem to have any doubts weakened his grip on his composure. Maybe he'd been hoping for a shadow of uncertainty, something to give him some hope.

But there was nothing.

He exhaled sharply, as if an unseen fist had just hit him in the belly.

"What can we do?" he demanded weakly. "Surely there is something we can do?"

Tarraby could see that the man was beginning that slow ascent into panic. "As I have explained to you, at some point, you must make a decision, my lord," he said. "I can cut into her and try to save her life, or we can let God's will be done and let the process come to its natural conclusion."

Will scowled. "Natural conclusion?" he repeated, aghast. "You mean death?"

"Aye, my lord."

"But if you try to take the child early, you can save her?"

Tarraby hesitantly shrugged. "We were unable to save the contessa," he said. "I cannot promise to save her, only to try. But the child… there is nothing we can do. I am sorry, my lord, truly."

Will stared at him. A dozen scenarios were running through his mind as his eyes flickered with an unsteady light. Pushing aside his grief and shock, he was trying to find some way to save both Lily and the child, but the truth was that he wasn't a physic. He knew warfare and tactics and politics among his many talents, but healing wasn't one of them.

However, he knew who was.

His father.

Scott de Wolfe was a healer, a man who had learned from Will's grandfather, Paris, who was also a skilled healer in his own right. Both men were well known to have the gift of health and healing and the family had often depended upon them for those talents. Perhaps they could help. Will wasn't going to bring Lily to them and, even now, had made the decision not to go to his grandfather's celebration of his day of birth, but that didn't mean he wasn't going to send for his father and grandfather to see what their opinion was of Tarraby's diagnosis.

To see if there was some hope.

He simply couldn't believe this was the end.

"I thank you for your skill and your honesty, Tarraby," he said, somewhat dazed. "Did… did you tell Lady de Wolfe any of this?"

Tarraby shook his head. "Nay, my lord," he said. "I assumed you would want to do it."

"To tell my wife that she is dying."

"Aye, my lord."

Those words hit him like a hammer. They were so… cold. Will knew Tarraby wasn't trying to be cold, but it all came out the same. Honesty was coldness right now and Will was trying to be calm and levelheaded about the situation. With God as his witness, he was trying hard. But so much was rolling through his mind that it was difficult to remain on an even keel.

"Thank you," he finally said, refusing to look at Tarraby. "You may go about your business, but do not speak of this to anyone. I must have your word."

Tarraby nodded. "You have it, my lord," he said. "I would never speak of your lady wife to anyone."

"Will you look in on her tomorrow? To see if there is any change?"

He was grasping at straws, as if a day might bring that hope he was trying so badly to find. Maybe Tarraby had been wrong. Maybe there was another diagnosis he simply hadn't realized yet. Maybe by tomorrow, this will have all been simply a nightmare.

Tarraby knew that. He could hear it in his tone. All he could do was play along, at least for now, until Will came to terms with the situation.

"If you wish it, I will," he said.

Will simply nodded, unable to articulate anything more, as Tarraby turned and headed back into the hall.

But Will didn't.

He didn't want to be around anyone at the moment.

Dazed, he headed back into Carlisle's keep. There was a small chamber off the hall that had formerly been used as a guard room but when he took possession of the castle, it became his private solar. It was a cramped chamber with an enormous hearth, but it was his and it was quiet.

At the moment, he desperately needed quiet.

There were only servants moving about the keep when he entered, sweeping the small feasting hall and making preparations for the night. Will walked right past them and into his small room, shutting the door. For a moment, he simply stood there, hearing Tarraby's words ringing in his head.

There is nothing to be done.

Lily was going to die.

Things like this happened to other people. Not to him. He'd already lost the most important woman in his life when he was younger, when his mother and his younger two siblings drowned in a terrible accident. It was true that he'd been a youth at the time, fostering at Lioncross Abbey Castle, but that didn't make the impact of his mother's death any less painful.

Unfortunately, he'd not been able to show it.

Will's brother, named Thomas but known as Tor, was three years younger and they'd fostered together. They had been, and continued to be, quite close. When news of their mother's passing had come, Tor had taken it hard and it had been up to

Will to show strength in the situation. He didn't have the luxury of exhibiting his pain because Tor had been such a mess about it. Will had been forced to mourn his mother privately, using his strength to comfort his brother. But inside, he had been crumbling just like his brother did.

That outward composure had come at a cost.

After that, Will became very good at bottling himself up and letting things fester. Outwardly, he was in control. Always in control. But inwardly, his guts ached and his heart burned, keeping his rather fragile emotions contained. He didn't speak much of his feelings and he rarely showed them.

Not even to Lily.

God, what a mess this was.

Now, he had a wife in trouble. Not merely in trouble, but facing a shockingly mortal situation. Never in a million years had Will imagined he'd be facing something like this again in his lifetime, but if what Tarraby said was correct, he was facing losing yet another important woman in his life. Even if their marriage had become something that simply existed for existence's sake and the fire of passion had burned out years ago, that didn't mean he didn't care for Lily. She was the mother of his children and he would always care for her. He would always be concerned for her. Truth be told, as he thought on the situation, he realized that he was much more concerned with his children's reaction to their mother's diagnosis than he was with his own feelings about it.

And that brought about waves of guilt.

Maybe more guilt than he could handle.

The small chamber contained a table with a half-filled pitcher of old wine and a couple of wooden cups that he and Marcellus had used for the wine two days ago. The servants simply never removed it because he didn't like them in this room. Picking up the pitcher, he drank straight from the neck.

Stale wine still got him just as drunk, but it didn't take away the anguish.

It only made it worse.

Buckling under the weight of his life collapsing before his very eyes, Will remained in the chamber all night and when morning came, a missive went out to Rule Water Castle, seat of Scott de Wolfe, and to Lioncross Abbey Castle, seat of Chris de Lohr.

He needed help.

CHAPTER FOUR

F OR THIS TIME of year, the day had dawned with a significant amount of dew and fog across the gently rolling hills of northern England.

Everything was wet as Adria emerged from the keep. These days, her chamber was an alcove off of Lily's main chamber, a tiny room used for servants in days past, but it had become her tiny haven. She really didn't mind because it was cozy and private, and more importantly, it was hers alone. She didn't have to share it with anyone. It kept her close to Lily, who slept alone in the big chamber except for Atticus, who had his own bed near the hearth and a corner of the enormous chamber to call his own.

Carlisle's keep hadn't been built for comfort or growing families. It had the one massive chamber and smaller servant's chamber on the top floor and then directly below that was the smaller hall. There were other small chambers off the hall, two in fact, and then there was a vault below the hall where they kept the stores. Visitors and knights either slept in the outbuildings in the outer ward or they slept in the small apartment block in the inner ward that was built along the wall next to the gatehouse.

That was where Adria's father was.

Truthfully, she was hoping he would become disgruntled with her refusal to participate in the schemes he'd come to her with and would soon be heading home. She'd stayed away from him last night and as the misty day dawned, she intended to stay away from him this morning as well.

The man's mere presence made her tense.

Still, she wasn't going to let him distract her. She had a task to complete with Warenton's gift and she intended to see it through. In her arms, she carried the blue woolen fabric with the intention of having it gently washed to remove the ammonia smell that Lily found so unpleasant. There was a type of herb used for the cleansing of clothing, called soapwort or even latherwort depending on the region or even the variation of the herb, that created a fine frothy liquid when crushed that was quite gentle on clothing and quite effective.

Adria had seen the washerwomen of Carlisle use the soapwort many times and even at this early hour, the women from the village who washed the clothing of the inhabitants of the castle were in the kitchen yard, heating big vats of water for the wash of the day. These women were paid well for washing clothing and Adria greeted them as they gathered around her, sensing a well-paying job with the fabric she was carrying. She was able to negotiate a good price for the washing with one of the women, turning over the fabric but not leaving the yard.

She wanted to make sure that lovely blue color wasn't damaged.

As the washerwoman began to work on the smelly fabric, Adria watched from a position over near the fire that was heating the big vats of water. It was warm there, heat against the cold morning. She was thinking about seeking something warm to drink, as the cook usually had something warm and simmering like watered wine, spicy and delicious, or even warm milk with cinnamon. That was Lily's favorite. As she mulled over collecting a drink, she saw a small body dart into the yard.

Atticus entered the yard, carrying his wooden sword. He wasn't well-dressed against the chill, meaning he'd slipped out while his mother was asleep. With Atticus, that happened quite a bit. When she saw the child, she immediately went to intercept him.

"Atticus?" she said. "What are you doing here? It's very cold this morning. Where is your heavy tunic?"

Atticus' teeth were chattering in the cold, his nose pinched red. He was wearing what he had been sleeping in – a tunic and a pair of breeches. He'd pulled his shoes on, but one of them was untied and he was dragging the ties through the mud of the yard.

He looked at Adria as if prepared to fight her off with his wooden weapon.

"I... I was looking for Bradford," he said. "Have you seen him?"

Adria shook her head. "I have not," she said. "Does your mother know you are here?"

Atticus frowned. "Where is my father?" he said. "I want my father."

"You just said you were looking for Bradford," Adria reminded him. "Do not lie to me, Atticus. Your mother does not know you are here because you are poorly dressed against the morning. That means you've not even washed your neck or ears. Your mother asks you to do that every morning before you dress."

Atticus' frown grew, looking very much like his mother in that gesture. "You cannot tell me what to do," he said. "Leave me alone."

He was defiant for a six year old. And naughty. But Adria didn't care how defiant or naughty he was; she knew how to take charge. Reaching out, she grabbed him by the ear, pulling him over to the fire with its boiling vats of water.

"Ooch!" Atticus cried as she dragged him across the yard. "Let me go!"

"Quiet," Adria hissed. "You are a wild and naughty lad, Atticus de Wolfe, and you disobey your mother far more than you should."

"Let me –!"

"*Hush*," she snapped softly, cutting him off. "There is no one to help you, so you may as well cooperate."

The washerwomen had already washed some of the linens that were used in the keep, either bedding or towels, and she grabbed one off the line that it was hanging on. Still dragging Atticus, she dipped the linen in the boiling water, waited a nominal amount of time for it to cool, before grabbing the child by the hair and using the warm, wet rag to wash his neck by force.

Atticus howled.

"Stop!" he demanded, trying to pull away from her. "Stop washing me!"

Adria ignored him. She scrubbed the boy's dirty face, having seen Lily do it a thousand times and having watched Atticus scream a thousand times. The boy hated to be washed, but Lily simply didn't have the strength to do battle with him these days, so Adria was happy to do it in her stead.

But Atticus was not happy to have her do it.

"You're hurting me!" he cried. "Let me go!"

Adria continued in her task, now washing his ears as he struggled to pull away from her. But she held his hair fast and he finally gave up pulling when he realized she wasn't going to let him go. He whined and groaned as she went back to scrubbing the back of his neck because it was so dirty. She didn't stop until she was satisfied.

"There," she said, finally releasing him. "Now, you will return to your chamber and put on warmer clothing. If you do not, I will drag you back into the chamber and dress you myself. Is that what you want?"

Rubbing at his stinging ears, Atticus hung his head and scowled. "Nay."

Adria pointed to the keep. "Go," she told him. "Do not come down until you are properly dressed."

Atticus dared to look up at her, sticking his tongue out at her before running off as fast as he could go. Adria shook her head at the cheeky child, catching sight of Will entering the kitchen yard just as Atticus ran through the gate like his arse was on fire. Puzzled, Will watched his son bolt as Adria went to him to clear up his confusion.

"He was out here looking for Bradford," she said. "He is ill-clothed for the chill morning, so I washed his face and neck and sent him back up to dress properly."

Will grinned, flashing that seductive de Wolfe smile that most of the males in the family seemed to have – dimpled, with prominent canines. It was a smile that thrilled a thousand female hearts and then some.

"Is that all?" he asked. "I heard him howling in the outer ward. I thought surely he was being tortured."

"He was."

Will chuckled. "I am sure he thinks so," he said, sobering as he looked at Adria. "Thank you for tending to him. I assume Lady de Wolfe is still asleep?"

Adria nodded. "I think so," she said. "She was when I left the chamber. She seems to sleep a good deal these days, understandably."

Will's humor left him completely as Adria inadvertently brought up Lily's condition. It was the entire reason why he hadn't slept last night and this morning, the situation didn't look any better. If anything, he felt worse. He glanced at Adria, seeing that lovely woman he'd always seen. Luscious titian-colored hair and green eyes were part of the beauty he was faced with every day, so he'd become accustomed to it and to her. She was a fixture in his family, something unnoticed when she was present but were she to leave, she would be terribly missed because she was incredibly devoted to Lily. She had been a great and loyal friend to his wife.

Lily was going to need that devotion now, more than ever.

"She is under a good deal of strain these days," he said. It was all he could manage to say on that matter. "Adria… you were with her yesterday when Tarraby examined her, were you not?"

Adria nodded. "I was."

"Did Tarraby… what I mean to say is did he express any concerns to you or to Lady de Wolfe?"

Adria cocked her head. "Concerns?" she repeated thoughtfully. "Nay, no concerns, but he did ask her many questions. Why do you ask?"

Will shrugged. "I was just curious if he said anything to her, or she to him."

"You've not asked her?"

He shook his head. "I've not seen her since last night," he said. "I will ask her when I see her, but I thought you might be able to tell me anything interesting."

Adria shook her head. "Nothing particularly interesting," she said. "Did Tarraby not tell you the results of his examination? He said that he was going to."

Will couldn't bring himself to tell her that he had indeed spoken to Tarraby. He was starting to feel anxious again, still shocked from the news, when he suddenly saw his son bolting across the inner ward again, heading for the gatehouse. The boy had a heavy tunic on, but his shoes were still untied, the laces dragging in the mud.

His focus shifted.

"Lady Adria," he said quietly. "I was hoping that you might be able to help Lady de Wolfe these days by tending to Atticus more closely. I know that my wife likes to tend her children herself, but in her condition, she should not be chasing after him. I realize that you serve my wife as her lady-in-waiting, but would you be willing to help more with Atticus? More than you usually do?"

Adria nodded. "Or course, my lord," she said. "I would be happy to."

"Would you be willing to take full charge of him?"

"If you and Lady de Wolfe wish it."

Will was trying not to convey what he was feeling. He was trying to keep his manner calm and composed like he always was, but given the subject matter, it was difficult. He didn't want to let on that there was a reason for his request beyond the normal concerns of Lily's obvious condition.

"I do," he said. "I will break the bad news to Atticus because he fears you are a tyrant, but I appreciate you tending to him so Lady de Wolfe does not have to worry over him. She should not be exerting herself so."

Adria smiled at the mention of a tyrant, for it was true. But something in those pale eyes studied him closely.

He could feel her scrutiny.

"Did Tarraby tell you something that we should be concerned with?" she asked.

He hadn't yet admitted he'd even spoken to Tarraby yet and he didn't want to fuel her curiosity, so he simply waved her off.

"My wife is pregnant," he stated the obvious. "That is always something to be concerned with. Now, I will go find my son, who I just saw run through the gatehouse, and bring him back here. I will tell him that you have full authority over him but I will request that if there is any punishment to be dealt out that you consult with me first. Will you do that?"

"Of course, my lord."

His gaze lingered on her as he wanted to say more but he ended up averting his eyes and turning towards the gatehouse.

"Thank you, my lady," he said quietly. "Your help is much appreciated."

Adria simply nodded even though he couldn't see her. She watched him walk across the small inner ward, studying the man. He had a kind of deliberate, proud gait. He was an enormous man with the future of the entire de Wolfe empire weighing on him. He was quite the handsome man; she'd always thought so. When he flashed that grin as he so often did, Adria could well understand how the gesture would make even the hardiest maiden faint with glee. With his hazel eyes and dark hair with a hint of auburn, he most definitely had that power.

But there was something gruff about Will de Wolfe, something hard and strong and unbreakable. He could bellow out orders that could be heard over half of England and he had a penchant for using hilarious insults when the mood struck him. They'd all heard Will call his men lumpish gecks when they didn't move fast enough or tell them that they were all a gaggle of musty parasites when something didn't go his way.

There was no one in all of England who could insult men better and get away with it.

Secretly, Adria had always had a bit of a fondness for him. She wouldn't even admit that to herself even though she knew it was true because Will was married to her lady and there would never be anything improper in her manner towards him. Adria wasn't in the habit of trying to seduce married men and she certainly wasn't going to start with Will de Wolfe, a man who was not only far above her station, but one she respected tremendously.

If there was a more perfect husband out there, she had yet to find him.

But it wasn't like the marriage was perfect in and of itself. It wasn't; being as close as she was to Lily, she knew that. Will and Lily rarely slept in the same bed – she in the big chamber and he in his private solar. Lily liked to sleep alone, so she said, and Will didn't fight her on it. They fact that they had three children and a fourth on the way was something of a miracle.

But there was a dark and dirty truth of it.

The reality was that Will and Lily had married too hastily, and too young, forced together by Lily's father who had wanted his daughter to have the de Wolfe connection. He wanted that link. Twelve years later, Lily and Will had a polite marriage, but it was more like two friends being thrust together rather than two lovers. Chris de Lohr's political marriage had consigned them both to a pleasant association and little more.

But no one acknowledged that. No one spoke of it.

Least of all Adria.

It was simply the way of things.

Pushing the state of Will and Lily's marriage aside, for there was no use thinking on something that really wasn't any of her affair, she turned back towards the washerwoman who was carefully scrubbing the blue fabric with the soapwort. She could see the woman from where she was standing. Around her, the castle was coming alive as the morning deepened, with men on the walls changing shifts and the servants below going about their duties.

The kitchens were in full swing by this time, preparing for the smaller nooning meal and then the feast that night. Adria could hear shouting on the walls and she shielded her eyes from the rising sun, looking up to see what the trouble was. There didn't seem to be anything of note more than soldiers yelling at one another so she lowered her hand as she reached the washerwoman and the blue fabric, now stretched out on a table.

"Good morn, my lady."

The greeting came from behind. Adria turned to see Hermes de Norville standing behind her, smiling timidly. She smiled politely in return.

"Good morn, Sir Hermes," she said. "What brings you to the kitchen yard?"

His smile turned genuine. "You," he said frankly. "I was wondering if I might have a word with you."

Adria nodded hesitantly, following him a few steps away from the washerwomen. When he turned to face her, she looked at him curiously.

"What is it?" she asked. "Is something wrong?"

Hermes shook his head. "Nay, my lady," he said. "Nothing is wrong. I was wondering... well, I hope you do not think I am being too bold by asking, but I was wondering if you would be interested in accompanying me to Gretna. I was passing through the other day and it seems that they are having a festival this week. There is food and music. It might be enjoyable."

Adria stared at him for a moment. It wasn't the first time Hermes had asked her to keep company with him. When they went to mass every week, he always tried to stand with her or get near her somehow. Last month, there had been a traveling entertainment in Carlisle, acting out stories from the bible on the backs of wagons, and he had asked her if she would like him to escort her. She told him no – always, no. Just as she'd told Lily, they had nothing in common but the truth was that she simply wasn't attracted to him.

Poor Hermes.

It wasn't that he wasn't handsome or kind. He was handsome, and very tall, with a crown of reddish-blond hair and blue eyes. He was a cousin to Will on both his mother and father's side, as Will's father's sister had married his mother's brother. Hermes was kind to her and the other women at Carlisle. But with the men, he could be a little... wild. She'd heard Will tell stories of how Hermes and his brother, Atreus, were veritable wild men when they got together, and in battle, Hermes was fearless – and not in a good way. *Reckless*, she'd heard Will say, but his skill saved him from losing his life.

The fact remained, however, that she didn't want to give him any encouragement where there was no hope.

She felt bad about it.

"It sounds most enjoyable," she agreed. "But I am sorry to say that I cannot leave Lady de Wolfe at this time. You know that she is nearing the birth of her child and, even now, Lord de Wolfe has asked me to take charge of little Atticus until such time as his mother can tend to him again. So, you see, I have a great many things that I am responsible for. I cannot leave the castle at this time."

Hermes was nodding even before she finished her sentence, perhaps embarrassed that he'd been refused yet again.

"I understand completely, my lady," he said. "Mayhap another time."

He said that every time she turned him away and, every time, she would simply nod and agree.

But not this time.

"Sir Hermes," she said hesitantly. "I pray you do not think me cruel for refusing your kind invitations, but I fear that I must be completely honest with you. May I?"

He eyed her with some apprehension, but like a gentleman, he nodded. "Of course, my lady," he said. "I would hope we are always honest with one another."

He said it, but he didn't mean it. Honestly would mean disappointment for him, but Adria had no choice if they were to end this uncomfortable and depressing dance they did on a regular basis.

"Then I must tell you that although I am very flattered by your invitations, I am afraid that I am simply not interested in anything other than a pleasant friendship," she said. "I have no intention of marrying you or anyone else at this time, so if you had something more in mind, then I am sorry to disappoint you."

He sighed, producing another forced smile as his cheeks turned a dull shade of red. "I had a feeling that was the situation," he said. "I was trying not to make a nuisance out of myself, but... well, I told myself it didn't hurt to ask. Mayhap one of these days you might agree."

Adria smiled at the man, seeing how embarrassed he was. "If you mean to invite me simply as your friend, I would be happy to agree should the situation warrant it," she said. "You and I have known each other for a couple of years and I have found you pleasant and good conversation, but I am simply not interested in anything more. I am sorry."

He scratched his head in a nervous gesture. "Don't be," he said. "You are being truthful and I appreciate it. If being your friend is all I can be, then I shall take it gladly."

"Good. I would like that."

"Then one of these days you might accompany me to an entertainment as my friend?"

"As your friend, I should like that."

There was nothing more to say at that point and he simply lifted a hand to beg his leave. Adria watched him go as he headed out of the kitchen yard, breathing a sigh of relief that this might actually be the last time she had to turn him down, at least in that sense. He was a nice man, but she simply wasn't interested.

She wondered how long it would be before he forgot that.

"Is he bothering you again?"

Yet another voice came from behind and she turned to her left to see Ronan standing there. She had no idea how he'd even gotten into the kitchen yard without her seeing him.

"Where did you come from?" she asked.

Ronan grinned. He was young and very handsome and muscular, with blond hair and glittering, dark eyes. He was usually the strong and silent type, having inherited his manner from his late grandfather, Kieran Hage. He also had Kieran's eyes, those dark eyes that seemed to look right through a man's soul. Or a woman's. Adria had never met the legendary Sir Kieran Hage, as he'd died several years earlier, but she'd heard enough about him. She'd also met his sons, Alec and Nathaniel, and Ronan definitely had that big, well-built look about him like the Hage men did.

But his intelligence, his skill, was purely de Wolfe.

"I came through the postern gate," he said, throwing his thumb over his shoulder. "What did that big dunce want?"

Adria had to fight off a grin. Ronan never really said much, but when he did, he was to the point. Hermes was not his cousin by blood, but the entire de Wolfe – de Norville – Hage families were so intertwined that they were really just one big family, so Ronan treated Hermes as he would a cousin.

An annoying one, but a cousin nonetheless.

"It is not of your affair," she said. "And he wasn't bothering me."

Ronan cast her a long look. "I've seen how he looks at you and how you want to run from him," he said. "Do not try and fool me."

"I am not trying to fool anyone."

"Should I chase him away for good?"

"I can chase him away myself if I wish, so I do not need your help."

Ronan snorted. "I think I'll find him and pound on him a bit," he said. "He's due for a beating, anyway."

Adria rolled her eyes. "He's taller than you are," she said. "And I know that he's a madman in battle, so do you really want to provoke him?"

Ronan puffed up. "I'm bigger and stronger than he is," he pointed out. "Hermes is a madman in battle, but foolish at times. Besides… he's only half the man without his brother around. The two of them together are like a tempest."

"It is a pity they cannot serve together."

Ronan frowned. "Have you met Atreus de Norville?"

"Once or twice."

Ronan shook his head. "You do not want the two of them together unless we are going into battle," he said. "It is well known that Hermes is the kindling and Atreus is the spark. The only safe thing to do is keep them apart unless we want an explosion."

Adria simply nodded, noting that the washerwoman were carefully rubbing in the soapwart to the fabric, testing sections to make sure the blue dye didn't fade out or run.

"Thank you for the stimulating conversation," she said, distracted. "I have tasks to attend to now."

Ronan nodded, but he didn't move away. "What did Hermes want?"

Adria sighed with frustration. "If you must know, he was speaking of an entertainment in Gretna," she said. "He had just come through town and thought I might like to hear about it."

"He invited you to go see it, didn't he?"

"What business is that of yours?"

Ronan grinned, eyeing her. "I have a better idea," he said. "Near Hexham, there is a tavern called The Temple. My father has taken me there before because it is known far and wide for the food it serves. Delicious and mysterious food that the lost legions used to eat. Men who built the walls along the Scots borders."

Adria looked at him. "I've heard of those men," she said. "If they're lost, then how do you know what they ate?"

Ronan laughed. "Because there are families in the north who have those lost legions in their blood," he said. "The secrets of their food have been passed down for centuries and The Temple prepares that food. I think you would like it."

Her brow furrowed. "How do you know what I would like?"

He lifted his big shoulders. "It's only a guess," he said. "The last time I was there, they had cabbage with vinegar and honey, and a soft cheese with a great deal of garlic and salt in it, spread upon bread. It was delicious."

Adria still wasn't convinced. "Too much garlic makes my belly ache," she said. "I am not sure that I would…"

She was cut off when she heard a shout, turning to see Gar entering the kitchen yard. The sight of her father had Adria's annoyance rising immediately. She was hoping the man wouldn't come out to wander the grounds of Carlisle, but she supposed that was too much to ask. Reluctantly, she lifted her hand in greeting.

"Who is that?" Ronan asked.

Adria sighed faintly. "My father."

"Good morn, Daughter," Gar said as he came near. "I did not see you last evening before I went to bed. Are you well?"

Adria nodded. "Quite well," she said, now seeing that Gar was looking at Ronan curiously. "Papa, this is Sir Ronan de Wolfe. Sir Ronan, this is my father, St. Ansgar de Geld, Lord Alcester."

Gar greeted the handsome young knight with more enthusiasm than he should have. "An honor, my lord," he said. But then he looked at his daughter. "I just saw another young knight leaving the yard. Another de Wolfe?"

Adria suspected what her father was fishing for. "Nay," she said. "A de Norville. Sir Hermes de Norville."

That apparently wasn't as much of a lure as a de Wolfe knight. Gar returned his attention to Ronan. "You are a brother to Lord de Wolfe?" he asked.

Ronan shook his head. "Nay, my lord," he said. "He is my cousin. Our fathers are brothers."

"Who is your father?"

"He was born Sir James de Wolfe, the fourth son of the Earl of Warenton and his wife, but through a situation too complex to quickly describe, he is known as Blayth," he said. "I am his eldest son."

"Blayth," Gar said thoughtfully. "That is Welsh for wolf, is it not?"

"It is, my lord."

Gar simply nodded, not delving into that curious name change because he honestly didn't care. All he cared about was the fact that he had a de Wolfe son in front of him. Not just any son, but a first born.

And unmarried. Young, but unmarried.

His hunting instincts took hold.

"How interesting," he said. "And you serve your cousin?"

"I do, my lord."

Gar looked up at the walls of Carlisle. "You and your wife do not mind raising your children in such a wild place as Carlisle, then?"

As Adria sighed heavily, knowing exactly what her father was up to, Ronan shook his head. "I am not married, my lord," he said.

"Oh?" Gar said. "You are young, that is true, but if a man is old enough to hold a sword, he is old enough to hold a wife."

"I have never heard it put that way before, but you may be right."

"I am sure your mother would think so," Gar said. "Does she not want grandchildren?"

Ronan laughed softly, slightly embarrassed. "I am certain she does, someday," he said. "Like most mothers, I am certain she wishes to see me settled and happy."

Gar smiled. "You are handsome and titled," she said. "I am sure a fine match will come along very soon for you. Mayhap it is even right under your nose and you do not realize it yet."

Adria stepped in; she had to. If her father kept on, she'd be betrothed to Ronan before the nooning meal.

"Papa, Sir Ronan has duties to attend to," she said, putting herself between Ronan and her father and taking the man's arm. "And I have something I must speak to you about. Sir Ronan, will you please excuse us?"

Ronan nodded, glad for the excuse to escape the man asking personal questions. Adria waited until he was nearly through the kitchen gate before dropping her father's arm and turning to him angrily.

"How dare you embarrass me like that," she hissed. "My God, Papa, have you no shame? Asking such prying questions?"

Gar's eyes narrowed. "You must marry," he hissed right back at her. "How dare *you* overlook an eligible knight in your very midst. And not just any knight – a de Wolfe son! Why not him?"

Adria growled in frustration and turned away. "I will *not* have this conversation with you," she said, leading him away from the washerwomen so they would not hear. "I do not wish to marry him or anyone else right now."

Gar was following her, pleading. "What is wrong with him?" he asked. "Why not?"

She came to a halt and whirled on him. "Because he is simply a knight who serves Lord de Wolfe and nothing more," she said. "I am Lady de Wolfe's lady-in-waiting. It is a good position and I will not have you embarrass me by trying to marry me off."

Gar was losing his patience. "I told you that if you do not marry de Brito, then you must marry a wealthy man to pay off my debt to Silas," he growled. "A debt I entered into for *you*, so you could find a position in life."

"You did not!"

"I *did*," he snapped. "The deal was that you would marry him when you came of age or I would pay him back the money – whatever the situation warranted. One way or the other, I will have my pound of flesh from you, so you had better quickly decide what that will be, for I am not leaving Carlisle until you either agree to come with me or agree to marry someone with wealth. What will your choice be?"

Adria was back to feeling angry and frustrated with her father. That was why she had avoided him the night before, why she had hoped to avoid him this morning. But here he was, back again, and his demands hadn't changed.

Anger gave way to disgust.

"It is always the same song with you," she muttered. "Your debts ruined you and borrowing money to educate me has put you in a position where you would see my life ruined to pay for your bad judgment. What happens if I marry de Brito, Papa? What happens then? Does he magically pay your debts? Is Alcester magically restored? Or do you simply intend to use me to get money from my husband to support your gambling habit?"

Gar gazed at her steadily. "What else are you good for?"

He may as well have slapped her. Adria looked at the man in utter revulsion, trying not to feel hurt by his statement.

But she couldn't quite manage it.

"Nothing," she said hoarsely. "Absolutely nothing. I was born to a vile beast of a father who killed my mother with his immoral behavior and has only sought to use me for his own repellent purposes. Do you know why I will not marry? Because I want to see you suffer. I want to see Silas de Brito punish you for not repaying your debt. I want to see you drown in the gutter, a victim of your own foolishness. That is why I will not marry and I swear, with God as my witness, that I will commit myself to the cloister before I marry anyone just because you want me to. Go home, Papa. I do not want to see you anymore."

With that, she pushed past him, heading from the kitchen yard. The blue fabric was forgotten; everything was forgotten.

Even her father.

But Gar was still standing there, watching her go. He had no intention of leaving. Adria was stubborn, but he was stronger. He'd stick around if only to break her down into doing what he wanted her to do. The time had come for that and he wasn't going to give up.

In fact, he had a de Wolfe son on his mind now.

The perfect husband, related to a perfect fortune.

He was going to see what he could do about it.

CHAPTER FIVE

"I DO NOT understand why he keeps coming to see me," Lily said. "It has been well over a week since he first examined me, but he comes back every day and performs the exact same examination as he did the first time. Why is he doing this, Will? What is he looking for?"

Will was standing in the big chamber, listening to Lily's question but also listening to Atticus whine and fuss because Adria was trying to clean the lad up before dressing him. It was a chilly morning on the borders, a clear morning after several days of an unseasonable rain. Everything was drying out under clear skies, at least for the moment.

But Will was facing a situation he'd been avoiding for an entire week.

Lily was growing suspicious.

Unfortunately, her physical situation hadn't changed, according to Tarraby. Lily's symptoms were still consistent with what he'd first diagnosed and only two days ago, she passed a significant amount of blood, something that had the midwife in a panic. She was so panicked, in fact, that she'd sent for Tarraby right away, whose diagnosis was only confirmed when the midwife told him what had happened.

More than ever, he believed Lady de Wolfe was in mortal danger.

Still, Tarraby went about the motions of listening for the child, trying to see just how much he was moving about. Lily didn't seem to think that the movements of the babe had slowed any, but Tarraby really couldn't tell. He didn't know her or the child well enough to be aware of any change. Even so, he told her that the child was still moving and avoided her questions about the show of blood. He knew that Will hadn't told her anything yet and he didn't want to be the one to break the bad news.

But Will knew that the time had come for total truth.

He simply couldn't keep avoiding it.

He'd had more than a week to think about how he was going to tell her, more than a week to mull over the words. He still couldn't belief it himself, so how was he going to convince her? All he knew was that he trusted Tarraby. The man wouldn't lie to him or lead him astray, and he certainly wouldn't be mistaken about something as serious as this.

When a man was about to lose his wife and unborn child.

"Will?" Lily said. "Did you hear me?"

Will had been staring off into the chamber, not really seeing anything, simply pondering the situation and trying to summon the courage to speak on it. Atticus picked that moment to bolt away from Adria, running across the chamber, naked, and disappearing into the stairwell. As Adria went in pursuit, Will grinned weakly.

"I think she has her hands full with that terror we are raising," he said. "I feel a good deal of pity for Adria these days. Atticus has been more than a match for her."

Lily waved him off. "She handles him better than I do," she said. "But you haven't answered my question. Why do you send Tarraby to me every day? What is he looking for?"

Will sighed heavily. With Adria and Atticus out of the chamber, he figured now was as good a time as any to do his duty and tell his wife what he knew.

He lowered himself onto the nearest chair.

"He is listening for the child," he said, but realized that sounded as if he were pretending everything was well. He was about to start off on that lie again. Scratching his head, he looked her in the eyes. "You and I must have a discussion, Lil. There is indeed a reason why I send Tarraby to you every day."

"What is it?"

He looked at her; *really* looked at her. She was still as pretty as she had been the day he'd met her. She had the de Lohr blue eyes, the fair hair, but the shape of her face was purely her mother's, a Welshwoman born Alys but who went by the name Kaedia as a tribute to her Welsh roots. It was something the women in her family did, having proper English names but adopting a Welsh name in tribute. Lily's name was, in fact, Lily Rhianne, only Lily refused to use her Welsh name. She had been born English and that was what she preferred. But her brothers – Morgen, Becket, Tobias, Rees, Dru, and Kade – all had the Welsh streak in them to varying degrees.

It made for some interesting dynamics.

One of those dynamics was the Welsh strength. Lily had that. She had the stubborn streak, the no-nonsense outlook on life. She was pragmatic. But she was also brusque at times, spoiled, and demanding. Will had never known her to lose her composure except when the situation didn't go the way she wanted it to. Lily didn't take disappointment well and she never had. He'd learned that very early in their relationship. Therefore, he really didn't know how she was going to react to the news.

There was only one way to find out.

"Tarraby told you of his education and qualifications," he

began carefully. "I've personally seen the man heal wounds that were quite severe and when he first came to Carlisle because I was injured, he healed a wound in my thigh that could have easily festered."

"I know."

"I could have lost my leg."

Lily was nodding patiently, which was unusual because she wasn't normally patient. "I know," she said again. "I was there. I saw it."

"Then you know the man has talent and experience."

"I do now," she said. "I'm sorry I thought he was simply a barber-surgeon. Clearly, he is much more. I suppose I just never took the time to find out more about him."

Will held up a hand to quiet her on the subject. "It is of no matter," he said. "What I am trying to say is that I trust him. That is why I wanted him to see to you because he has more knowledge than a midwife, as good as she may be."

Lily nodded again. "I agree," she said. "But you still haven't answered why he has seen me daily for the past week."

Will sat forward in the chair, elbows on his knees as he steepled his fingers thoughtfully. "I was concerned about your fall, as you know," he said. "Tarraby examined you and after he did, he told me that when he was an apprentice in Toledo, his master had a patient who was a contessa. She was pregnant and close to giving birth when she fell from her horse and started exhibiting symptoms just like you have been having. The aching back, the pains in the belly, the bleeding. The very same things."

Lily looked at him with interest. "Is that so?" she said, perking up. "So something did happen when I fell in the mud?"

Will nodded. "Apparently," he said. "That is why I have had him check you every day, to see if there is any change."

Lily pondered that for a moment. "Then what did he tell you about the blood two days ago?" she asked hesitantly. "I told him not to tell you this, but it wasn't the first time. Over the past week, it has been every day, only two days ago, that was the most it had ever been. I knew you were worried enough and I did not want to add to your concern."

Will took a long, deep breath. "That was noble of you, but unnecessary," he said. "The blood has some significance. When this happened to the contessa, the fall caused the nourishment sack that attaches the child to the womb to pull away from the womb itself. That is where the blood came from, like an open wound."

A light of understanding went on in Lily's eyes. "And that is what happened to me?"

"He believes so. That is why you have been bleeding and experiencing pain."

Lily digested what he was telling her, thinking she knew what he was going to say. "Then I must stay in bed until it heals," she said. "That is why you have asked Adria to tend to Atticus, because I am not permitted to leave my bed. I understand now."

Will was feeling increasingly despondent with what he had to tell her because he could see that she didn't understand at all. She thought she did, but she did not.

"Nay," he said softly. "That is not all of it. You see, when this happened to the contessa, she gradually weakened. Because the sack has pulled away from the womb, the child was slowly starving to death. There is no way to repair this injury, Lily. There is nothing to be done. It will not heal."

Lily stared at him for quite some time. He could see the thoughts rolling through her mind, her expression shifting as she began to piece together what he was trying to tell her. He watched her as the color drained from her face and she began to blink rapidly, as if blinking away tears.

"What are you telling me?" she asked quietly. "What happened to the contessa's child?"

"He died."

"And the contessa?"

"She died."

Her eyes widened slightly. "Am… am I going to die?"

Will could feel the pain of those words, stabling him like a million steely knives of anguish. He'd never voiced those words himself so to hear them coming from her was a shock. A painful shock.

But he'd come this far.

He couldn't stop now.

"The blood is because of the open wound in your womb," he said. "Because there is no way to heal the wound, Tarraby believes that you will eventually weaken too much to survive."

Lily simply looked at him, struggling to understand what he was telling her. "And my child?" she rasped.

Will simply shook his head, hanging it.

His silence told her everything.

The impact of the news hit her full force. Lily fell back against her pillows, looking at her husband's lowered head, dazed and in disbelief. As she realized the situation, her gaze moved away from him, to the window and the sky beyond. It was bright blue, a brilliant blue, and she could see birds flitting around. It was a gorgeous day, far too bright and lovely to be the day when she found out she was dying. It was an insult, this bright day, going along as if nothing was wrong in the world.

But, evidently, everything was wrong.

The news hit hard and she swallowed, closing her eyes tightly before opening them again, seeing that bright blue sky beyond again. A beautiful world that she would soon no longer be part of. Somehow, it all seemed terribly unfair.

She could hardly believe it.

"And Tarraby is certain of this?" she finally asked.

Will lifted his head, tears in his eyes. "He is," he said hoarse-ly. "He has seen it before."

Lily was staring out of the window. "He *could* be wrong," she said, grasping for the last vestiges of hope. "Remember last year when that foolish physic from Carlisle diagnosed me with a stomach tumor?"

"I remember."

Lily's breathing began to come in heaves as she struggled with her emotions while remembering that horrible time in her life. "That idiotic fool," she hissed. "He told me that I was dying of a tumor. He bled me and had me eat foods that rendered me so weak that I could hardly move. I was so... frail. But it was *his* fault because of what he did to me. I was weak *because* of him!"

Will simply nodded, feeling great sympathy for a wife who had to endure that horrible diagnosis that turned out to be incorrect. When the physic from Carlisle realized that he had been wrong, he did indeed weaken Lily with regular bleeding and tiny quantities of food, anything to prove she was frail and dying so his misdiagnosis would not be revealed. What had actually been a severe but non-lethal belly ache had turned into something quite darker.

The physic had tried to kill her to prove his point.

Needless to say, that man was no longer around to harm anyone else because Will had taken care of him in the worst way possible. In that sense, he didn't blame Lily for being wary of yet one more physic telling her that she was going to die.

This time, unfortunately, it happened to be the truth.

"I know," he said after a moment. "And although I do real-ize that terrible incident has made you leery of another physic's diagnosis, I will reiterate that Tarraby comes to us with a great education and great experience. Given your symptoms and his knowledge, he believes this to be the correct diagnosis."

Lily was still looking out the window, closing her eyes briefly as Will spoke those words. Somehow, she was hoping for doubt, but there was none.

"And you believe him?"

"I do."

She paused. "Very well," she finally said, resignation in her tone. "When... when will this happen?"

Will shook his head. "I do not know," he said. "He says the child's movements will become less and less until he moves no more and then with you... when your body decides it is time to give birth, that will be the time when..."

Lily turned to look at him. "That will be when I bleed to death from this wound in my belly."

Will nodded with deep regret. "Aye."

"And there is nothing to be done?"

Will sighed heavily. "He asked me if he wishes for him to cut into your belly and try to save the child's life, but that is almost certain death for you."

"But if we wait, the child will die and I will die, anyway."

Will could barely nod his head. Lily's hand found her way onto her rounded belly, feeling the babe moving. He was active today.

But he was dying, according to the physic.

God, this isn't happening!

But it was. According to her husband, it was. Will had never lied to her, so she knew he was telling her the truth as he understood it. She could see how painful it was for him to speak it. It was equally painful for her to hear it.

She simply couldn't believe it.

"Will," she said after a moment. "Will you leave me now? I would like to be alone and... think."

His head came up. "I will stay with you."

"Nay," she said firmly. "Please. Leave me for now. I want you to."

"Why?" Will sat up in the chair. "Lily, I realize we have not been too terribly close over the years, but this child is mine and you are my wife. You do not need to be alone at this time and I would prefer if it if I can remain. Please let me."

She grunted softly. "Not been too terribly close," she muttered, repeating his words. "It's ironic to hear you say that. Sort of the unspoken state of our marriage, I suppose. We've not been close over the years, that is true, but it is not as if I dislike you. Clearly, I like you. We have conceived children together even though I will admit it is a duty to me. Is it a duty to you?"

Will sat back in the chair, wearily rubbing his forehead as they touched on a subject that had been unspoken for years. It was difficult to speak of something you couldn't quite put your finger on, only that you knew it existed. But if she was being honest about it, he supposed that he could be as well.

"Aye," he said honestly. "A duty. We are married and we have an empire to sustain, and that is part of it."

Lily looked at him. "Tell me something, Will."

"If I can."

"When did you stop loving me?"

He was shocked by the question because it wasn't something they ever spoke of. Those were terrible words to acknowledge, but the truth was that he couldn't remember when he'd last told Lily that he loved her, probably because it had been ten years or more. But looking into her eyes, he could see that pragmatic side of her, the logical and sometimes emotional woman he had married. She wasn't asking in an emotional state, only a truthful one. She wanted to know.

Maybe the time had come to speak of it.

"I don't know," he said honestly. "You have been part of my life for nearly all of my adult life. I would not say that I do not love you."

"But you are not madly *in* love with me."

"And it is fair to say that you are not madly in love with me, either."

There was a glimmer of mirth in her eyes as she looked at him. "We are great friends, Will, but as lovers…" She shook her head. "When I first met you, I was smitten with you, but in fairness, my tastes were fickle back then. I was smitten with many men, but only briefly. Still, my father saw my interest in you and we were married within the month. Do you remember?"

Will smiled faintly. "Of course I do," he said. "Before I realized it, I had a wife and a responsibility."

"You were not ready for it."

"I was still a young man," he said. "It happened so fast."

"Do you regret it?"

It seemed to Will that this was the first real moment of utterly brutal honesty in their entire marriage. At this raw and terrible moment, Lily was asking for total truth. She was giving him total truth. Somehow, it made the moment beautiful. Tolerable.

Painful.

"When I look at Athena and Andrew and Atticus, most certainly I do not," he said. "But there are times when I wish I had been able to live as an adult unmarried knight longer than I had. There are things I wanted to do, things I wanted to see, but I had a wife and I could not leave her. I had responsibilities. We had Athena so soon after we were married that I think we were both thrust into something we were not ready for."

Lily nodded faintly. "That is very true," she said. "I was so young when we met. Honestly, before I met you, I had a new love every week, so falling in love with you was nothing new. But my father acted on it, which he had never done before. I am sorry if I have not been a good wife, Will. You deserve to have a wife who loves you madly and throws herself at your feet."

Will smiled weakly. "I would not know what to do with her if she did," he said. "But… do not apologize to me for not being a good wife. You did your best, as did I."

Lily continued to look at him, the gleam in her eyes growing faint. "Will you do something if I ask it of you?"

"You know I will."

"If there is no hope for me, then I want you to try and save the child. Will you do that?"

The warmth faded from his eyes. "What do you mean?"

"You said that Tarraby asked if you want him to take the child by force," she said. "If there is even a chance of saving him, I want you to do it. Please."

He looked at her in mounting horror when he realized what she meant. "Do you realize what you are asking?"

Lily nodded steadily. "Listen to me," she said, seeing that he was growing upset. "I will try to explain this to you if I can. I have given birth to three children and I love them all desperately. You will never know what it is like to grow a life inside of your body and see it emerge, becoming strong and vital. I cannot imagine my life without Athena or Andrew or Atticus. They deserve to live, Will, as this child does. This child is alive right now, in my belly, but if what you say is true, he is dying. How can I, as his mother, allow that to happen if I can save him?"

The tears were back. Will stared at her, tears pooling in his eyes and streaming down his face as he realized that she was more than willing to make the ultimate sacrifice. "But it will cost you your own life, Lily."

"If I do nothing, it will cost him his life, too."

Will blinked and the tears spattered. The problem was that he understood what she was saying completely. If they did nothing, he would lose them both. But if he allowed Tarraby to save the child, at least there was a chance that one of them might live.

"God, Lily," he muttered. "You must understand what you are asking. *Truly* understand it."

Lily was surprisingly in control as Will was threatening to come apart. "I do," she said. "Let me ask you this – if you are in battle with Tor or Jeremy or Nathaniel, or any of your younger brothers, and a situation arises where you can save them but you know it will cost you your life, what would you do?"

"It is not the same."

"Of course it is the same," she said. "I am willing to sacrifice my life to save my child. He deserves his chance to live, Will. I am going to die either way, according to Tarraby. Why let my son die, too?"

Will simply closed his eyes and looked away. After a moment, he got up from the chair and moved across the vast chamber, pacing to the other side of the room and looking from the windows that faced northward. Outside, over the walls, he could see the green hills, the blue sky. He could smell the river. He could smell the life of the land all around him and it all seemed so unfair when he was faced with a life or death choice at this moment. But there really was no choice at all. Lily had already made the decision.

The problem was that he understood it perfectly.

But he didn't want to.

"I will leave you alone now," he said, turning away from the window and moving sluggishly towards the door. "We do not have to make any decisions right now. Rest and think on it. I will speak to you again later."

He was almost to the door as she spoke. "I am not going to change my mind," she said quietly. "If I am going to die anyway, I want to save the child. You cannot take that away from me, Will."

He didn't say anything. He was afraid to. Just as he neared

the door, it opened again and Adria appeared, dragging Atticus behind her. The child had breeches on this time but nothing more. She nearly plowed into Will, quickly moving aside when she saw him standing there.

"He made it all the way to the outer bailey," Adria said, towing the unhappy child behind her like a barge. "My lady, after I finish dressing him, I will see to your morning meal. Do you feel like eating this morning?"

She was clearly oblivious to what had been happening in the chamber while she'd been gone, but that was for the best. Whatever was happening was purely between Will and Lily, and Lily's focus was still on Will as she spoke to Adria.

"I think I could eat something," she said. "Finish dressing Atticus quickly and let him go with his father, please."

Will was almost out the door but he came to a halt when he heard Lily, a command to him disguised as a reply to Adria. He stood in the doorway, unable to look at her, as Adria quickly put a couple of tunics on Atticus against the cold morning and yanked on his shoes, tying them tightly. The boy bolted over to his father, who put his big hand on Atticus' head and directed him out of the chamber.

Will shut the door, shutting out Lily and the terrible situation behind him. He was glad to leave her with Adria. He was so rattled with the conversation that he could barely walk, but Atticus was tugging on him, demanding attention.

"Papa!" he said. "I want mush!"

Will struggled to focus on his youngest. "Mush?" he said. "Very well. Let us go to the kitchens and see if they have it."

"I want bread, too."

"We'll find it."

Atticus had him by the hand, pulling on him as they came off the stairs. They made it out of the keep, but Atticus spied Bradford and a couple of other young pages over near the great hall and tried to run over to them, but Will held on to the lad and directed him away from his nemesis and towards the kitchen yard.

Even in a world of upheaval, some things never changed – like Atticus hating on Bradford.

Somehow, that was oddly comforting.

The kitchens of Carlisle were mostly outdoors, so everything they had cooking was evident as soon as they entered the kitchen yard. They were just passing through the gate when Will caught sight of Marcellus coming off the wall and heading in his direction. He didn't feel much like speaking to anyone, so he tried to ignore Marcellus, thinking the man would simply go away, but he had no such luck.

Marcellus caught up to him in the kitchen yard.

"Good morn, my lord," he said, grinning as Atticus ran straight to the cook and began demanding food. "He never stops eating, does he?"

Will watched his son make demands of the round woman, who immediately started handing over food. "He knows what he wants and how to get it," Will said. "Though I fear he is sounding like Hermes more and more every day. It's that wild, arrogant de Norville blood in him."

Marcellus chuckled as he looked at him. "You have that blood."

Will nodded in resignation. "Actually, he behaves like my mother," he said. "He even looks like her a little, I think. She had pale red hair."

"She was wild and arrogant?"

In spite of himself, Will smiled weakly. "She was a woman who knew what she wanted," he said. "She feared nothing. Hermes has that trait. That is very much my grandfather, Paris', trait. Wild, arrogant, and fearless."

Marcellus nodded, now looking to see Atticus stuffing his

face with bread and butter. "Speaking of fearless, how is Lady de Wolfe today?" he said. "I've not seen her out and about in several days. I hope nothing is amiss."

Will looked at Marcellus. He'd known the man for years. He'd come from Lioncross Abbey, so he was entrenched with all things de Lohr. He'd known Lily even longer than Will had, so in a sense, Marcellus was like one of the family, at least as much as a knight could be. He was also Will's second in command, meaning he should be aware of everything that went on at the castle.

The good and the bad.

Will thought he might as well tell the man what was going on because, at some point, it would no longer be a secret. He may need Marcellus' help at some point if he was emotionally unable to command.

It was only fair.

"I must speak with you about that," he said, looking at Marcellus and fighting off the emotion that the subject provoked. The pain from his conversation with Lily was still very fresh. "Please do not repeat this, not to anyone. When the time comes to speak of it publicly, I will do so."

Marcellus grew serious very quickly. "Of course, my lord," he said. "What is it?"

Will sighed heavily, sorrow evident on his face. "There *is* something amiss with Lady de Wolfe," he said. "Because I may be busy with her in the near future, I will need for you to assume full command. I cannot worry about commanding Carlisle and my wife's health at the same time, so please be prepared to assist me in any way you can."

Marcellus was clearly concerned. "You know I will be, always," he said. "May… may I ask what is wrong? I hope it is not serious."

Will couldn't look at him. He could hardly bring himself to

speak of it. "It is very serious," he said. "It is more than likely fatal. That is all I will say, so please do not ask me more. Just know that these next few months will be... difficult ones."

It was all he could say on the matter. He abruptly headed off to tend to Atticus, leaving Marcellus standing there, stunned with what he'd been told. He stood there watching Will and Atticus as the boy complained that he wanted "sweets" before finally turning around and heading out of the kitchen yard.

Dazed, Marcellus made it to the ladder leading up to the wall walk before taking a detour and ending up in one of the many shallow alcoves that lined the interior of Carlisle's wall. For a moment, he simply stood there in the shadows, rolling one word over and over in his mind. That one horrible word from his conversation with Will that he was hanging on to.

Fatal.

Putting his hand over his mouth, he closed his eyes tightly and wept.

CHAPTER SIX

Castle Questing

"I HAVE A message from Will, Papa. We must speak."
The statement came from a big knight, blond and handsome, aged in his fifth decade. He stood in the solar of Castle Questing, an enormous chamber that reflected the wealth and status of the de Wolfe family. It belonged to his father, the Earl of Warenton and Will's namesake, William de Wolfe, who was now looking up from the pile of vellum on the table in front of him.

William was the patriarch of a massive empire he had built himself, from the ground up, with eight children, dozens of grandchildren, and a tight network of close friends and allies. His properties, either owned or managed on behalf of the king, covered two-thirds of the Scottish border. There was no one more powerful, skilled, fair, just, or respected than William de Wolfe.

The Wolfe of the Border was legend.

"What is it?" William asked, sitting back in his chair and rubbing his forehead wearily. "He's coming to the celebration, isn't he?"

Scott closed the solar door. "Nay," he said quietly as he

made his way over to his father. "It seems that there is a… problem."

William stopped rubbing and looked at him seriously. "Problem?" he repeated. "With Will?"

Scott sighed heavily as he pulled up a chair opposite his father. He had the missive in his hand and he simply held it over the table, extending it to his father, who took it curiously. Unfolding the vellum, he proceeded to read the missive. He read it twice. When he was finished the second time, he lifted his eye to Scott over the tabletop.

"Oh, God," he muttered. "This cannot be right. It cannot possibly be right."

Scott could feel his father's horror. In truth, he had quite enough of his own and was struggling to remain on an even keel.

"I do not know," he said. "He is asking me to go to Carlisle and see to Lily personally. Papa, I'm a soldier's healer. I'm excellent with wounds or sickness, but a pregnant woman is not within my scope of expertise."

William sat back in his chair, heavily. "Sweet Christ," he mumbled. "Lily is *dying*? Her condition is fatal?"

"I do not know."

"Then you had better find someone who does," William snapped softly. "What in the hell is happening over in Carlisle?"

Scott could only shake his head. "I do not know, but I intend to find out," he said. "Needless to say, neither Will nor I will be at the celebration of your birth."

William was nodding before the words were even out of his mouth. "Completely understandable," he said. "I will miss you both, but I understand. I am sure your mother will, too. Will you take Avrielle with you?"

He was referring to Scott's wife, a woman who was not Will's mother but with whom Will had always shared a good relationship.

But Scott shook his head.

"Nay," he said. "She cannot do anything to help the situation. In fact, I do not even know if I am going to tell her the contents of the missive. She will worry too much and I do not want to worry her until I know more."

"She will want to know why you have gone to Carlisle in the midst of a celebration."

Scott sighed faintly. "She will," he said. "Papa… I'm wondering if I should take Mama with me. She's given birth to eight children herself. She understands the mysterious process of childbirth and, if for no other reason, she might be a strong and comforting presence."

"And you think she would be more help than Avrielle, who has also given birth to several children?"

Scott shrugged. "With Will's own mother gone, and her mother gone, Mama is the closest thing he has to a blood female relative," he said. "It might give him reassurance to have her there."

William's gaze lingered on the man in the candlelight, seeing the lines of stress across his forehead. With the initial shock of the missive fading, his concern turned towards his son's wellbeing.

A man who had also lost a wife, long ago.

"It might give you comfort, too," he said quietly. "I am sure she will not mind going, but you must tell her the truth. Your mother would not like to be kept oblivious to what is happening."

Scott nodded. "I will tell her," he said. Then, he sighed heavily. "Poor Will. First his mother, now his wife."

"You know what it is like to lose a wife."

Scott could only shake his head in sorrow. "Unfortunately, I do," he said. "I suppose I am the best person to comfort him at this time, but I must tell you that seeing his missive… it brought back memories, things I'd forgotten."

William suspected as much. Scott had lost Will's mother many years ago in a freak accident. Athena had been traveling in a carriage along with her younger sister, Helene, and four small children. Two belonged to Helene, who was married to Scott's twin, Troy, and two belonged to Athena. They were Scott's youngest children, Andrew and Beatrice. The carriage had gone over a bridge spanning a rain-swollen creek and the pylons had failed, dumping the carriage into the water.

No one had survived.

It had taken Scott years to come to terms with his grief. He'd alienated his family for the first few years after Athena's death, struggling with his guilt and anguish, before finally accepting what had happened. When William had first read Will's missive, he had to admit that his initial thoughts had been of Scott and how he'd reacted to his first wife's death.

He wondered if Will would do the same.

In any case, he knew it was important for Scott to go to his son at this terrible time. It was certainly more important than any birthday celebration.

"It was a long time ago," William finally said. "Athena would have been very pleased with how you continued to live your life. I'm convinced that she would have loved Avrielle. I've always thought that, wherever she is, she might have had a hand in bringing the two of you together. She would have wanted you to be happy, you know. She would have moved heaven and earth to ensure such a thing"

Scott nodded. "I know," he said. "Those feelings of grief were so strong for so many years but, nowadays, it is simply a gentle sorrow. She was such a strong woman, Papa. So very strong. Do you remember when she challenged Uncle Paris when I first asked for her hand?"

William's lips twitched with a smile. "Very well," he said. "I was there, if you recall."

Scott could hear the mirth in his father's voice. "It was a sight to see," he said. "She was prepared to fight for the man she loved – literally."

Humor was introduced into what could have been a sorrowful conversation. "She was fearless as she went after her father, who was a man of considerable skill and power," he said. "Paris would have never raised a hand against her, of course, but it was interesting to watch."

"True enough," Scott said. "If she went after her father like that, I often wondered if, as the years went on, we might have come to blows at some point."

William chuckled. "That is a very real possibility," he said. "Will and Tor do not have that bold, aggressive streak in them, but I remember that little Beatrice was very much her mother's daughter. You may have very well come to blows with her, too."

Scott grinned at the memory of his bold, sassy, but sweet daughter, his only daughter at that time. "That is more than likely," he said. "Between Bea and her mother, I would have lived in fear of my life on a daily basis."

They shared a laugh, fond memories and thoughts that created a warm sense of longing, of joy. In past years, that would have been difficult, but time and healing had a way of making painful memories a treasured and peaceful thing.

"I would not have been surprised," William said, glad they were speaking on the touchy subject without any angst. "For women with de Norville blood, they were quite strong. Not like their foolish father."

That had Scott chuckling for an entirely new reason. Paris de Norville, Athena's father, was William's best friend in the world. He had been for decades. William would kill anyone who openly insulted Paris, but that same rule did not apply to him. He insulted him happily and frequently, but then again, Paris did the same thing to William, so it was even dealings on both sides.

Old men who loved each other and took sport in harassing one another.

"The strongest," Scott said. "Helene didn't quite fit that, however. She was too much like Aunt Caladora."

William nodded. "She was, indeed," he said. "She was quite gentle."

"I miss them. All of them."

"We all do."

Scott sat there a moment longer, thinking of his long-dead wife and daughter, before drawing in a deep breath and shifting back to the subject at hand.

"I will leave on the morrow," he said. "Others will have to organize the celebration if I'm taking Mama with me and I'm sure people will wonder where she is. What will you tell them?"

"The truth," William said. "That Lily is pregnant and Jordan's presence has been requested."

Scott eyed him. "And if Uncle Paris asks? You know he will. And Will is his grandson, too."

"I know that. Let me handle Paris. I've been doing it for over forty years."

"No strong-arming the man."

"You'll not tell me how to deal with him."

"No fighting, either."

William rolled his eye. He only had one, as his left eye had been lost in battle many years before. "No promises," he said. "Now, find your mother and tell her the situation. Once she finds out, you'll be lucky if she waits to leave tomorrow, so you'd better be prepared to keep her at bay until you are ready to depart."

Scott stood up, folding the missive back up. The smile faded from his lips as he worked over the vellum, folding and refolding. William noticed.

"What is wrong?" he asked softly.

Scott paused in his folding. "I was thinking," he said. "I hope it is not our lot in life that the heirs to the House of de Wolfe should lose their first wives. First me, now Will. What of Andrew? He is Will's heir, named for his dead uncle. Truth be told, he's not had a great start in life with a dead grandmother and uncle, and now a dying mother. I worry for him."

William shook his head. "Don't," he said quietly. "Andy is a strong lad, in his mind and in his heart. He'll do well in life. You must have faith."

Scott wasn't sure if he did, but he nodded anyway. William was philosophical in his old age so he essentially humored him. It would do no good to argue. Not that he wanted to, but he was hoping this wasn't the beginning of some de Wolfe curse. First Athena, now Lily...

And the nightmare that he had to go through all over again with Will.

He hoped, this time, that he was strong enough to bear it.

CHAPTER SEVEN

Carlisle Castle

H E HAD TO wait until everyone was out of the keep. At least, he had to wait until Adria was out. Atticus didn't matter so much and, of course, he had to make sure Will was far away.

At the moment, it was a perfect storm of those factors.

He'd been watching the keep under the guise of supervising the sentries on the wall walk, which was his usual task, but he'd been watching the keep closely. The truth was that very few people went into the keep who were not invited, or part of the family, or servants because the keep only housed Will, Lily, Adria, and Atticus, so it wasn't a busy place. Not even the smaller great hall was much used. The bustle and business at Carlisle took place in the larger great hall, the outbuildings, and mostly in the outer bailey and gatehouse, so the keep, oddly enough, was a quiet place.

But that was a good thing where he was concerned.

He'd been speaking to a new soldier on the wall, a young man who had just come in from the country to pledge his oath in exchange for food, training, and a roof over his head when he saw Adria and Atticus come out of the keep.

That had his attention.

He already knew that Will was in the stable this morning with a new Belgian charger that was having trouble with its hooves and with Adria and Atticus leaving the keep, although Atticus was running away screaming as Adria chased him, he knew that Lily would be alone.

Quickly, he came off the wall and headed towards the keep.

No one was paying any attention to him. No one ever did; that was the beauty of it. A knight in the service of Will, a bold and brave man who was in the chain of command and no one would pay any attention to him anywhere in the castle. Seeing him cross the bailey was completely normal. Seeing him go into the inner bailey was also completely natural. Even seeing him enter the keep was natural.

He knew no one would question him.

They never had.

The keep, as he'd known, was empty. He didn't even see a servant. It was dark, mostly, as he bolted up the stairwell that was next to Will's solar. The stairs were wide and shallow, easy to navigate, as he made his way to the chamber on the upper floor. There was a small landing and a door, and he knew the door would be unlocked.

Quietly, he rapped on the panel before opening it.

The lavish chamber spread out before him.

"Lily?" he said softly.

He saw something stir on the bed. Lily's head suddenly lifted, her eyes wide when she saw who it was.

"Marcellus," she breathed. "I was wondering when you would come. Where is Will?"

Marcellus came into the chamber, over to the bed where she was struggling to sit up. "In the stable," he said softly, reaching out to pull her into a sitting position. "Adria is chasing Atticus all over the outer ward and I do not expect to see her any time soon. For the moment, we are alone."

Lily looked up at him, those words sinking in. This was the time she lived for, the moments when it was just the two of them.

Her eyes filled with tears.

"Oh, Marcellus," she whispered, crumbling. "Something awful has happened."

Marcellus put his arms around her as he sat on the edge of the bed, pulling her close. He knew exactly what she meant. He'd had his time to weep, and he had done so copiously. Now wasn't the time to put his weakness on display. That wasn't his right.

He had to be strong for Lily.

"I know," he said, holding her tightly. "Will told me."

She sniffled. "*What* did he tell you?"

"Only that there was a fatal issue."

"But no more?"

"Nay. Tell me what is happening."

Lily wept softly. "You know that I fell in the mud last month," she said. "I've been having pain and… blood. I've not felt normal in the least, although I've told Will that I did. I've told everyone that I did, but the truth was that I did not. I've been feeling terrible but unwilling to let anyone know. I hoped it would simply go away. But Will had Tarraby examine me and he has told me that my fall caused the nourishment sack that attaches the child to the womb to pull away. With the nourishment being cut off, the child is slowly dying and I am dying right along with him. There is nothing to be done."

Marcellus drew in a long, steadying breath. Things made more sense but his devastation was magnified. Now that he knew the truth, he was struggling desperately to remain composed.

It was worse than he could have ever imagined.

"That cannot be possible," he said quietly. "I do not believe you cannot be helped."

She wiped at her face. "Our choices are morbid," she said. "There is a possibility of saving the child if Tarraby cuts into me and takes him by force, but I will most certainly perish. Or, we can do nothing and the child will die a slow death and I along with him. Birth will not save him or me."

"But we cannot know that for certain – can we?"

"The only way to find out if Tarraby is right is to let the situation end naturally when I give birth," Lily said. "If I wait that long to see if he was correct in his diagnosis, it will be too late for me and too late for the child. I do not want to lose your child, Marcellus. I will sacrifice my life gladly if it will save him."

Those words hung in the air between them as the truth was spoken.

I do not want to lose your child.

Marcellus sighed faintly.

"'Tis a brutal, cold choice," he said. "Is Tarraby very sure this is the case?"

"Will seems to think so. He believes him. Do you?"

Marcellus grunted. "Tarraby is the most skilled physic I have ever seen," he said. "I suppose I do not doubt him, but this is something… I simply cannot believe it."

Because he was calm, Lily was calming, but she was still holding him with a death grip. "I do not wish to believe it, either," she said. "I do not want to die, but I do not want our son to die."

She was wiping the tears from her face with one hand as he gave her a squeeze, kissing the top of her head. He lay his cheek against her head.

"God, what a mess," he muttered. "A horrible, shocking mess."

"I know."

He fell silent, pondering fate and karma and God as having a hand in all of this. Surely they were being judged somehow, judged for the sin they had committed. When he spoke again, his voice was raspy.

"Mayhap this is punishment for our sins," he murmured. "The sin of loving a woman who is another man's wife. The sin of already having a child together and now, a second child. God can forgive one child, mayhap, but not two. Mayhap this is our punishment."

Lily closed her eyes, snuggling against him, drawing strength from the regular *thump, thump* of his heartbeat in her ear.

"I would like to believe that God is a merciful God," she whispered. "I would like to believe He is an understanding God. He understands that I was forced into marriage with Will because of my father. He understands that I have loved you since nearly the day I met you at Lioncross Abbey those years ago. He understands that we have a love that has never been broken."

"It is still a sin."

"But God created love, Marcellus," she insisted. "You were the man I should have married, but my father would not hear of it. A de Wolfe husband was far better than a mere knight, no matter how I felt about it. No matter how much you begged him for my hand."

Marcellus thought of those days when he'd spent several evenings on his knees in Chris de Lohr's solar, begging the man to permit him to marry his daughter. It had been a horrible, emotional time for him. Chris hadn't been unsympathetic, but he'd wanted a better husband for his only daughter. A de Wolfe husband, a man who could provide her with wealth and prestige.

It had been one of the more horrific times in Marcellus' life.

"He would not be swayed," he said softly. "My humble but noble birth could not compare to a de Wolfe. I understand that, but it took... time. I'm surprised he never told Will about me, though. I suppose he thought it would cause trouble in the knightly ranks."

"I know," Lily said softly. "It wasn't as if you made your quest for me obvious, either. You were very discreet."

"Out of respect for you and your family," he said. "There's nothing worse than a knight openly drooling over his liege's daughter. I've seen that happen before and it's disgraceful."

A smile flickered on Lily's lips. "You never did that," she said. "You were always quite mannerly. It only made me love you more."

He gave her a gentle squeeze. "It seems so long ago now," he said. "Those days at Lioncross before you married Will. But I never stopped loving you, not ever. Your father must have never guessed because he sent me north with Will when he took command of Carlisle."

"You and Will were friends," she said simply. "All of these years, you have been friends, but somehow, I wonder if my father knew you still loved me and that I loved you. Although I am glad you came north with us, if he suspected our feelings for one another had never died, I should think that he would have sent you to the far reaches of the earth."

Marcellus leaned back against the bed post, Lily still gathered up against his torso. "All I can say is that I am grateful he did not."

Lily didn't say anything for a moment, relishing the feel of him against her. "As am I," she said. "But Will still has not realized the situation between you and I after all of these years. It is true that our marriage is simply a polite association, so mayhap he does know and he simply doesn't care, but I do not think so. Mayhap he just chooses not to see it."

"We have been very careful," Marcellus said. "Unfortunately, Atticus is starting to look more and more like me, so there may come a time when suspicions will be raised. And now with this child, I fear it will only be a matter of time before Will figures out the truth for himself."

Lily put a hand on her belly, rubbing at it as Marcellus put his big hand over hers, feeling the life they had created together, a child who would bear the name of another man, another family.

Marcellus had long gotten over the bitterness of it.

As the man in the wrong, he couldn't afford to be bitter.

"If he has not realized it by now, then it's possible he never will," she murmured. "We have covered our movements well. When I realized that I was pregnant with Atticus, I made sure that Will did his husbandly duty as to make him believe the child was his. I did the same thing with this child. He will not bed me unless I ask him to, you know. Otherwise, he stays well clear."

"You have told me that," he said. "I still find that odd. He does not assert himself?"

"Nay," Lily said, shaking her head. "He has not in years. He views it as a duty, as do I, but I will admit that I have felt guilty letting him believe that Atticus and this child are his, but it would be worse if he knew they were not."

"Why do you say that?"

"Because the man's pride should be left intact," she said. "He did not ask for this union anymore than I did, but when I realized I was pregnant and asked him to share my bed… in a sense, I am protecting the de Wolfe reputation. I know it sounds so very strange to say that, but it is true."

Marcellus squeezed her gently. "It does not sound strange," he said. "You cannot help that you love another man, but to protect Will the way you have is noble, Lil. You may love me, but you do not want him publicly shamed."

She sighed heavily. "I do not," she said. "I never did. He is a good man. He does not deserve to be shamed, but I cannot help that I do not love him. We are simply making the best of a bad situation."

Marcellus knew that. He never once looked at Will with jealousy or scorn. In fact, quite the opposite. He respected Will tremendously, but he was in a difficult situation just as they all were. The only thing he and Lily were guilty of was dishonesty, only because telling the truth wouldn't solve the problem. It would only make it worse and there was a large part of them that didn't want to hurt Will in a situation of Chris de Lohr's making.

It wasn't as if they could do anything about it.

"If this child is born looking just like me, I fear we may find ourselves in a bind," he said after a moment. "We may not wish to shame Will, but we would be insulting him if he figures out that something is going on between us and we do not tell him everything."

"Mayhap," Lily said slowly. But her thoughts were shifting from Will back to the situation at hand as she felt the need to flesh it out further. "Marcellus, now that you know what Tarraby has said, what are your feelings on the matter? It feels so strange to speak of this so calmly, but I cannot help it. It is something we must face and mayhap a large part of me is still in shock, still thinking that Tarraby is mistaken. But if he is not… what do you want me to do?"

"What do you mean?"

"I mean do you want me to try and save the child?"

Marcellus was starting to tense up again. They were speaking of Lily's life now, and the life of his child. He'd come into the chamber shaken, had calmed somewhat with the ensuing conversation, and now he was feeling shaken all over again. He still couldn't believe they were speaking of life and death – Lily's. Her pregnancies were always easy and she delivered quickly, so this complication was a definitive shock.

By all convention, he had no rights in this matter.

But she was asking him just the same.

"What does Will say?" he asked quietly.

Feeling weak and exhausted, Lily was boneless against him. "I will tell you what I told him," she said. "I can feel this child moving in my belly daily. To know he is slowly dying is more horrifying than you can imagine. As his mother, I cannot stand by and do nothing. If I must sacrifice my life to save him, I will do so gladly. Not because I am some great martyr, but because I want my child to live."

He looked down at her, pain in his eyes. After a moment, he closed them and looked away. "Is this really happening?" he muttered. "Are we really having this conversation?"

Lily could hear the anguish in his voice, the pain of a man unable to do anything for the woman he loved. She craned her neck back, gazing up at him.

"Let me be clear," she whispered, the tears starting to form. "I do not want to leave you. I had always hoped… hoped we would be with each other into old age, but it would seem that God has other plans for me. Tarraby believes there is no hope for me no matter what, so if I agree to let him remove the child early, at least the child will have a chance at life. It gives me no great pleasure to know that his life will mean my demise, but I cannot stand the thought of him not being able to live his life. It does not seem fair."

She was being so calm about it except for the tears glistening in her eyes. That told him how brave she was being. Her tears triggered his and, soon, his eyes were filling with tears also.

"It is *not* fair," he said hoarsely. "And it is my fault."

"What do you mean?"

"Because I planted my seed in you. Had I not done that, we would not be facing this moment."

Lily pushed herself up and looked at him. "I forbid you to feel guilty for this," she said sternly. "As I recall, I was a willing participant, so this is not your fault."

Marcellus was trying, but not quite succeeding. He forced a smile at her, reaching out to cup her face in his big hand. For a moment, he simply stared at her, drinking in every feature, ever line.

It was agony.

"My sweet Lily," he whispered, lower lip trembling. "What am I going to do without you?"

Lily was starting to crumble because he was, but she fought it. "Then you want me to save the child? I want to do it sooner rather than later. Time is slipping away and every day that I delay is a day that his life slips from him."

She was trying so hard to sound logical about a situation where there was no logic. Only feeling. She was trying to be reasonable and unselfish, as if this were happening to someone else and not her. It was the only way she could get through it, something no woman should ever have to face. Marcellus understood that but it was still difficult to hear.

"I want you to do what you feel is best," he said hoarsely. "This is your life and no one else's."

Lily looked at him, knowing that Will's response would probably be the same thing. He would leave it up to her.

She already knew what she had to do.

"Then it is settled," she said tightly. She looked at him, drinking him in, studying every line to remember when she was in heaven and lonely for him. "But you... I want you to be happy, my love. I want you to marry a good woman and have many children. That is my wish for you, Marcellus. Please do not disappoint me."

He shook his head and looked at his lap. "I cannot even think on it," he said. "Do not force me to think about it, because I will not. But you must think of Will, for he is worse off than I am. You will be leaving him with children to tend to and no mother. He will be a wealthy widower and quite a prize for some unscrupulous woman."

Lily held her hand against his cheek, turning to kiss his palm. "Even at this moment, you are concerned for Will," she said. "That is sweet."

"Aren't you?"

She nodded. "I suppose I am," she said. "I have not thought on it, but now that you speak of it, I suppose I am. He needs a good woman who will not do to him what I have done."

Marcellus sighed faintly, hearing the same moral dilemma from her lips that they'd wrestled with for years. The truth was that their love for each other was stronger than their guilt. Love, in this case, was everything.

"You cannot fault yourself for listening to your heart," he said. "If you did not, you would be relegating yourself to a miserable life."

She sighed and pulled his hand away from her face. "That does not excuse what we have done to him," she said. "It makes us selfish because we have only thought of each other. We have done what our hearts dictated. Will is the only innocent here because he is caught up in it."

"As I said, you should be concerned for him. Mayhap... mayhap it will be your gift to him."

"What gift?"

"Would you not want to make sure he ends up with a good woman? And that your children have a kind and generous woman to take your place?"

"Of course I do," Lily said. "I would want him to be with a woman who will love him and love my children, but where would I find one? It's not so much the older children I worry about, but Atticus. She would need to tolerate Atticus' wildness and... *wait*."

"What is it?"

"I think I might have an idea."

"What idea?"

"*Mam!*"

They could both hear the shout from Atticus rushing up the stairwell. Thank God he had screamed because Marcellus was able to leap up off the bed and hide behind a dressing screen as Atticus rushed in with Adria on his heels. As Marcellus watched through the slats in the screen, he saw Adria come up behind Atticus as he tried to tell his mother how terrible Bradford had been to him. Marcellus should have thought something was amiss when Adria looked right at the screen, right at him.

He could see her through the slats.

He was fairly certain that she could see him, too.

CB

SHE HAD FORGOTTEN his little cap.

Atticus had a little woolen cap that Lily insisted on dressing him in when the mornings were cold and breath hung in the air, just as it was now. She'd come out of the keep with the boy on the loose, rushing off to find Bradford and food, in that order, but by the time she entered the kitchen yard, she realized she'd left the cap and Atticus' little face was pinched red.

He needed an extra layer of warmth.

Leaving Atticus with the cook, who distracted the boy with oat porridge and honey, Adria rushed out of the kitchen yard. As she came through the gate, she saw several soldiers milling around the inner gatehouse, including Marcellus. She didn't think anything of it because Marcellus was the commander of the walls and gatehouses during the day, so his presence was perfectly routine. She could also see Hermes and Ronan over near the outer gatehouse, putting some new recruits through their paces. She could hear Hermes bellowing at them.

Quickly, she ducked into the inner gatehouse before either knight could see her and headed straight to the keep.

The interior of the keep was cool and dark at this early hour. There had been servants sweeping out the ashes of the hearth in Will's solar, but they were gone now. She began to take the stairs quickly to the floor above where Lily's chamber was, but as she neared the open chamber door, she thought she heard voices.

At first, she thought it was Will. Somehow, the man had slipped past her, but as she came closer, she realized that it wasn't Will.

It was Marcellus.

Curious, she thought that Marcellus might have business with Lily and she didn't want to interrupt. She had just seen him going through the gatehouse, so he must have only just arrived in the great chamber to speak to Lily. Adria was about take the top step and knock on the open door when she heard Lily's voice.

I do not want to lose your child.

That brought her pause. Confused, she wasn't quite sure why she would be hearing such a thing. She stood on the second step from the top, baffled as she listened to a conversation she could have never imagined in a million years. As Lily and Marcellus spoke to one another and evidently wept with one another, it was becoming increasingly clear to Adria that all was not as it seemed with the two of them.

Something shocking was in the air.

Aghast, Adria leaned back against the wall as she heard Lily speak of so many things she'd never heard before – being forced into marriage with Will but of loving, of all people. Marcellus.

She was astonished.

Morbid curiosity had her frozen in place, listening to an intimately detailed conversation. Shocking, horrific, and deplorable. Absolutely deplorable. She'd gone from confused to astonished to outraged very quickly, but in the course of the conversation, she also learned that something was amiss with Lily's pregnancy, something that Tarraby had diagnosed.

Something terrible.

Lily was speaking of sacrificing her life for her child's. Marcellus spoke of Atticus growing to look much like him. There was so much going on that Adria was having a difficult time grasping such a staggering, private conversation. She knew she shouldn't be listening, but she simply couldn't help herself. It became readily apparent, from what she was hearing, that Lily and Marcellus had been carrying on for quite some time and that Atticus and the child Lily carried were not Will's, but Marcellus'.

She was so stunned that a gentle breeze could have blown her over.

When things began to come clear, self-preservation told her to leave the stairwell, to get out of there. She didn't want Marcellus or Lily discovering that she had eavesdropped, but she didn't feel guilty about it. She wasn't sure what she felt, but guilt wasn't part of it. She'd known Lily and Marcellus for years and she adored Lily like a sister, but she'd never had a clue that all of this was going on. Not one little clue.

Perhaps the greatest thing she felt, at the moment, was disappointment.

And pity for Will, who was apparently as oblivious as she was.

Making her way down the stairs, she was dazed as she headed for the keep entry. Her mind was on the conversation, unable to shake it, not even realizing that she didn't have what she'd come for.

The little hat.

It was still sitting in Lily's chamber where she'd left it.

Just as she set foot outside of the keep, Atticus came running in her direction and she found herself staring at the child, seeing Marcellus now that she knew who the lad's father was. She was so caught up in her observations that she was too slow to grab him as he ran by her.

After a moment's hesitation, she went in pursuit.

It seemed that all she did was chase Atticus. She ran up the stairs behind him, telling him to slow down, but he was shouting for his mother. He burst into the chamber, rushing for her bed as Adria came in behind him, looking around the chamber and seeing that Marcellus was nowhere to be found. Given that there was a privacy screen in the chamber, painted with a scene of mermaids and the ocean, she found herself looking right at it, suspecting that's where he was.

The cold burn of disapproval, of disgust, smoldered deep in her belly.

"He got past me, my lady," she said as evenly as she could. "I was only coming for his little cap. It is a chilly morning."

Lily smiled at her boy, running a hand over his head as he insisted that Bradford must be punished. "It is all right," she said. By this time, Adria had collected the cap and she held her hand out, taking it from Adria and pulling it down over Atticus' head. "Now, go outside and find your father. I wish to speak to Adria."

Atticus was not happy with that directive. "But Bradford is…!"

"Leave him alone," Lily said, giving him a shake. "You are

like a dog with a bone when it comes to Bradford. All you want to do is chew him down, but you will leave him alone. Do you hear me? If you harass him, I will see that you are punished."

She was holding up a stern finger in his face and Atticus frowned, but he didn't argue. He knew better than to do that when it came to his mother. After a reluctant shrug, which Lily took for an affirmative, she chased him out of the chamber. As he was heading down the steps, Lily turned her attention to Adria.

The woman had moved away from the bed, now over near the wardrobe pulling forth some garments that were hanging on the pegs. She seemed distracted, like she was finding something to do, for she certainly didn't need to be fussing with Lily's wardrobe right now. In fact, she'd seemed a little distant since she'd entered the chamber.

"Adria," Lily said. "Come here, please. I must speak with you."

Adria sighed faintly, setting aside the silk dress she'd been inspecting, and went over to the bed. There was a chair against the privacy screen and she resisted the urge to give the screen a shove, toppling the screen onto Marcellus, whom she knew to still be there. Whatever Lily was going to say, he was going to hear it.

Frustrated and gloomy, Adria pulled the chair up to the bed.

"Aye, my lady?" she asked politely. "How can I be of service?"

Lily couldn't help but notice that Adria wouldn't look at her. "What is the matter?" she asked. "You seem upset."

Adria was indeed having trouble looking at her after what she'd just heard, but she lifted her gaze and looked at her. "Forgive me," she said. "I... I suppose it has already been a trying morning with Atticus."

Lily smiled faintly. "Don't tell me that you are going off of my son."

Adria shook her head. "Never," she said. "But I will admit, he can be exhausting at times. He is very full of life."

Lily rolled her eyes. "You are telling me something I know all too well," she said. "That is why I am very glad you are tending to him now that I cannot. I know that Will asked you to tend to him and I am grateful."

"He did, my lady."

Lily hesitated. "Did he tell you about his conversation with Tarraby?"

Adria shook her head, but her gaze was guarded. As if she were wary, suspicious. "You mean the fact that he has examined you every day this week?" she said. "He did not speak of any conversation, my lady."

Lily wasn't quite sure why Adria was looking at her that way, but she didn't let it stop her from doing as she must. She averted her gaze, looking at her hands for a moment as she decided what she wanted to say.

"As it happens, Tarraby has been examining me all week because Will asked him to," she said.

"I assumed as much, my lady."

"There was more to it than simple concern," Lily went on. "There was a reason. As Will explained it to me, Tarraby was the apprentice to a great physic in his youth. This physic had a patient who had fallen from her horse when she neared the time to give birth and she exhibited the same symptoms that I have been having since my fall in the mud."

Adria was a little less wary and a little more interested. "You mean the pains in your belly and back?"

Lily nodded. "The same," she said. "And the blood. You know about that."

"I do."

Lily began wringing her hands a little. "The woman that fell from the horse had injured the child in her womb," she said. "Adria, I know you have never birthed a child so you would not know this, but when a child is born, there is a sack that attaches the child to the womb. It is where the nourishment comes from, as part of the mother. The child cannot survive without it and if it is damaged, it puts both the child and the mother in grave danger."

Now, Adria was starting to make sense out of the conversation she'd overheard between Lily and Marcellus. It didn't take a genius to figure out what Lily was trying to say.

"You injured this sack when you fell?" she asked.

Lily nodded slowly. "That is what Tarraby thinks," she said. "He has seen it before, and Will trusts him, so we have no reason to think that he is wrong. All of my symptoms indicate this injury."

"Then what will he do about it?"

Lily looked at her then. "There is nothing he can do about it," she said. "My child is slowly dying because the nourishment sack has come away from the womb. It has also left a gaping wound inside of me and that is where the blood is coming from."

Adria couldn't help it; she gasped, a hand flying to her mouth. "What does it mean?"

Lily could see the tears welling in Adria's eyes and she extended a hand to her. After a brief hesitation, Adria took it.

Lily squeezed her hand tightly.

"I am still coming to terms with this, so please be brave for me," she said, forcing a smile. "Adria, I will not survive this birth. As difficult as it is for me to say it, Tarraby believes it to be true. The only way to save the child is to have him cut out of my belly, so I have decided to do that. It will hopefully save his life, but it will not save mine. I will not be saved if he is taken by force or if I naturally give birth to him. Either way, I will not survive, so I am making the choice for my child's sake, to save him, and I must have your support. I must have your help."

Adria was staring at her with big eyes but the tears were beginning to trickle. "It's not possible," she breathed. "Surely... surely *something* can be done?"

Lily shook her head. "It seems that there is nothing to be done," she said, feeling pangs of grief even as she said it. "I suppose we could send for another physic, but he would take time to get here, precious time that could cost my babe his life. Do you see what I mean? If Tarraby is right, and Will believes he is, then there is no time at all. My son must be born soon if he has a chance of surviving."

Adria blinked and the tears spattered, but she didn't openly sob. All of the frustration and disappointment she felt at Lily and Marcellus had been pushed aside by painful grief for a woman she loved like a sister.

She was devastated.

"Oh, Lily," she whispered. It was rare when she called Lily by her name. "I cannot believe this. It cannot be true."

Lily squeezed her hand. "I wish it wasn't," she said. "I've wept over it, but not like I should because I feel such shock. As if none of this is real. It is almost as if I am watching someone else go through this, but then I remember it is me and I must make plans. I cannot leave this world without knowing my husband and children are taken care of."

"And you are so calm about it!"

Lily sighed faintly. "I can either become hysterical, which will do no good, or I can focus on what needs to be done. I choose to focus. For now."

Adria was struggling with her tears, struggling to stop weeping. "But what can I do to help?"

"Do you really want to know?"

"Of course I do," Adria insisted. "I will do whatever you wish, Lily. I will help however I can."

Lily's smile was genuine. "Good," she said softly. "Because I want you to marry Will. I want you to become his wife."

That stopped Adria's tears in an instant. Her eyes widened and she bolted up from the chair, looking at Lily as if the woman had just grown a second head.

"*What?*" she gasped. "Me?"

Lily nodded calmly. "You are perfect," she said. "You are from a good family and you need a husband. You love my son and my children know you and are fond of you. Will you not do this for me, Adria? It is the most important thing anyone could ever ask of you and I realize it is a great deal, but I beg you to consider it. Please."

Adria's mouth popped open and she gaped at her. So much shock that morning that she was unable to adequately handle. First the situation between Lily and Marcellus, then Lily's health, and now this.

Lily wanted her to marry Will.

Adria couldn't help it.

She fled.

CHAPTER EIGHT

"**Y**OU TOLD HER *what*?"

"That I wish for her to marry you."

Will stood in the center of Lily's chamber, dumbfounded.

It was mid-morning at Carlisle and, unfairly, the world was going on while Will and Lily continued to deal with catastrophic news. Everything around them was going on as normal and it hardly seemed right, but that was the situation they found themselves in.

And now this.

Lily had asked Adria to marry Will.

"Why on earth would you do such a thing?" he finally managed to ask. "You tell her what is happening and then you demand she marry me?"

Lily could see that his shock was turning to outrage, but she didn't back down. "I did," she said. "If you will stop posturing long enough to allow me to explain, I shall."

"I am not posturing. Speak."

Lily took a deep breath. "You will not deny me this last wish, William de Wolfe," she said, becoming angrier than he was. "I am the one who is suffering through something horrific and unimaginable, not you. I am the one who will not see my next birthday, so stop acting as if you are the one being wronged. It is not you. It is *me*."

She was shaking by the time she finished, spewing angrily, and he put up his hands in a gesture of surrender. "I am sorry," he said. "I am not trying to be difficult... but *marriage*? You want Adria to marry *me*? Why, in God's name?"

Lily wasn't going to let him off so easily. If she had any chance of bending the man to her will, she had to take a stand and make a good show of it.

The tears started to come.

"Because I want to leave this earth knowing that you are being taken care of," she said. "I want to know that Atticus and Athena and Andrew have someone they can turn to, someone that cares for them. I want to see my family tended to by a woman I love dearly, one I know will be good to all of you. Is that so much to ask?"

Will's outrage was gone, replaced by a distinct sense of remorse and sorrow. "Nay," he said hoarsely. "It is not."

"I want you to be happy, Will. Adria is a good woman and she will make you happy."

Will didn't even know what to say. It wasn't as if he could fight with her about it. He didn't have the heart. But he was still deeply shocked.

"Very well," he said after a moment. "If that is what you wish."

"It is."

"And she didn't say anything before she left?"

Lily dabbed at her eyes with her kerchief. "Nay," she said. "I know the news has hurt her. It has hurt all of us. I think asking her to marry you was too much, so mayhap you should find her and ease the situation."

Will frowned. "What do you want me to say?" he said. "Lily, I am as shocked as she is. I have never once looked at Adria in a romantic way. Not once."

"Then you do not think she is pretty?"

"She's damned beautiful, but that's not the point."

"Then what *is* the point?" Lily asked. "She's beautiful and sweet and she loves our children. I know she would grow to love you if you would only let her. Wouldn't you like to have a wife who was in love with you, Will? A woman who could give you something I never could?"

That was a harsh way of putting it, but it was true. Oddly enough, it gave him pause. Will thought that he and Lily would be married until he died. He'd always planned on that. It never occurred to him that she would die before him, so the loveless marriage they found themselves in was something he'd resigned himself to years ago. He thought that was going to be the rest of his life. To think that he might actually have a chance for happiness was a new and startling thought.

With Adria.

What Lily said was true. Adria was beautiful and sweet and she loved his children. She was young, with a curvy figure that most men gave a second look to. If he thought hard, he found her attractive, wildly so, but that was never anything he would have acted upon. He was loyal to his vows and always had been. But he had to admit that what Lily was suggesting was intriguing.

Perhaps a little too intriguing.

"I don't know," he muttered, turning away. "I must think on it."

"What is there to think about?"

"Lily, I cannot make lifelong decisions in a quick moment," he said, exasperated. "You must let me at least become accustomed to the idea. I never planned on another wife, but now you are demanding I have one, so I am allowed to think on it a little."

Lily did something at that point that she wasn't supposed to do. She got out of bed. She made her way over to Will, who was standing by the window overlooking the inner bailey.

"I would like to give you all the time in the world to think on it, but I do not have that kind of time," she said quietly. "I have decided to let Tarraby take the child from me in the hope of saving his life. If what Tarraby says is true, then every day that passes is a day the child is dying. Therefore, next week on a day of my choosing, I will permit the man to take the child from me. But between now and that day, I must know that you and my children will be taken care of. I want you to have a chance at happiness, Will, and I believe Adria will be that chance."

Will sighed heavily as he turned to look at her. "How can you even know that?"

She smiled faintly, gazing into his handsome face. "Because I do," she said. "Adria is almost part of our family, anyway. Would you prefer she marry someone else and you would never see her again? Our children would never see her again?"

He grunted. "It is of no matter to me because I do not have feelings for her," he said frankly. "She is your vassal, not mine. I am not the kind of man who goes around feeling things for women who are not my wife."

"You do not even feel anything for your wife."

He lifted an eyebrow. "That is not fair," he said. "Mayhap we have resigned ourselves to a marriage that has us friends and not lovers, but that does not mean I pine for other women."

Lily put a hand on his big arm. "I want you to think about pining for Adria," she said softly. "I give you my full permission, Will. Take this week and see if you find anything about her that you can have feelings for. Will you do this for me? Please?"

He rolled his eyes and looked away. "You cannot be serious."

"I am."

"You cannot force me to feel anything for her."

"I am not forcing you," she said. "All I am doing is asking you to try. Pretend I am not a factor, nor is your marriage, for soon enough, it will not be and you will be a widower. Pretend you are alone and can have any woman you want. All I am asking is that you try, Will. Please. I want you to."

He wanted to walk out of the room in protest. He really did. But something made him stay – confusion, curiosity, and perhaps even interest. He wasn't even sure what he felt. All he knew was that he couldn't walk away from her or what she was suggesting because it evidently meant so much to her.

He returned his focus to her.

"You are not going to leave me alone until I do, are you?" he said.

She grinned impishly. "Nay."

"But what if this isn't what Adria wants?"

"You will not know unless you ask her."

Will sighed sharply, looking her in the eyes. He seemed to study her for a moment, as if remembering that girl from long ago that he'd been so attracted to. He just didn't know what happened to that, but he did know one thing.

Lily was his friend.

She always had been.

"You are my closest friend," he said hoarsely. "I do not know how that ever came about, that you should be my friend and not a wife I love madly, but the loss I will feel of this friendship is greater than you can imagine. I do not know what I am going to do without you harping on me or ordering me around."

There was humor amidst the tears that came to Lily's eyes. "And you are one of my dearest friends, as well," she said. "I will miss you greatly, Will, and that is why I must make sure you are well taken care of when I leave. I want you to be happy. I want you to love. And I want you to remember me with some fondness as the years go on. I am sorry I could not be the wife I should have been to you, but I do not consider my life wasted. Not at all."

Reaching out, he grasped her hand and lifted it to his lips for a kindly kiss. "Nor I."

"Then please talk to Adria. It means a great deal to me."

He dropped her hand and nodded wearily. "I will try."

With that, he turned and quit the chamber, leaving Lily by the window, watching him go with tears in his eyes. She knew it was a huge burden she had given him, but she felt in her heart that it was the right thing to do. Everything was happening so quickly that there simply wasn't time for careful thought and lingering plans.

Next week.

She had until next week to find her husband a wife.

☙

"Ah," Gar said. "I have been looking for you. Sir Ronan, is it?"

Ronan looked up from the spear he'd been inspecting. He was standing outside of the armory built into Carlisle's massive outer wall, going through some old weapons they had found in a storeroom, when he saw Adria's father approaching.

"Aye, it is," he said. "How may I be of service, my lord?"

Gar smiled, being very friendly with him. He pointed to the spear. "Expecting trouble?"

Ronan shook his head. "Not any more than usual," he said, holding up the old spear. "These were found in a storeroom. I have no idea how long they've been there, but most definitely longer than Will has been in command."

Gar pretended to study the spear even as Ronan lowered it.

"I suspect you have more than your share of work here," he said. "You know – for things like weapons and protecting the castle in general."

Ronan nodded. "Being recently knighted, however, I am at the bottom of the chain of command," he said. "That will not last long, however. I can defeat Hermes and, somehow, I'll prove myself over Marcellus, or at least try to. I'll get to the top."

"Spoken like a true de Wolfe, I'm sure."

Ronan grinned. "Will is the heir to the kingdom," he said. "The best I can hope for is inheriting a grand post when he is the Earl of Warenton, but I want him to feel as if he can trust me. After I've beat down all of my competitors, of course."

Somehow, they got onto the exact subject Gar was hoping they could discuss. It had come organically, in conversation, and he was pleased. But he wasn't going to let them stray from it.

He'd come with a purpose.

"Then your father does not have any property to inherit?" he asked.

"He does," Ronan said, picking away the frayed leather at the head of the spear. "My father was granted the title Lord Sydenham and the Sydenham Barony, a small but strategic barony between Wark Castle and the town of Kelso. As a result, he commands Roxburgh Castle, a rather large bastion that is not unlike Carlisle in that it is a crown property manned by both de Wolfe and royal troops."

Sydenham. So Ronan's father had titles and land, which undoubtedly meant income. Given that he was part of the de Wolfe family, he had wealth from them, as well. Surely he was a rich man, indeed.

Gar could see gold coins floating before his eyes.

"Why do you not serve at Roxburgh?" he asked.

"Because my father wanted me to gain some experience outside of his influence," Ronan said. "My father is a great knight and I have no doubt that I will serve him one day, but for now, I remain at Carlisle."

"I see," Gar said. "And your mother? Where does she hail from?"

"She is a Hage," Ronan said. "Kieran Hage, her father, was the Earl of Warenton's second in command until his death a few years ago."

"Ah," Gar said. "I am sorry for your family. But I am sure he was quite proud of you."

Ronan smiled faintly. "I hope so," he said. "He was a great man. I miss him."

"Of course you do," Gar said, eyeing Ronan as the knight pulled off the rest of the frayed leather and separated the spear head from the shaft. "That shows a man of good character, feeling affection for friends and family. Certainly they must feel affection towards you, too. It is a pity you do not have a wife to share your affection. I must say I found it quite shocking to hear that you were not married."

Ronan lifted his eyebrows. "I do not know why," he said. "I have only seen eighteen summers. I have time still."

"True," Gar said. "There is no one special, though?"

"No one."

He was going back to his spear and the conversation was starting to lag, which was something Gar didn't want.

He had to go in for the kill.

"Sir Ronan, I would like to present something for your consideration," he said. "I realize we do not know each other, but given that you are a de Wolfe, I know that you are a fine and noble knight purely from the reputation of your family. You see, my daughter is in need of a husband. With her comes the Alcester title and properties upon my death, which would pass to her husband. She is my heiress. Would… would that be of any interest to you?"

Ronan looked at him. "Your daughter?" he said, dumb-founded. "Lady Adria?"

Gar nodded. "Aye," he said. "Lady Adria. Do not give me any answer now. Simply… think about it. You have known Adria for some time, I would imagine, so you know that she is a good lass. She is pretty and resourceful. I do believe she would make a fine wife and it is time for her to wed, so I am simply bringing it to your attention so that you may think about it."

Ronan was looking at Gar with bewilderment. He didn't even know what to say. Gar moved away from him, holding out a hand as if to beg pardon that he'd just dumped that rather heady proposal on his lap.

"Just think," he said. "I will leave you now. We may discuss it again at your leisure."

With that, the man scurried off, back across the outer bailey as Ronan watched in shock.

Did Adria's father just offer me a betrothal?

Scratching his head, he went back to work, but the thought of marriage to Adria stuck with him. As Gar had requested, he thought about it.

Maybe too much.

CHAPTER NINE

I T WAS TOO much.

All of it was too much. Adria had been sucked up by the overwhelming nature of the morning's events and, even now, she sat in the great hall of Carlisle by herself as servants worked in the shadows, because she knew it was the last place Hermes or Ronan or even her father would come looking for her.

She didn't want to see anyone at the moment.

Lily was dying.

Adria still couldn't believe it, but given that she'd heard Lily and Marcellus speak of it when they thought no one was listening, it must be true. She knew Lily wouldn't lie about that and given the signs that they'd been through all week, with Tarraby's visits and Lily's physical symptoms, she couldn't deny that it all made sense. Lily's fall had injured her and the child she carried to the point where the only option was to cut the baby from her belly and let Lily sacrifice herself to save the child.

Marcellus' child.

The entire situation had Adria muddled and distraught.

So, she sat in the great hall and wept. She wept for Lily, for the baby, for the fact that Lily had been lying to Will for so many years, and for Will himself. He was a noble and true man and he certainly didn't deserve what Lily and Marcellus had been doing behind his back. There was so much going on that she didn't know where she should be upset the most.

All of it was terrible.

Adria was sitting in one of the several alcoves in the great hall, bench seats built into the lancet windows that went from the floor almost to the ceiling. The seats faced each other and, in more genteel times, would have been for men and women to have a private place to converse with the cool breeze from the window making the ambiance pleasant. However, Carlisle was such a military installation that the alcoves were mostly used for men to sleep in or drink in. No genteel ladies, no great feasts with beautiful women and loud entertainment.

In truth, Adria missed that a little.

Lioncross Abbey was where she had fostered her last year. It was a massive, gracious castle that had feasts aplenty. Kaedia de Lohr, Countess of Hereford and Worcester, managed the castle with a velvet fist and Adria had always appreciated Lady de Lohr's kind but firm manner. She missed how Lady de Lohr would have her charges dress beautifully and present them to a hall of men who looked at the women as a feast for the eyes.

Will de Wolfe had been among those men. In fact, Adria had come to Lioncross well after Will had arrived, but he'd been kind to her from the start. That was about the time he married Lily. Adria really had no memory of Will before their marriage, for it seemed to her as though they'd always been married. But, as she'd so often observed, it had not been an affectionate marriage. Lily and Will had always been friendly with each other, like siblings more than husband and wife, because there had been no hint of love between them ever.

Now, she knew why.

At least, she knew why Lily had treated Will the way she

had. Perhaps Will only treated her the same way because Lily had set that precedence. It was difficult to know. But never in all of her years with them had she suspected there was anything between Lily and Marcellus. She was still having great difficulty with that. And now, Lily wanted to throw her into that very odd situation by forcing her to marry Will once she had departed this earth.

Adria didn't know what to think.

As she sat there and brooded, looking out of the window towards the kitchen yard and watching the servants move about, she caught movement in the corners of her eyes and turned to see Will entering the great hall. Swiftly wiping her cheeks, she climbed out of the window seat and began to make her way towards him, quickly.

"I am sorry, my lord," she said. "I did not mean to shirk my duties."

"What do you mean?"

"I thought Atticus was with you. Clearly, he is not. I will find him immediately."

Will put up a hand to stop her from moving around him. "He is with Hermes right now," he said. "My cousin is teaching him how to yell at men, so it should prove both hilarious and concerning."

Adria smiled weakly. "Then mayhap I should relieve Hermes from child tending duties."

Will shook his head. "Not yet," he said. "I've coming looking for you. It seems that we must speak."

Something in his tone put her on her guard. Adria looked up at him warily. "About what, my lord?"

Will's gaze lingered on her for a moment. "Lily told me."

Adria blinked. She wasn't prepared to speak on that yet and the longer she looked at Will, the more she remembered about Lily and Marcellus. The more it made her blood boil to know they'd duped such an honorable man.

She took a step back.

"What about, my lord?" she asked, lowering her gaze.

Will reached out and politely grasped her arm, turning her back towards the alcove. "Come," he said quietly. "Let us sit."

Adria let him turn her around but she didn't let him hold on to her. She pulled her arm away, gently but firmly, heading back to the alcove. Stiffly, she sat on one benches as he sat on the other, facing her. She kept her eyes averted, waiting for him to say something.

She wasn't sure she wanted to hear it.

"Lily told me that she informed you of Tarraby's diagnosis," he said softly.

Adria was still looking at her hands. "She did, my lord."

"She also told me what she has asked of you."

Adria couldn't help it; she started to tear up. "Then you know."

"I do."

The tears trickled down her face as she struggled for her composure. "May... may I ask you a question, my lord?"

"Of course."

"Is Lady de Wolfe truly dying?"

Will sighed faintly. "Tarraby believes so."

"And the child is dying, too?"

"So Tarraby says."

"Do you believe him?"

"I do. He is a man of uncanny skill. I have no reason to disbelieve him."

Adria's head lifted and she fixed on him. "But what if he is wrong?"

Will's brow flickered. "What do you mean?"

Adria quickly wiped at the tears on her face with a shaking hand. "If he is wrong, Lady de Wolfe will live and the child will live," she said. "Why must we make such decisions now? Why can we not wait to see? He is not God. He does not know what will happen in the end. He could be mistaken."

Will looked at her, sorrow in his eyes. "I wish he was," he said. "I hope he is. But I fear we have no choice but to believe him. He has knowledge that the rest of us do not."

Adria's features tightened. "Then I am to marry you the moment Lily passes on?" she asked. "I must go into the marriage bed with the husband of a woman whose body will still be warm? I do not like any of this, my lord. It feels… wrong. It feels opportunistic and wrong, as if I am stealing something from Lady de Wolfe even though she has made it clear that her marriage to you is…"

She stopped herself before she could go on, appalled that she'd run off at the mouth as much as she had. She dropped her head again, looking at her lap.

"Forgive me," she whispered. "Please forgive me. We are speaking of a woman I love as a sister and I find this whole thing… shocking and disorienting."

Will was watching her carefully. "I understand," he said. "I told her so. But she is determined to select a woman that I should marry who is worthy of the de Wolfe name. She feels that it is you."

Adria shook her head as if fighting off the very idea. "But I am no one," she said, emotion in her tone. "My lord, you know who my father is. *What* he is. He's a penniless lord who is looking for an opportunity for his daughter to marry well. I will not give it to him."

Will's brow furrowed. "What do you mean?"

Her head came up again, looking at him with great sorrow. "Alcester used to stand for something," she said flatly. "There was money and a lovely home, but my father took all of the money, and my mother's money as well, and gambled it all into the ground. He only had a daughter – me – so he knew he had to make sure I was positioned well for an advantageous marriage so he would have access to more money that he could squander. It would be his greatest wish for me to marry the heir to the House of de Wolfe because it would give him an endless supply of coin. He would bleed me dry and have me begging money from you constantly."

"Would you?"

"Nay!" she nearly shouted. "I would not, but he is like vermin that you cannot get rid of. He picks and picks until it drives you mad."

Will sat back in the seat, his focus never leaving her. "And that is why you will not consider Lily's request?"

She lost some of her anger. "Mostly," she said honestly. "May… may I be honest?"

"You are doing an excellent job so far. Continue."

"You have already had one unhappy marriage. I could not bring you another."

He cocked his head curiously. "You think my marriage to Lily is unhappy?"

"Isn't it?"

He shrugged. "It is a marriage by definition of the name," he said. "We do not hate one another. In fact, we are good friends. She wants for nothing. It is not a bad marriage."

"But are you *happy*?"

He sighed faintly. "I am not miserable if that is what you mean."

It was a surprisingly honest conversation between two people who had never really had a conversation at all, much less one like this. Even though they'd been acquainted for years, they really didn't *know* one another.

Perhaps it was time.

"What do *you* think of Lady de Wolfe's request?" Adria

asked after a moment. "After everything I have told you, surely you must tell her that a marriage between us is quite impossible."

"Why?"

Adria was surprised by his question. "I told you why," she said. "My father would look at such a union as his own personal fortune. I cannot allow him to do that to you."

Will shook his head. "And you do not think I can handle your father?" he said. "I do not care what he thinks. But if we were to marry and you ask me for money to give to him, I would do it. Would you ask?"

"Absolutely not."

"Then we have nothing to worry about."

Adria wasn't so sure. She shook her head. "It is not so easy," she said. "I told you that he picks. It would not be… pleasant."

"And I would not be pleasant if he annoyed you or, worse, annoyed me. He would be very, very sorry."

Adria looked at him curiously. Or, perhaps she was looking at him through new eyes. She wasn't quite sure, but his declaration somehow gave her hope.

Hope that Gar de Geld wouldn't get what he wanted, after all.

But that wasn't the only problem in her eyes.

"Even so, I am not a suitable match for you," she said, calmer and more quietly. "You are the heir to a great empire. I am the daughter of a very minor noble family. When you marry, it should be for wealth or position. I can't give you either."

"I do not want wealth or position, for I have both already," he said. "Wealth and position do not a happy marriage make."

She was quite curious about that comment. "Then it is not something you desire?"

He shook his head. "Strangely enough, I would like to marry a woman who isn't ambitious, who is unfailingly honest, and who would make an excellent companion," he said. "I've been around you for a few years now, my lady, and I have seen how you have been with Lady de Wolfe. You are faithful, true, honest, loyal, and unselfish. I know this for myself because Lily cannot live without you. Plus, you can run fast and chase Atticus down, so that makes you entirely suitable in my opinion. Lily did not have a terrible idea when she suggested a marriage between us. Mayhap she is right. Will you at least think about it?"

Adria stared at him, realizing that he was agreeable to his wife's mad scheme. Or perhaps it wasn't such a mad scheme, after all. Adria pondered his question a moment before answering.

"Are you sure this is what you want?" she asked.

His eyes took on a glimmer of warmth. "Knowing you as long as I have and seeing you through Lady de Wolfe's eyes, I think I could not find a more suitable lady were I to search far and wide," he said. "This is what Lily wants. I am agreeable if you are."

Adria didn't know what to say. She sat there for a moment, bewildered but not entirely hopeless. There was something in the way he looked at her that gave her confidence that, perhaps, this wasn't so insane, after all.

There was only one answer she could give him.

"I will think about it," she finally said. "I promise."

"Good," Will said, standing up. "We will speak again tomorrow. Is that acceptable?"

Adria nodded hesitantly. "It is," she said. "I... I do not think I have much time to think it over. I do not want to distress Lady de Lohr, so I promise I will think very hard."

Will nodded, stepping out of the alcove. "It is a big decision," he said. "You must make certain you are comfortable with it."

Adria stood up, too, following him. "Let us be honest, my lord," she said. "It is the request from a dying woman. I am not entirely sure there is any other option but the obvious. But I will most definitely think on it, very hard."

Will forced a smile. "That is all I can ask," he said. "Now, I intend to save Hermes from Atticus the Tyrant. I think he has spent enough time with his young cousin and is surely ready to beg for mercy."

"Nay," Adria said, pushing past him. "I will save Hermes. Atticus is my charge, after all."

"You are a brave, brave woman."

Adria couldn't help it; she grinned at him, flashing a big dimple in her right cheek, before quickly lowering her gaze and heading to the hall entry. Will followed at a distance, but as he did, he found himself taking a second look at the noble Lady Adria. He'd never really given her a second look in all of the years he'd known her, but now... now, perhaps he should.

His wife certainly thought so.

An odd situation, indeed.

CHAPTER TEN

"**I**T HAS BEEN a long time since I've been here," a soft female voice with a decided Scottish brogue spoke. "Carlisle Castle never ceases tae fill me with a sense of awe."

It had been a few days since Will's dire missive had been received at Castle Questing, forcing the House of de Wolfe into action. Scott, riding in full battle regalia beside a fortified carriage painted in the de Wolfe colors, turned to the woman looking from the window.

"How fortunate we were that Edward asked Will to be his garrison commander," he said. "That makes an unbreakable line of de Wolfe or de Wolfe allies from one end of the border to the other."

Jordan de Wolfe, the Countess of Warenton, gazed at the red-stoned bastion as it drew near. "When I married yer da those years go, who knew this would come about?"

"Papa did."

Jordan smiled at her eldest son. "I think he did," she said. "Ye've never seen a fiercer man in battle or when dealing with the politics of the border. It still amazes me that our life has become what it has."

"Regrets?" Scott teased her.

Jordan cocked an eyebrow. "Only with ye," she said, watching him laugh. But she sobered quickly. "I confess that I'm concerned with what we'll find here."

Scott's smile faded. "I know," he said. "Me, too. I wonder if Will has sent word to Chris. This is his daughter we are speaking of, after all."

Jordan fell silent for a moment. "Birth is part of life," she said quietly. "As men go intae battle prepared for death, women go intae childbirth prepared for the same. I've been very fortunate that my own children havena suffered dead children or wives throughout the years."

"But you had a stillbirth."

Jordan nodded. "Madeleine," she said, thinking back to that terrible day so many years ago. "It was strange, really – the babe had been very busy in my belly up until she was born, and when she came out, she was simply... dead. There was no chance tae revive her and I've always wondered what happened. Sometimes God's will is painful and mysterious, but when I die, that's the first question I'm going tae ask Him – what happened tae my Madeleine and where is she so that I may hug her?"

Scott nodded faintly, knowing that Madeleine's birth had always affected his mother so. She'd had many children, but each one was as precious as if it were the only child to her. "If you get there before me, hug her for me, as well," he said. "And then find Athena and Andy and Bea and tell them that I love them."

"I will, have no doubt."

The castle loomed closer.

The blue sky seemed inordinately bright against the silhouette of the structure as they came in from the south, as the road wound around to take them through the main gatehouse. There was an enormous moat between them and the walls, part of Carlisle's defense system, and the moat smelled – and looked –

like a sewer. It was all part of the deterrent.

Passing through the gatehouse, Baron Kilham was announced, Kilham being the hereditary title for the heir to the earldom of Warenton. Scott had brought two hundred men with him, unwilling to take a chance with his mother traveling with him. The entire party congregated in the outer bailey and by the time Scott opened up the door of the carriage so his mother could climb out, Will was upon them.

"Papa," he said, hugging his father fiercely. When he saw his grandmother's wimpled head emerging from the carriage, he reached out to help her down. "And Matha. I'm so happy to see you both."

Once Jordan was on her feet, Will hugged her tightly enough to lift her up. She grunted at his enthusiastic hugging as his father beat him off.

"Careful, lad," he said as Will set Jordan back to her feet. "Squeeze like that again and you may break something."

Will grinned. "I'm sorry," he said. "I'm just so glad to see you. Poppy let you come without him?"

Poppy was what all of the de Wolfe grandchildren called William de Wolfe and Jordan nodded. "He insisted I come," she said. "He thought I might be of some assistance, but I must tell ye that he sent word tae Paris. I wouldna be surprised if Bonny showed up as well."

Will's smile faded. "I'm so sorry to drag you away from Poppy's celebration," he said. "Every birthday celebration at his age is important."

Jordan waved him off. "This is important, tae," she said, looking towards the keep. "How is Lily? Where is she?"

Will took his grandmother by the elbow, helping her towards the keep as Scott took position on her other side. "She is as well as can be expected," he said. "Did Papa tell you everything?"

"Everything in the missive," Scott said, looking at his eldest son and seeing how much the man was starting to look like his mother. He hadn't seen him in about six months and even at Will's age, he changed and developed as he got older. His hair had taken on more redness to it and there was something with the way his mouth was shaped that looked just like Athena. "Now that we're here, tell us everything, Will. Everything that was in the missive and more that wasn't."

Will's joy in seeing his father and grandmother dampened at the thought of why they were actually there. There was comfort that they had arrived, of course, but there was also a sense of foreboding as to *why* they had arrived.

They'd arrived because of Lily's impending fate.

"There is little more to tell," he said. "Know that no one knows what is happening with Lily, so please do not speak of it to others. We have kept it private."

"Understood," Scott said. "Continue."

Will looked up at the squat, strong keep looming in the near distance. "My physic, Tarraby, is a man of great talent," he said. "Poppy sent him here last year when I was badly injured in a skirmish. He healed a wound to my thigh that could have just as easily gone wrong. I could have lost my leg."

"I know," Scott said. "The man is very skilled."

Will went on. "Last month, Lily was in the kitchen yard when she slipped and fell heavily in the mud," he said. "From what I understand, she landed on her bottom and left side. In any case, ever since then, she's been having pain in her belly and in her back, and she has been passing blood fairly steadily, sometimes a greater volume than other times. She did not tell me this, of course – I only knew about the pains – so I finally had Tarraby examine her and, based on his experience, he believes that the nourishment sack for the child has pulled away from the womb. He says the child is slowly dying and that Lily will bleed to death when he is born. That is why I sent for you, Papa – you are a great healer. I want you to examine Lily, too, and give me your opinion."

Scott drew in a long, if not remorseful, breath. "My skill is with illness and battle wounds, Will," he said. "A pregnant woman requires skill I do not believe I have. I am not entirely sure I can help in this case."

"Will you at least look at her, Papa?" Will asked. "I am willing to believe Tarraby. We all are. But I want you to examine her and tell me what you think."

Scott nodded in resignation, passing Jordan a long glance. "And Lily?" he asked. "How is she taking this?"

Will shrugged. "Lily has been surprisingly strong," he said. "She is trying to be logical and reasonable about it, but you should know something. Tarraby has told her that the only way to save the child is to take him by force, which will surely kill Lily. She has chosen to do this, for she wants her child to live. She has also decided to select a wife for me to take her place. She says that she must go to her grave knowing that the children and I are well-tended."

Both Scott and Jordan looked at him in surprise. "A *wife*?" Jordan said. "Who is this wife she has selected?"

"Lady Adria, her lady-in-waiting."

Jordan frowned. "Adria?" she repeated. "I believe I've met this lass, only briefly, however."

"Probably," Will said. "She accompanies Lily everywhere she goes, so I am sure you've met her at some point."

Jordan was still frowning. "So Lily wants tae make sure ye have a wife after she's gone?" she said. "I'm not sure I like that she insists upon selecting her. Ye have yer own choice of freedom as tae who ye'll marry, Will. 'Tis not Lily's decision."

Will nodded patiently as they came to the inner gatehouse. "I know," he said. "But she is concerned with what she leaves behind. She wants to make sure I am happy and that the children are cared for."

"It is still not her choice unless ye're comfortable with her making it," Jordan said. "Lily has exerted enough control in yer marriage, Will. The lass can be headstrong and ye've let her."

"This is not the time, Mama," Scott said, trying to head his mother off of any tirade against Lily. Jordan never had agreed with the way Will and Lily ran their marriage and wasn't shy about expressing that opinion. "Let us greet Lily and your great-grandson before we engage in any heavy discussions."

Jordan shut her mouth, but she turned her nose up at Scott to let him know she wasn't finished speaking her mind when it came to Lily de Lohr de Wolfe. The lass who had everything but never seemed to be happy about it.

"Where's my Atticus?" she said. "I must hug him before he can scream and run away. He doesna seem tae like hugs."

Will grinned weakly. "Do not feel bad about it," he said. "He doesn't like anyone to hug him."

"I'm not just anyone."

"That is true," Will said, lifting her hand and kissing it. "You are one of a kind."

Jordan let his flattery soften her and he laughed softly because she smiled at him, though reluctantly. The keep was looming ahead by now and they moved towards it, heading towards an encounter that would either give hope or give confirmation. That would either dispute Tarraby or support the fact that Lily de Lohr de Wolfe, Lady Irthington, was in a dire condition.

Somehow, stepping into that keep signaled life or death.

That dark, cool interior had them dreading what was to come.

⁂

"Sir Hermes, is it? I'm so glad I found you."

Hermes was moving between the stables and the outer bailey, heading back to check on a group of men he'd left with Ronan to work on battle tactics involving shields. He was in a hurry and not particularly paying attention to those around him, so Gar's sudden appearance caught him by surprise.

"Me, my lord?" he asked, confused, as he came to a halt. "I am sorry, but I do not remember your name."

"St. Ansgar de Geld," Gar said. "I am Adria's father."

That brought the light of recognition. "Of course," Hermes said. "I have seen you around over the past few days, but I could not place you."

Gar waved him off. "No trouble at all," he said. "I've not been very social since I've arrived. My daughter makes me stay mostly to my room, so I've not been out much. I've only been in the great hall once or twice."

Hermes nodded, but he didn't know why the man had stopped him. "Is there something I can do for you?"

Gar shrugged. "Possibly," he said. "May I beg a moment of your time?"

Hermes could see the men fighting and he knew that that Ronan was expecting him, so he struggled for patience with a man he'd only met once, really. That had been some time ago, which is why he hadn't recognized him. He'd certainly never had a conversation with him, so he had no idea what he could possibly want to speak with him about.

"I am afraid my time is very limited, my lord," he said. "Mayhap we can speak tonight at sup."

He started to walk away, but Gar followed him. "I only want to give you something to think on," he said, shuffling after Hermes, who slowed down but didn't stop altogether. "You can think about it and then we can speak when you have the time. Are you married, Sir Hermes?"

Hermes came to a stop, looking at him strangely. "Forgive me, my lord, but that is a rather personal question."

Gar could see that he'd offended the man. "I realize that, but I am asking for a reason," he said. "You see, my daughter is in need of a husband and if you are interested, I should like to know. If you are not married, then consider the prospect. She comes with the Alcester title and properties. We can speak more on it if you wish, but do not wait too long. Others are interested."

With that, he darted off, back the way he'd come, leaving Hermes standing there, looking baffled. But once that confusion passed, Gar's words sank in.

My daughter is in need of a husband if you are interested.

He'd been interested since he'd known Adria, but she'd made it clear that she wasn't interested in him. She was more than willing to be a friend, but not a bride.

Still…

He hadn't really tried to court her. He'd simply invited her to certain outings, offering to be her escort. He'd not really made his intentions clear because she'd made her intentions clear first. Maybe if he was able to be plain with her and explain himself, she might think differently. He really didn't want to give up if there was any hope of a chance.

Especially if her father was actively seeking a betrothal for her.

With that lingering on his mind, Hermes resumed his walk towards the training group.

CHAPTER ELEVEN

H E'D SPENT ALMOST an hour with her.

Scott and Tarraby, whom he knew because the man had served at Castle Questing before he went to Carlisle, spent nearly an hour with Lily. They listened, poked, prodded, and asked questions. Lots of questions, mostly from Scott to Lily, who hadn't wavered in any of her answers.

And that was concerning.

It was like putting the pieces of a puzzle together. Scott had conferred with Tarraby before they went to examine Lily and Tarraby had been precise in his assessment. In fact, Scott had been impressed with the man's scope of knowledge, something he'd been acquainted with before, but not to this degree. As he'd told his mother, a pregnant woman was much different from a wounded soldier or a sickly man. It was specialized, something almost always attended to by other women. Midwives had the market cornered on pregnant women, so a male physic was rather unusual.

But this was an unusual case.

The more Scott heard and the more he saw, the more he disliked. He couldn't contradict any conclusion Tarraby had come to, for he was seeing the signs, too. Most alarmingly, Lily's pulse was rapid and weak, which could signal internal bleeding. She was cold to the touch on a day that was quite mild. It was the little things that led him to believe that Tarraby was correct in that she had done irreparable damage when she'd fallen in the mud.

And then, there was the child himself.

Tarraby had examined Lily every day since his initial diagnosis and he mentioned to Scott that he believed the child was weakening, too. The movements were becoming less powerful with the child and even Lily had commented that he seemed to be slowing down. That frightened her and they didn't want her to be frightened, but she'd already made the decision that Tarraby was going to cut the child out of her body in the next few days. She was ticking the days off as they came. Her fear was that she couldn't wait too much longer to save her child.

That was Tarraby's fear, too.

But he would let Scott tell his son that.

Jordan had been in the chamber the entire time that Tarraby and Scott were examining Lily. She held Lily's hand as the two men pored over her, trying to determine if she really was facing such a terrible situation. Jordan was comforting and reassuring, but every so often, Scott would look at her and she could see from his expression that the situation was dire.

Still, Jordan smiled at Lily and spoke of her own experience with pregnancy, nine times, speaking of the joys of it and the aches and pains. It was chatter to distract Lily from what Scott and Tarraby were doing and when they were finished, Jordan kissed Lily's hand and let it go.

"Now," she said. "I'll chase the men out and ye can have a rest for a few minutes while I go tae the kitchens and find ye something tae eat."

"You don't have to," Lily said, laying back on her pillows and looking weary. "Truly, I do not eat much these days. You do not have to feed me."

"Of course I have tae feed ye," Jordan said, sounding as if she were scolding. "No wonder ye're tired and the bairn is sluggish. If ye dunna eat, how are ye supposed take keep up yer strength?"

Lily didn't really have an answer for her and Jordan's mothering manner essentially had her whipped into submission. But she was grateful for it. Leaving Lily lying in bed, Jordan followed Scott and Tarraby out of the chamber and down the stairs.

Will was waiting in the small hall below. Sitting at one of the feasting tables, he had his head down, looking at his hands, but when he heard the footsteps, he looked up to see them coming from the stairwell.

"Well?" he asked his father, standing up. "What did you find?"

Scott indicated the seat Will had been sitting in. "Sit down," he said. "I'll send your grandmother for food for Lily while you and I speak."

"I'm not going anywhere," Jordan said, moving to plant herself next to Will. "I saw what ye were doing and I saw the look on yer face. Ye have something tae say and I want tae hear it."

Scott eyed his mother, resigning himself to the fact that he couldn't get rid of her, so he sat down opposite his son. Tarraby sat down beside him.

For a moment, he simply looked at Will, trying to find the words.

"You were right to call me," he finally said. "Before I examined Lily, I spoke with Tarraby at length so I knew why he'd come to his diagnosis. I wanted to see the same things he did so I could understand his reasoning."

"And did you?"

Scott hesitated a moment before nodding. "I did," he said with some sorrow. "My expertise is not in women, Will. I can only observe and use my knowledge to make a diagnosis but, in this case, it was difficult. The problem is that we cannot see into Lily's belly to see what is really happening. All I can tell you is that I have listened to Tarraby and I have understood the symptoms. I can also tell you that Lily's heartbeat is fast and weak, and the fact that she is cold to the touch is indicative of a weakness of blood."

Will was listening intently. "What does that mean, weakness of blood?"

"It means that she is bleeding somewhere that we cannot see."

"You know that for certain?"

"I have seen it before with wounded men. Tarraby also says that he believes Lily is growing weaker as well. Have you noticed that?"

Will shrugged helplessly. "I do not know," he said. "She has been sleeping a good deal. I suppose I didn't stop to realize that it meant she was growing weaker, but she must be."

"That is what Tarraby thinks."

Will let that sink in. His father seemed to be confirming Tarraby's diagnosis and he felt sick to his stomach. There was a large part of him that was hoping Tarraby was wrong, but with Scott confirming the diagnosis, it was evident that Tarraby had been right all along. After a moment, he hung his head.

"Then Tarraby was right," he said. "She has mortally injured herself."

Scott nodded. "I believe so," he said. "I am so sorry, Will. Something like this... it is so unexpected."

"And there is nothing to be done?"

Scott looked at Tarraby, who shook his head. "Nay," Scott said. "I would not even know where to start. She's bleeding inside her womb and there is no way to save both her and the child."

"But we can save one of them," Will said hoarsely.

"What do you mean?"

He lifted his gaze, looking at his father. "She wants to save the baby, Papa," he said. "Tarraby said that it is possible to take the child from her. It will not save Lily, but it may save the baby. Now that you've seen Lily, do you agree that we could save the child?"

Scott wasn't sure. He'd never seen it done. After a moment, he simply shook his head. "I do not know," he said honestly. "If Tarraby seems to think so, then I will trust him."

Will was feeling such sorrow. Deep, saddening sorrow. There had been hope when his father had arrived, but that hope was gone.

He looked at Tarraby.

"Tell me what is involved in taking the child," he said, trying to be brave and rational. "And why can you not save Lily in the process? I do not understand *why*."

Tarraby could see that all eyes were on him, family members of the young woman with the death sentence hanging over her head. He tried to be as careful as possible when describing what had to happen in order to save the child.

"Right now, Lady de Wolfe is bleeding into her womb," he said, using his hands to illustrate what was happening. "The nourishment sack has created an open wound that is bleeding. When I cut into her belly to remove the child, all of that blood will escape and more besides. She will bleed far too much before I am able to sew her back up again. There will simply be too much blood loss and no way to replace any of it."

Will sighed heavily as he got a mental picture of what Tarraby was describing. "Does it matter where you cut into her?" he asked. "Mayhap if you cut on the top of her belly, the blood will not have a chance to escape."

He was gesturing to the top of his abdomen area, but Tarraby shook his head. "All of the blood in her belly has nowhere to go," he said. "It cannot go back into the body. If we leave it there, it will simply drain out another way when she is no longer pregnant and the womb no longer closed off. I wish there was another answer to this, but there is not. I am very sorry, my lord."

"Can we not drain it out and put it back into her somehow?"

Both Tarraby and Scott shook their heads. "I would not know how," Tarraby said. "It cannot be done."

Will stared at them a moment before lowering his head again. He'd asked the same questions he'd asked before and was getting the same answers. Nothing had changed. That meant there were no alternatives, but that didn't stop him from asking one last time.

"And you are *certain*?" he whispered.

"Aye, my lord."

"Do you feel the child is in danger the longer we wait?"

"Most definitely, my lord. Already, he is slowing."

Will grunted softly, closing his eyes briefly. Then, he looked at his hands for quite some time, contemplating what needed to be done, before speaking again. "We must try to save him sooner rather than later," he said. "But I want to make sure that Lily does not feel any pain when you cut into her belly. Can you make it so?"

Scott could hear the anguish in his voice and it was a struggle not to react. "We have nothing to give her that will take the pain away if that is what you are asking," he said. "We have nothing to make her go to sleep while the deed is done."

Will looked at him. "Then just how do you propose to accomplish this?" he asked, growing agitated. "Do you just cut into her while we hold her down and she screams in pain until she bleeds to death in front of us?"

Scott watched his son wrestle with the horror of what he was facing. "A sharp blow to the head will knock her unconscious," he said. "Do it hard enough and she will remain unconscious until the end. I am sorry I cannot offer anything better than that, but that is the truth of it."

Will grunted at that brutal solution, raking an agitated hand through his hair. "That is better than letting her bite on a leather strap as Tarraby cuts into her," he said, upset. "I do not want her to feel anything."

Jordan, who had been watching the exchange, could see how it had the potential to go badly. Will was growing upset and rightfully so. Reaching out, she put a gentle hand on his wrist.

"Ye'll knock her out yerself," she said quietly. "Dunna trust the job to any other man. In fact, dunna tell her what ye plan. Dunna tell her what day. Let her believe she is in control of her destiny when, in fact, it will be ye. 'Tis the merciful thing tae do, lad."

Will looked at her. "What do you mean, Matha?"

Matha was what all the de Wolfe grandchildren called Jordan. It meant "mother" in Gaelic and Will had been the first one to use the term. Now, he was using that term in a way that made Jordan feel like protecting him. There was anguish in his tone. She wanted to wrap that enormous man up in her arms and protect him, but she knew she couldn't. Therefore, she forced a smile at her eldest grandchild who looked like her husband through the eyes, his father through the cheeks, and his mother in the mouth. He was the best of all of them, now having to go through what no man should have to go through.

But he was strong enough.

She knew that without a doubt.

"Lily believes she has several more days until this is tae happen," she said calmly and quietly. "Can ye imagine knowing that ye only had a handful of days tae live? The closer she comes tae the end, the more upset she'll be. Ye heard yer da and Tarraby tell ye that the child is growing weaker. If ye want tae save him, then ye canna wait much longer. Pick the day, Will. Mayhap in two days, mayhap in three. Dunna tell Lily. Let her enjoy the day. Take her out of the keep and intae the fields. Let her feel the grass and smell the air. Let her watch Atticus run and play. Let her feel alive one last time. Then bring her back and while her attention is elsewhere, hit her across the back of the head with the butt of yer sword. And that will be the end of it. Let her last memory be one of a beautiful day and of her frolicking child. If that was my last day on earth, 'twould make me happy."

Tears were streaming down Will's face by the time she was finished because he knew she was right. He didn't want Lily being in distress when her self-imposed deadline came. That meant he had to make the decision for her, sooner rather than later.

That meant he had to help ease his wife into the next world.

"Oh, God, Matha," he said, putting his face in his hands. "Has it come to this? If this was happening to you, would Poppy have the courage to do it?"

Jordan smiled faintly. "There's more tae marriage than children and politics," she said. "There's real love. There's a love for Lily, as yer wife, as a mortal woman, as someone ye respect and value. If ye love Lily, then ye'll do it. Ye must help end her suffering."

Will almost said something, but he bit his tongue. No, he didn't love Lily the way a husband should love a wife, but he wasn't going to voice that, at least not to all of them. In the end, it really didn't matter. But as a friend, he did love her. As a human being, he respected her. She was the mother of his children.

He didn't want to see her suffer.

"If you think it is the right thing to do," he said hoarsely, wiping at his cheeks. "I think if she knew our reasoning, she would agree with it. She's stronger than you know."

Jordan reached up, wiping an errant tear from his face. "I know she is," she said softly. "And so are ye."

"I don't feel so strong."

"Ye are," Jordan said, patting his cheek. With nothing more to say, at least nothing more she could say, she stood up stiffly. "Now, I'm going tae go tae the kitchens and find her something tae eat. And then I'm going tae sit with her for a while."

With Will's help, she climbed over the bench and headed out of the keep. Will sat there with his father and Tarraby, thinking of what lay ahead. After a moment, he looked over at Tarraby.

"Thank you for your assistance," he said. "Know that I am grateful. But I would like to speak to my father alone now."

Tarraby immediately rose and moved quickly out of the hall. When Will and Scott were alone, Will looked over at his father.

"Thank you for coming, Papa," he said softly. "Thank you for confirming what Tarraby believes. I know it is not easy for you."

Scott forced a smile. "Don't worry about me," he said. "But, Will… I've been through a dead wife before. I did not behave nobly when your mother died. I realize you were fostering at the time and didn't know all of it, but you do know I ran. I ran away from everything and everyone I knew. I could not deal with what had happened, something I blamed myself for."

Will nodded. "I remember," he said. "I was young at the time. I remember thinking that you did not want to be my father anymore."

A look of pain washed over Scott's face. "Never," he said. "You and your siblings are my greatest pride. But I was certain I could have prevented your mother's accident and, in the end, I simply couldn't live with the guilt. It had nothing to do with you or your brother or my family. It had everything to do with me and my inability to handle the grief. Now... now, you are faced with something unimaginable. You must save your wife, but in a much different way. But know this... if you want me to be the one to knock her unconscious, I will gladly do it for you. That way, your hands are clean in all of this. You can look your children in the eyes and know that you had no hand in their mother's death."

Will looked at his father in shock. "You... you would do that for me?"

Scott nodded, his brow creased with distress. "Of course I would."

"But why? This is not your duty, Papa."

"I realize that," Scott said. "But I spent so many years running from your mother's death... and you were caught up in my behavior. I wronged you so terribly, Will. You were grieving the loss of your mother and the loss of your father at the same time, and I have always regretted that horribly. To say I am sorry is not enough. Let me do something for you when it comes to Lily. Let me help take that burden off of you."

Will could see that Lily's condition had stirred up the embers of grief in his father all over again. Since Scott had reconciled himself to Athena's death, which was several years after she had died, they'd not spoken of that event. It was one of those subjects to be avoided because of the dark and terrible memories it provoked. And now, Will could see that the fire of grief was starting to flare again in his father, just a little. Reaching out, he grasped the man's hands and held them tightly.

"Those were difficult years, to be sure," he said, looking his father in the eyes. "But no one ever blamed you. *I* never blamed you. You have nothing to atone for, though I love you dearly for wanting to help me. That means more to me than you will ever know."

Scott was emotional; that much was clear. He smiled weakly. "I want you to know that the offer remains until such time as it is no longer needed," he said. "I am so sorry you must endure losing a wife, as I did. It does not seem fair."

Will sighed heavily. "Nay, it does not," he said. "But... Papa, I want to tell you something I've never told you before. I've not spoken of it, not ever, but I feel as if I should tell you so you know the situation for what it is."

"Speak. I am listening."

Will was still holding his father's hands tightly when he lowered his head, struggling to come forth with the words.

"I cannot tell Matha this," he finally said. "To help Lily... to ease her into the next life... is not because I have a great love for her, as my wife."

Scott looked at him with some concern. "What do you mean?"

Will sighed sharply. "Papa, you know that Chris de Lohr all but tied me up and forced me to marry her," he said, looking at the man beseechingly. "You know that the moment I showed any interest in her, he was hounding me for a betrothal. I told you that. I am not saying that Chris is a terrible man, because he's not. I like him a great deal, but he wanted his daughter married to a de Wolfe no matter how Lily or I felt about it and the next thing I knew, I had a wife. There was no time for me to think about it and there was no time for me to fall in love with the woman. Suddenly, we were married and that was the end of it."

Scott knew that. He knew it all too well. "Marriages are not always love matches," he said. "You are surrounded by love matches, however, so that is what you know. You think that's normal. But it isn't always normal. Your marriage is an excellent one, bringing two major houses together. It is very important."

Will nodded, struggling through the conversation. "I know that," he said. "But Lily and I are friends. That's *all* we are. I love her, but only as a friend and as the mother of my children. There is no great love match here, Papa. Matha says that if I love her, I will do this... this *thing* to ease her suffering when the time comes and I shall do it because it is the right thing to do. Not because she is the love of my life and I do this because of my great passion for her. My biggest guilt in all of this is that Lily is dying because of the child I planted within her and I cannot even say I am madly in love with the woman. It wasn't a child conceived in love and that just makes it so much worse. That makes me a horrible man."

Scott shook his head as he squeezed his son's hands. "It makes you merciful and generous," he said. "It makes you a man among men."

Will refused to accept that opinion. "You must say that because you are my father," he said. "But know that Lily and I have never had a love match. She has spent her entire adult life trapped in a marriage with a man she does not love and who does not love her in return. That is no life at all, Papa. It is my fault."

Scott sighed faintly, watching his son go through the throes of guilt. He remembered those well when Athena died, but for much different reasons. He also remembered his father, among others, telling him that he had no right to feel guilty because the situation wasn't his fault. He never believed them. Therefore, he knew it would do no good to tell Will that none of this was his doing.

All he could do was to try and soften the blow.

"I will not tell you not to feel as you do," he said after a moment. "I will not tell you that you should not feel as if you are responsible for the state of your marriage, but I will say this. You made the best of it. You never disrespected your wife or this marriage, to my knowledge. You remained true to her no matter what you felt personally, and that makes you more noble than most, Will. That is something to be proud of."

Will lifted his head, looking at his hands as they intertwined with his father's. "Do you want to hear something truly noble?" he said weakly. "Lily is determined to ensure I am happy after she is gone. She feels as guilty as I do about the state of our marriage, so she has selected my new wife. I have tried to refuse, but she is insistent. She wants someone who will be good to me and who will love my children. She says she must know I am taken care of when she is gone."

Scott looked at him, brow furrowed. "Who is this woman she has selected?"

"Lady Adria."

That brought some surprise from Scott. "Her lady-in-waiting?"

"The same."

Scott mulled that over. "I seem to remember that she is quite pretty," he said. "I think Matha has said that Lady Adria has been a true and faithful companion to Lily, though you would know more about that than I would."

"She has been faithful and true," Will said. "She is all of those things. She is a good woman. And… truth be told, if I were not married and never had been married, and I had just met Adria, I might very well pursue her."

There was a hint in that statement. "But you feel that there is too much history with her? Being close to Lily as she is?"

Will lifted his shoulders. "I do not know," he said. "She is beautiful and kind, she loves my children, and she is quite faithful and resourceful. She has many good qualities that I have seen over the years."

"Then if it is what Lily wishes, what is the problem?"

Will looked at him. "That I might find happiness with Adria when I could not find it with Lily?" he said, more of a question than a statement. "That I could not love my wife, but that I could love a woman who was by her side through every hardship and every joy? Those concerns come to mind and the guilt is overwhelming. All I know is that I do not want to be forced into another marriage. That did not go well the first time."

Scott's gaze lingered over the man for a moment, trying to figure out where all of this guilt was really coming from. He was coming to the conclusion that it was too much for Will to adequately handle – a dying wife, a dying child, and now being told that he had to marry again immediately after his wife's death. It was more than the man could take.

But he also knew that Will was a strong man.

He was going to have to draw on that strength.

"Then you have a decision to make," he said, quietly but firmly. "Either you respect Lily's wish so that she can die happy and you follow through, or you lie to her and tell her you will and then forget about it when she's gone."

Will drew in a long, contemplative breath. "Is it better to lie to her and tell her what she wants to hear? Or is it better to actually do what she wants?"

"That is up to you," Scott said. "Could you live with yourself if you lied to her?"

Will shook his head slowly. "Nay."

"And could you live with yourself if you denied her dying wish?"

"Nay."

"Then you have your answer," Scott said quietly. "Does Lady Adria know of this request?"

"She does."

"How does she feel about it?"

"She seems to be more hesitant than I am, but at least she is not running away."

Scott scratched his head, thinking. "Then mayhap you should spend some time with the woman so you can both figure it out," he said. "That would be my advice."

Will simply nodded, giving his father's hands a final squeeze before letting them go. "Thank you, Papa," he said. "For your advice, for your skill... thank you."

Scott smiled wearily. "That is what a father is for," he said. "Now, I think I would like settle down in my chamber and mayhap even take a rest. We rode hard to get here."

"Of course," Will said, standing up. "I will have a servant take you to your bed. I suspect Matha may want to sleep in Lily's chamber."

"I am sure she will."

"Lily will be happy to hear that," Will said. "And before I forget, Lady Adria's father is here, also. He is staying in the knights' quarters where you'll be housed."

Scott cocked his head curiously. "Who is her father?"

"Lord Alcester," he said. "He came to visit, although I do not really know why, but it is not my business. I suppose he missed his daughter, but he came at a very bad time."

Scott cocked an eyebrow. "Mayhap not so bad," he said. "Mayhap it is fortuitous if you must ask the man for his daughter's hand in marriage. Do you know him well?"

Will thought of the conversation he and Adria had earlier about Gar and his ignoble manner. A gambler, a man out to find his daughter a rich husband. A man his daughter was clearly embarrassed about. He lifted his shoulders weakly.

"A little," he said. "I just wanted to tell you should you see the man and wonder who he is."

"And so you have. Does he know what is going on with Lily?"

"I've not told him and I doubt Lady Adria has," Will said. "Other than you, Matha, Tarraby, Lily, Adria, and me, no one knows. But I also sent a missive to Chris when I first found out. I knew he would want to know."

Scott nodded. "Of course he will," he said. "I feel for the man, truly. His only daughter."

Will nodded but he didn't say anything more. Truth be told, there wasn't anything more *to* say. With that, they moved out of the hall, each with a purpose now that the heavy conversation was finished. Now, they knew what needed to be done. It wasn't the best outcome, but an outcome nonetheless.

Life, it seemed, was going to get worse before it got better.

Ↄ

"DO YOU ALWAYS spend your time in the kitchen yard?"

Adria had been standing with the cook, discussing the stores they had because Lily was unable to attend to the duties that usually fell to her. She was an excellent chatelaine, but given her physical condition, she hardly got out of bed over the last few days much less came down to manage the kitchens and keep.

Therefore, it was up to Adria.

Not only was she tending to Atticus, but she was doing everything else Lily did and she really didn't mind. Her management skills were excellent, as well. However, when she heard her father's voice, she could feel herself tensing. He always had that effect on her. Taking a deep breath, she turned around to see him standing behind her.

"It seems that way," she said evenly. "Given that Lady de Wolfe is unwell, I have taken over her responsibilities. What are you still doing here?"

The cook, sensing trouble, discreetly slipped away, but Adria didn't notice. She was still waiting for an answer from her father.

He pointed up to the sky.

"The weather has not been cooperative," he said. "Too much rain and I do not travel well. I am waiting for it to dry up a little."

"You are purposely delaying."

"Think what you will," Gar sniffed. "I did not come to fight with you. I came with some good news."

"What good news?"

"You may have two possible suitors."

Adria's eyes narrowed suspiciously. "What are you talking about?" she said. "Who?"

Gar seemed pleased with himself. "There are two very fine young knights right here at Carlisle," he said. "Sir Ronan and Sir Hermes. I have presented them with the possibility of a betrothal with you and now we will see who comes back with the better offer. A little competition is never a bad thing."

Adria's eyes widened dramatically when she realized what he was saying. "You did *what*?" she nearly shouted. When a few of the kitchen servants turned in her direction, she quickly closed the gap between her and her father, lowering her voice. "What did you *do*?"

Gar was cocky. "I did what I told you I would do," he said. "If you will not marry de Brito, then you will marry someone else. I do not care who it is, but someone who will be part of our family and part of our fortune. Sir Ronan's grandfather is the Earl of Warenton and de Norville's mother is a de Wolfe. They are both part of the family and both part of that wealthy empire. If you marry one of them, your future is assured, as is mine."

Adria couldn't believe what she was hearing. She was so angry and embarrassed that she could feel the blood rushing to her face. In fact, fury didn't even cover what she was feeling at the moment. Had she been any less controlled, she would have punched him straight in the mouth.

"How dare you humiliate me like this," she hissed. "I always knew you were vile and low, but this goes beyond what I believed you capable of."

Gar's jaw ticked. "If you did your duty, as my daughter, we would not be in this mess."

Adria shook her head furiously. "Not we," she said. "*You.* You are the one who has spent all of your money. *You* are the one who drove the family into poverty. This has nothing to do with me and everything to do with you. You are in a mess – not me."

Gar did something then that he didn't normally do. Reaching out, he grabbed Adria by the arm. His fingers dug into her tender flesh as his snarling face focused on her.

"Is that what fostering has done to you?" he growled. "Has it taught you to be disrespectful to your father? Because if that is the case, you are going home with me immediately. I do not care if you do not want to marry de Brito – he is welcome to you. Let him deal with your insolence and I shall pretend I never had a daughter."

He was hurting her and Adria tried to yank her arm free. "Let me go."

Gar pulled on her so hard that he snapped her neck back. "Stop fighting. Stop fighting and obey me."

There was something decidedly dark in her father's tone. Adria had never heard that from him before, not like that. He often growled and grumbled, but the way he was speaking to her bordered on wicked. But her pause was only momentary.

"Let me go or I will scream my head off and you will have some explaining to do to the knights you have tried to peddle me to," she hissed. "How are you going to explain damaged goods to them?"

Gar's eyes flashed. "You have a mouth on you, Wench."

"And your character is as dirty as a sewer."

He yanked on her again, trying to pull her with him, but Adria reached out and slapped him across the face as hard as she could. It was enough to cause him to lose his grip and she dashed away from him, out of his reach, and picked up the first weapon she came across. Given that they were near the giant firepit where much of Carlisle's meals were cooked in the open, there was an array of iron rods used to keep the fire neat. She grabbed the first one she came across and held it up, wielding it like a club.

"Touch me and I will beat you to death," she snarled.

Gar came to a halt, eyeing her. Their fight was starting to attract some attention and that's not what he wanted. He took a few steps back.

"Put the rod down," he said calmly. "You're causing a ruckus, Adria."

She didn't lower the rod. "And you're not?" she said. "Did you think that I would just let you drag me around? I am not entirely sure you realize this, but I am a grown woman. I have a position and a purpose, neither of which include you. And since you are so insistent in marrying me off so that you can leech money from my husband, I am going to commit myself to the cloister at Carlisle Abbey. I'd rather be a nun than be your coin purse."

Gar looked at her in surprise. "You wouldn't dare do such a thing," he said. "You are not prepared for life in the cloister, you little fool."

"It is better than life as your daughter."

Gar realized that he had to rethink his plans. Adria wasn't making anything easy and that infuriated him. He glanced around, nervously, seeing that some of the soldiers were watching them from the wall walk above. Worse still, a knight was heading in their direction, urged on by the fearful cook. The tall, auburn-haired knight put himself between Adria and her father.

"I am not entirely sure what is happening here, but let cooler heads prevail, shall we?" he said, looking mostly at Gar. But he turned his attention to Adria. "My lady, surely you do not mean to use that against your father."

Adria didn't take her eyes off of Gar. "Tell him to go away, Marcellus," she said. "He is trying to hurt me. I want him banished from Carlisle, never to return."

Marcellus' gaze lingered on her for a moment. He'd never seen her in this state before. Adria de Geld had always been the kindest and most mannerly of women, so clearly, she felt threatened.

He turned to Gar.

"Please return to your chamber, my lord," he said. "Let this situation calm."

"She is my daughter," Gar said, agitated. "You will not tell me how to deal with her."

"I am telling you to return to your chamber. I will not tell you again."

Gar was quickly becoming humiliated and that didn't sit well with him. He took a couple of steps back, finally looking at Marcellus and smiling thinly.

"And you, my lord?" he said, almost gaily. "Are you married? I am seeking a husband for my daughter, but she does not seem to want to obey me in this matter. I have offered her to the two other knights here at Carlisle, but you look big and strapping. If you feel as if you can tame her, then she is yours. I will give her to you."

Marcellus' expression remained neutral at what could be considered an insult to his own daughter. "Go," he said quietly. "If you need an armed escort, I will be happy to provide one."

Gar sighed sharply, realizing the knight wasn't on his side. No one was. With a lingering glare at Adria, he turned and headed out of the kitchen yard. When he was gone, Marcellus turned to Adria but noticed she was still holding the iron rod. Reaching out, he gently disarmed her and tossed the rod aside.

"Normally, I would not ask what that was about, but it was a fairly public battle," he said. "It will get back to Will, I am sure. What should I tell him?"

Adria sighed heavily, running a trembling hand over her forehead to push away the stray tendrils. In truth, she was more shaken than she realized.

"Tell him that my father is a bastard," she muttered, watching Marcellus' eyebrows lift in surprise that she would use such a foul word. "I called him a bastard and I do not regret it. I am very sorry that he asked you about your marital status. He has debts to pay and wishes to marry me off to anyone who has the means to provide him with any money. He has already approached Hermes and Ronan and I fear that I must find them and apologize."

He put out a hand to stop her before she could get away. "Not now," he said. "They're with some new recruits, so let them finish their task before you speak to them. In fact, you may want to regain your composure before you do."

That was probably true. Adria put her hands to her cheeks, feeling that they were hot with shame and anger. But she was starting to calm down a little, thanks to Marcellus' intervention, but that also made her take a second look at him. The last time she'd heard the man speak, he was in Lily's chamber declaring his undying love for her.

A man she used to think was so terribly noble.

She didn't think that about him now.

"I'm well enough," she said stiffly, averting her gaze. "Thank you for your assistance, my lord. You do not have to worry over me any longer. I am quite well."

"My lord?" he said, grinning. "Since when do you address me so formally?"

Since I heard you speaking to Lily, she thought. But she didn't elaborate because this wasn't the time or the place to do it. There was too much happening with her to try and cast stones at someone else, but that still didn't mean she approved of what Marcellus and Lily had been doing. In fact, it just made her angry at Marcellus, a man who had never been anything but kind to her.

Shaking her head, she moved around him.

"I have duties to attend to," she mumbled. "I must find Atticus."

Marcellus frowned as she walked away from him. "Adria? What is the matter?"

She paused, but she didn't look at him. There wasn't any answer she could give him, at least not one that she was prepared to.

"Thank you again for your assistance," she said. "Can you please make sure my father leaves? I want him gone today. I do not want to see him again."

This time, Marcellus let her go. She was shaken up by the confrontation with her father, so he took that as the reason behind her manner towards him. Her father had embarrassed her by offering him her hand right in front of her, as if he were desperate to push her off onto someone else.

Perhaps that was why she couldn't seem to look at him.

Turning to the small group that had gathered to watch the

battle between father and daughter, he waved his hands and broke up the crowd, heading off to find Will and tell him what had happened.

He suspected that the man might want to know.

CHAPTER TWELVE

A TTICUS WAS SWINGING from a tree branch.

Seated on the grass on the banks of the River Eden, which carved a path on the north side of Carlisle Castle, Adria was sitting within full view of the castle. That was the rule when anyone went outside the castle walls – the guards had to be aware of where one was in case something unexpected happened.

Not that anything had happened in months, surprisingly. The Scots had been quiet for quite some time, but that didn't mean security at Carlisle was relaxed. It was just the same as it always was, men just as vigilant as they always were. They weren't prisoners in the castle, however, because every so often, Adria and Lily would stray to the river's edge to let Atticus play with Bradford and some of the other pages.

There was a little spot, shrouded in trees, where the children liked to play by the riverside. They liked it so much that Will had two big stone benches built so the women had something to sit on. There was even a wooden chair and a bed made of rope that was strung between two trees. Atticus liked that bed the best because he could lay on it and swing himself to sleep beneath the green canopy. Whenever Will accompanied them to the river's edge, he'd fall asleep in that swinging bed, too.

Even now, Atticus and Bradford and two other pages, Rufus and Edward, were playing in the trees and howling like wild men. Will and Marcellus had made a rope swing for the children and they were spinning around in it, having a marvelous time. Adria had the nearly finished blue tunic for the Earl of Warenton in her hands, a project that had been put off due to Lily's declining condition and Adria's increasing duties. But at the moment, she was finishing with the embroidery around the neckline. It was coming along marvelously. Though it was well after the earl's day of birth celebration, Lily still wanted him to have it.

Adria would make sure he did.

After her encounter with her father, and then Marcellus, she found that she was desperate to clear her mind. Just an hour or two of peace was all she wanted, but she'd located Atticus and he'd asked her if they could go to the river's edge. The sergeant at the outer gatehouse had given his permission, so they had. It turned out to be the break she'd needed to sort out what was going on. Lily and Will's issues were bleeding onto her, whether or not she wanted them to.

It wasn't as if she didn't have enough troubles of her own.

Adria hoped Marcellus had chased her father away, but she suspected he wouldn't do anything without Will's knowledge or blessing. Will, however, was not only occupied with Lily, but with his father and grandmother, who had arrived earlier in the day. Adria had seen them when they entered Carlisle. She'd met Scott de Wolfe several times and Lady Warenton, too, and she liked them both. They were nice people.

All the more reason to chase her embarrassing father away from Carlisle.

"I could hear the yelling all the way at the castle."

Startled from her thoughts, Adria looked up from her embroidery to see Will coming through the trees. Atticus saw him, too, and the sight of his father seemed to do something to him – his whooping and hollering grew louder as he and his three cohorts acted like wild men. When Will realized it, he grinned and shook his head.

"I see what the problem is now," he said. "My son is acting like his cousin, Hermes."

That brought a chuckle to Adria as she turned back to her careful embroidery. "Mayhap you should bring Hermes to the river's edge and let him wear Atticus out," she said. "I fear the lad has no limit to his spirit."

Will was forced to agree. "Indeed," he said, noting that the rope bed was unoccupied and making a break for it. "Do you mind if I utilize the rope bed in your presence?"

Adria grinned. "You needn't ask my permission. You've done it before."

"I know," he said, reaching for the rope. "But Lily was always here and I'm never terribly mannerly in front of her. I do not want you to think me rude if I lay in your presence."

"I do not think you rude. I think you weary."

The smile faded from his face. "That is quite true," he said. "Speaking of weary, I heard you had an eventful day in the kitchen yard."

Adria's warm expression left her as she carefully embroidered the golden leaves on the neckline. "Did Marcellus tell you that?"

"He did, but only what he witnessed," he said. "When he told me, I went to your father to make sure he leaves Carlisle today, but he is pleading illness. He insists he cannot leave while he is feeling poorly."

Adria rolled her eyes and stopped her needle. "He is *not* feeling poorly," she said. "He is only saying that so you will not force him to leave. God, I wish the man would just go away and leave me alone. I wish he had never come here in the first place."

"What did he do?"

She looked at him then. She hadn't told him why her father had really come to Carlisle and she supposed she couldn't avoid it now.

Perhaps he should know.

"Do you remember when we spoke of my father and how he wishes for me to marry well?" she asked, watching Will nod. "Then you will also remember that he wants me to marry well so that he can beg coin from my husband. Since I have refused to marry, he has gone to Hermes and Ronan and informed them of my availability as a bride. Evidently, he hopes they will agree and then he intends to create some horrible competition between them, the prize being my hand."

Will appeared surprised. "He did this?"

"He did," Adria said, fighting off the shame of the confession. "When he told me, I was outraged and told him to leave. He grabbed me by the arm to force me to go with him and I proceeded to fend him off with a fire poker. That is what Marcellus saw. And then he further shamed me by telling Marcellus he would *give* me to him. God... I just want the man gone."

Will was still standing next to the rope bed, listening intently to a rather shocking tale. "Why did he want you to go with him?"

She glanced at him, quickly. "I have not told you all of it, so you may as well know," she said. "Not to get too much into my family history, but since my father gambled away the family fortune, he had to find a way to regain it. He has only always viewed me as a tool in this quest, so he concocted a plan to have me foster at Kenilworth. That is where I met Lily."

Will nodded, finally sinking back into the rope bed. "I

know."

"Kenilworth is the finest castle for fostering and training in all of England, but it is only for the finest houses," she said. "My father knew this, so he borrowed money from a very questionable man named Silas de Brito, had fine clothing made for both of us, and then we attended a tournament where Lord and Lady Lancaster were the patrons. My father is very good with his flattery and he managed to present me to Lady Lancaster, who agreed to take me to Kenilworth. The object, of course, was for me to find a rich husband, which I did not."

Will could see her from where he was laying. He folded an enormous arm behind his head. "So that is why he is here, demanding you marry well?"

Adria nodded. "Exactly," she said. "The bargain he struck with de Brito was that my father pay the money back or give me over to de Brito as his bride. It is either a pound of gold or a pound of flesh, but either way, de Brito will gain his money. I gather that de Brito must be threatening him about it, so that has made my father desperate."

"And he is offering you to any bachelor who can pay him."

Adria lowered her head, sadly. "He is," she said. "One of these days, he will offer me to someone who will accept him and demand to marry me, but I have already thought of that. I told him that I would commit myself to the cloister at Carlisle Cathedral immediately. That will end any chance he has of marrying me off for money."

"Haven't you forgotten something?"

She looked at him curiously. "What?"

"Lily's wish."

She eyed him reluctantly. "Nay, I haven't forgotten," she said. "But surely now that you know everything, you cannot agree to it."

"Why not?"

"I told you why – because my father just wants money from you. That is all he'll ever want from you."

"And I told you that I can handle your father."

Adria sat there, looking at him with those big, pale eyes. Will stared back and the more he stared at her, the lovelier she became. He couldn't imagine her slipping through his fingers to someone else, someone who might not treat her well or, worse, abuse her. If her father was looking for a husband with anyone he could find, then her prospects were not vetted.

It could be anyone.

He didn't want to see that happen.

"We have discussed this," Adria said, breaking him from his train of thought. "You are the heir to the de Wolfe empire. I am no one important."

He cocked a dark eyebrow. "And I told you that it did not matter to me," he said. "I'd much rather have someone like you than a politically ambitious woman who only cares for the status of her family. You do not care about that, do you?"

"Nay, but…"

He cut her off. "Then you are perfect," he said. "Lily was right to select you. More than you know."

"Why would you say that?"

His eyes began to take on a distant twinkle. "Because I do," he said as an idea came to mind. "Let us start at the beginning, Lady Adria. Are you willing?"

"The beginning of what?"

"Just… humor me. Let us start at the beginning of everything, as if you and I have only just met."

Adria wasn't sure why, but she was willing to play along. "Very well," she said. "What do you want me to say?"

He was thoughtful a moment, made difficult because Atticus and his hoodlums were running after each other, right under the rope bed. When they ran back towards the river's edge, he continued.

"I want you to pretend you've never seen me before," he said. "Pretend that you are at a feast at Kenilworth. You know the ones – those big, lavish affairs with piles of food everywhere. Remember those?"

The same twinkle came to Adria's eyes at the memory. "Of course I do," she said. "I loved those so."

He watched her features soften at the memory. "Pretend I walk into the hall," he said. "Look at me. Do you think I am handsome?"

Adria looked at him in surprise, her cheeks flushing, which told him what he wanted to know before she even said it. "I do," she said, catching on to what she thought he was driving at. "And you would see me for the first time, too, dressed in a gown of pale blue with ribbons in my hair. What do you think of me?"

"You are the most gorgeous creature I've ever seen."

That caused her cheeks to grow even redder. "I am honored, my lord."

He fought off a grin at her enchanting reaction, a thrill he'd not felt in many years. He'd given up looking at women when he married Lily, so for him, this was something of an awakening. Feelings he thought were long dead in him were evidently only dormant.

Adria was stirring them.

He rather liked that.

"Now," he said. "It is crowded and smoky. Too many people pushing around, laughing and drinking, so I ask you to accompany me outside, to the gardens near the hall. It is quite proper, as there are people all over the grounds, and I am perfectly behaved. Will you come with me?"

Adria smiled shyly. "Must I?"

He laughed. "Aye, you must."

"Then I shall."

"Good," he said, his gaze lingering on her. "Now, we're outside sitting in the garden under a full moon. The smell of roses fills the air and, somewhere, a nightbird sings. I would like to know about the lovely Adria de Geld. What will you tell me?"

Adria shrugged, turning back to her sewing because she needed something to do other than look at Will and blush.

"I would tell you that I come from a minor noble family," she said. "I had a good childhood for the most part, though my mother died when I was young. Still, I was fed and tended to by an old servant, and when I turned eight years of age, my father bought me a white pony that promptly threw me."

Will smiled. "Ponies have a tendency to do that," he said. "What else?"

Adria shrugged. "I was taught to read and write by the local priest, who taught the children of the village every Wednesday and every Friday," she said. "I enjoyed it. My father commissioned a prayer book for me. I still have it."

"A pony and a prayer book," Will said softly. "It sounds as if your father wasn't always demanding and cruel."

Adria shook her head. "Not when I was younger," she said. "But as he grew older – as I grew older – he changed. He ceased to see a daughter and started to see a commodity."

The conversation threatened to take a downturn, but Will wouldn't let it. "You had a pony," he said, steering the subject back to her childhood. "Does that mean you like to ride for pleasure? I do not think I've ever seen you do that."

Adria cocked her head thoughtfully. "The white pony and I jumped many things," she said. "Rock walls, downed trees, anything we could find. It was enjoyable when I was younger, but as I got older, my tastes changed. Lady Lancaster thought all of her ladies should be quite accomplished, so we were taught poetry and painting, sewing and dancing and drawing. The ponies faded away, but I was not troubled because I love to draw."

"Do you?" he said. "I never knew that about you. I do not think I have seen any of your drawings."

Adria looked up from her sewing. "That is because I keep it to myself," she said. "But did you not notice scraps of vellum disappearing from your solar?"

He grinned. "Nay."

She fought off a sly smile. "Lily has been very discreet," she said. "She collects the scraps and pieces that you've torn away or discarded. I make my own charcoal to draw with, long and thin like a quill."

He thought that was quite interesting. "I'm intrigued," he said. "What do you like to draw?"

She shrugged. "People, mostly," she said. "I have drawn you and Lily, and Atticus and even Marcellus. I draw animals, too, but I find people the most interesting subjects."

"Why?"

"Because there is so much more than what you see on the surface," she said, setting her sewing in her lap. "A man can hide so much behind a smile or a cross word. If you look closely, you see pain or beauty or joy. I'm not sure why that has always fascinated me."

"What do you see when you look at me?"

Adria looked at him, thinking of several answers to that question and not one of which she wanted to voice. She was thinking of Marcellus and Lily and their deception, and how Will was a victim of their lies. She was thinking of the heir to a vast empire without a strong marriage or the right woman by his side. Soon, he'd be losing the wife he had and he'd be the most eligible widower in northern England.

Somehow, that didn't sit well with her. There was something about Will de Wolfe that needed protecting because the man had been greatly wronged by his wife, a woman she had loved so much. But somehow, that was changing.

Adria found herself wanting to protect him.

"I see a great knight," she said after a moment. "I see the future Earl of Warenton."

Will shook his head. "Nay, that is what I am," he said. "I want to know what you see *in* me."

"I do not know what you mean."

"Do you see a good man?"

She nodded without hesitation. "A good man, a good father, someone who always tries to do right," she said. "I have known you for almost as long as I have known Lady de Wolfe. She and I spent a few years at Kenilworth before I went with her to Lioncross and there you were. I know you are a man of good character. I have known that from the start."

"Then why will you not marry me? Am I not a better option than Carlisle Cathedral?"

He was. Of course he was. Truth be told, he'd never paid much attention to her, which was completely understandable, but now that he was, she rather liked it. She was starting to feel a pull to him, an attraction she'd never felt before, and she kept trying to avoid the thrill it was giving her. They were being thrown together because of a terrible situation, but the glimmer in his eyes took the edge off of the guilt and confusion she was feeling.

Perhaps she was having a moment of weakness, but she didn't care.

Perhaps she should simply agree with him.

"You are," she said. "There is no question that you are. But I am still afraid that my father will try to fleece you for coin."

"He can try, but he and I are going to come to an agreement. Quickly."

"And what about your father? Mayhap he will not approve."

"I do not need my father's permission to marry."

"You do if you want him to accept me. Surely he has something to say about this."

Will waved her off, turning to look at Atticus, who was yelling as he swung around on the swing. "I have told him already and he has no issue with it," he said. "He suggested we get to know one another, so that is what we are doing."

Adria was surprised to hear that Baron Kilham had no objection to his son marrying a woman of minor noble birth. "He did?" she said, incredulous. "He does not take issue?"

"Nay. You seem to be the only one who does," he said. "My lady, if you find me lacking in some way, I wish you would tell me.'"

Her eyes widened at the mere suggestion. "You?" she repeated. "Lacking? You are the most worthy man I have ever known."

"But I am not good enough to marry?"

"More than good enough."

"Then will you do it? Marry me, I mean."

Adria looked at him, long and hard. The question hung between them, filling the air, the only thing stronger than Atticus' yelling.

"Do you want me to, my lord?" she finally asked, almost pleading with him. "Truly?"

"You will address me by my name when we are in private, please."

She looked shock. "You wish for me to do that?"

"I do."

She tried to overcome that surprise. "Very well," she said. "Do you really want me to, Will? God's Bones, it feels strange to call you by your name. I feel as if I should beg your forgiveness."

He laughed, sitting up in the rope bed and sliding off, landing on his feet. "I like to hear you say my name," he said. "And, aye – I want you to. Have I not made that clear?"

He had. She was just being stubborn. After a moment, she nodded. "You have," she said. "If it is really what you want, then... I will."

He smiled at her, flashing that de Wolfe grin. "Excellent," he said. "Will you sup with me tonight then?"

She wasn't sure what he meant. "I sup with you every night, in the hall."

He shook his head. "Not that," he said. "Just you and me. If we are to marry, then we'd better become more acquainted quickly. I will admit that I am not unhappy about it, though I wish the circumstances were different."

She watched him for a moment, feeling brave enough to speak her thoughts. "If the circumstances were different, we would not even be having this conversation," she said. "The circumstances are what have brought us together, whether or not we are prepared for it."

He scratched his head, nodding. "That is quite astute of you."

"I told you that I did not want to be another unhappy marriage for you and I meant it," she said. "It is my sense that if we are to have any hope of not falling into that pit of despair, then we must be open and honest with one another. Would you agree?"

"I do," he said. "Very much. And since we are being honest, you realize I have the very odd task of trying to establish a relationship with you while Lady de Wolfe is... weakening."

"I know," Adria said softly. "It is very odd for you. For us both. Even as I stand here, all I see is Lily's husband. I am concerned that I may not ever be able to get past that."

"Understood," he said. "But I hope you try."

"I *will* try, I promise, but it does not seem right to even try until Lily is… until she is gone," she said. "God could bring about a miracle, you know. I would hate to fall in love with her husband in vain."

Will's focus lingered on her for several long moments. *I would hate to fall in love in vain.* Those were the only words he heard. The idea of love hadn't even been brought up yet, but here she was, speaking about it, and the mere mention from her lips had his heart pounding.

Love.

Was it possible he had a chance at love again?

"Then would you like to wait until everything is settled?" he asked after a moment. "If you would rather wait until it is over with, I understand."

Adria nodded, though there was distress on her face. "It seems as if that is the right thing to do," she said. "If we are to have any chance of coming together without the guilt of Lily's situation hanging over us, mayhap that is best."

Will sighed faintly, looking towards the river to see that the boys were splashing around in it now, up to their ankles. "This entire situation is so very strange and uncomfortable," he said. "Would it be wrong to say that the thought of coming to know you when this is all over is helping me focus on something positive?"

Adria watched his profile as he observed the boys in the water. That strong jaw, strong nose, and comely features had her softening to the entire prospect. She'd been very reluctant before this moment, but now… now, she wasn't reluctant any longer. He said that he was looking forward to coming to know her when all was said and done… truth was, so was she.

"It is not wrong of you to say so," she said. "I am glad if it helps you. I wish I could do more."

He looked at her, a grateful smile on his lips. "You are doing a great deal," he said. "I am appreciative, truly. But will you still sup with me tonight? Alone?"

Adria nodded. "If you wish."

"I do," he said. "We must be discreet about it, of course, since no one knows what is happening with Lady de Wolfe. I would hate for the gossipmongers to see us and think we are doing something clandestine."

Like Marcellus and Lily. Adria almost said it. She thought it was incredibly ironic that Will was worried about such a thing when that very situation was going on behind his back.

But she held her tongue.

"I will do whatever you wish," she said. "Tell me where to meet you and I shall."

"The small hall, I should think. At the usual supper hour."

"I will be there."

He nodded, looking at her as if he wanted to say more, but there was really nothing more he could say. They'd covered everything well enough and now it was time to get on with it.

"I am going to pull my son out of that water now," he said, turning to the river. "Will you come as my reinforcement?"

Adria giggled softly. "No need for you to pull him out," she said. "Wait here. I will get him out painlessly."

With a smile playing on his lips, Will watched her march over to the river where Atticus and his friends were splashing each other. He didn't hear what she said but, suddenly, the boys were bolting out of the water, running for their shoes. In little time, they'd pulled them over wet feet and were running back towards the castle with Adria trailing after them.

Will looked at her in astonishment.

"What on earth did you say to them?" he asked.

She grinned. "I told them that there were sweets waiting for them back in the castle and the first one to dry off and show up in the smaller hall would get an extra cream cake," she said, tapping her head with a finger. "I know your son. Trust me when I tell you that I know how to make him do as I wish without bloodshed."

Will lifted his eyebrows at her as they started back after the boys. "You are a sorceress, my lady," he said. "I am in awe of your power."

Adria broke down into soft laughter. "No magic, I assure you," she said. "I told you that I find people fascinating. I learn about them, what makes them who they are. I have figured Atticus out."

"Have you figured me out?"

It was a decidedly flirtatious question, the first such thing she'd ever heard out of his mouth. It would be a shame not to respond.

"If I did, I would not tell you."

"Why not?"

"And reveal my secrets? Never!"

They shared the first genuine laughter between them.

And it was marvelous.

CHAPTER THIRTEEN

"I SEND MY son out, dry, and he returns wet?" Lily said, a glimmer of mirth in her eyes. "Have you been trying to drown him again?"

Adria smiled weakly as she entered Lily's enormous chamber, the blue tunic in her hands. "Of course I tried to drown him again," she said. "I've been trying for years, but he is too clever and escapes me. Here – look at the embroidery and tell me if it is acceptable."

She handed Lily the tunic, who took it eagerly. She inspected the gold stitching all around the neckline, looking like laurel leaves, but all the while she was feeling anxious. It had been a day since Adria had run weeping from her chamber and although she'd seen the woman since then, they hadn't spoken of Lily's predicament again or her request. Lily hadn't wanted to stir up Adria's hysteria again, at least not immediately, but time was of the essence. She'd been planning to bring it up to Adria again today at some point, gently done, and now seemed as good a time as any.

Knowing where to start was the difficult part.

"It is beautiful, Adria," she said, appreciation in her tone. "Very beautiful. Well done."

Adria smiled politely as she went to Lily's enormous wardrobe and set her sewing kit down. But as she did so, she pulled out the scraps of dark blue fabric left over from the tunic.

"Do you still want me to make something for Lady Warenton?" she asked. "I think I can do something with these."

Lily put her index finger to her lips. When Adria looked at her curiously, she pointed to the alcove where Jordan slept. The door was cracked open, but it was dark inside.

"Lady Warenton is resting in there," she whispered. "I do not want her to hear."

Adria understood. She brought the fabric over to the bed and lowered her voice. "I can make her something to match him," she murmured. "Mayhap a kirtle?"

"If you have enough fabric."

Adria inspected the fabric and tried to figure out how she would make Lady Warenton a full kirtle using only scraps. She wasn't aware that Lily was watching her closely, wondering why the woman seemed so… hard. Not pleasant at all, which wasn't like her.

She suspected she knew why.

"Did Will speak to you?" she finally asked.

Adria looked up from the material. "About what?"

"Marrying him."

Adria sighed sharply when she realized the subject and looked back to the fabric. "He did."

She didn't elaborate and Lily reached out, grasping her hand. "I am sorry if I shocked you with my wish," she said softly. "I truly am. But it is very important to me that Will and my children are happy when I am gone. Will you not do this for me, Adria? For them?"

Adria couldn't help but feel that was an incredibly ironic statement. She tried not to think about Marcellus and Lily; God, she tried hard. It wasn't her right, her battle, or her business but, somehow, with Lily asking her to marry Will, it *was* her business.

Lily had made it her business.

And now Lily was pretending that she cared deeply for Will. As if his happiness in a marriage mattered to her. Adria found that incredibly offensive and she struggled not to let her feelings show. She didn't want to upset Lily because she didn't want to exacerbate her illness, but her illness had nothing to do with her behavior.

It was that behavior that had Adria shaken.

Adria turned away from her, fabric in hand. "We did speak at length about it," she said, going back to the wardrobe. "What you are asking, Lily... it is a great deal."

Lily tossed back the coverlet over her. "I know it is," she said. "But I have no one else to ask. You know Will and you know my children. Atticus loves you so. It would be so much better for my children to have a mother they know rather than one they do not. Don't you think so?"

Adria put the fabric back in the wardrobe and absently picked up her sewing kit again. "I do," she said. "Of course I care about your children. I have known them since they were born."

Lily sat up, swinging her legs over the side of the bed. "And Will," she said. "You have known him almost as long as I have. He is a good man, Adria. He will make a good husband."

"I know."

"Then you'll do it? You'll marry him?"

Adria came back over to the bed. There was a chair beside it and she sat down, sewing kit in her lap. Her manner was pensive, even distant, which had Lily worried.

"Sir Will and I have discussed your request and we have decided to wait until after the child is born," she said, opening up her sewing kit and pulling out a wooden spool with tangled thread. She started to untangle it. "There *could* be a miracle, Lily. You could come through perfectly well. Tarraby isn't God – he does not know everything."

Lily watched her lowered head. "Will's father agrees with him," she said, watching Adria's head come up. Their eyes met and Lily smiled sadly. "Scott agrees with Tarraby. The diagnosis has not changed."

"Who told you this?"

"Lady Warenton."

That changed things a bit. Will hadn't told her that his father had agreed with diagnosis. Adria remembered hearing that Scott de Wolfe was a great healer in his own right, now with a dying daughter-in-law. If he agreed with Tarraby, then that meant Lily was in a dire situation, indeed, and she knew it.

"I see," Adria finally said. "I did not know that."

Lily nodded. "You see that it is more important than ever for you to promise me to take care of Will and the children," she said. "Must I beg you, Adie?"

Adria didn't say anything for a moment. She returned her focus to the tangled thread, something to occupy herself with, anything but look at Lily and think how much she disapproved of her and what she had done. When she should only be thinking about Lily's health, she was thinking about Lily's morals or lack thereof. Perhaps it wasn't the right time, but she couldn't help it.

It was a struggle to stay on an even keel.

"Nay," she finally said. "You do not have to beg me."

"Then you will do it?"

"I will."

Lily put her feet on the floor, stood up, and put her arms around Adria, hugging her tightly. "Thank you," she said sincerely. "I knew you would do the right thing. I feel so much better knowing that you will make Will and my children happy.

Someday, you will be the Countess of Warenton."

"I do not care about that," Adria said, almost offended that Lily would say such a thing. "I do not yearn for titles. But I do love your children and Will is a good man. He deserves to finally be happy."

The word "finally" had been a slip, an accident, but not one missed by Lily. She sat back down on the edge of the bed as she thought on Adria's statement.

The joy between them cooled.

"Will and I have not been unhappy," she said after a moment. "I will not say anything more about it because there is no need. You know the state of our marriage so I will not elaborate, but given the circumstances, I did the best I could, I think."

That statement set Adria on edge. She'd heard it before. She'd heard Lily explain away the state of her marriage many times before and it had never bothered her until now. Now, she knew *why* the marriage had gone sour, with poor Will being duped and thinking he was equally to blame in the situation. But he wasn't. Now, Lily was going to go to her grave with a secret she had kept from her husband all of these years and Adria simply didn't think it was fair.

Those feelings of being protective over Will were starting to stir. In fact, they were starting to boil over. She couldn't stand the fact that Lily was going to play the innocent until the end.

When she was anything *but* innocent.

"Did you?" she muttered before she could stop herself. "Did you really do the best you could?"

Lily's brow furrowed. "Why would you say that?"

Adria sighed sharply and stopped fussing with the thread. "This morning, I came back up here to retrieve Atticus' cap because the morning was cold," she said, lifting accusing eyes to look at Lily. "I was coming up the stairs when I heard voices. I thought it was Will but I realized it was Marcellus."

She let that hang in the air, watching emotions of shock and fear ripple across Lily's face. "And?" Lily managed to ask.

"And I heard everything."

So there it was. Out in the open. Lily and Marcellus' dark secret, something they'd managed to hide for years was no longer hidden. Someone else knew. Lily swallowed hard, pausing a moment before sliding back on the bed and leaning against the pillows.

She couldn't even look at Adria.

Now, the woman's hardness was making some sense.

"I see," she said, but her voice was shaking. "Did you tell Will?"

That set Adria off. "How can you ask me that?" she hissed. "It is not my secret to tell, Lily. It is *your* secret that you have kept from him since the beginning of your marriage. It is not my place to say anything but, God knows, you and Marcellus have put on an astonishing act of deceit. I would have never guessed the two of you have been carrying on behind Will's back for the entirety of the marriage. How could you do such a thing?"

Lily was pale, looking at Adria with an expression of guilt and defiance that had become every line in her face, every pore. She was the living embodiment of the sorrow and rebelliousness she felt.

Her breathing was beginning to quicken.

"I have often asked myself that," she said, her voice weak. "All I can tell you is that we never meant to be deliberately deceitful. I loved Marcellus before I ever loved Will, but my father forced me to marry Will. Can you not understand that?"

"Nay!" Adria snapped. "I do not understand it. When you marry a man, you vow to be faithful to him. Marriage is about faith and loyalty. I could never understand why you and Will did not have a marriage like others who are fond of one another, and now I know. It was because you loved another man."

"And he loved me," Lily said softly. "I am sorry you do not understand what real love is, Adria. Mayhap you will someday."

It was a rebuke and Adria's head snapped back as if Lily had reached out and struck her. Astonished at the arrogance, she shook her head in wonder.

"That is the defense of every selfish person," she said, her voice hoarse. "No one understands you, so you justify your lies and deceit by trying to push the blame on others. Well, there is no blame to cast except on you and Marcellus. Nay, I will not tell Will, but I will not marry him unless you do. I will not let you take that secret to your grave."

Lily's eyes filled with tears. "To tell him now would only hurt him."

"So you will let him live the rest of his life with your lies?" Adria said. "Believing Atticus is his son? Believing the child you carry is his child? Worse still, he believes Marcellus is his friend. Is that fair to Will to let him believe that? You insult him by keeping him ignorant of your truth."

Lily blinked and tears streamed down her face. "Ignorance will give him peace."

Adria was infuriated with Lily's resistance. "What you and Marcellus did is disgusting," she hissed at her. "You're both selfish fools. You have been lying to Will and even to me, telling me that you want Will to be happy and your children to be loved. If you loved them the way you think you do, then you never would have done this. But since you have, the least you can do is tell Will everything. If the worst happens and you do not survive, then at least you have gone to your grave with a clear conscience. And at least Will will know the truth and he is not a man who has been lied to by his philandering wife."

They were such harsh words, but nothing she said was

untrue. That was the only thing that kept Lily from flaring at her, but more and more, she was being beaten down by Adria's rage. She thought the woman was her ally, but she was evidently wrong and that realization was a distinct blow.

Still, Lily was resistant.

"What if there is a miracle, like you've said?" she said. "Then I have confessed something that he did not need to know. Our lives will be in chaos."

"That will be *your* fault," Adria said. Lily couldn't take any more of Adria's anger and she lowered her head, sobbing softly. Adria watched the woman, struggling to compose herself. "Lily, I am sure Will feels that he is partially to blame for the state of your marriage. How can you let him go through life thinking you are innocent in all of this? How can you do that to him?"

Lily simply shook her head, sobbing into her hand. "I cannot help that Marcellus and I love one another," she said. "What you have never had, you cannot understand."

"I understand that what you are doing is wrong."

"I will not explain myself to you!"

"Then I have nothing more to say to you, either."

With that, she turned away, preparing to leave, but Lily stopped her. "Wait," she said, tears and mucus running down her face. "Do not leave, Adie, please. It's just that... do you know that Marcellus begged my father for my hand but he refused? He wanted to marry me badly, but my father wouldn't hear of it. He only wanted a de Wolfe. It did not matter what I wanted or what Marcellus wanted. Only my father's wishes mattered."

Adria was trying to see her side; she really was. But she simply couldn't. "I am sorry for you, truly, but poor Will is married to a woman who refused to give up her former lover," she said quietly. "And she lies to him about it. She bears the children of this man and lets Will believe they are his children.

Don't you see how wrong that is?"

"You do not understand!"

Adria could see that Lily was becoming increasingly worked up, which probably wasn't good for her. Adria may have been furious, but she wasn't cruel. She didn't want Lily to become ill and that was where they were headed.

Perhaps it was time for her to show a little compassion.

With a heavy sigh, she went in search of a bowl and a kerchief. She found the little bowl on the table with a few other things, like cups and knives, and filled it with cool water from the basin. Bringing it back over to the bed, she dipped the kerchief in it and put her hand under Lily's chin, tilting her head back and wiping her hot, tear-stained face with the cool water.

"Quiet, now," she said in a low tone. "Quiet yourself and rest. I will say no more about this, but you know how I feel."

Lily sniffled, letting Adria wipe her face off. "Please do not hate me, Adria," she said. "I could not bear it if you did."

Adria put the kerchief back in the bowl. "I do not hate you," she said. "But I am disappointed. So very disappointed. Just… rest now. I will tend to Atticus and the evening meal, so you rest."

Lifting up the coverlet, she helped Lily slide down into the bed and covered her up. Lily rolled onto her side, closing her eyes, as Adria gazed at the woman and felt a good deal of bewilderment and disenchantment. She had hoped that Lily might see the need to be truthful, but that didn't seem to be the case.

Time would tell if she changed her mind.

Quietly, Adria quit the chamber, heading out to go about her duties, trying to forget about the conversation, at least for the moment.

She had to clear her head.

When the chamber was still and Lily was dozing, the door to the alcove slowly opened. The panel swung back to reveal a rather stunned old woman.

Jordan had heard everything.

CHAPTER FOURTEEN

"**W**HAT ARE YOU doing in the bailey? I thought you were resting?"

The curious question came from Scott as he spoke to his mother, who had just found him near the stables. The small, elderly woman had ventured out of that sturdy keep where she was supposed to be sleeping, hunting down her eldest son.

And she did not look pleased.

"I must speak with ye," she said seriously. "Now."

Scott thought she sounded rather severe. "Go ahead," he said. "You have my attention."

Jordan waved him off sharply. "Someplace private," she said. "Someplace that is not the keep. I willna have anyone hear what I must tell ye."

He cocked his head. "Now you have my curiosity," he said. "Will the hall do?"

"Nay."

"The chapel?"

"Lead on."

Together, they crossed the outer bailey and back into the inner bailey where the small chapel was built against the wall from the same red stones as the rest of the castle. Scott took his mother inside the cool, dark structure with its dirt floor and precious glass windows by the altar. When they were well inside, he faced her.

"Well?" he said. "What is so important that I had to take you to a secret place?"

She was in no mood for his jest. "I have heard something most disturbing," she said. "There's no way tae be tactful about this, so I'll come out with it. I was resting in the alcove next tae Lily's chamber when her lady came in."

"Adria?"

"Aye," Jordan said. "Adria was quite upset and gave Lily quite a scolding."

Scott frowned. "God's Bones, what about?"

"It seems that Lily has been unfaithful tae Will."

Scott lost his mirth, his eyes widened with confusion and surprise. "*What*?" he said, rather loudly. "What on earth makes you say such a thing?"

Jordan lifted hand, indicating for him to keep his voice down. "Because I heard the conversation between Adria and Lily," she said. "It seems that Lily has been carrying on with Will's very own knight, Marcellus, since before they were married. I heard Lily say that she wanted tae marry the man, but her father wouldna hear of it. He wanted a de Wolfe husband for her and forced her tae marry Will."

By this time, Scott's features were pale with shock. "Oh, my God," he breathed. "I know Chris forced the marriage. That was never a secret."

"But did ye know that the knight Lily loves was also vying for her hand?" Jordan asked, her Scots temper building. "Chris turned the man down, but that dinna stop Lily from carrying on with him for all of these years. Worse still, Atticus and the child she carries are not Will's children – they are Marcellus'."

Scott's mouth popped open in outrage. "Christ," he

boomed. "You cannot be serious!"

Jordan's rage was taking hold. "So serious that it's all I can do not tae take a stick tae Lily," she said. "If I had any less control, I'd beat the lass tae a pulp and be happy for it. She's shamed our Will. She's shamed the de Lohr name. The lass has been whoring with another man!"

It was rare when Jordan used such strong language, but she was genuinely furious. Scott stood there, his eyes wide and his hand over his mouth, trying to absorb what his mother was telling him.

Atticus and the child Lily carries are Marcellus'...

He could hardly believe it. His hand came away from his mouth and went to his head as if to hold his brains in.

"And you're certain of this?" he asked, aghast.

Jordan nodded. "I wouldna tell ye if I wasna," she said. "Lily and Adria dinna know I was listening. In truth, it was difficult not tae listen because they were fighting about it. So much makes sense now – how Lily and Will werena a love match. How they were more friends than lovers, with nary a bit of affection between them. It was because of Lily!"

It certainly looked that way. Scott, who wasn't normally quick to temper, went from astonishment to a slow burn fairly rapidly when he thought of the bigger picture and how Lily had evidently been lying to his son. His beloved eldest boy.

His heir.

Rage began to sprout.

"Keep this to yourself until I find Will," he said, his jaw flexing dangerously. "We will tell him together."

Jordan was twitching angrily. "Lily asked Adria why she hadn't told Will and Adria said that it wasna her secret tae tell," she said. "Mayhap it's not Adria's secret tae tell, but I've no such restraint. 'Tis going tae be painful for Will tae hear it, but the man must know."

Scott nodded, thinking on his eldest son who had seen more than his share of heartache in his lifetime already. "I know," he said. "God, the more I think about it, the angrier I become. Will is blaming himself for Lily's condition. He blames himself for planting his seed in her and creating the child that is slowly killing her. He blames himself for so much."

"And Lily has let him."

Scott looked at his mother pointedly. "Aye, she has," he said. "That little… Christ, I do not use that language easily, but I cannot help myself. That little wench has let him go through so much and, all the while, she was bedding another man and bearing his children, letting Will believe they were his. That goes beyond anything I thought a well-born woman was capable of."

"Not just any woman, but a de Lohr woman," Jordan said. "A woman who cemented the alliance between two great families."

Scott nodded, sickened as his anger began to spread. "And now we find out that she's no better than a common whore."

Jordan was watching him carefully, knowing what he was capable of in a rage. Her anger had fed his own, so she calmed herself, fearful of what would happen if she didn't. "Breathe," she said. "Regain what ye can of yer composure because if Will sees yer anger, he may not be able to control his. Ye must be calm."

Scott took a long, deep breath. "I know," he said. "Do you know where Will's solar is in the keep?"

"I do."

"Go there and wait for me. I will bring Will."

Jordan left without another word, quickly leaving the chapel and leaving Scott standing there, stunned and furious. He could hardly believe any of it, but it must be the truth. His mother wouldn't lie to him. It was a situation he couldn't even wrap his head around yet.

Lily had been lying for all of these years.

It was time for Will to have a dose of that truth.

CB

"GREETINGS MATHA," WILL said, entering his solar with his father on his heels. "I thought you were resting."

Jordan had started the fire in the hearth. She was always cold, so a fire was always in order. Sitting next to the hearth on a small stool, she lifted her eyes to focus on her grandson as he entered the chamber.

"I was," she said simply. "But now I'm here."

Will came over to the fire to make sure it was blazing warmly enough for her. He was a good boy, always wanting to take care of those around him, especially his grandparents.

"Get out of my way," he teased her quietly, taking the poker from her and fussing with the peat. "You know nothing about a fire. Let a man do his job."

Jordan smiled faintly at her pushy grandson. "A man canna do his job without a woman telling him how," she said. "Ye've been listening tae Poppy tae much."

Will grinned. "I have not been listening to him enough," he said with one final poke. He set the poker aside. "Papa says you must speak with me about Lily."

Jordan's smile faded. "I do," she said, glancing at Scott. "Did he tell ye why?"

Will sat down on the floor next to her. "Nay," he said. "Why? Is something wrong?"

Jordan cleared her throat softly. "Ye could say that," she said. "Now, I want ye tae understand the circumstances of what I'm tae tell ye. I overheard something that ye should know."

"What did you overhear?"

"I was in the alcove next tae Lily's chamber and I heard her lady come in – Adria."

Will nodded. "I know Adria," he said. "What about her?"

Jordan sighed faintly, looking at the boy she'd loved since before he was born. In fact, she'd helped deliver him, so she had a special place in her heart for the lusty baby who had grown into a fine, strong man. "I wasna eavesdropping, Will," she said. "I was only in the next chamber. The door was open and I couldna help what I heard."

"*What* did you hear?"

"Lily and Adria were arguing," she said quietly. "Will, this will come as a shock tae ye, but it canna be helped. It seems that Lily has been unfaithful tae ye."

The warm expression on Will's face faded. "What in the hell are you talking about?"

"Lily and Adria were speaking of it," Jordan said, watching him carefully for his reaction. "Adria confronted Lily for being unfaithful tae ye. It seems that Lily has been carrying on with yer knight, Marcellus. It has been going on a long time, Will."

He looked at her, incredulous. "You *heard* this?"

Jordan nodded, her concern for his reaction growing. "I did," she said. "Adria accused Lily of being unfair tae ye, but Lily… she said that she loves Marcellus. The lass wasna remorseful about it."

Will rocked back on his heels as if the information had physically impacted him. He averted his gaze after a moment, obviously contemplating everything he'd been told. Brow furrowed, he returned his focus to his grandmother.

"What else did you hear?" he asked.

Jordan looked at Scott, who nodded curtly. Her sorrowful green eyes turned to her grandson. "I heard them say that Atticus and the child Lily carries are not yer children. They're Marcellus'."

With that load of bricks dropped on him, Will simply stared at her. For the longest time, he could seemingly only look at her before abruptly bolting to his feet. He started to walk, nearly crashed into the wall, but managed to turn himself and end up over by the lancet window that overlooked the inner bailey.

He just stood there, hand over his mouth.

Scott came up behind him.

"Will?" he said softly. "You know that Matha would not lie to you. If she said she heard this, then she did."

Will simply nodded. He was still looking out of the window, his hand still over his mouth, unable to speak. Scott looked at Jordan and they passed concerned glances, but they didn't say anything more.

Will would react when he was good and ready.

But that wasn't for quite some time.

The sounds of the bailey were floating in from the window, filling the stale air of the solar. Servants were calling to each other, going about their business, and life went on. It went on as Will stood there with his hand over his mouth, evidently too stunned to speak. Scott and Jordan stood by, waiting, watching.

Waiting for something to happen.

Watching for a breakdown.

Finally, Will plopped down into the nearest chair and the hand came away from his mouth. When he finally spoke, he was looking at the floor.

"I know," he murmured.

Scott's eyes widened. "You know?" he hissed. "You know about this… this *disgrace*?"

Will nodded unsteadily. "I know about Lily and Marcellus," he said dully. "I've always known. It has been going on since before we were married. I'm not that stupid, Papa. I know."

Scott was beside himself. He grabbed the nearest chair, pulling it up to Will and planting himself in it.

"And you let it go on?" he demanded, unable to comprehend what his son was telling him. "Why did you not put a stop to it?"

Will sat back in the chair, finally looking at his father. His face was lined with stress, with emotion. "Let me be clear," he said. "I knew about Marcellus. I did not know about Atticus or the child she carries. That is new information."

Scott wasn't any less bewildered than he had been moments earlier. "*Why* did you let this go on?"

Will shrugged, lowering his gaze. "It is... complicated."

"No doubt, but I still want to know. What in the hell is going on, Will?"

Will simply shook his head. "Lily never wanted to marry me," he said. "Frankly, I did not want to marry her. You already know this, so I will not go into it again. I knew they were carrying on when I was still at Lioncross and Chris knew, too. After Lily and I were married, Chris tried to do the right thing and send Marcellus away, but Lily tried to kill herself. Being that she is his only daughter, he brought Marcellus back. Meanwhile, he begged me not to say anything or do anything. He swore that she would overcome her feelings for Marcellus, but she never did."

Scott was gobsmacked. He sat back in his chair, his mouth hanging open. "De Lohr *knew*?" he repeated. "Worse still, he let it happen?"

Will nodded. "She was my wife by then," he said. "No one wanted a big scandal. Chris didn't want the de Lohr or de Wolfe names shamed, so he kept it quiet. We both did. As long as Lily and Marcellus were discreet, no one knew. Remarkably, no one ever found out."

Scott was still in disbelief. "So you both let it go on simply so the families of de Lohr and de Wolfe would not be swept up in scandal? That makes no sense."

"Aye, it does," Will said. "Papa, Lily and I do not have a marriage. We have a contract. I was not heartbroken by any of this and if that makes me sound cold and stupid, then so be it. I was more concerned with preserving the de Wolfe reputation than my own honor. Think about it – if I called Marcellus out, everyone would know. If I killed the man in an honor killing, not only would the truth come out, but Lily might actually jamb a dagger in her chest like she did before, only this time, she wouldn't miss. Then I would be known as the de Wolfe whose wife killed herself when her affair was discovered. I did not want that."

Scott was starting to see the light, no matter how much he didn't agree with it. "So you kept silent to preserve everyone's honor," he said. "Especially yours."

"Aye," Will said faintly. "Especially mine."

Scott was still astonished. He turned to look at his mother, to see how she was reacting to all of this, and all he could see on her face was distress. Pure, painful distress. That was enough to shake Scott to the bone.

"Oh, God," he muttered, standing up from the chair. "Is that what has happened here? Is this what you have had to deal with since de Lohr forced you to marry his daughter?"

"Aye," Will said, watching his father pace. "I never told you because there is nothing you could have done. I wanted to spare you that misery."

That only seemed to enrage Scott. "So I am to be kept in the dark while my son becomes a martyr?" he said. "I thought this was such a smart marriage but, as it turns out, the de Lohrs have been torturing you all along."

Will shook his head. "It is not like that, Papa."

"Isn't it?" Scott raged. "Chris forces you to marry his unstable and unfaithful daughter, and you have endured this silently for over ten years? I'd say that makes you a martyr and when I tell Poppy, it will change the relationship between de Wolfe and de Lohr forever."

Will lifted his hand. "Don't," he said. "Don't tell Poppy, I beg you. I did not even want you to know, but that cannot be helped now. There is nothing you or Poppy can do and if you try, it will only bring shame and quite possibly a war down upon us."

Scott didn't care. All he could see was that Chris de Lohr and his daughter had abused his strong, noble son all of these years and he was beyond furious about it.

"To hell with a de Lohr alliance," he snarled. "I don't give a damn what happens. They cannot get away with what they've done to you."

Will sighed heavily. "Papa, Lily is dying," he said frankly. "This is not a situation that will go on much longer, so there is no reason to start an incident over this. Please do not try."

"You're just going to let this go?"

"I am."

"Does Lily know that you know?"

"She does not."

Scott was prepared to blow up again but he found that he couldn't. He was far too upset to continue his unbridled raging. He plopped down in the nearest chair and put his head in his hands.

"You've let her lie to you for over ten years," he said. "Worse still, you've let a knight, a man sworn to you, lie to you as well. A man who showed you such disrespect that he impregnated your wife, twice, and has let you think those children are yours. Do you not feel any anger over this, lad? Because I have an abundance of it."

"Of course I feel anger," Will said quietly. "But not for the reasons you think. I feel anger at Chris because he married his daughter to the wrong man. I feel anger that two people who are clearly in love with one another cannot be together because of me. I feel anger that they cannot know true happiness because of what Chris did to them. His sins against them are far greater than his sins against me. At least he isn't keeping me from the woman I love."

Scott was listening to him intently, shocked by what he was hearing. But in the same breath, he'd never heard anything so utterly unselfish. That was a distinct blow, but not in a bad way. It was more that he had an epiphany.

After a moment, he shook his head in awe.

"I have been thinking you were showing such weakness in all of this," he muttered. "Forgive me, Will. It is not weakness you have been showing, but compassion. Generosity. I feel ashamed that I did not see that before."

"Ye remind me of someone I knew long ago," Jordan said, rising stiffly from her stool. She had been listening to the exchange carefully and now it was her turn to speak. Her eyes glimmered weakly as she approached her grandson. "Do ye know the story of how Poppy and I met, Will?"

Will looked at his grandmother. "Only that you were pledged to another man at first," he said. "Why?"

"Ye dunna know who?"

"Teviot?"

Jordan nodded. "Yer Poppy and I first met when I tended a wound he'd sustained in battle," she said. "'Tis fair tae say that it was love at first sight. There were wars going on across the borders back then, Scots against English, and months later, my own father pledged me tae marry the Earl of Teviot. As it turned out, Poppy served the earl as his captain."

"I think I heard that, once," Will said. "But you married Poppy instead."

Jordan nodded, pulling her old shawl more tightly about her shoulders now that she was away from the fire. "I did, but it wasna an easy path for us," she said. "We loved each other from the first and, much like Lily and Marcellus, we carried on in secret. We knew it was wrong but, sometimes, love willna be stopped. The earl knew all along until, finally, he confronted Poppy with it. Poppy admitted it and fully expected tae be punished, but the earl did something compassionate and generous – he permitted us tae marry in secret so we could be together. In a sense, that's what ye've let Lily and Marcellus do. Yer reasons are a little different, but the fact remains that ye've shown them the same compassion that Teviot showed Poppy and me. 'Tis true that Chris de Lohr was selfish – the man should have never forced Lily tae wed ye. But ye knew she dinna love ye, and even if ye dinna love her, ye showed her and Marcellus great understanding."

"Do you mean that?"

"Of course I do," Jordan said. "Now that I know the extent of their love, I canna condemn the lass for doing something I did myself. But I am upset that she did it tae my bonny Will."

Where there had been rage in the chamber only moments earlier, now there was the blessed relief of understanding, at least as far as Jordan was concerned. Will smiled faintly at her and she smiled in return, reaching out to take his hand. It was a moment of understanding between them. But Scott was still in the throes of confusion.

"Then you approve of what Lily and Marcellus have been doing?" he asked his mother. "What they have been doing to Will?"

Jordan shrugged. "As I said, I did it myself tae a very kind earl," she said. "It is not whether or not I approve. It is whether or not I understand, and I do."

Scott shook his head and stood up. "Well, I don't," he said flatly. "Chris de Lohr knowingly created this mess and the victim in all of this is Will. I'll not forgive him easily for this."

"Dunna say anything tae Lily or Marcellus," Jordan said sternly. "If we're tae be honest, they're victims as much as Will is, so dunna let on that ye know. This is Will's fight, Scott. Let him fight in his own way."

Scott simply shook his head and lifted his hands in defeat now that his mother was suddenly on Lily's side. Maybe she understood why Lily had behaved the way she had, but he still didn't. He understood that his son had been incredibly benevolent with his unfaithful wife, but that was about it. Bewildered and emotional, he quit the solar, heading out into the small hall.

Jordan and Will watched him go.

"I am sorry if I have disappointed him," Will said with sadness. "I would never knowingly do that."

Jordan shook her head. "He'll come tae terms with it, but dunna be surprised if he tells Poppy," she said. "In many ways, this involves the alliance between de Wolfe and de Lohr, so he has every right tae be concerned with it."

"I suppose," Will said. "But you were correct when you said this is my fight. It is not even a fight – it's simply my business."

Jordan looked at him. "May I make a suggestion?"

"Please."

Jordan cupped his bearded chin in one soft palm and forced him to look at her. "Tell Lily that ye know," she said quietly. "Tell her that ye have no ill feelings because of it. Make peace with the woman, Will, for yer own sake. And tell Marcellus that ye know, tae. Ye're raising the man's son. Mayhap ye should assure him that ye'll do yer best for the lad."

Will thought on that. "Atticus is *my* son," he said simply. "I swear to you that he looks like me and acts like the de Norvilles. It is possible that Marcellus is not his father."

"Mayhap," she said. "If ye really want tae know, I know someone who could tell ye."

Will knew that she meant Lily. He simply nodded. "I'll think on it."

"Will ye see her now?"

"Not now. I need some time to myself, Matha. This entire day has been… trying."

Jordan leaned down and kissed him on the cheek. "Ye've grown intae a fine man, William de Wolfe," she said. "I've never been more proud of ye than I am at this moment."

With that, she turned and wandered out of the solar. She found that she needed some time to reflect as well, perhaps take a walk out of the walls near the river where it was so lovely. There was no nearby river at Castle Questing and she didn't often get that chance.

She'd speak to Lily when she was good and ready, for she knew what it was like to love a man with all of her heart and find herself in a clandestine relationship because of it. Aye, she knew very well. Will's reaction to the situation was some of the greatest compassion she had ever seen.

A true de Wolfe heart, indeed.

Just like his Poppy.

CHAPTER FIFTEEN

S HE DIDN'T MUCH like the knights' quarters.

That was where male visitors were housed, including Gar. The entire structure was low-ceilinged and smelled of mold. It had a dark, dank feel to it and the chambers were very small, barely big enough for a bed.

Adria found her father in one of these tiny cells.

The door was partially open because the building had ventilation problems, so the door was open to help air circulate. Therefore, Adria didn't have to knock. She saw her father through the open door as she approached, sitting on the bed and looking at something in his hands.

She stepped into the chamber.

"I was told you were still here," she said.

Gar's head snapped up, his features registering surprise. "Aye, I'm still here," he said. "I... I could not leave until you and I made peace. I did not want to leave with our last words being harsh ones."

Adria wasn't convinced. "You told Lord Irthington that you were feeling ill."

"I was. Ill that we had such harsh words between us."

Adria had come to his chamber with a purpose and it

wasn't to make peace. She wanted him gone, now more than ever, and she was going to make sure he understood that.

No more excuses.

"As long as we do not have another discussion like the one in kitchen yard, there will be peace," she said. "I've come to tell you that you are to leave on the morrow."

Gar didn't react to that directive right away. He simply looked at her, shrugged, and looked at what he'd been holding in his hands. He held it up, a small, brown, leather-bound book.

"Do you remember this?" he asked. "It is your prayer book, from when you were a child. I always travel with it."

Adria did indeed recognize it. "I wondered what happened to it," she said. "I have not seen it in years."

"I had it," Gar said. "It reminds me of… better days."

Adria could understand that. "I am glad it gives you some comfort," she said. "But you are still to leave on the morrow. If you do not go of your own free will, you will be forcibly escorted out."

The pleasant expression faded from his features. "But I am not well."

"You are well enough."

"You would cast your own father aside when he is ill?"

She was losing her patience. "You are not ill," she said. "You simply want to remain here and become a burden to Irthington's good graces, which I will not allow. I do not want you here, Gar. I have told you that."

She couldn't even bring herself to address him as her father any longer. The man was a nuisance and a burden, and she was tired of it. He had become Gar to her. There was too much going on at Carlisle to accommodate his particular brand of foolery and she wanted him gone and out of her life, but that was more than likely too much to ask.

"I am your father and I have every right to be here," he said.

"Our business is not concluded, Adria, not in the least. There is still the matter of a marriage…"

She cut him off. "There will be no marriage to those you spoke to," she said. "I do not want to hear another word about it. You will leave at sunrise or I will have you bodily thrown from Carlisle."

With that, she turned on her heel, heading out of the knights' quarters.

Tossing the prayer book aside, Gar went in pursuit.

Adria didn't know her father was behind her until the man grasped her by the arm. Startled that someone was touching her, Adria yanked her arm free and spun around, fists balled, only to see Gar standing behind her.

Her eyes narrowed.

"You will not touch me," she hissed. "I told you that once. Do it again and I will find the nearest weapon and use it on you."

Gar wouldn't be intimidated. In fact, he'd had quite enough of his daughter's attitude. "There is no knight to save you now," he said, his eyes narrowing. "I am your father. In this world, a man's word is law and I will no longer tolerate your refusals. I do not care who accepts my offer first, but whoever it is, you shall marry. If you refuse to do it, I shall take my case to the church and they will force you."

Adria stood her ground. "I told you I would join the cloister before I allow you to marry me off like a prized mare."

"Do you really think they'll accept your pledge when I tell them of your disobedient and stubborn nature?"

She cocked an eyebrow. "Then I'll run away to someplace where you cannot find me," she said. "This is a battle you cannot win, so I suggest you not try. Leave me alone, Gar. That is all I ask."

Gar took a menacing step in her direction. "I'll teach you

who is in command of your destiny, you silly cow. I'll…"

"My lady?"

They both stopped in their brewing battle, turning to see Scott standing a few feet away. He was looking at them with a mixture of curiosity and concern, a very big knight who happened to be armed. Wearing a broadsword in a sheath at his side was as natural as breathing, but to Gar, it signaled danger. Yet another Carlisle knight to protect Adria. As he stepped back from his daughter, Adria forced a smile.

"My lord," she said. "This… this is my father, Lord Alcester. Father, this is Baron Kilham, Lord Irthington's father."

Gar blinked in surprise. "De Wolfe?" he said. "You are a de Wolfe brother?"

Scott nodded. "I am," he said, looking Gar up and down. "I had heard you were here."

"Indeed?" Gar seemed excited about that. "I came to see my daughter, of course, but we have family business to attend to."

"Of course you do. I'll not keep you."

He started to turn away, but Gar stopped him. "Sir Ronan's father is your brother, correct?"

Scott looked at him. "My younger brother, aye," he said. "You know Ronan?"

Gar shrugged. "We have met," he said. "We have business together that I should like to discuss with you."

"Papa," Adria said quickly, putting herself between Gar and Scott. "Baron Kilham is much too busy to discuss business that does not concern him."

Gar knew she was trying to prevent him from bringing up a betrothal, but he wasn't going to let her. "Surely Baron Kilham has an interest in his own nephew's future," he said. "Especially when the man could inherit a title by marrying you. Surely he will put in a good word to his brother."

Adria was so embarrassed that she prayed the ground

would open up and swallow her. But that wasn't possible, so she did the only thing she could do. She looked straight at Scott, knowing she had to tell the man the truth. She knew that he was aware of Lily's request of her and Will because Will had told her. She didn't know Scott personally, but if he was anything like his son, she knew that he must be a noble and understanding man.

She prayed her assumption was correct.

"My father feels that I am too old to be unmarried, my lord," she said plainly, even if it was a bit of a lie. "Because of that, he has been made attempts with Ronan and Hermes to offer a marriage contract even though I have told him to cease. I have also instructed him to leave, several times, and he has refused. It should be noted that he does not know of current events at Carlisle. He knows *nothing*."

The words hung in the air between them and, after a few moments, Scott's eyebrows lifted in understanding.

"I see," he said, focused on her in a way that suggested he did indeed comprehend what she was trying to tell him. His attention shifted to Gar. "My lord, Ronan is too young to marry, so I will not speak to my brother on such an issue. As for Hermes, his father has his own plans for him. If you wish to broach the subject with Hector de Norville, then I suggest you go to Northwood Castle. It is unwise to discuss the issue directly with Hermes."

Rebuked, Gar didn't seem particularly dissuaded, but he did seem annoyed. Mostly at his daughter for opposing him in front of someone as important as Scott de Wolfe.

"Then I seem to have troubled you, my lord," he said. It sounded like an apology, but it wasn't even close. "Forgive me then. Thank you for your time."

With that, he turned away with the intention of returning to the knights' quarters, but Scott stopped him.

"You have been asked to leave," he said. "It would be the polite thing to do, since you are here on my son's good graces."

Gar's pleasant expression was completely gone. "Can a man not visit with his daughter?"

"She says that she has asked you to leave. I would say that your visit is over."

Gar didn't say a word; he just continued walking. Both Scott and Adria watched him as he headed back to the knights' quarters, disappearing into the small, stone building. When he was out of sight, Scott turned to Adria.

"We've not met formally, my lady," he said.

Adria sighed heavily, smiling as if hoping he'd see the humor in the situation. "And this was not the way I had planned it, my lord," she said. "I sincerely apologize for my father. I am his only child and he can be quite... stubborn. He has plans that I do not agree with."

Scott put up a hand to ease her. "Not to worry, truly," he said. But his gaze remained fixed on her for a moment. "Will told me about Lily's request. Clearly, your father does not know."

Adria shook her head. "He does not," she said. "If I do marry your son, then I suppose he will know at some point, but not now."

"Why not? It is clear that he is trying to broker a betrothal right now. Would it not be better for him to know?"

Adria averted her gaze, sadly. "I do not know, my lord," she said honestly. "You may as well know that my father, although titled, is not a noble man at heart. He squandered the family fortune and looks at any marriage as a chance to regain coinage to feed his bad habits, mostly gambling. That is why he is trying so hard to find a husband for me – he wants a man he can bleed money from."

Scott nodded faintly. "I see," he said. "Does Will know

this?"

"He told me that he can handle my father."

"He can."

Adria swallowed hard, lifting her eyes to meet his. "If your son has told you anything about our discussions about Lily's wish, then you must know that I have been reluctant," she said. "Much of the reluctance is because of my father. It is not fair to Will to have to deal with a shameful father-in-law, but Will does not seem to care."

A gleam came to Scott's eyes. "Rather than hide the truth, you have come forth with it," he said. "Rather than accept Lily's request with any hint of deceit on your part, you are completely truthful about the challenges Will may face even though it may cost you an excellent position. You are to be commended."

She smiled timidly. "He has suffered through one unhappy marriage," she said. "I would not want to be the cause of another. He must know that I come with an ambitious, greedy father."

"He does now."

"And I am sorry for it, truly," she said. "That is why I have asked my father to leave. I want him to be home when he receives word that Will and I have married, *if* we marry. I do not want him here where he can start his campaign of begging money from my new husband."

Scott cocked his head thoughtfully. "Why do you say 'if' you marry?"

Adria shrugged. "Lily has not yet given birth," she said. "A miracle could still happen."

Scott forced a smile, not wanting to delve into why that was more than likely not going to happen. "I appreciate your optimism," he said. "And I look forward to more conversations with you, Lady Adria."

Her smile turned genuine. "As do I, my lord," she said.

"Now, I must see to Atticus and Lily, in that order. When your grandson is out of my sight for too long, I worry that he is off burning down a village somewhere."

Scott laughed softly. "A reasonable and completely understandable fear where he is concerned," he said. "If you need help taming him, please send for me. Good day to you, my lady."

"And to you, my lord."

With that, Scott and Adria went their separate ways, but with a better understanding between them. At least, Adria felt better about it. If she could only get her father out of Carlisle, then perhaps she'd feel better all the way around.

You are to be commended.

Perhaps she was, but she was still nervous that her father wasn't finished with her yet.

CHAPTER SIXTEEN

A TTICUS WASN'T BURNING down a village somewhere.
In fact, he was near the stable yard, building a small city with Bradford and a couple of other pages, with Ronan helping him. It was quite an elaborate city, with buildings made from sticks and stones, and time would tell if he actually burned this one down in a fit of youthful destruction. Meanwhile, he seemed to be having a marvelous time with his friends as they built a cathedral with pieces of wood that Ronan had confiscated for them. As long as Atticus and his mob were playing peacefully, Adria was satisfied.

At least, for the moment.

But seeing Ronan brought about a reminder of her father's embarrassing proposal, so she pulled the knight aside and apologize for her aggressive father and begged him not take offense or take his actions seriously. Ronan didn't seem too troubled by it, but he warned her that Hermes had also been on the receiving end of the same offer and could very well pursue it. That made Adria determined to find the knight and head him off after she had seen to Lily. She didn't want Hermes pursuing something that would only end in her declaration of friends – again.

After her argument with Lily, Adria was feeling some guilt about how she'd handled it. She had been harsh with the woman but, in her opinion, Lily had deserved it. She was still angry, still upset about the deception, but that didn't mean she didn't care about Lily. Of course she did and she always would. Therefore, she wanted to check in on her to see how she was faring. Perhaps she was still asleep. If she was, well and good. But if she wasn't… well, Adria wasn't sure an apology was in order, for she didn't regret anything she'd said, but perhaps she should apologize for being so forceful about it.

She didn't want any hard feelings.

Making her way over to the keep, Adria caught sight of Marcellus on the inner wall. She gave the man a lingering glance, seeing both him and Atticus through new eyes after the revelations of the day. She still didn't think Atticus looked like him, but he did have hair that resembled Marcellus' color. Then again, Will had a hint of red to his hair color, as well.

It was difficult to know what to think.

Heading through the inner gatehouse, she went straight to the keep. It was dim and cool inside, like it always was, and quite empty. The servants had done their cleaning and sweeping for the day, as Lily insisted that they at least keep the floor swept even if the smaller hall wasn't used, so the keep was empty – and clean – as she made her way up the stairs.

The keep was also deathly still and quiet, which was excellent for Lily. The woman didn't need any further excitement than she'd already had. Adria wasn't sure where Lady Warenton was, but she knew the woman was around somewhere. In any case, everything was peaceful and silent as she came to the top of the stairs and carefully pushed the door open.

From her line of sight, which was only one eye at this point, she could see the end of the bed but nothing more. Pushing the door open further saw a bloody, empty bed with Lily on the floor next to it, propped up by her arms as a red stain spread out over the linen shift she was wearing.

There were blood smears on the floor.

Adria bolted into the chamber.

"My God," she gasped as she ran to Lily. "What happened?"

Lily was struggling to stay conscious. "I… I do not know," she said weakly. "I was sleeping and I felt a strong pain in my belly. Then there was a rush of… something. It… it was blood. I tried to summon help but I could not… I cannot…"

Adria didn't listen to anything else. She ran back to the doorway and screamed down the stairwell at the top of her lungs.

"Bring help! *Help!*"

Rushing from the doorway, she ran over to the big windows that faced out over the inner bailey where she knew there were several people. She screamed as loud as she could.

"Bring help!" she cried. "Send for de Wolfe! *Hurry!*"

It was all she could do. She wasn't about to leave Lily alone, so she raced back to the distressed woman and reached down, laboring to pull her off the floor.

"Come along, my lady," she said, struggling to stay calm. "We'll go back to bed. You must lie down."

Lily was clumsy and weak. She clung to Adria, who had to heave her up, not an easy task since Adria was smaller than Lily was. But she was lifting the woman with as much strength as she could.

"I'm sorry, Adie," Lily said faintly. "I am so sorry for this."

Adria had her to her feet, trying to help her over to the bed. "Not to worry, my lady," she said steadily. "Lean on me. Back to the bed we go."

Lily was trying to, but her knees gave out. Adria grunted as she heaved her up enough to get her over to the bed, but not onto the mattress. She wasn't strong enough to lift her all the way. As she was trying desperately to get her into the bed, Marcellus suddenly appeared in the doorway.

"Christ," he hissed, rushing into the room. "What happened?"

Adria didn't care that Marcellus had been the first one to come; she simply needed help. "I do not know," she said. "I came in to find her like this. Help me get her onto the bed."

Marcellus reached down and scooped Lily into his arms, gently depositing her in the bed. Unfortunately, there was a slick puddle of blood beneath his feet and he slipped in it, nearly falling, as he set her down.

"Oh, my God," he breathed, horrified when he saw all of the blood coming from Lily. He patted her on the cheek, trying to force her to come around. "Lily? Do you hear me?"

Adria could see that he was starting to panic and she grabbed him, yanking him away from Lily.

"Find Tarraby," she said evenly but urgently. "Marcellus, listen to me. Find Tarraby. Find Will. *Go!*"

Marcellus had Lily's blood on his hands, literally. He looked at Adria, looked at Lily, and then looked at his red-stained hands. Hysteria was near the surface, but he fought it. In a flash, he was gone, tearing down the stairs as Adria tried to figure out what to do until help arrived. Lily was bleeding to death before her very eyes and, suddenly, Lily let out a groan and lifted her knees.

"The baby," she gasped. "I know he is coming. Adria, the baby! Help me!"

Adria had been present for the births of Lily's other children, but she'd been assisting the midwife. She'd never delivered a child on her own. Lily let out a cry of pain, her hands to her stomach, and Adria knew she couldn't just stand there like a dumb fool. She was terrified, but that was no excuse for inactivity. Besides... there was no one else.

She swung into action.

Rushing to the wardrobe, she grabbed anything she could find by way of towels or linens, hauling an armload over to the bed where Lily was bleeding all over the coverlet. Lily cried out again as a pain hit her and Adria tossed up the skirt of the woman's shift, pulling her legs apart and being confronted with a mess.

A bloody, gory mess.

The child was being born right that very moment, the head already having come through. But there was blood spilling from Lily's womb, along with the child, and Adria thought she might become ill. She'd never seen anything like it in her life. Lily cried out again.

"Adie!" she gasped. "The babe is coming!"

After a moment of dazed shock, Adria began to move quickly. "The babe is here," she said as calmly as she could, grabbing a piece of drying linen to wipe the baby's face and mouth so the child wouldn't suffocate on the blood. It was such a tiny baby that one more strong pain and it slipped right out into Adria's waiting hands.

Shocked, she found herself looking at a child no larger than a cat.

"'Tis a boy, Lily," she said, frightened and joyful at the same time. "Do you hear me? It's a boy!"

Lily was deathly pale, but she managed to smile. The blood was still rushing and the child began to mewl. Adria focused on the baby, who was in a bad way. He was so very small. She cleaned his mouth and nose and face as best she could, cleaning away his mother's blood.

"Breathe, little man," she told him, patting his back enough to jar him a little. "That's a good lad. *Breathe!*"

The baby let out a weak cry and Adria began to gasp in delight. But no sooner had the baby drawn his first breath than the chamber door flew back on its hinges and she looked up to see Scott, Will, and Tarraby in the doorway.

Her eyes filled with tears.

"Oh, God," she begged. "Help me, please."

The men flew into action. Tarraby and Scott went to help her with the baby while Will, horrified and stunned, went to the head of the bed. He had no idea what he could do, so he simply stood there and watched events unfold. Lily was unconscious by now as Tarraby cut the cord on the infant so Adria could take him away. She did, her last sight of Lily on the bed was of Tarraby and Scott trying to stop the bleeding and deliver the nourishment sack that was quickly killing her.

Adria took the baby into the alcove where she slept and began to weep.

Deep, painful, frightened tears.

She could hear them in the main chamber, trying to save Lily's life. Adria wept as she bathed the baby in the only water she had, cold water from a nearby basin. But for the moment, it was all she had and she wanted to remove the blood from the child. By now, the baby was crying as lustily as it could. She wept for the baby, who might or might not survive. She simply didn't know. All she knew was that he was fighting for his life just as his mother was fighting for hers.

It was devastating.

Gently, she cleaned away the blood and swabbed his face until it was rosy, mostly because he was screaming so much. At least his lungs sounded strong. She knew how to swaddle a child because she'd done it with Lily's other children, so she swaddled the baby tightly, holding him close for warmth as she went to stoke the fire in the small hearth of the chamber. A little blaze was beginning to spark when she heard a voice behind her.

"Let me have him."

She turned to see Will standing there, looking positively

ashen. Adria couldn't help the tears as she stood up, handing the little baby over to his father. Or at least the man who believed he was his father. Will looked the child in the face for a moment before he sat down on the edge of the bed, all the while unable to take his gaze from the baby.

Adria watched him for a moment before she turned back to the fire, putting more fuel on it and stoking the blaze. When she was finished, she stood up and simply watched him, still hearing Scott and Tarraby in the other chamber, now joined by servants who were helping them out. She could hear all of that commotion but she was terrified to ask about Lily. Somehow, she already knew the answer.

Her friend was gone.

Lowering her head, she wept.

"You were brave, Adria," Will murmured. "So very brave. My son would not be alive right now were it not for you."

That only made Adria weep harder. She wept aloud, turning her face to the wall, so shocked and sickened and terrified that she couldn't conceal it. When next she realized, she felt a warm hand on her back, comforting her.

"Turn around," Will said gently. "Turn around and look at me."

Adria turned around, but she wouldn't look at him. Will put the baby in her arms.

"Here," he murmured. "Hold him. Hold him and love him. I do not know if he will survive and I want him to know warmth and comfort and love. Will you do this for me?"

Adria thought her heart might truly break at that sad request. She took the infant without question, who had quieted down by now.

She held him tightly.

"He's so beautiful," she whispered, tears dripping off her nose onto her lips as she looked down at the little face. "He's perfect."

Will had agony in his eyes as he gazed upon his son. "He is quite perfect," he said. "Perfect and loved."

Adria rocked the child gently. "We must feed him," she said. "Even if he is not long for this world, we cannot let him starve. He is hungry."

Will nodded weakly. "I have already sent a servant to summon the midwife from town," he said. "The woman will bring a wet nurse."

The baby was still mewling, which gave Adria an idea. If the child was hungry now, there was no telling when the wet nurse would come and she couldn't stand the thought of a hungry baby. Without a word to Will, she went into the main chamber where Scott and Tarraby were doing something to Lily. Adria didn't even look to see what it was because it really didn't matter. While they were working at her bottom end, she went to Lily's head.

The woman was as pale as the linens she lay upon. Adria didn't know if she was alive or dead and she didn't ask. The top of Lily's shift was bound by ties and she loosened the ties enough to expose a breast. Will, who had followed her into the larger chamber, saw what she was trying to do and helped her, peeling back the top of the shift to expose both of Lily's breasts. Carefully, Adria lay the baby against Lily's breast, putting the little mouth on the nipple.

"Come along, little man," she whispered to him. "You must feed. You can do it."

Instinct took over in the infant, who immediately latched on to the breast and began to suckle. Breathing a sigh of relief, Adria held the infant to Lily's chest as the baby suckled furiously. She wasn't even sure if he was getting any nourishment, but she thought so. A little was better than nothing at all. Then, and only then, did she dare to look at Lily's face.

Her skin was gray, her lips blue, and Adria knew that her friend of many years was gone. The tears, which had somewhat abated, returned.

"Oh, Lily," she breathed. "He is beautiful. I know you would be so happy and proud."

Tears popped from her eyes, sprinkling the skin of Lily's chest, as Adria returned her focus to the infant, who was feeding eagerly. She knew that Will was somewhere behind her, but it occurred to her that Tarraby and Scott had stopped working on Lily. Her legs were down now, and closed, and they'd pulled the skirt of her shift down. Someone tucked a blanket around her hips and legs, covering the bloody stains as much as they were able. Behind her, the servants were quickly wiping up the blood from the floor.

For a room that had been so chaotic only moments earlier, now it was eerily silent.

It had become a tomb.

For the longest time, they simply stood and watched as Adria fed the infant his dead mother's milk. Adria switched breasts, letting the infant feed until he was sated, before collecting him back into her arms and pulling up the top of Lily's shift to cover her up. Adria could see a second pair of hands helping her, old but delicate hands, and she looked up to see Jordan.

The elderly woman was stoic in all things. She fastened up Lily's bodice and pulled the coverlet up to her neck, smoothing back Lily's hair and generally tending kindly to her. Then, she held her hands out for the infant.

"I'll take the wee bairn now," she said softly. "Ye did well, lass."

Adria handed over the infant. Jordan put the baby on her shoulder, burping the child as she headed back into the alcove, which was warm now with the fire burning. When she disappeared into the chamber and shut the door quietly, Adria simply sat down in the chair next to Lily's bed.

She was dazed to the core.

What she didn't realize was that every man in the chamber was looking at her. There she sat, covered in Lily's blood, pale from tears and distress, but she had done something incredibly brave in a terribly stressful moment.

She'd earned their respect.

"Papa," Will said faintly. "Will you please take Adria from here? She's had a terrible shock."

Scott nodded, going to Adria, who quickly resisted.

"Nay," she said, looking between Scott and Will. "I do not wish to go. Please do not make me. I have been at Lily's side nearly every day for over ten years and I am not going to leave her now. I am her lady-in-waiting. It is my right to stay."

Scott looked at Will, but his focus was riveted to Adria. "Your loyalty is touching," Will said softly. "I know Lily loved you, but it is my wish for you to find Atticus and remain with him. Do not let him come up here because you know he'll want to. I do not want him to see his mother before I've had a chance to tell him."

Adria understood, but she still didn't want to leave. In that moment of indecision, Scott spoke up.

"I'll find Atticus," he said. "I'll help him burn down villages and swing on his rope by the river. Do not worry about him, Will. I will take care of him for now."

Will was still looking at Adria as his father motioned to Tarraby, who followed him from the chamber. The servants had finished cleaning up the floor and they, too, quit the chamber, leaving Will and Adria alone with Lily's corpse. Adria turned her focus to her friend, reaching out to touch the woman's cheek.

She burst into quiet tears.

"She is still warm," she sobbed. "Is she truly dead? She cannot be. She is still warm."

Will went to her. He wanted to comfort her, perhaps with a touch or an embrace. But somehow, he didn't think that would be appropriate in the room with his dead wife. Perhaps Lily had never shown any respect for him during their marriage when it came to Marcellus, but that didn't mean he was going to start showing attention to Adria. At least, not at the moment.

It just didn't seem right.

"There was nothing they could do," he said quietly. "It was as we feared. She had been bleeding inside and when the child came, all of that blood drained out of her and more besides. Can you tell me what happened? Were you here when it started?"

Adria wiped at the tears on her cheeks, smearing them with the dried blood she had on her hands. "I came in to see if she was still sleeping and found her on the floor," she said. "Lily said she felt pains in her belly and then she started bleeding. By the time I got her on the bed, the child's head was already out. One more strong pain and he was in my hands. That is when you came in."

Will started to say something but a noise caught his attention. Adria heard it, too. It sounded like singing or a distant chorus, but when he followed the sounds to the door and opened it, they realized the sounds were coming from Marcellus as he wept softly on the top stair of the landing. The man was simply sitting there, weeping into his hand.

Will stood there for a moment, looking at him.

It was a pathetic sight to see, the impact of Lily's death upon one who had kept his feelings for her deeply concealed. Perhaps Will had only loved Lily as a friend, and Adria loved her as a sister, but Marcellus had loved her as the wife he'd never had. Those feelings were never more evident than they were at this moment.

Even Will could see that.

"Marcellus," he said quietly. "Get up and come inside."

Adria heard him. Eyes wide, she stood up from the chair, moving away from the bed as Marcellus came in. The man was absolutely shattered. As Adria watched, Will took him by the arm and directed him over to the bed, to the chair that Adria had been sitting in. Marcellus sat heavily, looking at Lily with tears streaming down his face. Adria was standing by the wall as Will went back to the door, motioning for her to follow him.

She did.

The two of them headed down the stairs, to the smaller great hall below. Will went to the nearest table, sitting wearily, as Adria stood at the bottom of the steps, looking up into the stairwell as if wondering why Will had left Marcellus with Lily. Did he even know how foolish that was? Of the lies those two had perpetrated upon him?

Her confusion had the better of her.

"Adria," Will said softly. "Come here."

Adria did, moving over to the table. He silently indicated for her to sit and she did. Head hung, she caught sight of her dress, a light woolen garment that had been dyed a medium shade of green, only now it had bloodstains all over it. She sat there looking at Lily's blood on her when Will spoke quietly.

"Do you know why I permitted Marcellus to sit with Lily?" he asked.

Adria's head came up, her gaze fixing on him. "I... I was just thinking on that," she said. "He has known her for many years."

"He has loved her for many years."

Adria's shock registered. She had no idea what to say to that and Will didn't torture her. He held up a hand to ease her surprise.

"I know that you know about them," he said. "My grand-mother heard you and Lily arguing about it."

Adria couldn't deny it, but she had no idea how Will was going to react to the fact that she knew. "Aye," she said honestly. "Just a little while ago, we were arguing about it. I knew your grandmother was sleeping in the alcove where I usually sleep but I did not know that she heard us."

"How did you find out about them?"

Adria couldn't tell if he was angry or not. "I heard Lily and Marcellus speaking," she said. "I did not mean to eavesdrop, mind you. I had gone to retrieve a cap for Atticus. I was not even sure what I had heard at first, but by the time I realized what it was, I had heard quite a bit."

Will looked away, thinking on what she said, his eyes taking on a distant gleam. "And you heard them say that the child she carried was Marcellus'?"

"Aye, Will."

"Atticus, too?"

"Aye, Will."

He looked at her again. "Is that what you and Lily were fighting about?"

Adria averted her gaze. "I was... angry," she said. "When someone you trust falls from grace, it is a difficult thing to bear. I told her that she was wrong and that she needed to tell you the truth."

"Why?"

"Because it is not fair to you," she said, feeling strongly about a sensitive subject. "Mayhap that is assuming too much, that I should not involve myself in your business, but you and Lily made me a part of your business when Lily asked me to marry you. I am supposed to have no feelings about her behavior? About Marcellus? What they did is wrong."

Will did something at that moment on impulse. He reached

out and grasped one of her hands, holding it tightly in his big fist. It was an impulse because, for the first time in his life, he saw a woman leaping to his defense. He'd been married to Lily for many years and never saw her leap to his defense like that. Something in Adria's reaction to Lily and Marcellus' deception touched a chord in him, a chord he didn't even know he had.

He grasped her hand in silent gratitude.

"Under normal circumstances, it was very wrong," he said calmly. "What did Lily tell you about it? Why she and Marcellus carried on?"

Adria could only seem to look at his hand as it closed over hers. It was warm and strong, causing her heart to race. Something about that hand over hers awakened something in her.

Something needful and giddy.

"She said that her father had forced you two to marry," she said, struggling to focus on something other than her hand in his. "She said that she had loved Marcellus before she married you."

"She did."

It took Adria a moment to realize that Will didn't seem surprised by all of this. It further occurred to her why.

"You *knew*?" she asked, incredulous. "You knew about them the entire time and you never tried to stop them?"

He nodded. "My father asked me the same question," he said. "I will tell you what I told him – Lily's father should have never forced us to marry. He forced his daughter to marry one man when she loved another. I have never been in love with a woman, but I should imagine that being forced to marry someone other than who I loved would be a terrible thing. Lily never asked for a marriage to me. She wanted to marry Marcellus but her father had other ideas."

Adria stared at the man. "Then... then they had your approval to carry on in secret?"

He shook his head. "Not approval," he said. "But they had my understanding. As long as they did not publicly shame me, as long as they were discreet, I did not trouble myself over it. But my mother heard you say that Atticus and the child Lily just gave birth to were not my children."

"That is what Lily told me."

He squeezed her hand and let it go. "I should be irate," he said. "I should be furious. I should kill Marcellus. But that would not solve the problem, nor would it destroy the feelings they have for one another."

"But what they've done to you is *wrong.*"

"It is," Will agreed. "But do not look at me as a victim in all of this. The real victim is Marcellus. Can you imagine having children with the woman you love, only for them to bear the name of another man?"

Adria was coming to realize that he really *wasn't* troubled by any of this. At the very least, he'd reconciled himself to it. She wasn't sure how she felt about it.

"Are you truly so unselfish?" she asked. "Or are you truly so callous? Does the sanctity of marriage mean nothing to you?"

He met her confused gaze. "It means everything to me," he said. "I never took a mistress, not in all of the years Lily and I were married. Even if Lily did not honor her vows, I did."

"But you never banished Marcellus."

Will shook his head. "Nay," he said. "As I said, removing him would not be the answer. How do I know? Because Lily's father tried to send him away, once, and she attempted to kill herself, so if I sent Marcellus away, she might try again and then everyone would know that my wife had shamed me with another man. To preserve my honor, and the honor of the houses of de Lohr and de Wolfe, I did nothing. They kept it secretive so no one ever knew. Did you?"

Adria shook her head. "Never."

"And you were close to Lily," Will pointed out. "If you did not know or suspect, then no one did. That was my only concern."

Adria was truly baffled by the entire situation. She couldn't believe he was so complacent when it came to his wife and her lover, but in listening to his reasons and the situation from his perspective, she could understand why he did what he did. That was generosity and compassion that went beyond anything she ever thought a man was capable of.

Was Will de Wolfe truly so forgiving?

Lost to her thoughts, Adria didn't realize that Will was watching her. He knew the situation was shocking and unconventional, and even though he'd known Adria for several years, he didn't really *know* her. He didn't know how she would react to his position on the matter because she was absolutely right – it was wrong. All of it *was* wrong.

But Will wasn't sorry for his actions.

Far from it.

"Adria," he said quietly. "If you view that as foolish, then I am sorry you feel that way. But I will not apologize for my decision for the greater good."

Shaken from her train of thought, Adria looked at him. "It's not that," she said. "I was simply thinking… if you let Lily do as she pleased, then my loyalty to you would mean nothing. I could do whatever I wished and you would let me do it in order to preserve the de Wolfe honor."

Will shook his head, his gaze intense. "Your loyalty would be the only thing that mattered to me. I will not tolerate a disloyal wife a second time."

"Nor would I tolerate a disloyal husband."

"I would be faithful to you until the day I died, Adria."

"But that loyalty would only be out of honor?"

"What else is there?"

That wasn't the answer she was looking for. There was something about Will that had conveyed he expected more from their marriage, something that would make him glad to be married.

Perhaps he was expecting what Lily and Marcellus had.

But Adria could see that she had been wrong in that assumption. With the events of the day, she couldn't take another emotional or spiritual blow. She'd just been through the most horrific event of her entire life and had lost a dear friend in the process, and now... now, Will was speaking about honor, the only thing that evidently mattered to him. Perhaps that was all he had left because Lily's lack of faithfulness had hardened him, had left him in a rock-solid fortress of self-protection where there was no emotion, no sentiment, only duty and loyalty. Only honor. Things that were cold and without feeling.

No love.

Adria realized that it was something she had hoped for with him.

Love.

Without another word, she quit the small hall, heading out into the inner bailey with her bloodstained dress and a broken heart. When people saw her coming out of the keep, gore-splattered, the rumors and whispers began to fly, but Adria didn't hear anything. Even if she had, she wouldn't have cared.

All she cared about at that moment was her own quagmire of grief.

CHAPTER SEVENTEEN

THE MORNING AFTER Lily's death brought an unexpected event.

It was just after dawn when the sentries on the walls began taking up the call. A contingent had been sighted coming in from the south and by the time the sentries were aware of it, a small army of about five hundred men was already halfway through town, heading straight for the castle. The buzz began to move through the men.

De Lohr standards.

Will hadn't slept all night, and what a harrowing night it had been. Adria had disappeared after their conversation and he had been torn between going after her and letting her deal with the situation in her own way. Going after her finally won over, but he was distracted by the arrival of the wet nurse and the midwife, who promptly went to Lily's chamber to help with the baby. The burden had been on Jordan through the night and although she was quite capable, the one thing she couldn't do was feed the tiny infant who was still alive. The wet nurse took over and the baby received the first of what would be many excellent meals.

There was hope he would live.

With the child well-tended, Will's focus turned to Lily and funeral arrangements. Will had sent word to her father when he'd first been told of her deadly diagnosis, but Chris de Lohr was far to the south on the Welsh Marches. Will had asked him to come but, even so, he couldn't be sure that the man would respond.

He had his answer the morning after Lily's death as the de Lohr contingent approached.

Meanwhile, Atticus had taken the news of his mother's death hard, so hard that he didn't want to sleep in the big chamber where she was and Will allowed him to sleep with the other pages. They had their own small chamber in the knights' quarters and he seemed to be happier surrounded by boys his own age, including his nemesis, Bradford.

Marcellus, however, was another matter altogether.

After saying his farewells to Lily the day before, he'd spent the entire night wandering the walls of Carlisle. Will knew that because he'd seen him. The man hadn't said a word to Will, not one bloody word, but he saw him in the torchlight sometime before morning wiping his face of tears as he walked his rounds. Clearly, the man was devastated but Will couldn't muster the energy to become emotionally involved in Marcellus' comfort.

That would have been an odd thing, anyway.

The husband comforting the lover.

It was a strange night for Will, mostly because of how he found himself feeling about Adria and her disappearance. The poor woman had endured something horrific the day before and she'd risen to it. She'd shown incredible bravery and clarity of thought when everything else around her was chaos. He found that both endearing and attractive, and even though the hours after Lily's death were the most inopportune times to realize his strong attraction for her, that was exactly what happened. He felt sorrow for Lily's passing, of course, but he found himself more interested in the living than in the dead.

And he suffered some guilt because of it.

News of Lily's passing, of course, had been spread by the servants who had cleaned her blood from the floor and, in little time, everyone at Carlisle knew what had happened. Oddly enough, no one really expressed their condolences to Will, perhaps fearful of his reaction. Hermes and Ronan did, however, and they were quite saddened by it, but everyone else seemed to avoid Will, afraid to look him in the eyes, whispering to each other of their pity for him.

It was a tragic situation all around.

Late in the night, when Will could no longer stand it, he'd gone looking for Adria only to find her sleeping in the stable loft. Ronan had seen her go in but not come out, and Will found her curled up in the loft, cozy in the hay that surrounded her. He'd found a blanket and gently put it over her, but she hadn't awakened. He left her there with Ronan keeping watch over the stable area. In fact, none of the Carlisle knights, including Scott, slept that night and most of the soldiers seemed to be up and moving, too.

It was a tense and sorrowful night after the death of Lily de Wolfe.

Given the chaos going on in and around Carlisle Castle, the arrival of de Lohr on the morning after was something of a surprise. Will was in his solar with Scott when he heard the sentries, emerging into the outer bailey just as the portcullis in the main gatehouse began to crank open, the massive iron grate straining on its chain. The de Lohr contingent began to pour in through the gates, looking muddy and weary and worn out. They looked as if they'd done nothing but ride straight through, from the Welsh Marches to Carlisle, and that went especially for Chris de Lohr as he rode in astride his expensive cream-colored war horse.

Will and Scott went out to meet him.

"My lord," Will greeted him as he came near. "Why did you not send word of your impending arrival? I would have sent an escort out to greet you."

Chris had the faceplate flipped up on his helm, his sky-blue eye ringed and weary. Those who had known his grandfather, like William de Wolfe, said that Chris was nearly the exact image of him with his blond hair and trim beard. He wasn't as fair as Christopher had been, but he had the man's size and eyes.

He was a de Lohr to the bone.

"There was no time to send you anything," he said, dismounting his horse stiffly. "We simply wanted to come. Come and embrace me, Will."

Will did. It was like being hugged by an angry bear who only wanted to squeeze and shake. He was a little larger than Chris, and a lot younger, so he could have easily fended the old man off, but he let him squeeze and pretend he was still the strongest. When Chris caught sight of Scott, he embraced him, too, and held him as if he were the man he loved best in the entire world.

"Scott," he said, even kissing the man on the cheek. "How I have missed you, my dear friend."

Scott was pleasant. He was polite. He even smiled at Chris and patted him on the cheek. But he was feeling decidedly unfriendly given the actions of the man's daughter towards his beloved son, no matter if Will had been resigned to the situation. It was a situation that should have never happened.

If Will was edgy from being up all night, that was nothing compared to his father.

Unfortunately, that set the stage for what was to come.

But Chris was oblivious to what was going on and what had happened. For all he knew, everything was still as it was when he had received Will's missive. He indicated the two large knights behind him.

"Greet my sons," Chris said, yanking off his heavy gloves. "Becket and Morgen have attended me. They wanted to come and lend their support."

Will greeted Lily's older brothers. Becket had the blond de Lohr looks, while Morgen took after his Welsh mother. He had dark hair and striking blue eyes, an even-tempered man who was well liked. But Becket was someone Will had always bonded with.

"Beck," Will said, extending his hand in greeting. "Welcome to Carlisle."

Becket had his helm off, smiling wearily as he took the man's hand. "It's been a long time, Will," he said, sliding out of the saddle. "Are you still screaming at your army with loud-mouthed insults to motivate them?"

Will smiled weakly. Even the de Lohrs knew of his reputation for slick insults that were both hilarious and accurate. "Not lately," he said. "I leave the army to Marcellus and Ronan and Hermes these days. I'm a lord, you know. I have others scream at my army for me."

Becket grinned. "Come this way," he said, motioning the man around his horse to one of his saddlebags. Will didn't notice that he'd put the horse between them and his father as he untied the saddlebag. "My father has been frantic to get to my sister. Tell me she's well."

He was whispering, pretending to show Will a new dagger when he really wanted to lay the foundation for his father's mood. But Will couldn't lie to him. He couldn't even soften the blow.

"We lost her yesterday," he muttered. "You must help me with your father if he is on edge."

Becket closed his eyes tightly for a moment, steeling himself, before putting the dagger back in the saddlebag.

"God help us," he breathed. "I will do what I can. Was she... was she in pain?"

Will could see the pain of an older brother asking about his only sister. Discreetly, he put his hand on Becket's arm. "She gave birth, so there was some pain," he said. "We did everything we could. That is why my father is here. But you should also know that there have been some... developments in relation to Lily. My father is on edge also."

Becket looked at him, frowning. "Why? What's happened?"

Will shook his head. They couldn't risk whispering any further without someone figuring it out, so Will came around the horse and greeted Morgen. As the de Lohr army began to disband around them, the sons joined their fathers and Will made a gesture towards the keep.

"Come," he said to Chris. "Let us go inside and you may rest. My men will disband your army."

Chris was nodding, handing off his helm and traveling robe to the nearest soldier as they began to walk in a group towards the inner gatehouse.

"Where is my daughter?" he asked. "I am anxious to see her."

Will looked at Scott, expecting some kind of help from him, but Scott remained oddly stiff and silent. Will could see that it was up to him to handle the situation, at least as much as he could.

"Let us go inside the keep," he said again. "You must have made incredibly good time to have arrived here as quickly as you did. I assume the weather was on your side?"

Chris nodded. "Fortunately for us," he said. "I pushed my men to do thirty-five, mayhap forty miles a day, so they've hardly slept and they've eaten while they were traveling mostly. After I received your missive, I knew I had to come. Lily's mother insisted."

Will was glad the man hadn't asked for Lily again, but they still weren't to the safety and privacy of the smaller hall yet. They were just approaching the inner gatehouse drawbridge when Atticus suddenly appeared, running in Chris' direction.

"Avus!" he shouted. "*Avus!*"

Avus was the Latin term for grandfather, something the de Wolfe grandchildren had called Chris from the beginning. Delighted to see his youngest grandson, Chris came to a halt and opened up his arms. Atticus stopped short of throwing himself into his embrace and the old man roared with laughter, grabbing the boy by the hair and pulling him into one of those angry bear hugs.

Atticus howled.

"It is music to my ears to hear his screams," Chris said, laughing. "Atticus, lad, I'm so happy to see you. Have you missed me?"

Atticus was throwing fists to try and break his grandfather's hold, so much so that Will had to step in and still the flying fists. He pulled Atticus out of Chris' embrace and set him on his feet.

"What did you bring me?" Atticus demanded.

Chris and Becket and Morgen were grinning, getting a good look at the lad they'd not seen in at least two years. He'd been young then, but still full of fire. At six years of age, he was positively a terror.

"I'm not sure," Chris said, putting a big hand on Atticus' head. "We'll go through my saddlebags and see if there is anything you want to keep."

The mere idea lit Atticus up. "Now?"

"Nay," Chris said. "After I have seen your mother."

"But Mama is in heaven."

Chris froze. In fact, they all did. His eyes widened as he

looked at Atticus. "What did you say?"

"We lost Lily yesterday," Will said softly. He had no choice. "I was trying to take you into the keep where I could tell you privately. She gave birth to another grandson, but she did not survive the birth."

Chris looked at him with such horror that Will was physically struck by it. He could see the grief filling every line of the man's face.

"My angel is gone?" Chris said. "She is dead?"

Will nodded. He wasn't unsympathetic about it, a father losing a child, so he put his hand on the man's shoulder to ease him as Becket and Morgen came up alongside him, each man trying to be of some comfort to his father.

"She is," Will said. "She passed away yesterday afternoon and there has been no time to send you word. I was planning on doing it this morning, in fact, but you have arrived and must hear the terrible news from my lips. Mayhap it is best this way."

Chris was trying very hard to keep his composure. He paused, struggling, digesting every horrible word that Will had delivered.

He simply couldn't believe it.

"Tell me what happened," he finally said. "Tell me everything that happened."

Will nodded, but he was trying to direct the man inside. "Shall we go into the keep?" he asked, looking at Becket with silent encouragement to move the man forward. "Let us go where we can speak privately. You do not want the soldiers to witness your grief, my lord."

Chris started to walk, but it was stiffly. "Tell me now," he said. "Tell me as we walk. What happened to my angel?"

"As I said, we lost her in childbirth, yesterday. We..."

"Nay!" Chris roared, interrupting him. "From the beginning!"

It was the desperate cry of a father and Will took up pace beside him as Becket and Morgen crowded in around their father.

"I told you in the missive that Lily injured herself when she fell last month," he said as steadily and clearly as he could. "My physic believed that the fall caused the nourishment sack for the child to pull away from the womb. Lily was bleeding internally and when the child was unexpectedly born yesterday, there was nothing to be done. Lily lost consciousness because of the loss of blood and simply never woke up. Her passing was... peaceful."

They were in the inner bailey by now with the keep straight ahead. Everyone was herding Chris into the keep, into the small hall, where he could grieve in private. Scott was bringing up the rear with Atticus, but before the child entered the keep, he sent him off to the kitchens to tell the servants to bring refreshments for their visitors. It was simply a ploy to remove Atticus from a situation that was sure to get worse before it got better.

As Atticus ran off, Scott followed the others into the keep.

"My sweet angel," Chris was saying as he sat heavily at the nearest table. "What am I going to tell her mother? Kaedia will be shattered by the news. *What* am I to tell her?"

"Tell her that Lily met her death bravely," Becket said, sitting next to his father with his arm around the man's shoulders. "Death in childbirth is like the death of a warrior – it is glorious and for the right and true cause. Mother will understand that."

"*I* do not understand that," Chris said, slapping his hand on the table as the tears began to come. "I do not understand why this has happened. Lily was a good lass, true and compassionate. I do not understand why God took her from us."

Neither Becket nor Morgen had an answer for him. They simply sat with him, their arms around him, trying to give him some comfort. Will and Scott sat across from them, watching the sorrowful scene.

"You have a new grandson," Will said. "He is small, but he is strong. I have every faith that he will survive."

Chris had his head in his hands, elbows on the table. He didn't say anything to the news of a new grandson; he hadn't the first time, either. He just sat there with his head in his hands.

All he seemed to focus on was Lily's death.

"I was not here to comfort her," he said mournfully. "My God... is that what I will remember for the rest of my life? That I was not here to comfort my daughter when she needed me?"

"Lily was not without comfort," Will said. "My own grandmother is here and she spent a great deal of time with Lily yesterday. It is my grandmother who is tending to the new child, so Lily was comforted. She was well tended to."

Chris looked at him. "I notice that you do not mention that *you* gave her comfort," he said. "I hoped that things would be better between you when you assumed command of Carlisle, but I will go on the assumption that I was wrong. Why were you not there to give her comfort, Will? You are her husband. You should have never left her side."

"I was with her a great deal," Will said, hearing hazard in Chris' tone. "There was only so much I could do."

Chris growled. "Then it is like it was before, is it?" he said. "When you were at Lioncross, serving me, and you ignored Lily. Do not deny it, for I saw it myself. Is that what happened here at Carlisle? You ignored your wife and she was condemned to die alone?"

"She did *not* die alone," Scott suddenly hissed. Before Will could stop him, Scott began spewing venom straight at Chris. "She had her lover to comfort her, as you damned well know. A knight you permitted her to fornicate with throughout her marriage to my son, so do not sit here and put the blame on him when it was you who created this mess. Will is a victim of your daughter's infidelity!"

Chris' face turned red and his tears vanished unnaturally fast as the insults and accusations began to fly hard and fast. "What's this?" he demanded. "What's this you say to me?"

"You heard me," Scott growled. "Your daughter was an adulteress with your full knowledge, so you will not tell us what a pure angel she was. She was anything but a pure angel."

"Bite your tongue!"

"She was a whore!"

Everyone at the table bolted to their feet as Scott practically threw himself over the tabletop to get to Chris, who was equally eager to get at Scott. Will and Becket and Morgen had to throw themselves between the old men, struggling to pull them apart as meaty fists began to fly. Scott made contact with the side of Chris' head, and also his own son's head, as Will manhandled his father away from the table.

"The child your daughter died giving birth to was not even her husband's child," Scott roared. "It was her lover's child!"

"I will kill you for saying such things!" Chris bellowed.

Will was having a hell of a time restraining his father because Scott would not be stopped. He had been stewing about the situation ever since he found out about it and to hear Chris put any onus on Will had him exploding in defense of his son.

"Do you deny that you allowed Marcellus to continue at Lily's side even after you forced her to marry Will?" he shouted. "Do you deny that you sent Marcellus north with Lily and Will to Carlisle so that Lily would not be without her lover? You know this to be true, de Lohr, so you will not deny it. Cast blame on my son again for your failure and I will destroy everything you hold dear. Do you understand me? *This is your fault!*"

Chris was so enraged that he kicked at his sons to try and

break their hold so he could get to Scott.

"Bastard!" he screamed. "I will kill you, de Wolfe! I will release my armies on the north and I will wipe you from this earth!"

Will was trying desperately to push his father into the second portion of the hall where he could shut the door and separate him from Chris, but Scott wasn't having any part of it.

"No one defeats William de Wolfe in battle and especially not the sorry descendants of Christopher de Lohr," he seethed. "You caused this situation with your greed and ambition, marrying your daughter to a man she didn't love, yet you refuse to take any responsibility for it. Damn you to hell, de Lohr!"

Will managed to get his father through the open door into the second part of the small hall, slamming it behind him and bolting it. There was nowhere for Scott to go except a servant's alcove and a smaller secondary access door to the inner ward. He pushed Scott so hard to get him away from the door that Scott nearly fell over the nearest table. Enraged, he straightened himself up and faced his son.

"I will not let that bastard accuse you of any wrongdoing," he said through clenched teeth. "If he believes you are at fault here, I will kill him."

Will, deeply concerned with the turn of events, put up his hands to try to ease his father. "Papa, I…"

"His daughter ruined your life!"

"Papa, I will not fight with you about this," Will said, louder. "You are going to remain here and behave yourself, do you hear me?"

"I'll not let him blame you!"

Will sighed sharply. "He's upset," he said. "He has just lost his daughter. How would you feel if you lost Sophia or Sorsha or Seraphina? Can you not relate to some of the man's pain?"

Scott's eyebrows flew up in outrage. "You *defend* him?"

Will shook his head. "I'm not defending him, but he's mad with grief right now and you did not help matters," he said. "Please… just stay here for a moment. Will you please?"

Scott waved him off and turned away, struggling to compose himself. Will eyed his father nervously for a few moments before daring to go back to the door he'd just bolted and return to the first section of the smaller hall. Just as he stepped through the door, he could see Becket and Morgen escorting their father from the hall.

"Wait," Will called. "Wait, please."

Becket and Morgen came to a halt, eyeing Will with some concern as he approached them. As Will drew closer, he could see that Chris had broken down into a flood of tears.

The man was shattered.

"I'm sorry," he said, looking at Chris with great sympathy. "My father… he's quite distressed about everything. He loved Lily, you know. He did not know about Marcellus until recently."

"What's this about Marcellus?" Becket hissed, looking to Will. "What does it mean?"

Will held up a hand to silence him, at least for the moment. He was more concerned about Chris.

"Your father will tell you about Marcellus when his wits return," he said, but his focus was on Chris. "My lord, I swear he did not mean what he said. He's mad with grief and confusion. You see, I lost my mother many years ago and the grief of that loss drove my father into abandoning his family for a few years. He simply could not handle the anguish and guilt of my mother's passing. I'm afraid that Lily's death has brought about those memories he's tried so hard to forget. Please forgive him."

Chris was wiping the tears on his face. "I remember," he said. "The fair Athena. I remember it all."

"Then you know how badly it hurt him."

Chris nodded, but the longer he looked at Will, the more his composure fractured. "I am sorry," he whispered. "Your father is right. I wanted to keep my Lily happy, but it was at your expense. Everything was at your expense. Forgive me, Will."

Will drew in a long breath, one of relief that the old men were calming down, glancing at Becket and Morgen, who seemed more confused than ever.

But he didn't have the time to explain.

"It was not only my expense," Will murmured. "Lily and Marcellus paid the price, too. But what is done cannot be undone, so there is no need for forgiveness. I never blamed you for anything, truthfully, except for forcing us to wed, but I understand why you did it. You wanted the de Wolfe marriage."

Chris wiped at his face again. The tears wouldn't seem to stop falling. "Where is your father?"

"Through that door. I told him to wait."

"I will go to him."

Will wasn't so sure that was a good idea, but he stood aside. He and Becket and Morgen made a nervous trio as Chris went to the door, opened it, and went through. After that, the three knights were coiled, waiting for the first sound of a struggle.

But the chamber remained silent.

"What do we do?" Becket whispered. "Do we go in?"

Will kept listening, but he didn't hear a thing. Gesturing for Becket and Morgen to remain where they were, he silently made his way over to the cracked-open door and peered inside. It was dim in the chamber and it took him a moment to see Chris and Scott, sitting over near the darkened hearth.

Scott had his arm around Chris' shoulders.

That was all Will needed to see. Making his way back to Becket and Morgen, he gestured to the keep entry.

"They do not need us," he said quietly. "They are working it out between them. Now, let us go into the great hall. I'll have food brought to you."

"Will you tell us what Marcellus has to do with this?" Becket asked.

But Will shook his head. "That must come from your father," he said. "He will tell you when he is ready."

Without another word, the three knights slipped from the keep, out into the deepening morning.

CHAPTER EIGHTEEN

"**C**AN I LEAVE you alone with him?" The round, full-breasted wet nurse was gathering up swaddling clothes and blankets that had been hurriedly gathered for the infant. "I want to wash a few things out. Whatever goes against his little body should be clean. I will not be long."

Adria waved the woman on. "I've spent time with all four of Lady de Wolfe's children," she said. "I know what to do."

The woman nodded and collected the last of the items, heading from the alcove that had now become a nursery. Adria was seated next to the bed where the tiny infant lay sleeping on his back, tightly swaddled. The child's birth may have been harrowing, but he was still alive and, in fact, seemingly thriving. He ate well and slept well, and both Tarraby and the midwife thought the child had a good chance of surviving.

Alec de Wolfe had a hopeful future.

It was the morning after the death of Lily and things still seemed strange and surreal, at least to Adria. After spending the night in the stables because she couldn't bear to return to the keep, she awoke with thoughts of Lily on her mind and wept yet again for the loss of her friend. For a few minutes, she let the grief wash over her, but when it was finished, she sat up, wiped her face, and climbed down from the loft. Adria had always been a woman of action and she knew that she would be needed today.

There was much to do with the arrival of a new baby.

Dawn was just breaking as she made her way back to the keep. The smell of baking bread was heavy in the air and her stomach rumbled, as she had missed the evening meal the night before. In fact, with everything that had gone on, she didn't even know if there had been an evening meal. She doubted many people felt like eating. But she stopped at the kitchen yard on her way to the keep, collecting bread and cheese and part of a cold meat pie the cook had saved for her. Stuffing food into her mouth as she walked, she made it into the keep.

By the time she reached the great chamber, she could see that all traces of Lily had been removed. The bed had been stripped of the bloody linens and Lily's body was gone. The chamber was quite warm, as the servants had stoked the fire, and she found Lady Warenton and the wet nurse in the alcove with the infant.

Neither one looked as if they'd slept all night.

Adria called to the servants and had them not only put fresh linens on Lily's bed, but she had them move it to the far side of the chamber, closer to the hearth. That took some doing because the bed had four carved posts and wooden rods that connected them at the top, meant for curtains. Not only did the servants have to move that bed, but they had to reattach the rods because Adria had them put up the curtains that Lily had never liked. The object was to let Lady Warenton sleep there, in comfort and privacy, and Jordan was quite touched at Adria's effort.

After a night tending a baby that seemed to have a strong will to live, she was ready for some sleep. She was an old woman, after all, and the stress of the past few days was catching up to her. Therefore, she took to the big bed and drifted off to sleep without much of a fuss.

With Jordan sleeping after her long and tense night, Adria changed out of her bloodstained dress, washed her face and arms and hands, brushed her hair and braided it, and changed into a fresh shift and a durable gown of undyed linen and an apron that made her waist look tiny. It was a new day, a new future, and even if she hadn't approved of Lily's deception, that didn't dampen her sense of compassion and forgiveness. When she'd awoken this morning, all of that didn't seem so important any longer.

Perhaps that's what she needed to do most – forgive her friend.

With Jordan asleep and the wet nurse out doing wash, Adria pulled out the blue fabric in the wardrobe, the pieces she'd meant for Lady Jordan, and brought them back into the alcove to work on them. It helped her to focus on something Lily wanted, piecing together the kirtle for Lady Warenton at one end of the bed while the baby slept peacefully on the other. She kept looking over at little Alec, thinking that he really was a beautiful child.

She knew Lily would have been so proud of him.

"Are you well this morning, my lady?"

Will was standing in the doorway, his gaze on his son even though his words were meant for Adria. She looked at him, thinking that he looked absolutely exhausted. Setting down the blue pieces, she went to him, studying his stubbled face.

"I am well enough," she said. "But you look as if you've not slept in weeks. Sit down and I will send for food and drink."

He shook his head. "I have eaten," he said. "I was just in the hall with our visitors."

"We have visitors?"

He looked at her then. "Did you not see an army come

through the gates a short time ago?"

She shook her head. "I have been here or in the kitchens," she said. "Who came?"

"Lily's father."

Adria gasped softly. "Does he know?"

"He does."

"The I'm so sorry for him. He was too late to see her."

Will nodded faintly. "I know," he said. "But my father has taken him down into the vault where we put Lily's body, so he is visiting her now. I am sure he will want to see his newest grandson at some point. Is the child doing well?"

Adria looked over at the infant, sleeping between two fat pillows. "The wet nurse says that he is eating very well," she said. "I've not spoken much about him with your grandmother, but he seems to be doing quite well."

Will stood over the infant, looking down at the sleeping face. "Poor little lad," he said. "How close we came to losing him."

Adria stood next to him, also looking at the infant. "This is what Lily wanted," she said quietly. "She wanted her child to be saved. Her prayers were answered."

She was still looking at the infant when Will looked at her. He was at least a foot taller than she was, probably more, so he was mostly looking at the top of her head. Much of what was on his mind last night had been Adria and to see her clean and groomed this morning did his heart good.

With Lily freshly gone, perhaps it still wasn't the right time to let his attraction to Adria run wild, but given he'd not felt anything for Lily for a very long time, it was difficult to restrain the emotions that were starting to bubble up. It felt good to have his heart leap a little when he saw a woman.

He thought he'd lost that ability long ago.

"I am sorry that I caused you to run off last night," he said quietly. "I did not mean to upset you."

Adria looked up at him, realizing that he was quite close. She hadn't really noticed until this moment and she found herself mesmerized by his gaze.

"It was not your fault," she said, her cheeks growing hot because of his proximity. "It was only foolishness, really. I think the events of the day simply overwhelmed me."

He scratched his head, moving over to the chair she'd been occupying and sitting heavily. "It could not be because of something I said?"

"What did you say?"

He kicked his big legs out, leaning back against the chair. "I was thinking about that," he said. "You asked me if my loyalty to you would only be out of honor and I asked you what more could there be? Clearly, that upset you."

Adria remembered the exchanges verbatim, but she was ashamed of her reaction. "Everything upset me yesterday," she said, averting her gaze. "Pay no attention to me."

"But I do," he said. "I want to pay a great deal of attention to you if you'll let me. I still want you to marry me, Adria. That has not changed. Has it changed for you?"

She looked at him then. "Nay," she said honestly. "It has not, but we should not marry anytime soon. That would reflect poorly upon you to marry so recently after losing your wife."

He sighed wearily, looking at the child on the bed. "I know," he said. "Adria, may I ask you a question?"

"Of course."

"What expectations do you have for this marriage?"

She was back to fussing with the blue strips of cloth. "Nothing more than the usual," she said. "Being a wife, hopefully a mother, and living a respectable life."

"Is that all?"

"What else is there?"

He paused. That's what he had said to her yesterday when they spoke of loyalty in a marriage. There was something both defiant and harsh to that question, as if there were no room for options. He had a feeling he knew what might be bothering her, a young woman who more than likely hoped for something far more than a respectable life.

He was going to take a chance that maybe he was right.

"I don't know," he said. "Mayhap there is a good deal more that neither one of us knows about."

"Like what?"

He sat back in the chair as he began to feel his fatigue, but he didn't want to give up this moment with her. They had agreed to wait until Lily was gone before engaging in any kind of courtship and, right or wrong, he wasn't going to wait. His interest in Adria was growing by the minute.

"I have sisters," he said. "Three of them. I seem to recall that young women like dreams of handsome husbands and of falling in love. Is that something you hope for?"

Adria's movements slowed. She had the blue strips laying side by side, but she couldn't seem to focus on them. He was asking her an honest question and she only had two options at that point – either lie to him or tell him the truth. Since she wasn't a liar by nature and she'd made quite a big deal out of Lily not being truthful, she wasn't going to start masking the truth and hiding her feelings now. Will had already had one wife who hadn't shown him any consideration or honesty.

She wasn't going to do it, too.

Slowly, she lifted her head and looked at him.

"Not if you don't."

Will was looking at her when she spoke, feeling something radiating from those pale eyes. It was something that gave him hope that somewhere, deep inside, Adria had the potential to feel something for him.

He realized that he wanted her to.

"I do," he murmured. "I very much do. I would like to have a wife who loves me."

Adria began to feel quivery, giddy. It was not a familiar feeling, but she'd already experienced it with Will and was at least somewhat prepared. But his answer, which had been honest, fueled her bravery.

"And I would like to have a husband who loves me," she said, sitting on the bed and facing him. "I am, if nothing else, truthful. You will always know what my thoughts and opinions are because those are things I have never been any good at concealing. I ran from you last night because your answer about loyalty – whether you would only be loyal to me out of honor – wasn't the answer I was hoping for. I was hoping to hear you would be loyal to me because you wanted to be, not because your reputation was at stake. Will, you have had one cold marriage. I do not want this to be another one. I will be warm and kind and caring if you'll let me. But I cannot be warm and kind and caring to a man who does not show me the same things in return."

A smile played on his lips. "I appreciate your honesty," he said. "I will give you more of the same. We had a delightful conversation the other day when Atticus was playing down by the river. That is more of a conversation than almost anything I've ever had with Lily and it made me realize that I want that kind of bond with my wife. With you. I want to be able to sit with you and talk to you, to share my hopes and concerns, and I want you to do the same with me. My parents have a marriage like that. I have always been quite envious of it."

Adria smiled. "Me, too," she said. "What an astonishing way to live. With someone who cares about you and wants the best for you."

"I cannot think of anything finer."

She bit her lip, still smiling at him, in a gesture he found utterly charming. He chuckled. "Even if we delay our marriage for propriety's sake, mayhap… mayhap you will let me court you," he said. "Discreetly, of course. I simply do not want to waste any time coming to know you because this is a moment I never thought I would have."

"What moment?"

"The chance to find happiness. With you."

Adria thought that was the sweetest thing she'd ever heard. Will, a man she'd known for years, a cold man by most accounts, had a romantic streak him.

And she loved that.

"I would like that," she said softly.

He smiled at her, a gleam of real hope in his eyes. Then, he yawned, spoiling the moment, but she laughed. He grinned sheepishly but he was prevented from saying anything when the baby on the bed began to mewl like a cat. Immediately, Adria was up, turning the baby on his side and patting his back gently to soothe him.

Will got up from the chair and went to stand beside her, watching her gently tend to the tiny infant. It was very sweet and he was gaining new respect for her, seeing things about her that he'd never seen before. When the baby settled down and she turned to him, finger to her lips for silence, all he could see was those lips. He couldn't help himself. Bending down, he slanted his lips softly over hers.

Startled, Adria gasped, but she didn't pull away. Will had only meant to kiss her briefly, but the moment his lips touched hers, he knew this wasn't going to be a brief or chaste kiss. Not even close. She was warm and soft and before he realized it, he was pulling her into his arms.

Adria let him.

His kiss was curious at first, but the moment he pulled her

to his chest, the kiss turned hot. He suckled her lips, tasting her, squeezing her so hard that he squeezed the breath right out of her. Adria's arms ended up around his neck, her hands on the back of his head, her fingers intertwined in his hair.

Searing.

That's what it was. Searing.

The baby let out a weak cry and Will abruptly let her go, but it was reluctantly. He still had his arms around her as they both looked at the baby and Adria finally had to gently pull his arms away so she could get to the child. Will was still hovering over her, still very close, and when she settled the baby down again and turned to him, he moved to kiss her again. He nearly made contact, his lips against hers, but noise in the other chamber had them putting immediate distance between them.

The wet nurse was back.

"You came to see your son, my lord?" she said, coming into the alcove. "He's doing quite well. He's a strong lad."

Adria was trying desperately to look as if she weren't breathless or disheveled. "He's beginning to stir," she told the wet nurse, smoothing at the braid that Will had managed to muss. "I believe he is hungry again."

The wet nurse leaned over the bed, peering at the child. "I'm sure he is," she said. "I'd better feed the lad all he can eat."

"Where is his wash?" Adria asked.

"Down in the kitchen yard with the washerwomen."

"I'll see to it.

As the wet nurse went to pick up the baby to feed him, Adria and Will left the alcove together. Adria put a finger to her lips, indicating the bed where Jordan was sleeping, so Will remained silent until they shut the door and reached the bottom of the stairs.

The small great hall loomed before them, empty.

"Are you really going to check on the wash?" he asked.

She nodded. "I am," she said. "And do you know what you should do?"

His eyes glimmered with mirth. "I am afraid to ask."

She pointed to his solar on the opposite side of the small hall. "Sleep," she said. "You've not slept all night, I would guess, so you should try to get some sleep now. It is a quiet morning, Will. Nothing is happening that you need to attend to right now."

He grunted. "That's what you think," he said. "My father and Chris de Lohr nearly came to blows this morning. I should really find them and make sure they have made nice with each other."

Adria frowned. "Why should they fight?"

Will waved her off. "I'll tell you the whole story later," he said. "Suffice it to say that grief does strange things to men."

She looked at him closely. "And you?" she asked quietly. "How are you feeling? Above all, Lily was still your wife. Surely you must feel some sadness."

"Of course I do," he said. "She was a friend to me, you know. In spite of everything, we were friendly with one another."

Adria smiled sadly. "I know," she said. "I have seen it for years. You were always pleasant with one another. If you could not be with her at the end, I am glad that I was able to spend her last moments with her. She was with someone who cared about her and she knew she had given birth to a son. I know she was happy about that. Those are her last memories and they are good ones."

She was starting to tear up and he pulled her into his arms, holding her tightly. "She loved you," he said huskily. "We all take comfort knowing you were with her."

Adria embraced him, their first real embrace and one that was so completely satisfying. She never knew being held by a man could be so warm and comforting. As big as Will was, it was like being swallowed up by a mass of flesh and heat and safety.

It was bliss.

"I am just glad that I could be there," she whispered against him. He didn't seem keen to let her go and she was afraid that they might be seen, so she patted him on the chest and gently pushed herself from his embrace. "Now, I am going to check on the wash and then I will find Atticus. I think I should spend the day with him, don't you?"

Will nodded. "He will need your comfort," he said. "I am grateful."

Adria thought of the little boy who was now motherless. She felt overwhelmingly protective over him because of it. "I will take care of him, I promise," she said. "And speaking of comfort... given that I have railed against him, it may seem strange for me to suggest that you might see how Marcellus is. I still have visions of him crying in the stairwell when Lily died, unable or unwilling to come inside the door where she was."

Will nodded faintly. "I will find him," he said. "And your show of compassion does not surprise me."

She shrugged. "I suppose, in the end, it is not my place to judge them," she said. "I still feel that it was wrong of them, but that does not matter any longer. If you have not judged them, what right do I have to do it?"

He smiled at her. There wasn't much he could say to that because she was right. He was just glad that she'd come to that conclusion on her own. He was starting to see how kind and rational she was.

It was something he appreciated, very much.

"Then I shall go about my duties and see you later," he said. "Mayhap you should take Atticus back to the river today. He likes it so much there."

She nodded. "I was just thinking the same thing."

"And mayhap I will join you."

"I was just thinking the *same* thing."

He laughed softly. "Good," he said. Then, he headed towards his solar, but not before blowing her a kiss. "Until later, my lady."

Adria just smiled. Her heart was pounding a mile a minute and all she wanted to do was smile until her face split in two. It was the effect Will was starting to have on her.

A joyous moment in a day that was badly in need of such things.

Leaving Will to go about his day, she quit the keep and headed out into the sunshine.

℣

LADY DE WOLFE was dead.

That was all anyone could talk about this morning, but Gar didn't really care. All he cared about was his daughter, who seemed to have disappeared.

He was on the hunt.

A large contingent of soldiers had rolled in just past dawn, flying blue and yellow standards with a lion on them. Gar had heard the soldiers talking and it seemed that Lady de Wolfe's father had arrived, though too late to see his daughter alive. She had evidently given birth to a son, a very precious commodity given that the child had de Lohr and de Wolfe blood.

In some circles, much more desirable than even royal blood.

But Gar wasn't concerned about any of that. His daughter was caught up in the chaos that was going on in the wake of Lady de Wolfe's death, given that she had been the woman's lady-in-waiting, but he was determined to find her. She wanted him gone on this very morning, as she'd so adamantly told him, and he would go – but only after he'd made his final stand.

Gar had been given a good deal of time to think last night while the castle was still for the most part, as whispers of Lady de Wolfe's death were flying but there had not yet been a confirmation. There had been no formal evening meal, as there usually was, so the servant who was in charge of the knights' quarters brought Gar cold beef and bread, certainly not the rich meals he'd been enjoying since his arrival.

The night itself seemed to have a strange, unsteady feel.

As if the stars themselves had changed.

During that odd stillness, Gar had made a decision. He wasn't going to beg for his daughter's permission any longer. If he wanted her wed, she would be wed to whomever he chose. He'd tried to talk to Ronan yesterday, but the young knight avoided him at every turn. Hermes did the same, though he was not as rude about it as Ronan had been. When Gar had asked him if he'd had a chance to think about his offer, Hermes had simply changed the subject before moving on to his duties. He wouldn't give Gar any time to ask more questions or persuade him.

That meant that Gar had little choice left.

Adria was coming with him.

He wasn't sure how he was going to achieve it, only that he was. He would take her back to Silas de Brito and let him deal with her insolent nature. Silas was old, rich, childless and widowed, and he wanted sons to carry on the family name. That was the only reason he wanted to marry Adria. Of course, it was about the money, but it was more about establishing his legacy. Like it or not, that's where Adria was heading.

Gar didn't want that debt hanging over his head any longer.

The time had come to act.

He finally spied his daughter about mid-morning, herding several young boys into the kitchen yard. She had one of the boys by the hand and as Gar drew closer, he could see that it was a de Wolfe son. He'd seen the boy running about with his band of hooligans, a loud child who had everyone at Carlisle under his thumb. At least, it seemed that way, because Adria was most certainly under the lad's thumb.

He ruled Carlisle more than his father did.

The boys were running into the kitchen yard with Adria bringing up the rear, but Gar hurried to catch up with her before she disappeared completely. If he wanted to convince her to leave with him, he was going to have to be careful.

And clever.

He knew she wouldn't go willingly.

"Adria," he called to her. "Adria, sweetling!"

Adria was about to step through the gate when she heard her father behind her. By the time she turned around, there was a decidedly unfriendly expression on her face that Gar pretended to ignore.

"I have heard about Lady de Wolfe," he said with mock sympathy. "What a great tragedy for both families."

Emotionally brittle, Adria had little patience with her father this morning. "It is, indeed."

"I heard that it was childbirth?"

"Aye."

"And the child?"

"He is small, but he survived."

Gar nodded as if he really cared. "God is merciful then," he said. "Have you been tending him?"

"I have, along with a wet nurse and Lady Warenton."

"And how is Lord Irthington?"

"Grieving, as you can imagine." She stopped him before he could ask any further questions regarding people he didn't care about. "I told you to leave this morning. Why are you still here?"

He frowned. "It would hardly be considerate of me to leave after such a tragedy," he said. "I thought to remain. Mayhap I may be of service."

Adria's patience vanished. "With what?" she demanded. "Gar, you are no longer welcome here. I want you to gather your things immediately and leave. We do not want you here. I am not sure how much plainer I can be."

In the kitchen yard, the boys were yelling, running around and chasing one another. They had bread in their hands, as Adria had brought them into the kitchen yard to find food to bring down to the river. Gar pointed to the boys.

"Surely you do not need to be tending these children," he said. "I can watch over them. Surely you are needed elsewhere."

Adria rolled her eyes. "Nay, you cannot watch over the children," she said. "I would not leave you in charge of dogs much less children. Gather your things and leave. If you do not, I will tell the knights and they will make sure you do."

So much for trying to be helpful. Adria turned away from him with the intention of passing into the kitchen yard, but he grabbed her by the arm. Furious, she came to a halt and raked her nails over his hand. He drew back quickly, in pain.

"I told you never to touch me," she growled. "Get out and leave me alone."

Gar looked at the two scratches on his hand, already oozing blood. He smiled thinly. "I want you to listen very carefully to me," he said. "I will leave you alone, on one condition."

"Say it and go."

"You will listen to me one final time."

"Speak."

Gar looked pointedly at her. "You have refused to marry de Brito," he said. "You will not marry any of these fine young knights so that I may repay de Brito for the life he gave you."

"He did not give me a life!"

"He *did* give you the life you lead by loaning money to me so that I could put you in front of Lady Lancaster at the proper place and the proper time," he said. "Think about it and stop being so self-righteous. Had we not attended the tourney at Kenilworth, you would probably be married to a farmer with ten children to take care of by now. Your life would be difficult and harsh. You might even be hungry. Instead, he provided us with the money so that you could have a better life. No matter how much you want to tell me that this is all my problem, think about what I did to ensure you had a life with the heir to the House of de Wolfe. Had I not incurred the debt, you would not be here."

Unfortunately, his logic was sound. It was the truth. Adria was gearing up to turn her back on him again, but she couldn't manage to do it because he was absolutely right. She did owe him the life she was living.

She sighed sharply.

"I will acknowledge that," she said. "But I am still not marrying him."

"Then give me money to pay him off. How much do you have?"

Adria suspected it might come to this. She opened her mouth, but Atticus and his friends suddenly rushed up to her, food in their hands.

"May we go to the river now?" Atticus asked excitedly.

Adria nodded. "Tell the gate guards where you are going," she said. "I will be there shortly."

The boys rushed through, running for the gatehouse with pieces of bread falling to the ground as they ran, tumbling from their overloaded hands. When they were out of earshot, Adria looked at her father.

"How much do you need?" she asked, resignation in her tone. "Let us come to the crux of your visit, Gar. How much do you need to give to de Brito?"

"Ten pounds."

Her eyes widened. "Ten pounds?" she repeated. "That is a good deal of money. I remember everything you bought for me in order to foster at Kenilworth and it was not ten pounds' worth of items. Where did the rest of the money go?"

Gar shrugged. "I had other debts to pay off," he said. "But I need ten pounds to pay the man off."

Adria shook her head. "I do not have ten pounds."

"How much do you have?"

"Not quite half."

"Then ask your liege," he said. "Surely de Wolfe has the money. Surely his wife had the money. Mayhap there is money you could take from her. She no longer needs it."

Adria looked at him in outrage. "I am not going to steal the money and most certainly not from a dead woman," she said. "I will give you what I can, but you will have to work for the rest. Go find a rich lord and tell him you'll mind his wine stores or be a liaison to his merchants for a price."

"I will *not* work for anyone," Gar fired back. "I am a nobleman from an old family. I do not work for anyone."

He said it with such disdain. The man would rather steal or beg money than work for it, and Adria rolled her eyes.

"Then do whatever you want," she said bitterly. "Steal it and hope whoever you steal it from doesn't catch you. In fact, if you're going to embark on a life of crime, why not make it easy for yourself? Steal a man's wife and ransom her back to him. The truth is that I care not how you get the money because that *is* your problem. I will give you what I have and then wash my hands of the entire thing, but whatever you decide to do, you will leave Carlisle before sundown. I have given you enough warning and I will not warn you again."

With that, she turned to follow the boys' path to the river.

Gar watched her go, the wheels of thought turning in his mind. She'd given him an idea, unknowingly, and he needed to consider it further.

Ransom.

It was true that he would not work for his money. He never had. The only thing he had really ever done to earn money was gamble and, at the moment, he had nothing to gamble with. But ransom had always been a way for men to make money, especially knights who tended to ransom their enemies. At tournaments, mass competitions were all about ransoming men who had been defeated, so ransom was a very good idea.

… but *who* to ransom?

There were two very wealthy families at Carlisle at the moment – de Wolfe and de Lohr. De Lohr owned about half of the Welsh Marches while de Wolfe controlled or owned most of the Scottish Marches. There was massive money to be made were he to ransom one of their own.

The problem was that he wasn't a good enough warrior and there were only men to ransom.

… *or were there?*

He'd heard that Lady Warenton was in residence, an elderly woman who was the matriarch of the entire de Wolfe empire. She was a possibility, but she also had sons and a husband who controlled thousands of men and he could very well find himself drawn and quartered if he tried to abduct her for ransom.

Lady Warenton was out.

The next possibility was his own daughter, but surely they wouldn't pay for her return and Adria would give him too much of a fight.

His daughter was out.

That left him with two weaker possibilities, but they were possibilities that both families would pay handsomely for. Why only ransom to one family when he could ransom to two? There were two children at Carlisle that were of de Wolfe and de Lohr blood, and both of them were sons of the heir to the entire de Wolfe empire and son of a de Lohr daughter. There was Atticus, the older son, but Gar had been watching him for a while and the child was a terror. More than likely, he would make it very difficult for Gar to abduct him and hold on to him. A child like that would make a lot of noise and fight back.

But there was a second child who couldn't fight back.

The newborn.

Aye, the families would pay well to have the baby returned unharmed.

Adria had said that she and a wet nurse and Lady Warenton had been tending him, so he knew the child wasn't well-guarded. But he was in the keep and Gar would have to get in and get out without being seen. He didn't worry about the women because he could silence them easily enough, but he did worry about the guards at both gatehouses. He'd have to be fully packed, ready to depart, and then abduct the child and put him in one of his saddlebags. It would be a nice, comfortable hiding place for the infant while he rode from the outer gatehouse and to freedom beyond.

Then, he'd set about ransoming the infant.

Ten pounds? More like one hundred pounds. If this was his chance to finally make the money that his daughter had denied him, then he was going to make as much as he could.

The wheels of the plan were in motion.

CHAPTER NINETEEN

"M ARCELLUS?"

Seated in the dusty, cluttered armory upon a stool, looking at the floor, Marcellus lifted his head when he heard his name. He blinked because the door was open and the light from outside was shining in, but he could see a silhouette standing in the doorway.

He knew the voice.

"My lord," he said, realizing it was Will. Standing up, he grabbed the nearest weapon, pretending to be busy. "How can I be of service?"

Will came into the armory, his gaze fixed on the auburn-haired knight. He'd been looking for him for about an hour but no one seemed to know where he was. Usually, Marcellus was at one of the gatehouses, always in command, always vigilant and visible.

But Will found him hiding in one of the old armories built into the outer wall.

That wasn't like him.

"I've not been in here in a long time," Will said, looking around the dirty, dusty mess. Reaching out, he picked up a spear and looked at the rusty tip. "All of this was left from the previous command. I thought we'd cleaned it all up."

Marcellus shook his head. "There are three such armories like this one," he said. "We've been working on the other two because they're larger. The weapons in this one are mostly crumbling. I'm not sure how much we can improve upon them."

Will peered at the rusty head before setting the spear back against the wall. "Hopefully, we can salvage them before the Scots try to take the castle back," he said in jest, picking up one of the wooden shields only to discover that it was broken. Gingerly, he set it down. "I think some of these things were used by the Romans."

Marcellus smiled weakly. "I would not be surprised, my lord."

Will looked at a broken mace before turning his full attention to Marcellus. "And it would probably also not surprise you that I've not come to discuss broken weapons."

"My lord?"

"I came about Lily."

Marcellus' entire expression changed; Will could see it. He couldn't shut the armory door without shutting out the light and plunging them into darkness, so he went to stand by the opening to make sure no one was around to overhear their conversation.

Marcellus didn't give him the opportunity to speak first.

"You have my deepest sympathies, my lord," he said, seemingly struggling with his composure. "We all had a great deal of respect for Lady Irthington. I have known her for many years and I know she will be missed."

He was prattling on, perhaps nervously, and Will put up a hand to silence him. "Marcellus," he said, his voice low but firm. "I know. I have always known."

Marcellus coughed as if choking on the words that he was

preparing to give forth. His head came up and he looked at Will, his eyes wrought with confusion and emotion.

"Know... know what, my lord?" he said feebly.

Will kept his hand up to ease the man, who was clearly shaken by the direction the conversation had taken.

"I know that you offered for Lily's hand long ago," he said quietly. "I know that Lily loved you. I know that she continued to love you for the duration of our marriage. Marcellus, I've not come to condemn you. In fact, I have always had a great deal of sympathy for you. You and Lily loved one another, but her father demanded she marry me. I had about as much choice in the matter as you and Lily had, so I've come to tell you something that I've always wanted to say to you."

Marcellus looked as if he were about to become ill. "My... my lord?"

Will took a deep breath. "I wanted to tell you that I am sorry," he said. "Had I not come along, it is very possible that Chris would have allowed you to marry Lily, but he did not and, for that, I am sorry. I am sorry that I had no voice in the matter. I was young at the time and it didn't occur to me to refuse. I had my own father to consider, as you know, and refusing a de Lohr marriage would have probably seen him come down on me harder than most. I am sorry that I came between you and Lily."

Marcellus' expression moved from apprehensive to shocked. He stared at Will for several long moments before sinking back onto the stool he'd been sitting on. He seemed rather dazed.

"I... I do not even know what to say," he said, his voice quivering. "For you to apologize is... madness. Pure madness. You are Lily's legal and true husband. If anyone should apologize, it should be me. I should apologize for my less than noble behavior. I should apologize for loving your wife when I had no right to. I thought that I would overcome my feelings for her when she married you, but I never did. They are stronger today than they were when I first fell in love with her. I knew I was doing wrong by carrying on with her in secret, but I loved her. I will never love another."

Will could hear the anguish in the man's voice and it only made him feel guiltier that he'd kept him from the woman he loved. It had been such a terrible and complicated situation for them all.

"You needn't apologize," he said. "I never blamed you. As for carrying on behind my back, you were so careful about it that not even Adria knew and she slept in the same chamber as Lily did for years. How on earth you conceived both Atticus and the new baby is something I shall never understand."

Marcellus closed his eyes tightly and hung his head. "Did Lily tell you that?"

"Nay."

Marcellus sighed heavily. "Then I will not ask how you know," he said. "But please know that we never enjoyed deceiving you. There was always a great deal of guilt about it, but our love was stronger than our guilt."

Will knew that. In times past, perhaps he wouldn't have understood the strength of love, but since the introduction of Adria and the delicate relationship they were building, there was a glimmer of comprehension there. He couldn't imagine loving a woman and not being able to be with her. He couldn't imagine loving Adria only to see her marry another man.

That was a scenario that Marcellus had to face for many years.

"Marcellus, none of this was fair, least of all to you and Lily," he said. "You have given your life to a woman you could never have and that is either an incredibly stupid man or an incredibly selfless one. I choose to believe the latter because you and I have served together for many years. I know you and I know your character. Because none of this was fair to you or to Lily, I am going to ask you a question and I want a completely honest answer. Will you do this for me?"

Marcellus looked at him, nodding firmly. "Of course, my lord. I swear it."

"Do you wish to return to Lioncross with Chris and take the infant with you to raise as your son?"

Marcellus gasped as if an unseen hand had hit him in the gut. "*What*?" he hissed. "You... you want me to take the child?"

The man's shock was a palpable thing, causing Will to pity him more than he already did. "It seems only fair to me that you should be allowed to raise your child with the woman you love," he said. "Atticus is too old, but the infant... he would only know you as his father. You can simply tell everyone that your wife perished in childbirth, which is mostly the truth. I am certain Chris would never say differently."

"But what about the people at Carlisle?" Marcellus asked. "They know Lily gave birth to a living child. How would you explain his absence?"

"Infants are fragile beings. They die frequently. No one would disbelieve the infant died shortly after birth."

Marcellus stared at him for a moment before rising to his feet. The emotion was gone from his face, replaced by something strong and appreciative. Will's understanding of the situation had been like a salve for Marcellus' grieving heart.

But his actions, his offer, meant more than words could say.

"My lord, I have never heard of a more gracious or noble offer in my entire life," he said, choked with emotion. "To express my gratitude would seem woefully inadequate, but please know that my respect and gratitude for you is endless. However, I must decline. It is enough to know that you asked me."

Will frowned. "Why would you decline?"

Marcellus smiled faintly. "Because the babe was born a de Wolfe," he said simply. "He will remain a de Wolfe. You can provide him with more than I ever can and he will bear the honorable name of de Wolfe for the rest of his life. Let me be proud from afar, my lord, for I shall be. My son will have a better life in your hands than in mine. Both of them will."

Will nodded faintly, understanding a father's desire to have the very best for his children and Will took that responsibility very seriously.

"If that is your wish," he said. "It seems strange that Atticus and the infant should have two fathers who love them, but I suppose that makes them more fortunate than most."

Marcellus blinked back tears. "I do not know what to say except that it is unfortunate that men will never know just how generous you have been all these years," he said. "Lily knew it. She always had the greatest admiration for you."

"And I, her," Will said. "Speaking of Lily, I believe that Chris will want to take her back to Lioncross for burial and you may go with him, if you wish. I think you'd be happier close to Lily than here in the wilds of the north."

Marcellus smiled weakly. "That is very understanding of you," he said. "If Worchester will have me, I shall return to Lioncross."

"I am sure he will."

With nothing more to say, Will turned for the door, but Marcellus stopped him. "I hope you will tell Atticus and Alec the truth one day," he said. "Mayhap you'll tell them of a man who loved their mother, and them, so much that he only wanted the best for them."

Will paused by the door, looking at him. "Someday," he agreed. "I will tell them of their guardian angel who was one of the most selfless men I have ever known."

"The same could be said for you, my lord."

With a smile on his lips, Will headed off into the sunlit outer bailey. The keep lay before him and, suddenly, he felt as if he could sleep a little. The conversation with Marcellus had lifted a weight off him that he didn't even know he had.

But it was gone now.

Perhaps everything was going to be all right, after all.

CHAPTER TWENTY

"**W**OULD YOU LIKE me to watch out for them, my lady?"

Sitting in the wooden chair beneath the canopy of trees and watching Atticus swing on his rope swing, Adria turned to see Hermes standing a few feet away. The last she'd heard of Hermes, her father had been proposing marriage to him, so she forced a smile at the young knight who had crept up behind her and she hadn't even noticed.

"That is kind," she said, rising from her chair. "Don't you have duties to attend to?"

Hermes nodded, seemingly as uncertain and uncomfortable as she was. "A few," he said. "But there is a new infant and I know you are needed to attend it. I can watch over Atticus and his gang of ruffians for a while. I may even join them."

As if on cue, Atticus bellowed as he swung around on the swing, being chased by his friends. Adria did indeed have things she could attend to, so Hermes' invitation was attractive.

"I told Will that I would stay with Atticus today to make sure he was not sad about his mother," she said. "But I think he might like playing with you even more. You're much more fun than I am."

Hermes grinned, embarrassed. "I would not say that, my

lady," he said. "I am certain that you are just as much fun when you have time for recreation."

"I do not swing from ropes and yell."

"Then I have the advantage."

Adria giggled as she stood up from the chair. She looked into Hermes' freckled face and found the need to come clean with the man in the hopes they wouldn't be so awkward with each other in the future.

"Hermes, I am glad you're here. I've been meaning to speak to you about my father," she said. "I know he offered you a betrothal and I want to apologize. I know it must have been uncomfortable for you."

Hermes flushed a little around the ears. "It wasn't uncomfortable," he said. "But your father did seem rather eager about it."

Adria grunted unhappily. "Eager because he is foolish and greedy," she said. "You should know that all he wants is access to your money and your family's money. That is why he is trying so hard to marry me off. It was not something I agreed to or asked him to broker on my behalf. I am just sorry you were caught up in his attempts."

Hermes smiled, but not one of humor. Perhaps one of disappointment. "I did not think you had given him permission," he said. "That is why I've not accepted him. I did not think it was what you wanted."

Adria could see his disenchantment. "It wasn't," she said. "But we can still be friends, can we not?"

"Of course, my lady."

Her smile turned genuine. "Good," she said. "Thank you for understanding. And thank you for offering to tend to Atticus. Should you need to return to your duties, just send for me."

With nothing more to say, Hermes simply grinned, nodded, and moved towards the group of frolicking boys. With Atticus attended to, Adria headed back towards the castle, perhaps more relieved than she cared to admit.

Relieved that Hermes wasn't going to push the betrothal offer.

It was just after the nooning hour and the castle seemed a little more normal than it had that morning, when the fog of grief was as heavy as the morning dew. People seemed a little more lively, going about their business, and she stopped into the kitchen yard to see how the washerwomen were getting along with the infant's wash. The blankets and swaddling for the baby had been carefully washed with the soapwort and dried in the sun. Gathering the wash, she headed back for the keep.

The outer bailey was a little more crowded than normal given the de Lohr army had set up an encampment inside the walls. Adria kept an eye out for Will, but she didn't see him around. She hoped he was somewhere catching up on sleep. When she thought about their heated kiss earlier in the day, a smile came to her lips. It had been such an unexpected thing and, truthfully, the very first kiss she'd ever had from a man. She would be quite open to more such unexpected kisses and she giggled to herself when she thought of actually telling Will that.

She hoped he wouldn't think her too bold.

Crossing through the inner gatehouse, she came face to face with Chris, Becket, and Morgen coming out of the keep. The smile vanished from her face when she saw how upset Chris was, his features ruddy and his eyes watery. But he caught sight of her almost immediately and lifted a hand to her in greeting.

"Lady Adria," he said, sounding pleased and relieved. "I was hoping to see you."

Adria liked Chris. He was a little loud and could be intimidating, but he'd always been very kind to her. She smiled warmly at him.

"My lord," she said, talking a moment to nod to Becket and Morgen. "It is very good to see you all. I hope your journey was pleasant."

Chris nodded. "It was uneventful, but then we arrived to... *this*," he said, starting to tear up again and trying desperately not to. "My sweet angel is gone."

Adria reached out to take the man's hand, a comforting gesture. "I know," she said softly. "Lord Irthington told you everything?"

Chris nodded, steeling himself against his grief. "He did," he said. "We were just in the vault visiting her. She looks as if she is sleeping. It is difficult to believe that she is gone."

Adria patted his hand. "For me, also," she said. "I loved her like a sister."

Chris squeezed her hand. "And she loved you," he said. "You two were friends for a very long time."

"We were."

"Were you with her when she passed, Adria?" he asked, sounding earnest and sad. Like a man trying to reconcile himself to the death of his child. "You two were so close. She would have been comforted by you."

Adria wasn't quite sure how much to tell him. She wasn't sure if he could take it. She looked to Becket and Morgen, men she had known fairly well, to see if they could give her some silent indication on how to answer. Becket nodded faintly, encouraging her to reply.

"Aye," she said after a moment. "I was with her. I was the only one, for the baby came quite unexpectedly. How *much* did Irthington tell you? I will not repeat it if you already know."

Chris shook his head. "Only that she perished in childbirth," he said. "I suppose I do not need to know more than that, but I just want to make sure she was not alone."

"She wasn't, my lord. I was the last one to speak with her and they were words of joy."

Chris wiped at his eyes. "That is good to know," he said. "I can tell her mother that, at least."

"You can both be at peace," Adria said. "Lily simply went to sleep and never woke up, but her last feelings were those of joy as her son was born. She was very happy."

Chris simply nodded, accepting that explanation. It gave him comfort. "Thank you," he said hoarsely. "May I ask a final task of you?"

"Or course, my lord."

"I have decided to take Lily home to Lioncross so she can be buried in the chapel with her ancestors," he said. "Will you dress her for her final journey?"

Adria had never dressed a corpse before, but she couldn't deny him. "If you wish."

Chris squeezed her hand one last time and let it go. "Thank you," he whispered.

Adria stood aside, watching Chris and his sons continue on through the inner gatehouse and to the outer bailey beyond. She felt sorry for the man who had doted on his only daughter.

It was a tragic thing, indeed.

With Chris on her mind, she continued to the keep. The familiar dark and quiet greeted her as she headed up the stairwell to the great chamber at the top. The door was open, sending rays of light into the stairwell, and she entered to find the chamber quite warm.

Not strangely, she could still feel Lily here.

Adria had done well at dealing with her grief today but, for some reason, she felt Lily heavily at that moment as she stood in the chamber. She looked around, to Lily's possessions, to the things that meant something to her.

It made her sad.

"Everything will be well, Lily," she whispered. "The baby is doing well and I just left Atticus. He is sad, but he will be well in the end. I also saw your father and he is saddened, but I spoke with him. I told him you were happy in the end. Please don't worry about them."

There was no reply, of course, but she felt better speaking the words to any remnants of Lily's spirit that might still linger. Lily had been worried about her family and if her spirit was still about, Adria didn't want her to fret.

She would take care of Lily's world... and make it her own.

That was what Lily wanted.

Returning her focus to the living around her, Adria noticed that the big bed was still on the far side, curtains still drawn. Assuming Lady Warenton was still sleeping, she headed into the alcove where the wet nurse was feeding the tiny infant again. Her big, lovely breasts held a wealth of nourishment for the weak child as she clutched him to her breast and sang to him softly.

Adria stood in the doorway for a moment and watched.

"That is so kind of you," she said softly. "I know his mother would be so happy with your nurturing."

The wet nurse grinned, a gap-toothed smile. "I raised eleven children of my own," she said. "My youngest has seen three years and he doesn't need me like he used to. I'm happy to do what I can for your young lad."

"You know his mother died giving birth to him, don't you?"

The woman nodded, her smile fading. "I do," she said. "That's why I sing to him. So he knows he's loved."

Adria thought that was quite touching. She watched the woman as she finished feeding the baby and gently burped him. Changing the child's swaddling, she wrapped him back up tightly, from his head to his toes, and handed him over to Adria.

"Will you mind him while I sleep?" she asked. "I was up all night with him, as Lady Warenton was. I think I need a bit of a rest."

Adria nodded. "Of course," she said. "Use this bed and I will shut the door to give you some peace."

The wet nurse thanked her gratefully as she began to disrobe. Adria went out into the great chamber, closing the door to the alcove softly. With both Lady Warenton and the wet nurse sleeping, she didn't want to disturb them in case the baby fussed, so she grabbed a basket with a pillow fashioned in the bottom of it, one Lily had specifically made for an infant to sleep in, and headed from the chamber to the smaller hall below. She could sit in the alcove near the hearth, where it was warm, and let the baby sleep next to the fire.

Sweet little Alec, she hoped, was going to get stronger every day.

She was going to do her best to ensure it.

CB

HE'D BEEN WATCHING the inner gatehouse all morning.

Gar's window had a good view of the drawbridge and part of the gatehouse and he'd been keeping an eye out for his daughter in between packing his saddlebags. Even as he'd gone out to the stable to load his saddlebags on his horse, he'd still kept an eye out for her.

He wanted to know when she went back into the keep.

He had a reason for loading his saddlebags before he actually intended to leave Carlisle. The saddlebag on the left contained his clothing and he'd managed to create a very nice bed for a tiny infant right on the top. All he had to do was lift the flap, drop the infant in, resecure the flap, and he'd be out of Carlisle before they realized what had happened.

But none of it mattered if he couldn't get to that baby.

So, he continued watching the gatehouse, hardly taking his eyes from it. The nooning hour came and went, but still, he was riveted to the gatehouse.

And then, he saw her.

Adria was coming from the direction of the kitchen yard, heading through the inner gatehouse, and Gar knew he had to move swiftly. Since the great hall was in the inner bailey, he would make that his excuse if anyone stopped him. The great hall and the keep were in close proximity, so he could only hope no one watched him go for the keep instead of the great hall.

It was a chance he'd have to take.

Quickly, he began to move.

His heart was pounding as he approached the inner gatehouse, passing through without anyone questioning him. In fact, no one was even looking at him. Once he passed through, the great hall was to his left and the keep was to his right. He ducked to his right, looking straight ahead, not even looking to see if anyone was around who might question him.

No one was.

Into the keep he went.

The dark mustiness of the stone building greeted him. He didn't know where Adria went, but he guessed up to the great chamber. Quickly, he ducked into the darkened smaller hall, positioning himself in a dim corner so he could watch the stairwell. He did it specifically to watch for his daughter, so he could catch her unaware, but he didn't retreat into that corner without a weapon of some kind. There were fire pokers and shovels near the hearth and he quickly grabbed a shovel, mostly for defending himself from his angry daughter.

Perhaps even to use against her if he needed to.

And so, he waited. He wasn't sure how long he would have to wait before she came downstairs, but it wasn't long. She appeared shortly after he'd settled in, but what he didn't expect was for her to come down the stairs with an infant in her arms.

The very infant he was hoping for.

Adria didn't see him as she went to the hearth. She had a basket in her hand and she set it down, making sure it was sturdy and comfortable before she lay her precious prize in it. Then, she began to put fuel into the hearth from the wood bin, kindling and peat, before striking a flint and stone. The blaze sparked almost immediately and she used the fire poker to settle in the fuel so it wouldn't spill out. As the blaze took off, someone lay the flat end of a shovel across the back of Adria's head.

It was a sickening, loud sound. Adria fell onto her face, hovering above unconsciousness as she heard the shovel hit the floor beside her. Stars dancing in front of her eyes, she struggled to shake them off and roll over so she could see what was happening.

Who had attacked her.

She noticed immediately that the basket was gone. As her vision cleared, she could see Gar holding the woven basket with the baby inside.

"Nay!" she cried weakly. "Put the child down!"

Gar was just standing there, looking at the infant. "So this is the lad that killed his mother?" he said. "Uninteresting and unspectacular, but I suppose he'll do the job."

Ears ringing and the world rocking dangerously, Adria struggled to sit up. "What job?" she demanded. "Gar, put the child down. What do you think you're doing?"

Gar looked at her. "Exactly what I told you I was going to do," he said. "I am going to get the money I need to pay off de Brito. If you will not do it for me, then I must do as I see fit."

"*What?*"

"You heard me. And remember – this is your fault."

Trying not to vomit, Adria managed to push herself into a sitting position. "Make sense," she said. "What are you going to do?"

Gar had a hint of a smile across his lips. "Ransom the child, of course," he said. "It makes the most sense, truly. Thank you for the suggestion."

Horror swept Adria. "My *suggestion*?" she repeated, appalled. "I only said it with sarcasm because you refused to work for your money. I never suggested you do it!"

Gar chuckled, but it was without humor. "I know," he said. "But it was a good idea. I do not know why I did not think of it earlier. How much do you think the de Wolfe and de Lohr family would pay in ransom to have Lily de Lohr's last child returned to them?"

Adria was beyond dismayed with what he was saying. Never did she imagine the man had it in him to abduct an innocent baby in exchange for ransom. That went beyond anything she thought he was capable of, but in the same breath, she should have known. She should have known that her desperate, immoral father would have something equally desperate and immoral in mind. She refused to pay his debt, so he was right – she *was* to blame – and little Alec was going to pay the price.

She had to regain control of the situation any way she could.

"The infant is very sick," she said, trying to sound reasonable and not afraid. "He may not even survive the day, so taking him will not help you. The family will not pay you for a corpse."

Gar looked at the child and as he did, Adria caught movement out of the corners of her eyes. Will had appeared in the doorway leading into his solar, his features as tight and focused as Adria had ever seen them. Gar's back was to the solar door, so he couldn't see Will standing there with a very big broadsword in his hand. But Will looked at Adria, who quickly shook her head at him. Were he to attack Gar, the child would be in the line of fire. Gar might drop the baby, or worse.

From the look on Will's face, Adria was aware that he knew that. But she also knew that Gar's life was forfeit from this moment on. If Gar realized that, the baby was most certainly in mortal danger.

Adria had to act fast.

"The child looks healthy enough to me," he said. "A little small, mayhap.'"

"He is very small," Adria said, putting her hand to the back of her throbbing head and coming away with blood from where he'd split her scalp. "I am telling you that he will not survive the day, so he is not a good hostage. And... and the fact that you have gone this far tells me that you are serious, indeed."

Gar looked at her. "Did you think I was not?"

Adria was feeling sick and weak and dizzy, but she struggled to her feet, gripping the nearest feasting table to steady herself.

"I suppose I did not believe it until now," she said. "You do not need to take the infant, so set him down. I... I surrender, Papa. I will go with you and marry de Brito."

She'd called him Papa for a reason – hopefully to ease the tension between them. To remind him that she was, in fact, still his daughter.

Gar looked at her in surprise.

"You will?" he said.

"I said I would."

"And all of this has changed your mind?"

She sat down, heavily. Her head was killing her. "I am stubborn like you are, so you only have yourself to blame," she said. "Put the baby down and I'll go pack my things. I will go with you today."

Gar's gaze lingered on her for a moment before returning to the child. "I am not certain I want you to," he said. "I can get more money for this child than I could ever get for you from de Brito."

Adria glanced at Will, still in the doorway. He hadn't moved, but she could see from his expression that he was ready to kill. She didn't care about her father; he'd signed his own death warrant.

But the baby hadn't.

She had to get that baby.

"Silas de Brito is one of the richest men in the shire," she said. "You may be able to get a fortune for the baby, but it would be a finite amount. If I marry Silas and he dies anytime soon, I will have control of his entire fortune. Remember that."

That had Gar's attention. "True," he said. "I had not thought on it that way."

"Of course I'm right," Adria said, trying to sound as if she were finally on his side. "Come along, now. Put the baby on the table. We'll leave today."

Gar wasn't so sure. That was the horrible part. He still wasn't sure he wanted to let the child go. Adria watched him anxiously as he just stood there, looking at the baby. Over to her right, the hearth popped and crackled, and a big piece of glowing wood flew out, missed the stones of the hearth, and landed on the wood floor. Weakly, Adria got up, picked up the poker, and tried to flip the wood back into the fireplace.

All the while, watching her father.

Then, he began to move.

Gar wandered over to the table where she had been sitting, closer to her. He didn't sit down, and he didn't put the baby down, but from the way he was standing, even if the basket fell, it would only fall onto the tabletop. Not to the floor. If she was going to act, now was the time.

There might never be another chance.

Adria still had the poker in her hand. The wood hadn't gone

back completely into the hearth, so she pretended to fuss with it, trying to shove it back, when what she was really do was calculating her next movement. Will was still over by the solar door, unmoving because he didn't want to tip Gar off, so it was up to her at this point.

There was no time to waste.

As Gar stood over the table, Adria suddenly threw herself in her father's direction. She ended up on her belly, the fire poker arcing over her head. The poker was shaped like a halberd, which was a type of ax with a blade on one side and a sharp, blade-like hook on the other. Adria hurled the hook end of the poker right at her father's lower legs, slamming it into his left foot.

The hook went straight through his foot, bones and flesh, all the way to the wooden floor.

As predicated, Gar dropped the basket to the tabletop, howling with pain. Adria lurched to her feet, going for the basket, but Gar reached out and cuffed her across the face, sending her flying. His foot was essentially staked to the floor, so he couldn't run, but even if he could there was nowhere for him to go. Will, bolting from the solar door when he saw Adria act, was already on top of him. Gar's last memory was of a searing pain to his neck as Will sliced his head off.

A head that rolled right into the hearth and caught fire.

It was all over in a flash.

Adria was on her back several feet away, her nose and mouth bloodied from where Gar had brutally struck her. Will took a half-second to ensure his son was well and undamaged before rushing to her side and picking her off the floor.

She was only half-conscious.

"The baby," she said, over and over. "Is he well? I must see him. Is he well?"

Will had her up in his arms, carrying her to the table where the baby was just as Jordan, who had heard the commotion all the way up the stairs, came into the smaller hall with a dagger in her hand. The spry, elderly woman was fully prepared to fight. Even though the mother and grandmother of dozens of knights was fairly unshakeable, even she was a bit put off by what she saw.

Blood everywhere and a headless body.

"God's Bones," she gasped. "What happened here?"

Will was gently wiping the blood from Adria's nose and mouth. "Everything is well, Matha," he said, though his voice was quaking. "Nothing that will not heal."

Jordan practically pushed him aside to get to Adria. "My God," she said, seeing the blood. "What happened tae her?"

"My father," Adria said feebly as she came around a little. "He... he tried to take Alec. He wanted to ransom him, but I stopped him. I had to stop him."

"You did," Will said soothingly. "You were very brave, my lady. The bravest woman I have ever seen."

Jordan looked at her grandson, who was verging on tears. The man was shaken to the bone. The body was on the ground, the head smoking in the hearth, and she could see that something horrible had happened.

And little Alec slept through it all.

Peering into the basket, Jordan could see that the child had hardly stirred. His nose was moving around a little but other than that, he was sleeping most peacefully. From what she could see, Will had everything else in hand.

She plucked the infant out of the basket.

"I'll take him back upstairs," she said. "Will, it sounds as if we owe everything tae Lady Adria. Make sure ye tend tae her properly."

With that, she scurried out of the smaller hall, heading for the stairs. As she began to carefully mount them, Will found himself gazing into Adria's pale eyes.

She was gazing back.

"How do you feel?" he managed to ask.

Adria was a little more lucid, certainly lucid enough to see that Will was having a difficult time with his composure. She could feel him trembling as he held her.

"I will be fine," she said. "Give me an hour, and I shall be quite fine. Truly, Will, it is nothing to worry over."

He nodded. Then, his face crumpled and tears popped from his eyes. Quickly, Adria wiped them away.

"Why the tears?" she asked gently. "No harm has been done that cannot heal."

He shook his head, feeling like a fool. "I do not know," he said honestly. "All I know is that I have never been so terrified in my entire life. Not ever. I've faced dozens of battles in my life and never felt anything close to what I just felt when I watched your father toy with you. I was frightened for Alec, of course, but you... you tried to exchange yourself for a baby that is not even of your blood, but you did it because it was the right thing to do."

She continued to softly wipe at his wet face. "I did it for Alec, for Lily, for Marcellus, and for you," she murmured. "You have already suffered so much loss, Will. I could not let you suffer through something like that."

He sniffled, kissing her hand when it came close. "But don't you see? I would have lost you. As I heard you offer yourself up in exchange for the infant, I realized that I could have lost you and it occurred to me that losing my chance at happiness with you would destroy me. You've given me such hope, Adria, such joy and hope that my brightest days are in front of me as long as you are by my side. I... I just couldn't stomach losing you."

Adria smiled faintly. "You told me once that you wanted a wife who would love you," she said. "I feel as if I am well on my way. You will never lose me, Will de Wolfe. Come what may, I will be by your side for the rest of your life and forever after."

Will grinned; he couldn't help it. "I think I've been waiting all my life to hear those words but I simply didn't know it."

"You know it now."

"Indeed, I do. And I think Lily would be very happy for us."

Adria wrapped her arms around his neck, holding him close. "I know she would."

The kiss that followed, however gentle because of Adria's bruised mouth, was the most precious kiss either one of them had ever experienced.

For the rest of your life and forever after.

She meant it.

CHAPTER TWENTY-ONE

Four days later

THE DE LOHR contingent was ready to return to Lioncross Abbey.

It was a gloomy morning after days of rain, but the de Lohr army was assembled and ready to depart. The delay in departure had been due to a coffin having been built for Lily, a simple box made from strong Scottish pine and filled with fresh rushes, rosemary, lavender, and other aromatics for the journey home.

Carefully dressed by Adria and Jordan, with help from the wet nurse, Lily was placed in a woolen gown the color of bluebells, her blonde hair washed and braided, with a circlet of flowers on her head made by Adria from flowers that Atticus and his gang had picked at Hermes' direction. Wrapped in her burial shroud, she was gently placed in the coffin by her brothers, father, husband, and Marcellus. When no one was looking, Will gave Marcellus a dagger with which to cut a few locks of Lily's hair because the man had desperately wanted a keepsake.

Yet one more act of generosity from Will.

With Lily secure in her new coffin, Will had produced a wagon for them to put the coffin on, with Hermes and

Marcellus making sure it was tethered securely to the wagon bed. Given the weather, they also covered it with a large piece of oiled canvas to protect it. It was as safe and secure as they could make it.

Will, Scott, Jordan, Adria, and Atticus had turned out to bid the de Lohr group a farewell. Jordan had spent a good deal of time with Chris, comforting the man and sending him home with some of Lily's possessions so her mother could have them. Atticus had spent the morning screaming because Uncle Becket and Uncle Morgen were taking great delight in harassing a child who both loved and hated to be teased. Given the procession had a somber purpose, it did everyone good to watch Atticus and his antics.

It gave them comfort in a child who still found joy in life.

When everything was finally set and Jordan was bidding her farewells to Chris, Becket came to say his goodbyes to Will. They smiled at one another as they joined hands, reaffirming both friendship and family bonds, something hysterical fathers could never break.

"I will send you word when we return home," Becket said. "My father has not sent word to my mother about this, as he prefers to tell her in person."

Will nodded. "Understandable," he said. "I wish I could come with you."

Becket waved him off. "No need," he said. "My mother never much liked you, anyway."

They both burst into soft laughter. "Lady Kaedia is a fine and loyal woman," he said. "Tell her I love her and that I miss her."

"I will *not*."

More laughter. Kaedia had never thought any man was good enough for her daughter, so there was some truth to what Becket had said. As they smiled over a moment of levity, Becket caught sight of Marcellus. The man was in full protection, his baggage stashed on Lily's wagon. He was returning home with her, as Will had given him permission to do so, and he seemed both pleased and relieved about it.

Becket's gaze lingered on him.

"My father finally told us about Marcellus," he said quietly. "I must say that I wasn't surprised to hear it. He wanted to marry my sister very badly."

"And she wanted to marry him."

Becket looked at him. "I am sorry, Will," he said quietly. "Sorry my father forced you to marry Lily. I never acknowledged what he did, but I am now. He should not have done it. He knows that now."

Will patted Becket on the shoulder. "It is of no matter," he said. "I have four enviable children, so there are no regrets."

"Even if two of those children belong to Marcellus?"

Will shrugged. "Marcellus was cheated out of marrying the woman he loved," he said. "He and I have spoken. He would be honored to have them raised as a de Wolfe, with their other siblings, and I will not deny him. But do me a favor."

"What?"

"See if you can find Marcellus a good woman. He deserves that."

Becket shook his head. "You are too forgiving for words," he said. "And what about you? What happiness will you find?"

Will's gaze trailed over to Adria, standing by herself and watching the farewells between the de Lohrs and the de Wolfes.

"I think I've already found it," he said, his focus lingering on her. "I did not tell your father that Lily's dying wish was to have me marry her lady-in-waiting. She wanted her family taken care of by someone she knew, a woman she loved, and Adria and I have agreed to wed."

Becket, too, was looking at the lovely woman with the long,

lustrous hair and doll-like features. "I've always thought she was a beauty," he agreed. "And I am not surprised Lily made that request. No matter what you think of her, Will, I know she cared for you in her own way."

"I know," he said. "We both did. Ours was not a love match, but that did not mean we did not like one another. She had her love and it wasn't me. Now, I am going to have mine – and it is not her."

Becket smiled. "I hope so," he said. "I truly do. I am sure my father will hope so, too."

Will squeezed his hand and released it as Becket headed over to where the de Lohr men were gathering, shouting at everyone to mount up or prepare to march out. Half of the men were mounted, the other half were on foot, and the great gates of Carlisle's outer gatehouse began to swing open.

For a moment, Will watched his father and Chris speak before embracing. Whatever trouble had erupted between them was clearly gone and the rock-solid alliance of de Wolfe and de Lohr was once again intact.

The world was right again.

Turning away, he was heading over to where Adria was standing, now holding Atticus by the hand, but he was stopped by a mounted knight. He looked up to see Marcellus beside him, looking as if he were about to go to war.

"Well?" he said to the man. "Do you have everything?"

Marcellus nodded. "I think so," he said. "If you find I have left something behind, either take it for yourself or give it to someone who can use it. I'm fairly certain I have everything that I need."

Will nodded. "Then if I come across anything, I'll do with it as I please." He paused a moment, studying Marcellus. "In spite of everything, I will miss you. I wish you the best in your return to Lioncross. I hope the memories there are those of comfort."

Marcellus smiled faintly. "It is where I met Lily and where she will always be," he said, reaching into a purse on his belt and pulling forth the strands of her hair, all carefully tied up in a piece of blue cloth. "This is the most valuable thing I own. Thank you for everything, Will. I will never forget your kindness, in all things. If you ever have need of me, send word. I will come."

Will smiled, waving the man off. As Marcellus charged back towards the de Lohr group, Will caught movement out of the corners of his eyes.

"Papa," Atticus said. "I must find Bradford now. Can I go, please?"

Will looked up to see Adria standing a few feet behind Atticus, a smile playing on her lips. "What does Adie say?"

Atticus stomped his foot. "She says I must ask you!"

"Then you have my permission."

As Atticus tore off, Adria came to stand next to Will. She wasn't close enough so he took a step to ensure that he was standing right up against her, feeling her body next to his.

She took a step away.

"Restrain yourself," she said warningly. "We have already decided that being obvious about courting so soon after Lily's death is not the right thing to do. We must wait."

He sighed heavily. "I know," he muttered. "But I cannot stand not being near you."

"You must show some self-control."

"How long do we have to wait?"

She looked at him. "I would say at least six months before the men can know that we are courting."

"What about marriage?"

"At least a year."

He scowled. "A year?" he repeated. "That is ridiculous. I will not wait that long."

"Aye, you will and you will like it."

"I will *not* like it."

Adria fought off a grin. "Stop sounding so petulant," she said. "Out of respect for Lily, we must do this. Do you agree?"

He rolled his eyes. "Aye," he said begrudgingly. "Can I at least tell my father?"

"I suppose so."

Will could see his father, waving as Chris and the others began to ride out. But thoughts of his father turned to thoughts of Adria's father. He looked at her.

"And how are you feeling after everything?" he asked quietly. "I am sorry I have not asked you yet today."

She looked at him, her gaze soft on him. "You have asked me every day since that terrible moment and I love you for it," she said. "But, truly, my answer has not changed. I am well. I feel relieved. More relieved than I have felt in my entire life. Gar was my father, but in name only. He killed any affection I had for him long ago. What happened to him was nothing less than he deserved, so please do not worry that I will resent you for it. That will never happen."

His gaze was soft on her, too. "Say it again."

"Say what again?"

"That you love me."

She flushed to the roots of her hair. "In time, my lord," she said, moving past him. "I think I hear Atticus calling me."

He turned to watch her walk past him. "You do *not* hear Atticus calling to you," he said. "Come back here. I demand it."

She simply looked over her shoulder, grinned at him, and kept walking.

Will just stood there and laughed.

As it so happened, he told his father of his intention to marry Adria later that day, when the sun was setting and they were in the great hall with cups of fine wine in their hands. He told both Scott and Jordan of Lily's request and how, in the end, Will couldn't have been happier about it. Somehow, Lily must have known what he needed and the joy he felt in Adria was something he'd never experienced before.

Mayhap I'll finally have a love like you have, he told his father.

Truly, it was all Scott could do to contain his happiness. He remembered wondering if he and his son were cursed with their first wives, perhaps made to suffer in the end. But much like his father, Will was finding love in his second marriage.

Most definitely, a love like his father had.

A love for this life… and forever after.

EPILOGUE
MY MOON AND STARS FOREVER

Year of Our Lord 1294
Castle Questing
July

"There once was a lady fair,
With silver bells in her hair.
I knew her to have,
A luscious kiss… it drove me mad!
But she denied me… and I was so terribly sad.
Lily, my girl,
Your flower, I will unfurl
With my cock and a bit of good luck!
Your kiss divine,
I'll make you mine,
And keep you a-bed for a fuck!"

*T*HE NAUGHTY WEDDING *song.*
Everyone knew about the naughty wedding song. It was legendary in all the de Wolfe weddings and even some ally

weddings. Somehow, it was always sung, like some terrible tradition. Currently, it was being sung by Ronan's father, Blayth, and Apollo de Norville, the groom's uncle. Blayth could sing, Apollo could not, so there was a good deal of laughing and cheering and, ultimately, food throwing going on.

It was one of the most boisterous weddings yet.

Unfortunately, those singing the song had the groom in a bind. His uncles on the de Wolfe side – Troy, Patrick, Blayth, Edward, and Thomas – had Will surrounded, feeding him cup after cup of the very good Scottish ale that their mother had sent down from her Scottish relatives. In fact, some of those relatives were present in the great hall of Castle Questing, singing their own drunken wedding songs, as Adria sat with a sleeping Alec in her arms and watched it all in the company of the women on the dais.

It was wedding chaos at its finest.

"How in the world the bairn can sleep through this noise is a mystery," Jordan said, peering at Alec, who had his first birthday a couple of months prior. "Is the lad drunk like the rest of them?"

Adria grinned, looking down at Alec as he drooled all over her arm. "He is exhausted," she said. "You saw how hard he played today."

"And how much he screamed through the wedding mass."

Adria laughed softly. "So you understand how he would sleep through anything," she said. "Atticus is already fast asleep upstairs, but Alec is at that age where he cannot be separated from me. I'm sure you remember what that was like."

"I do," Jordan said. "I remember it well. It seems that Scott and Troy and Atty all went through that age at the same time, so I had tae carry three little boys around or they'd all scream."

Atty was the nickname the family had for Patrick, the largest and most fearsome de Wolfe brother. Adria grinned.

"They are close in age?" she asked.

Jordan nodded. "Scott and Troy are twins, as ye know, and Atty was born when they were a little over a year old, so they were all mostly of the same age," she said. Then, she puffed her cheeks out wearily. "At least, it sure seemed like it at the time."

Adria smiled as the woman relived her exhausting memories. "But it was fun, wasn't it?"

Jordan looked at her, smiling. "I'd give the world for my sons tae be small again."

Adria could well understand that. As she gazed down at the sleeping baby, a big and healthy boy these days, massive hands suddenly reached over her and scooped him out of her arms. She looked up to see the Earl of Warenton himself collecting his great-grandchild with the gentleness of a mother.

"I shall put him to bed alongside his brother," William said quietly. "He does not need to be here and neither do I."

Adria smiled up at the enormous knight, the Wolfe of the Border, who had a surprising soft touch with children. Even though he knew all about Atticus and Alec, and the fact that they weren't of true de Wolfe blood, it didn't matter to him. It hadn't from the start. He had loved them as if they were his own blood, now wandering off with one of them.

Adria let him go.

"I'll go with him," Jordan said, rising. "He'll be fine until the lad soils himself and then he'll beg for help."

Adria laughed softly as Jordan and William headed off, carrying Alec from the great hall. That left her with Scott's wife, Avrielle, and an array of Will's aunts in Evelyn de Wolfe de Norville, Katheryn de Wolfe Hage, and Will's step-grandmother, Lady Jemma Hage de Norville. Given the marriages within the de Wolfe – Hage – de Norville families, it seemed like everyone was married to someone in those families, so there was a good deal of overlap in relations. Jemma had married Will's grandfather, Paris, back in the summer, though she was also the matriarch of the Hage clan. In fact, it was Jemma who took Jordan's seat.

Her scowl was evident as she watched the singing and drinking going on.

"Listen tae them singing that dirty song," she growled. "I apologize tae ye, lass. They turn these celebrations intae drunken orgies, so I'm sorry they're singing such a disrespectful song."

Adria could see that Jemma was quite upset about it and she fought off a smile. "It makes them happy, I suppose," she said, pointing to the heart of the group where her husband was. "Will is in the middle of it. He's probably singing the song, too."

Jemma shook her head in disapproval. "'Tis unseemly for the bridegroom tae be singing of whores," she said, then realized the naughty word she used and looked at Adria apologetically. Then, she hiccupped loudly from too much of that fine Scottish ale. "God's Bones, I sound like a drunken fool myself. Forgive me, lass."

Adria laughed softly, taking the old woman's hand. "There's nothing to forgive," she said. "I'm glad you feel comfortable enough to curse in my presence. I've used that word once or twice myself before."

It was Jemma's turn to fight off a grin. "How disgraceful of ye."

Adria winked. "I know."

As they shared a laugh, Scott abruptly appeared. He had to fight his way past several groups of happy, drinking guests, like a battle he'd finally emerged from. He appeared a bit harried and drunk himself.

"Come with me," he said, holding out a hand to Adria. "The vultures are starting to circle and I must take you to your wedding chamber."

Adria let him pull her out of the chair. "What vultures?"

Scott pointed to the group of men around Will. "Them," he said. "They are my brothers and I love them, but they are vultures when it comes to a wedding night. They'll stand at the door all night and drink, or they'll even try to push into the chamber if you let them."

"Wait!"

Paris de Norville was suddenly at Adria's side. He'd been speaking to another group of men near the hearth, but he saw when Scott came to claim Adria. Elderly but still quite spry and strong, he tried to put himself between Scott and Adria.

"Where are you taking her?" he demanded.

Scott tried to push his former father-in-law aside. "To her chamber," he said. "Get out of the way."

Paris frowned. "You know nothing," he said, trying to take Adria from him. "I will do this."

Scott pulled Adria towards him as he pushed Paris away. "If you truly wish to help, then help Will make it to his wedding chamber. I fear that Troy and Atty and the others will try to abduct him for the night as a joke. We'll find him chained in the vault in the morning."

Jemma was on her feet. "They wouldna dare," she said. "Both of ye take Adria up tae bed. I'll deal with the lads."

That was the best offer they had, and probably the only one that would really work, so Scott took Adria by the hand and led her from the hall with Paris bringing up the rear. That movement had Will moving to follow, but his uncles and cousins were determined to hold him up.

Jemma swooped in.

"Back, all of ye," she said, swatting at Thomas and her own son, Nathaniel, when they tried to block Will. "Leave him be, ye pack of dogs. The man has a wife waiting for him, a wife he's waited a whole year for, so dunna delay him."

A chorus of congratulations went up as the men began to slap Will on the back, sometimes quite hard. Will found himself virtually pummeled, including by his own brother, Tor, who leapt on his back and kissed him on the cheek. The entire de Wolfe Pack was full of drink and deliriously happy, but Will managed to extract himself from the group and, with Jemma's help, headed up to the chamber where his wife was waiting.

But the group was following. When they saw the tide of happy men coming their way, Jemma stood her ground.

"Go," she said. "I'll hold them off, but hurry. And when ye get up there, send Bonny down tae me. I'll need him tae help fend off the horde."

Bonny was what the grandchildren called Paris. When he first became a grandfather, he wanted his grandchildren to call him *bon père*, but somehow that got twisted into Bonny. Not exactly the auspicious name Paris had wanted, but it couldn't be helped. Will kissed Jemma on the cheek and darted off, rushing up the stairs to find Bonny and send him down as reinforcements.

Not that Jemma needed them.

Jordan had put the newlyweds in the top floor of Castle Questing's enormous keep, which wasn't like a traditional keep. It was shaped like the letter "H", with wings and stairwells and corridors. It was a maze. It had been built by the Dudforth family many years ago, a very large family, and they had added to it over the years until it sat derelict for a while until William de Wolfe brought his family to live there.

Jordan had put Will and Adria in the very last room at the top of the northeast wing, overlooking the bailey and the gatehouse, and the door was open when Will arrived. Scott and Paris were standing in the doorway, waiting for him.

"Well?" Paris said. "Are you being followed?"

Will nodded. "Unfortunately," he said. "Aunt Jemma told

me to send you down to help her. She's holding the line."

Paris lifted his eyebrows. "She does not need my help," he said. "She is quite capable of holding off a hundred angry men all by herself."

"Then go down and protect them."

He was trying to get rid of his grandfather, who grinned. "I'll go down in good time," he said. "I thought you might have some questions about what is to take place now."

Will clapped a palm to his forehead in embarrassment. "Bonny, my wife is in the chamber," he said. "She can hear you ask such foolish questions."

Paris was trying not to laugh. "She is not paying any attention to me," he said. "Do you have any specific questions?"

Will grasped him by the arm and pulled him out into the corridor. "I do not," he said. "And if I did, you are the last person I would ask."

"How cruel of you to say so."

"I do not mean to be cruel, but you told me once that women liked biting and spanking, and I found out neither was true." He watched Paris nearly double over with laughter and he fought not to do the same. "It is *not* funny. You told me those things before I'd had any experience with women and, God help me, I believed you, so I am not asking advice from you again, ever. Now, go downstairs and help Aunt Jemma."

Paris was still laughing when he kissed Will on the cheek and headed towards the stairs. That left Scott standing there, shaking his head at Paris' antics.

"You did not really think women liked to be bit and spanked, did you?" he asked.

Will came over to his father. "Unfortunately, I did," he said. "Lily nearly knocked my teeth out on our wedding night."

Scott burst into soft laughter, pulling Will into the warm, lavish bed chamber where Adria was waiting for him. She was bent over the hearth, stoking it, as Scott softly closed the door and bolted it. Will looked at him questioningly.

"Papa, I adore you, but I do not plan to spend this night with my new wife and my father," he said. "You can go, too."

Scott shook his head. "I will in a moment," he said. "But I wanted a chance to speak to you both. I wasn't present when you married Lily, if you recall."

Will's smile faded. "I remember," he said. "I missed you."

Scott looked at his eldest son, seeing a great deal of his mother in those handsome features. "Did I ever tell you about the night I asked Bonny permission to marry your mother?"

Will shook his head. "I do not think so," he said. "Although I remember hearing something about the time when Uncle Troy asked to marry Aunt Helene."

Scott smiled faintly. "Aunt Helene was pregnant with your cousin, Andreas," he said. "Bonny, Poppy, and Kee proceeded to invoke the Helm of Shame to punish Uncle Troy for, shall we say, taking liberties before they were married. Kee sat on Troy's head with his naked arse to punish him while Bonny shaved his head. It was truly spectacular punishment."

Over near the hearth, Adria's eyes widened at the terrible mental image Scott was painting for them. "Kee?" she said. "Who is that?"

"Kieran," Scott said. "Kieran Hage, Jemma's first husband. He was my father's best friend next to Paris and the wisest, most gentle soul I've ever known."

As Adria nodded in understanding, Scott continued. "On the night Troy and Helene were married, which was the same day as the Helm of Shame, your mother and I were summoning the courage to speak to Bonny about our marriage," he said. "Your mother was pregnant with you and we were running out of time to tell him. As you can imagine, Bonny was not pleased. Not in the least."

Will had a smile playing on his lips. "Don't tell me," he said. "You were also a victim of the Helm of Shame."

Scott shook his head. "I was not," he said. "Bonny tried to kill me at first. He chased me all over Castle Questing's stable yard with an iron rod and tried to kill me. But as he chased me, he insulted me – greatly. I finally had enough and walked away. That brought your mother to defend my honor. Someday, you should ask Poppy how your mother tried to kill Bonny by chasing him around with a sword."

By this time, Adria had come to stand next to Will and he put his arm around her, laughing softly at the idea of his mother trying to kill his grandfather.

"Mother was not a shy or retiring woman," he said. "She was tall and strong, so she surely must have been formidable."

"She was," Scott said. "I thought you should know that it was your mother who fought Bonny for permission to marry me. She was as fearsome a woman as I have ever known."

They were venturing onto the very sensitive subject of Athena de Norville de Wolfe. Even Adria knew that. She and Will had visited Athena's crypt earlier in the day, talking to Athena and explaining their courtship.

It had been a bittersweet and poignant moment.

Will thought it was very important to include his mother in the day of their marriage and even though she wasn't present, Paris had given Adria a blue dress that had belonged to Athena, long ago. In fact, it was the same dress Athena had been married in and Adria had worked furiously for three hours, along with Jordan and Jemma, to alter the dress so that she could wear it for her wedding to Will.

In spirit, Athena had been there.

It had been important to them both.

"I was happy to honor her by wearing her wedding gown," Adria said, her eyes glimmering warmly at Scott. "It made her a part of this day."

Scott looked at Adria, such a lovely woman with a lovely disposition who had completely and wholly captured his son's heart, and he reached out to take her hand.

"You must understand that we de Wolfes get very attached to one another," he said. "We love our family and the people in our lives. Understand that for that reason, I loved Lily, but were I to search the entire world for a bride worthy of my son, I could never find anyone as worthy as you are. We are so happy to have you."

Adria went to him and gave him a hug, smiling gently at the emotional man. But Scott wasn't finished yet. He dug around in the pocket of his tunic and pulled forth an object. Taking Adria's hand, he put it in her palm.

"On the night I asked for Athena's hand, I gave her that ring," he said as both Adria and Will looked over the ring with great interest. "That was hers. The stone is a moonstone set in a star-shaped mount and on the inside of the band, it says *my moon and stars*. I used to tell Athena that she was my moon and stars. Will, I want you to give it to your bride. Your mother would want that."

Deeply emotional, Will took the beautiful ring and slipped it onto Adria's finger next to the small gold band she already wore. The ring was a little large, but not too terribly. The two rings fit well enough together.

"Thank you, Papa," Will said sincerely. "That means more than you'll ever know."

Scott looked at the ring on Adria's finger and felt quite emotional about it himself. The last time that ring had been on a finger, it had been Athena's corpse. William had the foresight of mind to remove it and save it for his son. But Scott didn't want to think about that – he only wanted to think about the happiness that ring brought him.

The happiness it would bring Will and Adria.

"I will leave you two now and see you on the morrow," he said. "You have my blessings and my love this night."

Will hugged his father tightly before the man quit the chamber and shut the door softly behind him. Will threw the bolt, turning to his wife.

"Well?" he said. "Here we are."

Adria grinned broadly. "Indeed," she said. "Here we are."

"No more sneaking out of your chamber so the servants won't see me," he said, snorting. "No more hiding you under the coverlet when Atticus comes in early in the morning and wants to climb into bed with me."

Adria laughed softly and went to him, sliding her arms around his neck as he bent down to kiss her. Fourteen months of courtship had brought them to this moment, but the truth was that they already felt married. They had for the past several months. They slept in the same bed nightly but tried to keep it discreet. What wasn't discreet was the fact that Adria was already four months pregnant with their first child.

Will hadn't quite shared that with his family yet.

He would when the time was right and hoped he wouldn't be on the receiving end of the Helm of Shame. Even though Kieran was no longer around to deliver it, there were plenty of eager arses to take his place.

But for tonight, no thoughts of shameful helms or drunken relatives. No thoughts of what had happened over a year ago, only what was coming with the future. Tonight, they could hold each other with all of the rights a marital couple had. Will was so eager to taste her that he immediately reached out and pulled Adria into his arms, his warm mouth slanting over hers.

Adria fell against him without resistance, her soft body against his. They craved each other so much that they were intuitive when it came to the needs and wants of one another. They knew what was to come and made all due haste to ensure that it happened. Her arms around his neck tightened, pulling herself closer to him even as he nearly crushed her in his embrace.

Her scent.

Something sweet and musky filled Will's nostrils as he kissed her and his arousal was instant. It always was when it came to her. He'd spent most of his adult life bedding a woman who didn't mean anything to him in the romantic sense and, in truth, he knew that he was sharing her with another.

Now, he was with someone who belonged only to him.

Forever after.

Will was consumed with the smell and feel of her, his mouth on hers, his arms around her, but soon enough, his grip loosened and his hands began to roam. She was dressed in his mother's wedding gown but that that did not deter him. He was a man used to getting what he wanted and he was not subtle. His lips still fused to hers, he pulled at the fastens on the dress, loosening it enough to pull it over her head. She was left in a fine silk shift and Will could feel her hard nipples when he dragged his palms across her breasts.

Something in him unleashed.

With a growl, he grabbed her by the waist and lowered his head, suckling her nipples through the fabric. Adria gasped as he suckled and bit and tugged at her breasts, her hands finding their way into his hair, holding his mouth against her breast as if to nurse a starving child.

Still holding her by the waist, Will lifted her up onto the table behind him, the one that contained wine and fruit and had been so artfully arranged by Jordan. They couldn't even make it to the bed. One big arm lashed out and everything was swept onto the floor. Adria's legs were parted as he yanked her to the edge of the table, wedging himself between them. One hand left her waist and lifted the shift over her head, tossing it to the floor with the food, while the other hand moved for the glistening flower between her legs.

The moment he touched her, he groaned.

"God's Bones," he muttered, his mouth now on her bare nipples. "You are already prepared for me, Wife."

Adria didn't have a chance to answer as he thrust fingers into her quivering body, first one and then two. She groaned softly, throwing her head back as she lifted her knees higher, giving him unhindered access to her tender core.

Her movements had him foaming with lust. All Will could think of was thrusting himself into her slick folds and he fumbled to untie his breeches as his throbbing erection strained against them. His tunic was getting in the way, so he yanked it over his head and lowered his breeches, freeing his enormous manhood. Pulling Adria forward so that her buttocks nearly hung off the side of the table, he arched his big body over hers and thrust into her quivering, slick body.

Adria was so highly aroused that she bit off a cry into his chest as he plunged into her. It was the most uncontrollably pleasurable thing she had even known and, predictably, her body began trembling with what was the first of several releases. That was something they'd discovered since Will first bedded her – she was easily aroused, leading to more than one climax, and that excited Will terribly.

A woman whose body finally understood his.

Will, feeling her body react to him in a most erotic way, didn't wait to extend his pleasure. He could feel her body milking his, demanding his seed, and he was so highly stimulated that in little time he was answering her, climaxing so hard that he bit his tongue. But the moment was more than worth it. The love he never thought he'd have, now with his wife, made every stroke as he made love to her completely worth it.

She was worth his life and more.

Beneath him, Adria was still twitching, still gasping softly with the ripples of release as Will gently thrust into her. He wanted to stay that way for the rest of his life, buried in her sweet body, feeling her flesh react to his. He cupped her buttocks in his big hands, holding her pelvis against his as he kissed her gently.

"I am so sorry," he whispered. "I should not have taken you on the table."

Adria started laughing. "Why not?" she said. "You have taken me everywhere else – the bed, the floor, the chair in your solar, the…"

He kissed her to shut her up. "Stop it this instant," he growled. "I was trying to be gentle and polite with you. God's Bones, I did not even make it to the bed."

"We can still make it to the bed."

He snorted, a bit dastardly, and picked her up while still joined to her body, carrying her all the way across the floor and to the bed against the wall. He lay her down carefully, still embedded deep within her.

"There," he said, looming over her. "Better?"

Adria laughed softly and he shifted, attempting to find a position with more traction, but he ended up withdrawing accidentally. The mere stimulation from his movement caused her to climax again and when he realized that, he thrust into her again with his semi-flaccid member, soaking up every last quiver from her body.

It was utter, complete delight.

Gasping as the tremors died away, Adria lay beneath him, satisfied and boneless and exhausted, but knowing Will, that wouldn't be the last time he bedded her before morning. The man had an insatiable appetite when it came to her, often bedding her twice a night or more. He didn't even care when she was on her monthly cycle – nothing deterred him or bothered him – so there was no reprieve. Not that she wanted one. But when her monthly cycle finally stopped about four months ago, she realized his seed had taken root. Not surprising, considering how much they craved one another.

Knowing a child was on the way, she'd never seen the man so happy, about anything.

As she'd predicted, he made love to her once more before midnight, and afterwards they finally climbed beneath the feather-soft coverlet, snuggling down for sleep, listening to the sounds of the night outside of the nearby window. In fact, Adria could see the sky beyond the window, with a full moon and a million stars twinkling back at her.

Lifting her hand, she looked at the ring with the moonstone in the star-shaped mount. Spooned against Will, she felt him stir.

"What's wrong?" he mumbled.

"Wrong?" she said. "Nothing. I was just looking at your mother's ring."

He lifted his head from where it has been pressed into the back of hers, looking over her shoulder to see the ring she was holding up on her finger. Reaching out, he touched it, watching it catch the light from the fire in the hearth.

"I did not even realize that my father kept my mother's ring," he muttered. "That's a very special thing."

"Do you remember your mother well?"

"Very well. I had seen fifteen years when she died."

"What do you remember about her?"

"Everything," he said softly, kissing the side of her head. "She was kind, loving, but firm. And she would have been mad about you."

"Do you think so?"

"I know so." He lifted the ring off of her finger, looking at it. He couldn't quite see the inscription. "I like that inscription. *My moon and stars.* That's what you are to me, too. My moon, my sun, and my stars."

Adria turned to look at him as he loomed over her, reaching up to touch his face gently. "You are all that and more," she whispered. "Forever after."

He put the ring back on her finger. "I think I'll add that to the inscription. My moon and stars isn't quite enough. I must add my own meaning to it."

"What do you mean? Add what?"

"You'll see."

She did. Before their first child was born, Will took the ring away for several days and when he returned it to her finger, two new words were added to the inscription.

My moon and stars… forever after.

Truer words were never spoken.

ᑕ THE END ᗡ

De Wolfe Pack Generations:

WolfeHeart

WolfeStrike

WolfeSword

WolfeBlade

WolfeLord

Children of Will and Adria

Athena (with Lily de Wolfe)

Andrew (with Lily de Wolfe)

Atticus (with Lily de Wolfe)

Alec (with Lily de Wolfe)

Titus

Lucas

Leonidas

Edward (b. around 1299, mentioned in Swords and Shields)

Amalia

William III

THE PARENTS, CHILDREN, AND GRANDCHILDREN OF DE WOLFE

(Note: Don't be intimidated by these family trees – refer to them if you need clarification on a relationship)

William (deceased 1296 A.D.) and Jordan Scott de Wolfe

Total children: 10

Total grandchildren: 75 (including 4 deceased, 7 adopted, 3 step-grandchildren)

Scott (Troy's twin) – (Wife #1 Lady Athena de Norville, has issue. Wife #2, Lady Avrielle Huntley du Rennic, has issue)

With Athena

- William "Will"
- Thomas "Tor"
- Andrew (deceased)
- Beatrice (deceased)

With Avrielle

- Sophia (with Nathaniel du Rennic)
- Stephen (with Nathaniel du Rennic)
- Sorcha (with Nathaniel du Rennic)
- Jeremy
- Nathaniel
- Alexander
- Seraphina
- Jordan

Troy (Scott's twin) – (Wife #1 Lady Helene de Norville, has issue. Wife #2 Lady Rhoswyn Kerr, has issue)

With Helene

- Andreas
- Acacia (deceased)
- Arista (deceased)

With Rhoswyn

- Gareth
- Corey
- Reed
- Tavin
- Tristan
- Elsbeth
- Madeleine

Patrick – (Married to Lady Brighton de Favereux, has issue)

- Markus
- Cassius
- Magnus
- Titus
- Thora
- Kristiana

James – (Wife #1 Lady Rose Hage, has issue. Wife #2, Asmara ap Cader, has issue)

With Rose

- Ronan
- Isabella

With Asmara (as Blayth)

- Maddoc
- Bowen
- Caius
- Garreth (known as Garr)

Katheryn (James' twin) – (Married to Sir Alec Hage, has issue)

- Edward
- Axel
- Christoph
- Kieran
- Christian

Evelyn – (Married to Sir Hector de Norville, has issue)

- Atreus
- Hermes
- Lisbet
- Adele
- Aline
- Lesander (goes by Zander)

Baby de Wolfe – (Died same day. Christened Madeleine)

Edward – (Married to Lady Cassiopeia de Norville, has issue)

- Helene
- Phoebe
- Hestia
- Asteria
- Leonidas
- Dorian

- Dayne
- Stephan
- Pallas

Thomas – (Married Lady Maitland "Mae" de Ryes Bowlin, has issue)

- Artus (adopted)
- Nora (adopted)
- Phin (adopted)
- Marybelle (adopted)
- Renard & Roland (adopted)
- Dyana (adopted)
- Alexander
- Cabot
- Matthew
- Wade
- Tacey
- Morgan

Penelope – (Married to Bhrodi de Shera, Earl of Coventry, hereditary King of Anglesey)

- William
- Perri
- Bowen
- Dai
- Catrin
- Morgana
- Maddock
- Anthea
- Talan

Kieran and Jemma Scott Hage

- Mary Alys (adopted) – (married, has issue)
- Baby Hage, died same day. Christened Bridget.
- Alec (married to Lady Katheryn de Wolfe, has issue)
- Christian (died Holy Land 1269 A.D.) no issue
- Moira (married to Sir Apollo de Norville, has issue)
- Kevin (married to Lady Annavieve de Ferrers, has issue)
- Rose (widow of Sir James de Wolfe, has issue)
- Nathaniel

Paris and Caladora Scott de Norville

- Hector (married to Lady Evelyn de Wolfe, has issue)
- Apollo (married to Lady Moira Hage, has issue)
- Helene (married to Sir Troy de Wolfe, has issue)
- Athena (married to Sir Scott de Wolfe, has issue)
- Adonis
- Cassiopeia (married to Sir Edward de Wolfe, has issue)

Holdings and Titles of the House of de Wolfe and Close Allies as of 1293 A.D.

Scott de Wolfe – Baron Kilham, heir to the Earldom of Warenton (Heir: William "Will" de Wolfe)

Troy de Wolfe – Lord Braemoor (Heir: Andreas de Wolfe)

Patrick de Wolfe – Earl of Berwick (Heir: Markus de Wolfe, Lord Ravensdowne.)

Blayth (James) de Wolfe – Baron Sydenham (Heir: Ronan de Wolfe)

Edward de Wolfe – Baron Kentmere (Heir: Leonidas de Wolfe)

Thomas de Wolfe – Earl of Northumbria (Heir: Alexander de Wolfe, Lord Easington)

Wark Castle (Wolfe's Eye):
Larger outpost for the Earl of Warenton. Literally sits on the border between England and Scotland.
- Titus de Wolfe (son of Patrick de Wolfe) commander

Berwick Castle (Wolfe's Teeth):
Massive border castle, strategically important, de Wolfe holding and seat of the Earl of Berwick, Patrick de Wolfe
- Alec Hage, commander
- Edward "Eddie" Hage, commander

Castle Questing (Wolfe's Heart):
Massive fortress, seat of the Earl of Warenton, Scott de Wolfe.

- Apollo de Norville, second
- Nathaniel Hage
- Owen le Mon

Rule Water Castle (Wolfe's Lair):

The largest outpost in the de Wolfe empire, known as The Lair. At this time, commanded by Thomas "Tor" de Wolfe.

- Magnus de Wolfe, second
- Adonis de Norville, second
- Perri de Shera, son of the Earl of Coventry and Penelope de Wolfe de Shera (squire)

Monteviot Tower (Wolfe's Shield):

Smaller outpost in Scotland, strategic. Holding of Troy de Wolfe.

- Brodie de Reyne, commander

Kale Water Castle (Wolfe's Den):

Larger outpost on the England side of the border, strategic.

- Troy de Wolfe, Lord Braemoor, commander
- Troy also commands Sibbald's Hold, former home of Red Keith Kerr (his wife's father). A minor property commanded by son Gareth de Wolfe.

Kyloe Castle (Wolfe's Howl):

Seat of the Earl of Northumbria, Thomas de Wolfe

- Christoph Hage, second

Roxburgh Castle (Wolfe's Claw – unofficially)*

Large royal-held castle near Kelso, formerly manned by knights from Northwood, but awarded to the House of de Wolfe by royal decree for meritorious service to the crown. Volatile location, often attacked by Scots, and is manned by both royal and de Wolfe troops.

- Blayth (James) de Wolfe, Lord Sydenham, commander
- Axel Hage, second

*Note: Because of the extreme volatile location and nature of this garrison, Blayth (James) de Wolfe was given the title Lord Sydenham and the Sydenham Barony, a small but strategic barony between Wark Castle and the town of Kelso.

Carlisle Castle (Wolfe's Fangs)

Massive and large royal-held castle, perhaps one of the largest castles in the north. Awarded to the House of de Wolfe by royal decree. Very volatile location, often attacked by Scots, and had changed hands many times in its history. The castle is manned by both royal and de Wolfe troops.

- Will de Wolfe, Lord Irthington, commander
- Hermes de Norville
- Ronan de Wolfe

Northwood Castle:

Massive border castle, very important and strategic. Belonging to the Earls of Teviot. Not part of the de Wolfe empire, but strongly allied to de Wolfe by marriage and blood. The Earl of Teviot is John Adrian de Longley, Adam de Longley's eldest son. Adrian's mother is Cayetana Fernanda Teresita Silva y Fausto de Longley, Princess of Aragon.

- Hector de Norville, captain of the guard (also Lord Bowmont)
- Atreus de Norville, second
- Tobias de Bocage, second

Castle Canaan (Kendal) Wolfe's Bite:

The Earl of Warenton's southernmost holding, not directly related to the Scottish border but a source of additional troops if needed. Inherited the property when he married the widow of Castle Canaan.

- Stephan du Rennic, commander

Seven Gates Castle (Kendal):

- Seat of Edward de Wolfe's Barony – Kentmere in Kendal that adjoins brother Scott's lands at Castle Canaan
- Isleworth House, Surrey

Hell's Guardhouse (The Hermitage)

- Andreas de Wolfe, commander
- Theodis de Velt, second

KATHRYN LE VEQUE NOVELS

Medieval Romance:

De Wolfe Pack Series:
Warwolfe
The Wolfe
Nighthawk
ShadowWolfe
DarkWolfe
A Joyous de Wolfe Christmas
BlackWolfe
Serpent
A Wolfe Among Dragons
Scorpion
StormWolfe
Dark Destroyer
The Lion of the North
Walls of Babylon
The Best Is Yet To Be

De Wolfe Pack Generations:
WolfeHeart
WolfeStrike
WolfeSword
WolfeBlade
WolfeLord

The Executioner Knights:
By the Unholy Hand
The Mountain Dark
Starless
The Promise (also Noble Knights of
de Nerra)
A Time of End
Winter of Solace
Lord of the Shadows
Lord of the Sky
Splendid Hour

The de Russe Legacy:
The Falls of Erith
Lord of War: Black Angel
The Iron Knight
Beast
The Dark One: Dark Knight
The White Lord of Wellesbourne
Dark Moon
Dark Steel
A de Russe Christmas Miracle
Dark Warrior

The de Lohr Dynasty:
While Angels Slept
Rise of the Defender
Steelheart
Shadowmoor
Silversword
Spectre of the Sword
Unending Love
Archangel
A Blessed de Lohr Christmas

The Brothers de Lohr:
The Earl in Winter

Lords of East Anglia:
While Angels Slept
Godspeed
Age of Gods and Mortals

Great Lords of le Bec:
Great Protector

House of de Royans:
Lord of Winter
To the Lady Born

The Centurion

Lords of Eire:
Echoes of Ancient Dreams
Blacksword
The Darkland

Ancient Kings of Anglecynn:
The Whispering Night
Netherworld

Battle Lords of de Velt:
The Dark Lord
Devil's Dominion
Bay of Fear
The Dark Lord's First Christmas
The Dark Spawn
The Dark Conqueror

Reign of the House of de Winter:
Lespada
Swords and Shields

De Reyne Domination:
Guardian of Darkness
A Cold Wynter's Knight
With Dreams
The Fallen One
Black Storm

House of d'Vant:
Tender is the Knight (House of
d'Vant)
The Red Fury (House of d'Vant)

The Dragonblade Series:
Fragments of Grace
Dragonblade
Island of Glass
The Savage Curtain
The Fallen One

Great Marcher Lords of de Lara
Dragonblade

House of St. Hever
Fragments of Grace
Island of Glass
Queen of Lost Stars

Lords of Pembury:
The Savage Curtain

Lords of Thunder: The de Shera Brotherhood Trilogy
The Thunder Lord
The Thunder Warrior
The Thunder Knight

The Great Knights of de Moray:
Shield of Kronos
The Gorgon

The House of De Nerra:
The Promise
The Falls of Erith
Vestiges of Valor
Realm of Angels

Highland Warriors of Munro:
The Red Lion
Deep Into Darkness

The House of de Garr:
Lord of Light
Realm of Angels

Saxon Lords of Hage:
The Crusader
Kingdom Come

High Warriors of Rohan:
High Warrior

The House of Ashbourne:
Upon a Midnight Dream

The House of D'Aurilliac:
Valiant Chaos

The House of De Dere:

Of Love and Legend

St. John and de Gare Clans:
The Warrior Poet

The House of de Bretagne:
The Questing

The House of Summerlin:
The Legend

The Kingdom of Hendocia:
Kingdom by the Sea

Regency Historical Romance:
Sin Like Flynn: A Regency
Historical Romance Duet

Gothic Regency Romance:
Emma

Contemporary Romance:

**Kathlyn Trent/Marcus Burton
Series:**
Valley of the Shadow
The Eden Factor
Canyon of the Sphinx

**The American Heroes Anthology
Series:**
The Lucius Robe
Fires of Autumn
Evenshade
Sea of Dreams
Purgatory

**Other non-connected
Contemporary Romance:**
Lady of Heaven
Darkling, I Listen
In the Dreaming Hour
River's End
The Fountain

Sons of Poseidon:
The Immortal Sea

**Pirates of Britannia Series (with
Eliza Knight):**
Savage of the Sea by Eliza Knight
Leader of Titans by Kathryn Le
Veque
The Sea Devil by Eliza Knight
Sea Wolfe by Kathryn Le Veque

Note: All Kathryn's novels are designed to be read as stand-alones, although many have cross-over characters or cross-over family groups. Novels that are grouped together have related characters or family groups. You will notice that some series have the same books; that is because they are cross-overs. A hero in one book may be the secondary character in another.

There is NO reading order except by chronology, but even in that case, you can still read the books as stand-alones. No novel is connected to another by a cliff hanger, and every book has an HEA.

Series are clearly marked. All series contain the same characters or family groups except the American Heroes Series, which is an anthology with unrelated characters.

For more information, find it in **A Reader's Guide to the Medieval World of Le Veque.**

ABOUT KATHRYN LE VEQUE

Bringing the Medieval to Romance

KATHRYN LE VEQUE is a critically acclaimed, multiple USA TODAY Bestselling author, an Indie Reader bestseller, a charter Amazon All-Star author, and a #1 bestselling, award-winning, multi-published author in Medieval Historical Romance with over 100 published novels.

Kathryn is a multiple award nominee and winner, including the winner of Uncaged Book Reviews Magazine 2017 and 2018 "Raven Award" for Favorite Medieval Romance. Kathryn is also a multiple RONE nominee (InD'Tale Magazine), holding a record for the number of nominations. In 2018, her novel WARWOLFE was the winner in the Romance category of the Book Excellence Award and in 2019, her novel A WOLFE AMONG DRAGONS won the prestigious RONE award for best pre-16th century romance.

Kathryn is considered one of the top Indie authors in the world with over 2M copies in circulation, and her novels have been translated into several languages. Kathryn recently signed with Sourcebooks Casablanca for a Medieval Fight Club series, first published in 2020.

In addition to her own published works, Kathryn is also the President/CEO of Dragonblade Publishing, a boutique publishing house specializing in Historical Romance. Dragonblade's success has seen it rise in the ranks to become Amazon's #1 e-book publisher of Historical Romance (K-Lytics report July 2020).

Kathryn loves to hear from her readers. Please find Kathryn on Facebook at Kathryn Le Veque, Author, or join her on Twitter @kathrynleveque. Sign up for Kathryn's blog at www.kathrynleveque.com for the latest news and sales.